I0818211

THE PILATE SCROLL

PRAISE FOR THE PILATE SCROLL

“It has everything—a strong heroine, a sweet younger brother, a true hero, and pesky villains . . . I won’t give away the details, but it sure touched me! I highly recommend this book!"

- Lenora Worth
New York Times Best-Selling Author

“WARNING: Sleep deprivation likely. This Christian thriller is a page-turner; more like a page burner. Think *Indiana Jones* meets *God’s Not Dead*!”

- David Jeffers, Amazon Best-Selling Author of
Man Up! What the Bible Says About Being A Man

“...Lewis weaves into the story a spiritual dimension that is filled with the author’s excellent knowledge of the Bible, his deep understandings of the teachings of Jesus Christ, and the virtues of Christianity found in forgiveness, redemption, transformation, and healing.”

- Dr. Karl K. Stegall, Pastor Emeritus
First United Methodist Church Montgomery,Alabama

"...a story that lifts both the soul and the heart rate."

- James R. Hannibal,
Award-Winning Author of The Gryphon Heist

"...an engaging action-filled romp through Europe and the Middle East steeped in religious symbolism and history..."

- Publisher's Weekly's The Booklife Prize

"Lewis courageously steps away from the mainstream to answer a higher call to deliver this epic Christian thriller. Well done!"

- Gary Westfal, Best-Selling Author, Goal Mind

"...let me just say there haven't been many action novels that moved me to tears. This one did... highly recommended novel for believers and nonbelievers alike."

- Jason E. Fort, Creator and Author of Fortress Books

"A little Indiana Jones, a little Da Vinci Code, and a whole lot of fun. "*The Pilate Scroll*" is the most exciting fiction I've read in years."

- Drew Allen, Author of Uncommon Sense

The Pilate Scroll

M. B. Lewis

SATCOM Publishing

DISCLAIMER: The views presented in this fictional work are those of the author and in no way reflect the views of persons, places, or institutions mentioned in the manuscript.

Characters and incidents are products of the author's imagination and are used fictitiously while locations and names of historical figures may be used as reference to ground the reader. Any resemblance of characters and incidents to actual events and persons, living or dead, is entirely coincidental.

First Printing: April 2021

SATCOM Publishing

Hardcover ISBN: 978-1-7330989-3-9

Trade Paperback ISBN: 978-1-7330989-1-5

E-Book ISBN: 978-1-7330989-2-2

Cover Design by DaMonza

Printed in the United States of America

BOOKS BY M.B. LEWIS

The Pilate Scroll

THE JASON CONRAD THRILLER SERIES

WRITTEN AS MICHAEL BYARS LEWIS

Retribution

Surly Bonds

The Right to Know

Veil of Deception

The Quiet Professional

AWARDS WON BY THE PILATE SCROLL

- 2022 Killer Nashville Silver Falchion Award - Winner - Action/Adventure
- 2022 Illumination Book Awards - Gold Medal - Mystery/Thriller
- 2022 National Indie Excellence Awards - Winner - Religious Fiction
- 2022 Book Excellence Awards - Winner - Christian Fiction
- 2022 Independent Press Awards - Winner - Christian Fiction
- 2022 American Best Book Awards - Winner - Thriller: Religious
- 2022 Pinnacle Book Achievement Award - Winner
- 2022 eLit Book Awards - Silver Medal - Religious Fiction
- 2021 American Best Book Award - Finalist - Fiction: Religious
- 2021 Best Thriller Book Awards - Finalist - Action Thriller
- 2021 Readers' Favorite Book Awards - Finalist - Fiction - Tall Tale
- 2020 Killer Nashville Claymore Award - Finalist (unpublished manuscript)
- 2022 Military Writers Society of America - Bronze Medal - Mystery/Thriller

For my wife Kim, my son Derek, my daughter Lydia,
and my grandson, James...

THE PILATE SCROLL

1

Port Said, Egypt
The Market District

Samuel Jacobson was a dead man. Or at least *he* thought so. His phone call had been erratic, anxious—almost in a panic.

"Brian, we have to go." Kadie Jenkins stood and slid her iPhone back in the pocket of her tan 5.11 cargo pants. She grabbed her purse and rose from the table in the back of the tiny restaurant, dragging her nineteen-year-old brother out before they had a chance to order their dinner. The restaurant sat tucked between shops selling hookahs on one side and women's clothes on the other. The aroma of fresh bread and grilled meats dissipated, replaced by the pungent scent of car exhaust and camel dung.

"It's only a fifteen-minute walk back to the hotel," Kadie said. "I bet we can make it in ten."

Brian stumbled behind her as they hurried along dusty streets. They turned into the *souk*, or open-air market, the brick-laid section of the market that was pedestrian-only this time of night. While many of the shops had their "roll-up" metal security doors pulled down, the market bristled with life.

Vendors waved items in their faces, children tugged on their pant legs, and beggars held their palms up hoping for a handout. Her eyes studied everyone who came close, gauging their intentions in a moment's glance. She was one of only a few women in the market not wearing a *hijab*.

"Kadie, slow down," Brian said. His breathing came deep and awkward, despite being a regular participant in the Special Olympics.

"Sorry, Brian. We could get a cab at the other end of the market. But by the time we find one, describe our hotel, and negotiate a price, we could walk to the hotel." While she relished the exercise, she worried her pace was too much for him. He was fit for a young man with Down syndrome, but she moved swiftly.

Their team had been in Egypt for almost three weeks. Starting in Cairo, the small group of seven from GDI, the Global Disease Initiative, had been scouring the city for clues to an ancient cure. Their quest had led them from the United States to Cairo, then to Port Said. Their four days here had not yet proven fruitful.

The goosebumps on her skin reminded her of Samuel's phone call. His message was brief yet concise: his life was in danger because he knew what they were *really* searching for. What did he mean? Their team was one of four positioned across the Middle East in search of their goal. Now, for some reason, Samuel questioned what that was.

GDI had been contracted by the United States government to locate an ancient cure for an even older virus—the hantavirus. Kadie researched the topic before they left for Egypt. Rodents generally spread it, and this strain was a particularly virulent "Old World" virus that had proven resistant to modern medicine.

The Central Intelligence Agency learned that ISIS weaponized the hantavirus in aerosol form and planned to unleash it across the West. The virus was known at the CDC to cause hemorrhagic fever with renal syndrome. Initial symptoms include fever, chills, blurred vision, back and abdominal pain, and intense headaches known to bring a grown man to his knees. Later, those exposed would experience shock, low blood pressure, kidney failure, and vascular leakage —all in all, a nasty virus to thrust upon any population. The logistics involved in treating the virus were obvious.

The unique thing about the "Old World" hantavirus, was that it had predominantly appeared in Europe and Asia. GDI discovered that the virus had been eliminated in the Middle East, which was odd, as rodents were prevalent throughout the region.

Through one of their many connections, GDI learned of a legendary cure developed in ancient Israel around 30 A.D. The virus had a different name back then, but the symptoms were the same. The cure was a simple combination of plants and minerals. The formula was stored in a vase with Aramaic writing on the side and lay hidden for millennia. That was why she was here. Kadie was fluent in Latin, Greek, and Aramaic. The executive vice president for the Science and Technology Division of GDI had contacted her personally, telling her she was "uniquely qualified" for this job. Kadie was enthralled to join the team when the offer came.

Samuel was in his early sixties, and he and Kadie had struck up a friendship at the beginning of their journey. He became her mentor and father figure, occasionally giving her advice on what to do with her career. Samuel was the team's expert on carbon dating. His equipment was state-of-the-art, but other than testing its functionality the day after they arrived, he hadn't used it. So, what *did* he discover? What did he know that was worth killing for?

Halfway to the hotel, she mumbled something she shouldn't have as she pulled out her phone and dialed. Her eyes darted toward her brother.

"Do not c-cuss," Brian said between heavy breaths.

Brian. Her moral compass there to steer her back on course. She squeezed her brother's hand. Brian always kept her grounded. What would she do when he was gone? But he was here now, and she needed to make sure he would be safe, something she had done for him since the day he was born.

"Sorry, Brian. I just remembered I need to call Curt. He's probably on his way to the restaurant to meet us."

"He is probably s-still wor—king." Brian's eyes darted back and forth. His speech impediment that made his 'r's sometimes sound like 'w's wasn't nearly as bad as it was when he was younger, and his stutter only showed up when he was nervous.

Kadie grimaced. Curt Baxter didn't answer his phone. He was GDI's security man and the only full-time employee on their team. Kadie left a message, telling him she was sorry, but she had to leave the restaurant. They'd talk later.

Next, she called Samuel. He didn't answer either. She slipped her phone back in her pocket and glanced at her brother. He was doing all he could to keep up with Kadie and avoid the distractions of the numerous shops in the marketplace. Gasping, his jaw jutted forward, brow furrowed, and his eyes bulged. He had been reluctant to leave the restaurant; he must be starving. She had to plead with him to get him to budge.

"We did not stay—for food. I am hungry," Brian said.

"I know. I'm sorry. I am, too." Her eyes darted back and forth in search of something they could eat. A few moments later she smiled. Near the end of the market, a vendor baked and sold bread. They stopped next to the giant metal oven that extended back into a yellowing mud-brick building. The bread rolled out of the front like doughnuts at Krispy Kreme, and two men placed the warm food on a rack woven out of sticks to cool. Her limited vocabulary in conversational Arabic helped her in situations like this. Kadie bought two loaves of *Aish Baladi*, an Egyptian flatbread made with whole wheat flour, similar to a pita. Handing the bag of bread to Brian, they turned and sped off.

The dust of the market peeled away as they rounded the corner, and their hotel came into sight. Well-lit against the black sky, it sat on the edge of the water where the Suez Canal merged into the Mediterranean Sea. An outdoor restaurant sat to her left; the numerous tables had their umbrellas open, lit candles centered on each table.

To her right, a small mosque lay nestled amongst other buildings. This street was far less crowded than the *souk*.

"What do you think about Curt?" Her chestnut-brown hair bounced as she slowed her pace so Brian could keep up. She needed a conversation to take her mind off Samuel.

"He is okay." Brian looked away when he answered. Kadie knew what that meant. Brian's instincts on people were spot on, and he wasn't very fond of Curt. She wasn't sure why; she was still trying to figure him out herself. Curt was a few years older than her. He was handsome, dashing, and brave—former Delta Force. There was something to be said for that.

They entered the newly renovated hotel, leaving the Third World atmosphere behind them. Kadie sighed as they weaved through the crowded lobby and lumbered up the stairs to their room on the second floor. She dropped Brian off in their room before she went to check on Samuel.

"Don't leave," she said. "I'll be back in a minute."

"Okay." Brian moved to the couch and pressed the big green button on the television remote.

Kadie closed the door; the hairs on the back of her neck bristled, and her heartbeat raced higher than usual. She hurried down the hall to Samuel's room. Inside, she heard a loud crash and the sound of something hitting the wall, followed by a solid thud.

That's not good, she thought.

Kadie tried the door handle. Locked. She pulled a small FOB out of her pocket. It was called a Gomer, a new device that opened almost any electronic lock. It had wreaked havoc on the hotel industry, but she had picked one up back in the States knowing she'd be living in hotels abroad for three months.

She was hesitant to use it. She shouldn't just barge into his room. Then came a second thud, followed by a muffled cry.

Kadie swiped the FOB across the lock and pushed hard against the door. The door cracked open about two inches and abruptly stopped; the chain secured on the inside.

"Samuel?" She peered through the gap; a body lay on the floor.

Oh my, he's had a heart attack. Kadie lowered her shoulder and bulldozed the door. It started to give way. On the second try, the chain burst free from the wall and the door flew open.

Kadie gasped. In the center of the room, a large man stood over Samuel's body, wearing a faded brown *futa,* the traditional Yemini male shirt, and black pants. A black *keffiyeh* covered his face, with only his eyes exposed.

The man stood over Samuel, the bloody knife in his hand dripping on the floor.

2

Port Said, Egypt
Resta Port Said Hotel

Kadie wanted to scream, but her survival instincts kicked in. She was a fighter and had been for years. Perhaps the assailant picked up on that. When she burst through the door, he hesitated for a moment, then fled out the window. Kadie started to follow him but realized he might not be the only one in the room.

She scanned her surroundings until her eyes focused on the bedroom door. Picking up a small but dense statue off the coffee table, she crept toward the bedroom. As she had done at the entrance, she flung open the door and barged in.

Empty.

Rushing back to the window, she found the assailant gone. Kadie set her ad-hoc weapon on the credenza and ran to Samuel. His skin was pale, and his eyes stared blankly at the ceiling, the once white shirt now a deep crimson in front. Her two fingers pressed against his jugular vein, searching for a pulse. There was none. She pulled her portable compact out of a cargo pocket on her pants and placed the mirror under his nose. He wasn't breathing.

Her eyes watered with the realization her friend was dead. Could this be related to his phone call? He was on to something, but what? It was too coincidental for this to happen.

Kadie rose and scurried to the bathroom to wash her hands. She turned on the water and picked up the soap. The blood sullied the white porcelain before disappearing down the drain. She breathed deep, and for the first time, noticed how rapid her heart pounded. After several deep breaths, she washed her face.

She dried her face and hands and hurried back into the living room. She needed to call the police but not until she gathered Samuel's computer and cell phone—in case the police confiscated them for evidence. Their mission was classified. The last thing the team needed was their data in the hands of local police.

The laptop had a flash drive inserted in the USB port. She pulled it out and stuck it in her pocket. Slipping through Samuel's broken door, she scurried down the hall to her room, opened the door, and stepped inside.

Brian was on the couch, tinkering with his drone. The television was on, but he wasn't watching.

He looked up as Kadie slipped inside. "Hey—is that computer fow me?"

"No, it's Samuel's. I'm borrowing it for a while." She didn't have the heart or the time to explain what happened to him yet. She was still trying to figure out what to do. Setting the computer and his phone on the desk, she tugged on the window and ensured it was locked. If the killer had come through Samuel's window, there was no reason he couldn't come through hers.

"I'm going back to Samuel's room," she said as she trotted to the door. Her eyes seeped, and she wiped them with the back of her hand. "Lock the chain behind me and don't open it for anyone but me. Don't even answer it. Okay?"

Brian's head tilted. "Okay. What is wrong?"

"Nothing's wrong. I'm just worried about you."

"I am okay—but something is wrong. I can tell."

Kadie opened the door and peered into the empty hallway. "I'll tell you when I get back. Lock the door behind me, okay?"

Brian nodded and rose from the couch, his drone clutched in his left hand. When she shut the door, she stayed until she heard him lock the chain from the inside. It provided little protection—she had just proved that herself—but it made her feel better. She turned and raced back to Samuel's room.

Inside, the scene hadn't changed. Bending down, she rechecked Samuel, sure that hadn't changed either. He was still dead. Kadie found the phone on a small table by the door and dialed the front desk. She explained there had been a murder and to please send the police to room 212. The clerk didn't understand her the first time, and she had to repeat it. Shocked, the clerk said he'd call the police right away.

Kadie sobbed as she hung up the phone. She spun back toward Samuel and gasped as the Middle Eastern killer crawled through the window again. Tall and filled out, he still had the *keffiyeh* covering everything on his face but his eyes. Her mind took in as many details as possible when the man's arm shot out like lightning. She retreated until her back butted against the wall.

Something glittery and shiny flew toward her.

Everything moved in a dreamlike state until . . .

THUNK!

The shiny object struck the wall inches from her ear. Her head rolled to the right. A thin-handled silver throwing knife with a wide blade and a stylish, engraved logo remained embedded in the doorframe. The shape reminded her of a fish.

She looked back toward the killer, who pulled another knife from his sleeve. Kadie grabbed the door handle, flung it open, and raced out of the room, slamming the door behind her as a second blade pierced the door. She darted past the tiny clerk creeping toward

Samuel's room. The man swiveled to speak to her as the killer burst through the door and crashed into him.

Kadie dashed away as the two men tumbled to the floor. At the top of the staircase, she found an overweight Middle Eastern man halfway up the stairs struggling with an oversized suitcase in each hand. Down the hallway, the killer climbed back on his feet and rushed toward her. Kadie started down the stairs a few steps, then hopped on the sturdy mahogany banister and slid down the rail to the first floor.

The man on the staircase seemed both annoyed and amused as he watched her glide down. When he turned back, the Middle Eastern killer plowed into him, and the two tumbled down the staircase to the bottom step. The long shirttail of the Kurta rode high, and she noticed the belt around the black pants for the first time.

Kadie searched the lobby for more threats. None in sight.

I've got to lead him away from Brian, just in case.

Without a second thought, she bounced out the front door and into the shadowy streets. Once outside, two more men with *keffiyehs* hiding their faces pointed at her. She ran the opposite direction, away from the water and toward the small nighttime market she had left only minutes before. Glancing over her shoulder, the killer from Samuel's room was right on her tail.

It had been three years since she had been a star on the Princeton women's volleyball team, but she was still in shape. She easily outran the killer, her chestnut-brown hair flowing in the wind, and weaved through the market's crowd once she reached it. Two small boys occupied the middle of the street selling something, and she leaped over their display at the last second. Landing on the balls of her feet, she glanced behind her; she didn't see anyone following her as she accelerated forward.

Finally, she thought, *I've ditched these guys. Need to find the po—*

She slammed into a vendor's cart as he pulled it across the street, and she fell to the old stone roadway. The cart, filled with Mediterranean fruits and vegetables, wobbled on its rickety wheels. The vendor, a weathered man wearing blue jeans and a green and white athletic jacket, was stunned, though angry words in Arabic soon followed.

Didn't see that coming. Kadie shook her head and felt for injuries. No sooner had she pushed herself off the ground than Samuel's killer was upon her. The man had a *jambiya* in his hand, its curved blade glinting in the early evening streetlight. He reached her as she turned to run, thrusting the knife toward her as she took her first step. She backed up against the cart she had run into; the vendor continued cursing her in Arabic. When the vendor saw the *jambiya*, he stopped berating her and retreated to the other side of the cart.

Kadie dodged to the right at the last second, and the *jambiya* lodged into the wood siding. She ripped a heavy iron pan free and swung it at the attacker. When the dense pan slammed into his head, he crumpled to the ground.

The vendor sidled around the cart and yelled at her again, pointing to the attacker on the ground.

"Sorry," she said, handing him the pan. Glancing back up the street, she quickly realized the other two had found her.

Worse than that, they had her trapped. Each man hurried to load a crossbow, guaranteeing she could never outrun them.

Of course, they have crossbows.

The cart and its dislodged contents cut off any easy escape. Once the bolts locked in place, the two men raised their weapons and fired simultaneously. Kadie dropped to the ground, pounding her elbow on the bricked street. The bolts screamed by at incredible speed, splitting the wood on the cart behind her.

Rolling on the soiled cobbled surface underneath the cart, Kadie rose on the other side and sprinted down the street. She found an unlit alley and ducked in. Peering through the shadows, she had to decide—leave the market or find a way to blend in.

The decision was an easy one. Kadie could never blend in; even if she threw a *hijab* over her head, her Western-style clothes and boots would identify her immediately. Her feet slid side to side, as she edged along the wall, keeping an eye out for her assailants.

Something rubbed her hair, and she brushed her hand to push it away. She twirled to the right, and the faint netting increased in both density and resistance.

Spiderweb!

"Eeeeeaaaahhh!"

Her arms flailed, peeling away the wispy cobweb from her hair and face. From a distance, it might appear she was dancing, but this was no dance. Kadie hated spiders. She had even refused to watch any of the Spider-Man movies, from Toby Maguire through Tom Holland.

When the cobweb finally wiped away, she checked the entrance of the alley. Her two assailants blocked her only way out.

Way to go, Kadie. Screaming like a little girl is going to get you killed.

Kadie twirled and raced down the dark alley, figuring it was better to run into the darkness than stay exposed in the light. She used the blackness creeping over the alley to her advantage. She veered left at the end and slipped into an alley between two small buildings. The alley expanded into a clearing and she screeched to a halt.

It was a dead end.

Her head swiveled in all directions and her breathing was heavy. Sweat dripped down her face and her shirt clung to her back. A small stable sat behind one of the buildings, and across from that, stacks of pottery and tools. She wedged herself between a pair of large pots, praying she could hide as the two assailants ran into the alley. Pulling her scrunchy off her wrist, she pulled her hair back into a ponytail. Despite no breeze, the change made her feel more comfortable. She then lifted an over-sized ceramic saucer to hide her face, hoping the object would break up her profile.

Peeking around the edge of the saucer, the two men chasing her meandered across the street. Their heads swiveled in both directions, then strode down the street toward her.

Across the clearing from her, a small, covered stall held a donkey, who ate from a tiny trough of hay. The two men stopped there, searching around the stall. They continued down the along that side of the clearing, looking at every conceivable hiding place, when the unthinkable happened.

TING!

The phone in her cargo pants lit up with a text message.

Brian.

There was no reason to check the phone. When she peeked around the ceramic saucer, the two men taunted her as they reached for new bolts to load their crossbows.

3

Port Said, Egypt
The streets of Port Said

Kadie's heart raced. The two attackers pulled the strings back on their crossbows so they could load their bolts.

She hurled the ceramic saucer at the two men. They ducked the projectile and snickered. But the saucer smacked the donkey in the head, which then did what donkeys do—it kicked backward at the perceived threat. The kick dislodged the vertical pole that propped up the overhang above the stall. The residents of this house must have used the overhang for a storage area because everything crashed down on the two men.

Kadie didn't wait around to see if they were okay. She spun and sprinted back down the alleyway, then turned toward what she believed to be the direction back to the hotel. She ran for several blocks and when she rounded a corner, she skidded to a stop once again.

The murderer she slugged over the head with the heavy pan was back.

Who is this guy? Michael Myers?

The *Halloween* reference wasn't far off. This guy wanted to kill her and wasn't going to stop.

She pivoted to her left and sprinted toward another house, this one surrounded by a small wall. With the grace of a cat, she swung her legs over the stonework and raced across the dark yard, weaving around several carts and tools left overnight in the dust. She cleared the wall on the other side as easily as the first and found herself in a larger compound.

The killer trailed not far behind, and she approached another wall in front of her, this one much higher, at least eight feet tall. Four feet from the wall, she leaped forward, planted her right foot in the center, and grasped the top with both hands. Her feet bicycled up the wall, slipping as she did so. Eventually, she managed to get high enough to get her elbow on the ledge, the push up to her waist. As she swung her right leg over, the killer grabbed her dangling left foot. She shook her foot violently, attempting to break free, but he held on, even tightening his grip. Shifting her weight, she checked her side of the wall— nothing but dirt below.

Kadie used her body weight and leaned toward her side of the wall. Gravity took over, and the assassin lost his grip on her foot, unable to stop her as she fell to the other side. Her foot hit first, and she twisted her body, using her thigh and backside to absorb the impact.

She felt a slight twinge in her left knee; rolling to her side, she rose slowly, checking for any other injuries. Her shoulder also ached from the fall, but otherwise she seemed unscathed. She heard a noise and looked up to see several goats clamoring to their feet and hurrying to the other side of the compound.

After wiping away her sweaty bangs from the front of her face, she peered through the dust that stung her eyes. Across the courtyard stood a two-story house. That was unusual around here. Whoever owned this property had money. Kadie took a step and discovered the twinge in her knee was a little more than that. She hobbled toward the home when the killer reached the top of the wall.

Doesn't this guy ever quit?

Her breath came in large gasps; she couldn't do this forever. Across the yard, she discovered a small ladder leaning against the house, which gave her an idea. Kadie limped to the ladder as the killer landed on the ground behind her.

Fear gave her a second wind. Kadie climbed the ladder, her knee aching with every push. The delay let the killer catch up with her. He grabbed for her foot again, but Kadie, having no other choice, leaped to the roof, and spun around, gritting through the pain to kick him in the face. The impact sent him off the ladder, sailing toward the ground below.

Kadie dragged the ladder to the roof so he couldn't climb after her. Tossing it aside, she noticed a ladder to the second floor. She scaled this one as well, pulling it up behind her. The Middle Eastern killer moved to the middle of the courtyard as light spilled out of the house. Angry Arabic voices emitted from the courtyard below, ending only when her assailant sprinted across the compound and escaped into the night.

With her fingers locked behind her head, Kadie tried to slow her breathing. Three people in the courtyard pointed in her direction. She rubbed her scraped elbow, wiping away the dirt and grime while they argued back and forth for several minutes. In the distance, blue lights flashed on the horizon, growing brighter as they moved closer. Eventually, sirens accompanied them. The owner of the home must have notified the police. Kadie slid her cell phone out of her pocket and called Brian.

"Where are you, Kadie?"

"I'm a few blocks away." Her free hand brushed the matted hair from her eyes.

"When are you coming back?"

Kadie bit her bottom lip as two police cars stopped outside the compound fifty yards away.

"I'm not sure, Brian. Maybe thirty minutes. Whatever you do, don't answer the door for anyone."

The owner reached the gate and rattled on incessantly to the police, then pointed toward her. One of the policemen used a handheld spotlight to illuminate her on the roof. Kadie waved a subtle wave waist high.

"On second thought, I may be a few hours."

4

Port Said, Egypt
Resta Port Said Hotel

It took almost three hours for the police to release Kadie. Unfortunately, their English was about as effective as her Arabic. Two of those hours entailed finding an English interpreter, apparently not an easy task at this time of night. They had taken her to the Port Police Station next to the water, a vast white three-story building with a white cement tower extending another fifty or sixty feet. In the darkness, it reminded her of the Aloha Tower in Honolulu she saw on her high school senior trip, minus the clock. Initially, she was interrogated as if she were a thief, attempting to break into a family's home. As her story unfolded, the owner of the house she had climbed on was forgiving of her intrusion. Once she told her story, the owner confirmed that he *did* see a man running from his compound. The police were surprised when Kadie divulged the story of Samuel's murder at the hotel. She sobbed as she recounted the story. By this time, the police were very familiar with the crime. It wasn't every day a tourist was killed at one of the more posh hotels in Port Said. After a phone call to the U.S. Embassy, all charges against her were dropped. When they finished, one of the officers gave her a ride back to the hotel, which had police swarming everywhere.

When she entered the lobby, she had to go to the front desk to verify her identity.

"Dis is her!" the clerk said.

Kadie cracked a faint smile. "Yes, it's me."

The officer at the desk glared at her. "Missus, you are de one to call dis in?" His broken English wasn't too much of a distraction. He was much better than the interpreter at the station.

"Yes, I saw the man who did this." Kadie explained what happened, her hands whirling about as she weaved her tale. The officer marched her upstairs to Samuel's room, the second floor filled with activity. Samuel's body was gone, replaced by police officers standing around talking to each other. Kadie walked them through the series of events, even explaining the two knives still embedded in the wall and door. Her stomach turned as the police removed the knives and placed them in a plastic bag. The knife in the door protruded all the way through. No doubt it would have shattered the front of her skull and left her body next to Samuel's.

Kadie went on to describe the chase through the market and her eventual arrest. The officer called the station to confirm her story. While he was on the phone, a familiar voice carried down the hallway. She stole a glance outside.

"Curt!" Kadie rushed down the hall, bursting past the two policemen who stopped him, and wrapped her arms around the neck of the six-foot-tall GDI security man.

"It's okay," Curt said to the police in Arabic. "She's with me." Curt was one of the two team members who spoke the native language. Unfortunately, Samuel was the other.

"Are you okay?" he said with a toothy smile, squeezing her hard.

"I'm fine." Kadie pushed away as if suddenly aware of her actions. After what she'd experienced, seeing a familiar face was overwhelming. She glanced at him and gasped. "What happened?" A small cut in the middle of his forehead dripped blood.

Curt grinned. "Well, I texted you I'd be late for dinner because I was still here taking care of some security issues." He pointed to Samuel's room. "Clearly, we still have a problem. Anyway, I ran after the guy who chased you out of Samuel's room, but another guy slammed me into the wall. We struggled for a couple of minutes. He got away, and I got this."

He ran a hand through his blond hair. It was far worse than just a cut. The side of his head bore several bruises.

"You poor thing. You should put some ice on that."

Curt shook his head. "No time. I notified Doctor Hastings about what has happened. She wants our team in Istanbul in the morning. We've got to pack up and depart as soon as possible."

"When do we need to leave?" Kadie said.

Curt glanced at his watch. "In four hours. We head south to Ismailia and catch a flight."

"Why the rush? Four a.m. is awfully quick. I mean, it's doable, but I'm exhausted, and I desperately need a shower. What about the airfield in town?"

Curt nodded. "I understand. Mister Thorndike called Doctor Hastings after she reported this to the company." Graham Thorndike was the CEO of Alligynt, the parent company of GDI. "His contacts in the DOD have advised him of the increased threat in Egypt. ISIS is very active here and makes repeated threats against all foreigners, particularly Jews."

Kadie knew exactly what Curt meant. Samuel was Jewish and somehow had been targeted by ISIS. "Okay, we'll get packing." She wanted to hug him again but wasn't sure if that was appropriate. Given their work situation, she didn't want to come on too strong. When she turned to go to her room, he followed, never leaving her side. Kadie smiled. That was a good sign.

When they reached her room, she opened the door with the Gomer. The chain stopped the door from going any further. "Brian, it's me," she yelled through the crack and closed the door.

"Okay," Brian said from inside.

A few seconds later, Brian unlocked the door and let her in. Her brother stared at them with sunken eyes.

"Did you bwing me a gweat big hambuwgew?"

Curt's forehead scrunched, his mouth tilting downward. "What did he say?"

Kadie spied the crumpled bag the bread came in laying on the coffee table. "Nothing," she said. "He's just hungry."

She stepped in and glanced back at Curt as she closed it. "We'll meet you in the lobby at four." She slid the chain back in place and chuckled to herself, aware it wouldn't prevent anyone from getting in. When she turned around, Brian stood with a stern expression on his face.

"Where—have you been? Did you go—have food with him?"

She recognized the problem immediately. "No, no. Brian, I'm sorry. I ran into him in the hallway a few minutes ago. I've been speaking to the police most of the night." Brian stared at her, skeptical. How would he take this? He was familiar with death; in fact, he was facing it himself. But murder was different. He stared at her awkwardly.

"Why are you so dirty?"

Kadie glanced down at her filthy pants and her untucked, tattered shirt. Her hand drifted to the side of her face; aware it was probably smeared with dirt. "Brian, Samuel was killed earlier."

"Killed?" His eyes drooped and watered, showing a sadness that broke her heart. Samuel had been so good to Brian the past few weeks.

"Yes. We're not sure why." She decided *not* to tell him what happened to *her*. That might scare him too much—both for his safety and hers. Still, he needed to understand their situation better. "The company believes we're all in danger. We're leaving the hotel in a few hours and driving to an airport in another town."

"Ugh, I am so sleepy. I do not want to go."

She ran her fingers through his hair. "I know, but we have to pack.

Curt says the security threat is too high to stay here. It's too dangerous."

Brian shook his head and returned to the couch. He seemed aggravated when he thought she and Curt had dinner alone. Thankfully, his disposition changed once she told him what had happened, but Brian remained stubborn. She trusted Curt and felt like he was attracted to her and maybe her to him. Curt had taken them to lunch and dinner a couple of times. Of course, Brian would be upset if they went to eat without him.

"What do you think of Curt?" she asked him again. She found his answer earlier that night too non-committal.

Her brother glanced at her. "He is okay." He focused back on the television.

Kadie sighed. His answer was the same as before. "*Just* okay?"

He looked back and nodded. "Yeah," then returned his attention to the TV.

"Well, we're leaving in a few hours. Whether we like it or not."

Brian focused on the television. Kadie shook her head, then checked the locks on the windows and door before strolling to the bathroom. She'd take a fast shower to remove the filth from earlier. They had a long night ahead, and the killer may return.

5

The Egypt team gathered in the lobby well before 3:30 in the morning. In front of the hotel, a vintage, battered bus that appeared like it belonged on a California hippie compound in the 1960s waited for them. The team consisted of five more besides Kadie and Curt. Abdul Hassan from Cambridge, England was an expert in Egyptian hieroglyphics. Andre LeBeau was a DNA specialist from Paris. Biological disease specialist Dr. Jedediah Hamilton and general practitioner Dr. George Upton both of whom worked at the CDC in Atlanta. Added to the small group was Kadie's brother, an honorary member of the team.

Bringing Brian had been her go-no-go position. She was quite surprised GDI went along with it. Kadie let them know upfront that aside from having Down syndrome, Brian had a brain tumor. A cyst had formed on his pituitary gland and had grown substantially over the last year. The doctors at the Kirklin Clinic at the University of Alabama, Birmingham, had given him a few years to live. When this opportunity arose, Kadie refused to leave him on his own. She was going to spend whatever time he had left with him. When they agreed to her demand, she offered to take a salary cut and pay his way to Egypt, but GDI said none of that was necessary. They made Brian part of the “team,” paid his way there, and made special arrangements for Kadie to have a suite with two rooms at every location.

That sealed the deal. The job was perfect for a recent graduate student. It would boost her resumé for the faculty position at Princeton. Everyone on the team was very welcoming of Brian, and most, given their medical backgrounds, were more than familiar with Down syndrome.

Reflecting on it, she didn’t know what to expect. Typical images of an archeological dig swirled in her head—dirty, dusty, and hot. So, that’s what she packed for. The team was a rather peculiar collection of specialists to fight a virus, she thought when she learned who would be joining her. Everyone had a unique skill that didn’t relate to anyone else’s. They all engaged in the initial search, of course, scouring museums and ancient sites. If they found anything, Kadie would be the one to confirm it was potentially the correct vase, translating the Aramaic inscription believed to be on the vase. She wasn’t sure why they had a DNA specialist on board, but the two doctors from the CDC were present to ensure the vase didn’t contain any traces of disease inside the vessel. Samuel was supposed to do the preliminary carbon dating to confirm the age of the vase.

Curt announced everyone was accounted for, and the ragged bus pulled out of the hotel parking lot at precisely four o’clock. The plastic-covered seats split at the seams, the disintegrating foam spilling on the floor. Kadie felt every bump and crack in the street as the driver struggled with the transmission. They hit a bump that launched them all upward in their seats.

“Shock absorbers must be optional in Egypt,” she said, causing Brian to chuckle. She smiled at him and rubbed her knee. The soreness had dissipated in the last hour. She had wrapped her knee with an Ace bandage after her shower and downed a couple of Motrin. Brian sat next to the window and stared at the dark and silent city streets; his drone secured in the small Pelican case that sat on his lap. Kadie placed her arm around his shoulders, and within minutes, he dozed off. It had been a long, rough night for everyone.

Her thoughts had drifted back to Samuel. They met when GDI first organized the team in New York City. Samuel became very protective of her, like a father to his daughter, and Kadie clung to that, a feeling she hadn't had in years. Having a father-figure to confide in lifted a huge burden off her shoulders. Not only did he admire her plans to become an associate professor at Princeton, but he also reassured her that her decision to bring Brian on this trip was the right one. But Samuel was gone, and there was no one here who could ever take his place.

They drove south out of town along the Suez Canal. Once Brian fell asleep, Curt slid in the seat in front of her and started to open his go-bag. He pulled out a small rifle resembling an AK-47 and inserted the magazine. Then he donned a tactical vest that had extra magazines and a pistol strapped to his chest.

"Is all that necessary?" she asked.

"We're leaving the city. Could be dangerous." He shifted in his seat looking back at her. "How are you doing?" he said.

Kadie shifted in her seat so she could see him better. She wasn't comfortable with Curt brandishing his weapons the way he was, but perhaps it was necessary. "I'm okay. It's been a crazy night. I can't stop thinking about Samuel. It-it's so horrible."

Curt's gaze dropped to the floor before shifting back to her. "Yes, it is. I-I'm sorry you had to see something like that."

"What will happen with Samuel?"

"I contacted the U.S. Embassy. They will send a representative tomorrow to claim his body."

"But he's from Israel."

"Yes. Given the circumstances, this was the best we could do. Our embassy will arrange for Samuel's body to be sent to Tel Aviv as soon as possible."

Kadie glanced down before she returned her gaze to Curt. "I'm stunned the police let us leave so soon after. You'd think they would want to question us further, interview everyone, investigate *what* happened to find out *why*?"

"Well, they spoke to you. They didn't have any other witnesses, and you didn't really see anything."

"Didn't see anything? The guy stood over Samuel with a bloody knife! He threw a *knife* at my head!" Her voice came out in a harsh whisper, and she recognized she needed to be a little more discreet. "He and his gang would have killed me if they caught me."

"Gang? What are you talking about?"

The ragged bus shuddered violently as the driver applied the brakes at a stoplight.

Kadie grabbed the back of the seat in front of her. "Two other guys chased me. They tried to shoot me with crossbows."

"Really? I didn't know that." There as a brief pause. "Tell me about them."

Kadie explained what they looked like and how she got away. Her voice became louder the more she relived the experience. The explanation she gave was thorough, ending with her on a roof when the police arrived.

Curt put his hands forward to calm her down. "So, let me get this straight . . . you saw the man in the room but didn't actually observe him killing Samuel?"

"I don't believe I needed to. It was obvious what happened."

Curt tilted his head to the side. "You had quite an evening. I'm just grateful the authorities let us leave. They seemed to think another attack by ISIS was imminent, so us skipping town made sense."

"Hopefully ISIS is asleep."

"Don't count on it. I have no doubt our hotel is under surveillance around the clock. While it feels like we're safe right now, this trip is very dangerous. We must stay alert."

Kadie shifted her attention outside. If that were the case, she needed to pay attention to what they were doing and where they were going. The roads became less bouncy as they went further outside the city, but the transmission creaked and groaned every time the bus changed gears.

They left M40 and joined M67, which led them straight to the Ismailia Airport. The entire trip took about an hour and a half, and the abandoned airfield sat right off M67, just west of town. The bus left the main road and took a left up a side street, the trees lining either side visible for a second only as the bus headlights rumbled by. At the end of the street, the fence to the airport had been removed. The bus trudged through the packed sand until it climbed back on to the asphalt of the taxiway and eventually came to a stop.

Kadie nudged Brian to wake him up.

"Brian, we're here." She wasn't quite sure where "here" was. This wasn't what she expected when Curt said they were going to the airport. They appeared to be next to the runway, but regardless, they were alone in the darkness, a long way from the terminal, from any building for that matter. Throughout the ride there, Curt told her the trip was dangerous, yet he didn't seem nervous. Perhaps that's what they taught these Delta Force Commandos—how to have nerves of steel.

The bus sat in the blackness of the taxiway. Everyone remained quiet, scanning outside, and knowing they were defenseless if ISIS attacked. Curt checked his watch and directed everyone to exit the vehicle.

"Take everything with you," he said. "If anything happens and we need to leave in a hurry, bring only the Pelican cases and your go-bags."

It took a few minutes for the team to unload everything and even longer to stack their bags and Pelican cases on the side of the runway.

Kadie noticed Curt was still checking his watch. No doubt he had timed the pickup to perfection. After thirty minutes of them standing by the edge of the runway, her perception began to change, and she shuffled next to him.

"How much longer?"

Curt shook his head. "I don't know. They should have been here ten minutes ago."

"Is there a reason why we can't wait in the terminal? It's going to be miserable out here when the sun comes up."

"We won't be here that long."

"How can you be sure? We—" She stopped as the roar of an

aircraft raced to the southeast of their position at a very low altitude. Stunned by its immediate and intense appearance, Kadie fell silent, unable to yell over its deafening pitch. The plane had no exterior lights on and was almost impossible to see. She caught a glimpse of it in the ambient light before it disappeared in the darkness once again.

"There he is," Curt said.

Kadie lost sight of the plane in the inky void, but it sounded like it banked left and was coming back toward them. The blacked-out plane showed up on short final, landing on the runway and rolling a short distance before turning around and taxiing back toward them.

It wasn't a small airplane, but it would never pass for a commercial jet. A twin-engine propeller airplane taxied toward them and did another one-eighty-degree turn, pointing down the runway as if ready to take off again.

"Okay, everyone," Curt hollered over the engines' sound. "Load the cases and go-bags first."

The team moved steadily toward the aircraft, bags and cases in hand, Kadie and Brian led the way. Kadie held one of Brian's hands while the other clutched the small Pelican case containing his drone. Curt marched next to her, his eyes scanning their surroundings every step of the way.

They were twenty yards from the aircraft, when the first sign of trouble arrived. On the southeast side of the runway, dashes of light streaked across the runway. A POP-POP-POP could be heard over the aircraft's humming engines.

Everyone appeared to notice it at once and huddled together short of the airplane.

"Tracer fire!" Curt yelled. "Get moving! Now!"

"What about our luggage?" LeBeau said.

"Leave it. Go!"

Kadie and Brian were the first to move. They reached the airplane in seconds. The door flew open. A grizzled older man, wearing a worn, tan flight suit with Under Armor tennis shoes, leaped outside. He brandished a small weapon with a big, curved magazine. Moving beyond the wing on the left side, he knelt and started shooting in the direction of the gunfire. The muzzle of his rifle spit fire with each shot, highlighting him in the darkness.

Brian boarded first. The poor boy's eyes bulged, mouth open, his body visibly shaking.

"It's going to be okay, Brian," she said. "Pull the case inside, then find a seat." Brian did, and Kadie assisted the others. When Dr. Upton passed, she grabbed him by the arm. "Check on Brian for me." Upton nodded and hurried into the plane.

She faced Curt, who motioned for everyone to hurry onto the plane. "Who is shooting at us?"

"ISIS . . . Must have followed us!"

They both yelled to overcome the roaring engines of their rescue plane. Curt moved down the line, encouraging them to speed it up. Hassan hollered and fell to the ground. The report of a rifle boomed from behind them. Curt swung around and squeezed off a few shots at the muzzle flashes behind them. He snarled as his rate of fire increased, shifting from left to right, then left again. His shoulder jolted with each pull of the trigger.

Kadie helped Hassan onto the plane. She scurried back and dragged his Pelican case to the door. LeBeau climbed out and loaded it on the plane. Once everyone was on board, Kadie ran back to Curt.

"Everyone's on!" she yelled.

Curt kept shooting until he ran out of ammunition. The receiver on his rifle locked back; he deftly swapped out magazines, threw the bolt forward, and continued to fire. "Okay, get on! I'm right behind you!" More and more shooters seemed to appear, muzzle flashes and deadly tracers coming from all directions.

She whirled and raced to the waiting plane and climbed aboard. Brian sat in his seat, anxious, nervous, scared. When she poked her head through the door, he beamed.

"Kadie!"

She pulled herself into the plane and slid next to him, wrapping her arms around his shoulders. "We're going to be okay," she said, hugging him. "We're safe now."

Soon after, Curt climbed aboard, and Kadie felt the aircraft lurch but not move as the pilot pushed the engines forward and back twice. That must have been his partner's cue because moments later, he jumped through the door and closed it behind him. Kadie heard the engines advance, but the aircraft didn't move.

The second pilot climbed in, shut the door, and crawled over the cases and bags that littered the tiny aisle to the cockpit. Halfway there, he hollered ahead.

"Let's go!"

The aircraft leaned forward. The pilot was holding the brakes while he pushed up the power. Kadie cradled Brian in her arms as she searched out his window. Tracers still zipped through the air.

A few seconds later, bullets riddled the airplane.

Maybe they weren't so safe after all.

6

Ismailia, Egypt
The abandoned Ismailia Airport

Duke Ellsworth shoved the throttles up. "Set takeoff power," he said.

Mac reached over the throttle quadrant and adjusted the power. "Ignition lights—off. Auto-feather lights—on. Power—Set." He climbed into the co-pilot's seat.

Duke released the brakes, and the King-Air lurched forward and accelerated rapidly. Tracers from ISIS AK-47's zipped in their direction from the left-forward quadrant. Mac was still buckling in when they passed sixty knots. He called out the speed, but Duke didn't reply. As they approached one-hundred knots, Mac started to call that out when Duke yanked back on the yoke, and the King-Air leaped from the ground. He transitioned to the artificial horizon on the instrument panel and set the pitch at ten degrees nose up. Mac raised the gear, and the aircraft shuddered as it struggled to avoid a stall. The airspeed reached one-hundred-ten knots, and Duke held that speed as the aircraft climbed away from the ground at the best rate. There would be a brief window of time where his plane would be in range of the 7.62mm rounds that flew toward them. And judging from the amount of tracer fire, that could be dangerous.

"We must have woken them up in the terminal," Mac said.

"I think they're awake everywhere now," Duke replied over the passengers screaming in the back. Tracer fire came from behind them, peppering the airplane.

I hope we make it out of here in one piece. God help us.

"Should be out of range soon." Duke checked the airspeed indicator. "One-hundred-thirty-knots."

"Passing two-thousand feet," Mac said, fidgeting in his seat.

Duke's eyes shifted from his airspeed and the altitude to the tracers that zipped around them. Most of them fell short, but he felt the ones that impacted the plane. A right turn would have placed more distance between him and the shooters, but he elected to maintain his climb. He thought it would get them out of the firing envelope quicker vertically than if he lowered the nose and moved away horizontally at a faster speed—no way to know for sure, even after this was over.

The airspeed settled at one-fifty, and Duke continued his climb. When he reached six-thousand feet, he nudged the nose down and accelerated away from the airport.

"I'm heading for the Suez Canal," Duke said. "Keep an eye out for MANPADS," the man-portable-air-defense missiles, or shoulder-launched projectiles of death. Their airplane was equipped with a rudimentary flare system to counter heat-seeking missiles; they just had to see the missile first. If they did, the flares were very effective against early generation *heaters*, as they were called. If they didn't, well . . .

Once they reached the coast, Duke climbed to ten-thousand feet. That would give them a few more seconds to detect a missile launch. Duke coupled the autopilot, set his power, then pulled out a can of Wintergreen-flavored, long-cut Skoal out of his pocket. He twisted off the lid, grabbed a pinch between his thumb and forefinger, and stuck the smokeless tobacco between his cheek and gums. His body shuddered as the minty nicotine gave him a rush.

Duke spit in an empty water bottle, then looked at Mac. "Check on our passengers and look for any battle damage. I want to pressurize and go higher, but I'm worried there are too many holes in the fuselage."

"You got it." Mac unbuckled and stepped to the door. "Everyone okay back there?" Duke heard voices, but they were drowned out by the engines. After a minute or so, Mac slid back into his seat and buckled back in.

"One of the guys was shot in the leg, but they've got a med-kit broke out and looks like they got him cleaned up. Everyone else is okay. There are a lot of holes in the back, though. Don't think we can pressurize. Shocked that more of them didn't get hit."

Duke nodded. "It's a blessing, for sure."

Mac broadcast their position on the Israeli frequency as they flew offshore past the international boundary of Egypt. The last thing they wanted was a couple of Israeli F-35's chasing them down. It would be a very short chase.

"Uh-oh," Mac said.

Duke checked the engine instruments and immediately saw the problem. The oil pressure on the left engine fell. Fast.

"Must have shot up the engine," Mac said. "Maybe they shot a hole in the sump?"

"No telling. Doesn't matter—we won't have the engine for long anyway. Let's keep our altitude at ten-thousand for now." Duke leaned forward and checked the engine on the left wing. Ambient light from the stars allowed him to see black streaks over the engine cowling. "Yup, it's oil."

The two pilots kept the engine running until the pressure hit red line, then they shut it down. They proceeded with their checklists when someone stuck their head in the cockpit door.

"It sounds like one of the engines quit," a female voice said.

Duke glanced to his right. *Hmmm. Cute.*

"Lady," Mac said, "one of our engines got shot up. Had to shut it down. We're busy. Please sit down and let us handle it."

"Are we going to crash?" she said.

"Only if you don't go back to your seat," Mac replied.

The woman disappeared.

"You're mean," Duke said.

"Not mean. Efficient. I got rid of her with minimum discussion."

Duke nodded with a grin. "We're going to have to head to Israel. Contact them and let them know we're an emergency aircraft and need to land at Tel Aviv."

"Big international airport. Think that's a good idea?"

Duke shrugged his shoulders. "Left engine crapped out after twenty minutes. There's no telling if anything is wrong with the right one. If there is, we'll be ditching this thing in the Mediterranean."

Mac coordinated with Israeli air traffic control, giving them the nature of the emergency, the number of souls on board, and flight time remaining based on their fuel.

Fuel.

Duke checked the fuel for the first time since he had leveled off at six-thousand feet. They still had fuel pressure—the quantity was just several hundred pounds less. Mac did some back-of-the-napkin calculations and confirmed it with their flight plan. They *were* leaking fuel.

"Must have taken rounds to the oil tank," Duke said. "That sits aft of the compressor air inlet and the forward end of the accessory gearbox. Probably had a fuel line or two nicked in there to boot."

"Well, with one engine or two, we won't make Istanbul leaking fuel at this rate," Mac said. "We'd most likely need to land in Cyprus."

"Thank God Israel is here."

Mac smiled. "Yes, indeed."

The two men prepared for landing. When they were fifteen minutes away from the airport, the distant plumes from two jet afterburners shimmered against the onyx black sky. The jets turned and headed in their direction.

"Here they come," Duke said.

"You can bet their air-defenses on the ground will be tracking us the whole way in."

"Yup. I'm sure the IDF will be waiting for us when we land." The entire Israeli Defense Force would be active, unsure if the approaching aircraft was friend or foe. The Israelis would not be shy about blowing them out of the sky at the slightest provocation.

Runway 08 was the active runway at Ben Gurion International Airport in Tel Aviv, but the controller wanted them to land on Runway 03, so they wouldn't shut down the primary runway. Duke followed the controller's directions and established himself on a visual straight-in for Runway 03. Two F-35s intercepted them when they leveled off at two-thousand feet and confirmed they were who they said they were. One of the jets broadcast the King-Air did indeed have an engine shut down and commented that they had bullet holes in the cowling and fuselage.

"Well," Mac said, "at least we know what caused the oil leak."

"As if there was ever any doubt."

Mac chuckled. "Felt safer in the combat zone back in Iraq."

"Yeah." Duke was ambivalent about Iraq. The on-again/off-again approach to combat operations in Iraq had gotten beyond ridiculous. He was there for only one purpose: To help the guys on the ground. It wasn't like his days flying the AC-130J gunship, raining death and fire from above, but his role as a contractor flying ISR missions was still rewarding. The intelligence, surveillance, recon planes they flew were similar to this old King-Air.

Duke slowed the aircraft and delayed extending the landing gear. He didn't want any more drag on the airplane until the last possible second. The fuel leak increased, but they would have enough to land, even at this rate.

To his left, one of the F-35's hung on his wing fifty yards away, flaps down, and the thrust vectoring nozzle in its most downward trajectory. Cool. That meant his partner was behind them, ready to shoot them down at the first sign of something suspicious. Mac broadcast their intentions every step of the way. He also told them they had an injured passenger onboard and requested medical assistance.

At about one-thousand feet, Duke lowered the landing gear to configure for the no-flap landing. He didn't use any flaps because he didn't want the extra drag on the plane in case the other engine quit, and he had to glide the remaining distance in. With 9,094 feet of concrete ahead of him, he would have more than enough runway to stop the plane with no flaps.

The King-Air touched down a thousand feet down the runway and taxied off at the end and turned right, just like the controller directed. He taxied down the Tango taxiway to the dark Apron VC where the IDF waited for them. Every vehicle on the ramp illuminated their headlights, and Duke interpreted that to mean they wanted him to stop. Setting the parking brake, he feathered his remaining engine. The numerous Humvees, ATV's, motorcycles, and MRAPs with troops bailing out of the back closed in. Thirty-seconds after Duke shut down the right engine, they were surrounded by countless weapons of different calibers pointed directly at them.

7

Tel Aviv, Israel
Ben Gurion International Airport

Kadie squinted out the tiny window as she and Brian observed the swarm of military vehicles approaching the crippled plane. They just got shot at after taking off from one airport; now they were surrounded by an army after landing at another. She joined GDI to help save the world using science and technology, but she quickly realized that bombs and bullets ruled in this region of the world.

In the back of the small plane, Doctor Upton treated Abdul, who had been shot in the leg. Curt was back there too, checking on him. Within moments, the seasoned co-pilot stepped out of the cockpit without a rifle this time.

"Hi, folks," he said as he crawled over the bags and Pelican cases that blocked the small aisle. "Welcome to Israel. My name is Mac. Sit tight and give me a few minutes to talk to the folks outside. We'll have to clear Customs and Immigration, but that's going to take a while. Anticipate a long and painful process once we get started." He glared at Curt, still holding his AK-47 in the back of the plane. "I'd unload your rifle and break it down best you can. And whatever you do, *don't* bring it off the airplane." Mac stepped out the door.

Kadie couldn't see anything that took place outside, but inside the plane, Brian was upset. He struggled to process everything that was going on.

"Did we have—an engine f-fire?" he said.

Kadie shrugged her shoulders. "I'm not sure, but they shut it down. I'm sure it got shot up by bullets. That was scary."

Brian's eyes went wide, and he smiled. "That was awe—some! There were glowing bullets flying every—where."

Kadie cringed. *I guess he's processed this okay*, she thought. She wasn't sure if he understood the gravity of the situation. They had come very close to dying, and Abdul was still in pain.

"That was a g-good pilot," Brian said.

Kadie glanced behind her toward the door Mac had exited. "Yes, he was."

"Not that one—the other one who flew it." Brian pointed to the front. Yes, there was still another pilot, but they hadn't seen him yet.

She ran her fingers through his hair. "You're so smart. There *are* two pilots on this plane."

Curt left his seat and slid behind her and set a hand on her shoulder. "Are you okay?"

"I'm fine. That was a lot more excitement than I bargained for on this trip."

"Well, we knew ISIS could be a problem. That's why I'm here." Curt spoke with a confident swagger, but it didn't sit well with Kadie after what they just experienced. Regardless, she chose to say nothing. There might come a time when his being here would come in handy.

"What about you, Brian? How are you doing?" He spoke louder and slower to her brother. She cringed again. He's not deaf; he's Down syndrome. Kadie had spoken to Curt about Brian's condition when they first met. Curt was rather flirtatious. *When Curt first met Kadie and Brian, he told her, "Down syndrome is not normal."*

"It's normal to me," she replied. She wanted Curt to understand upfront: she and Brian were a package deal.

"I am fine," Brian said, shifting his gaze out the window. "How—long—awe—we going to be here?"

"What?" Curt said. "I don't understand."

Kadie intervened. "He asked how long we are going to be here?"

"He—I don't know. We just landed. We'll be here for a couple of hours. Once we're done, I'll contact corporate and have them work on transportation to Istanbul."

Her eyes drooped. "How about a hotel and a nice hot shower?"

Curt's eyes lit up, and he started to say something but stopped himself. She hoped her comment wasn't seen as an invitation because it wasn't.

"You might be right. It's been a long night for everyone. We'll secure a hotel, then work out transportation for tomorrow."

Mac climbed back on the airplane and stood in the doorway. "Folks, we're going to exit the plane now. Bring your go-bags with you but remove any kind of weapon and leave it on your seat. No guns, knives, hammers, chisels . . . nothing you wouldn't get through TSA in the States."

"We need to get Abdul off of the plane," Upton said. "I can't suppress the bleeding any further."

Curt examined the crowded aisle. "He'd have to climb over all these bags." He motioned to everyone in the front. "Unload these cases and bags so he can have a clear path."

Mac slid back out the door, and the GDI team grabbed their bags and went through them, just to make sure they had none of the items that might be considered dangerous, then took them off the airplane. After three minutes, they formed a line to hand the bags off the plane. Several of the bags and Pelican cases had bullet holes in them, and the GDI team realized just how fortunate they were.

To the East, the sun rose over the horizon, painting a captivating mosaic of warm colors across the horizon. The gentle breeze that flitted in from the ocean compensated for the warm temperature. *Odd*, Kadie thought. *It is much more comfortable here than in Port Said. And both are on the coast.*

A pair of medics climbed into the airplane and brought out Abdul, followed by Doctor Upton. Curt was the last of their team to leave the airplane. The small group gathered aft of the left wing, about fifty feet away from the plane. Mac roamed around the airplane to assess the damage. Kadie started to pivot away when she saw movement on the plane but stopped when the mysterious second pilot appeared in the doorway. Kadie caught herself, mumbling, "Oh."

The pilot stepped off the plane and approached the small group. He was the tall, rugged type; almost a stereotype of what one might expect to be a pilot, only he dressed like Indiana Jones, minus the hat and leather jacket. He checked on Abdul in the ambulance before they drove off, then returned to the rest of his passengers.

"Is everyone okay?" the pilot said. He searched the faces of the small team and strolled down the line and introduced himself to each team member. *He's smart*, she thought, *he's trying to get us to relax*. They still were surrounded by a small contingent of soldiers, all heavily armed.

When he got to her, she expected him to turn on the charm. It wasn't ego. It was just what always happened to her. Curt wouldn't stop talking to her for ten minutes when they first met a few weeks ago.

"Hello. I'm Duke Ellsworth." She shook his hand. He was rough and needed a shave and a shower. Even his clothes appeared to have been worn for days.

"Kadie Jenkins." She placed her arm around her brother. "And this is my brother, Brian." She squeezed Brian, whose attention drifted. He fidgeted, his short arms bent at the elbows, and the fingertips of each hand tickled the tips of the other.

Duke knelt and stuck out his hand until Brian shook it. He looked Brian straight in the eye. "That's a strong grip you've got there. How's it going, buddy?"

Brian's face broke into a smile. "G-good. Awe you the pilot?"

Duke smiled. "One of them. You've already met my partner, Mac."

"You awe—a good pilot."

Duke rested a hand on Brian's shoulder. "Well, thanks, Brian. But don't let my partner hear that. He'll insist he does everything." Duke's smile was genuine, and Brian picked up on that immediately. "I've got to do a quick inspection of my airplane. Do you want to walk around with me?"

Brian gazed at Kadie, his eyes pleading to go. Kadie faced Duke. "Will the guys with the guns mind?"

"No," he said as he stood. "They're harmless unless we start to cause trouble."

Curt slid over to them. "Is there a problem?" he said, his voice stern.

Duke glanced at him. "Nope." He pivoted on his heel and strutted toward his airplane with Brian in tow. Duke inspected the engine with the bullet holes while Brian stood back and watched, his hands on his hips. The pilot pointed at the bullet holes in the engine and spoke to Brian, who nodded eagerly. Brian asked a question, and Duke knelt next to him and tried to answer it with his hands. She wished she could hear what they were saying. It warmed her heart that Duke paid attention to him. Too many people stare at Brian with pity, disgust, and even fear. And they're so wrong.

Curt moved closer to Kadie and shook his head. "Typical pilot. All ego, no common sense."

Her eyebrows raised. "Why do you say that?"

"All pilots are the same. You know, girl in every port."

"I thought that was sailors."

"Same thing. You know how these guys are . . . try to impress you with their daring deeds. They're all jerks. I don't trust any of them."

Kadie smiled. Curt acted like an overprotective teenager. "Sounds like the green monster is rearing his head."

Curt jerked his head toward her, grinning. "Oh, a Red Sox fan. We're more compatible than I thought." He slid an arm around her shoulder and gave her a gentle hug.

Ugh. He missed that one by a mile.

"Sorry, Curt. I grew up with Derek Jeter posters on my wall."

Her tone was a little sharp. Curt dropped his arm and backed off; perhaps aware he may have pushed a little too far. Maybe she was too harsh.

"I'm sorry that came out a little stronger than necessary." She tapped his arm. "You don't have to try so hard. Just be yourself." A subtle smile crept across her face.

Curt blushed. "Yeah. That's easier said than done sometimes."

About the time Brian returned, an Israeli officer approached the team with Mac.

"*Shalom*. I am Major Ben Shahim of the Israeli Defense Force. I'm sorry for your predicament, but we are doing everything we can to accommodate you. If you can gather your bags, we will process you through Customs and Immigration. Once clear, we will need to take statements from each of you. I realize you've had a long day, but I will tell you upfront, it's going to get longer. Please be patient, and things will work out."

Major Shahim spoke to Duke. "Please, come with me. We understand you have weapons on board the aircraft." The major escorted Duke to another group of men, who appeared to hurl question after question. Major Shahim returned. "If the rest of you will follow me, we can start."

Kadie picked up her go-bag and slung it over her shoulder and grabbed Brian's hand. Her terrifying night was about to evolve into a miserable day.

8

Kadie trudged her way through the security line as she waited for her turn. Jedidiah Hamilton had been first, followed by the pilots and everyone else. Her focus was on Brian to help him overcome his nervousness. He was fine when he met the pilot, but the slow process of security coupled with the lack of sleep, food, and water started to overwhelm him.

Curt rolled his bag through the X-ray machine and walked through the portable metal detector. He was patted down on the other side, even though the detector did not go off. These guys were taking no chances.

Kadie put Brian's bag and the Pelican case with his drone on the rail, pushed them into the X-ray machine, then sent her bag through.

Curt lingered beyond the rails.

"Go ahead, Brian." She encouraged him to walk through the metal detector. He marched through, was also patted down, then turned around on the other side. Kadie followed Brian through and waited for her bag.

The technician working the machine looked up at her. "Do you have a laptop in here?"

Kadie's eyes widened. "I'm sorry, I should have removed them. I'm so tired. It's been a long night."

"No problem." The officer handed her a plastic container to set them in. "Just run it all back through."

Kadie pulled out two laptops from her backpack. One was hers, the other belonged to Samuel.

Samuel.

She hadn't thought about him in hours. Their whole predicament began with his murder at the hands of ISIS. What could he have discovered? Was it related to ISIS? If so, why would they kill him for his discovery? Too many questions clouded her thoughts as she laid the two computers in the plastic bin. She left his phone in the backpack, along with her own, and sent everything back through the X-ray machine.

Everything came through with no issues, and Kadie gathered the laptops to put back into the backpack.

"What's that?" Curt said.

"What's what?" His stern voice rattled Kadie.

"The laptop. You've got two. Where'd you get the other one?"

His disposition surprised her. "It's Samuel's."

His eyes narrowed; his forehead scrunched. "What are you doing with Samuel's computer?" Curt grumbled through clenched teeth.

"I-I don't know. He left it in my room by accident." It was a lie, but she just blurted out the first thing that came to her mind.

"That's company property. Give it to me." Curt snatched the laptop from her hand. Kadie stood wide-eyed. Where was the caring guy jealous of the competition from a few minutes ago?

"Take it," she said, the anger in her voice evident. "Here, you can take mine, too." She held her laptop at arm's length.

Curt shoved Samuel's laptop into his backpack. When he saw her face, he must have realized how mad she was.

"I don't need that one. I just needed to account for Samuel's. The company—"

"Save it," she said, stuffing her laptop back into her bag. She zipped it up and stormed past Curt with Brian right behind her. Duke and Mac stood off to the side, watching the entire exchange.

Once the group gathered again, they were all taken to separate rooms for an interview with Immigration. Who were they? Why were they in Egypt? Why did their plane leave so early in the morning? How did ISIS know they were going to the airport? Why were they shot at? How did they end up in Israel?

Some interviews lasted longer than others. Kadie and Brian were the first to finish and sat in the bland hallway on a bench to wait for the others. Duke exited a room, saw them sitting on the bench, and walked over.

"You two doing okay?" he said.

"Yeah." Brian forced a smile, but his droopy eyes gave him away.

"How about you?" Duke asked Kadie.

She nodded. "I'm fine. Just tired."

Duke sat next to her. "I understand." He paused. "I know it's none of my business, but what set that guy off about the laptop?"

Kadie sighed; embarrassed Curt's actions were so obvious. "It's the company computer issued to our colleague who was murdered last night. I-I guess he'd been looking for it."

"I understand that, but he was kind of a jerk."

Kadie remained silent for a moment. "Curt is . . . Curt is kind of intense. It's his background, I think."

"What's his background?"

"He's a former Delta Force Commando." Kadie felt herself speaking with the same pride and confidence Curt had when he'd told her.

Duke laughed, deep and hearty. "Delta Force Commando? Is that what he told you?"

Kadie's head tilted to the side. "Well, yes." She squinted, and her lips tensed. "I don't see what's so funny."

Duke continued to laugh. "I'm sorry, miss, but no self-respecting Delta guy would ever refer to himself as a *Delta Force Commando*."

Kadie got angry for the second time this morning. "Well, he is. You didn't see him fighting off ISIS outside the plane."

"Oh, you mean the guys shooting at us from a mile away?"

Her face flushed, and Brian leaned over to watch them. "You're just jealous. You pilots are all alike. Your egos are bigger than your airplanes."

Duke's eyebrows raised. "Oh, I clearly hit a nerve I wasn't aiming for. My apologies." Duke stood and meandered to the end of the hallway and poured a cup of coffee.

Kadie then realized that Brian had been paying attention to the entire conversation. The sadness in his eyes broke her heart. "Why w-were you mean?" The disappointment in his voice made her eyes water. "I-I want to invite him to my—birthday pawty."

"I'm sorry, Brian . . . I don't know." His birthday was eight months away. That was something that probably wouldn't happen, but people with Down syndrome loved their birthday and cherished the people they invited to it. She glanced down the hallway at the lanky pilot, as confused by her actions as his.

THREE HOURS AND TWELVE MINUTES AFTER LANDING AT TEL AVIV, Duke and Mac were on a bus with what remained of Team Egypt from Global Disease Initiative on their way to the closest hotel with rooms for all of them, the Market House Hotel in Jaffa. The oldest part of Tel Aviv, Jaffa, is linked with the biblical stories of Jonah, Solomon, and Saint Peter. The small but lovely hotel stood next to the Jaffa Tower and flea market a couple of blocks from the coast.

The sun perched well above the horizon, and the heavy traffic made moving slow. The morning commuters were on their way to work in Tel Aviv. Duke turned to Mac. "I think we're gonna be here a while."

Mac nodded. "Yeah."

"Any plans?"

Mac shook his head.

"I was thinking about going to Jerusalem tomorrow. Visit the Garden Tomb."

The smile on Mac's face seemed to wake him up. "That would be good for you. The Garden Tomb is an incredible experience. You might call it the pinnacle of your spiritual journey."

Duke focused straight ahead. "There's no telling how long it will take to fix the plane. It may take one day; it may take two weeks. I wish I had a better idea of how long we'll be here. There is so much to see in the Holy Land."

Mac patted him on the shoulder. "Well, my friend, if you only had one day and one place to go, the Garden Tomb is the right place as far as I'm concerned. I've been there several times. It's reaffirming."

"Meaning?"

"You'll see."

"How many times have you been to Israel?"

Mac gazed into the distance. "Six. Three times with the Air Force and three times on tours. First tour was with an independent outfit. Fantastic, first-class operation. The second and third times were with my church. They were not as well-organized as my first excursion, but good nevertheless."

Just talking about it got Duke excited. He had begun his Christian journey three years ago and going to Jerusalem would be a bonus. For most of his life, he had been what most Americans had evolved into—a casual Christian. He had never read the *Bible* and only went to church on Christmas Eve and Easter—maybe. Like most Americans, he never thought about God or salvation until something drastic happened. And like most Americans, something drastic *did* happen to him.

"Have you talked to the security guy from GDI?" Duke said.

"No."

Duke checked behind him for anyone close enough to hear what they said. "So, I was talking to the young lady—"

"That a boy."

Duke grinned. "Stop. Please. Anyway, I was talking to the young lady about the jerk and the laptop coming through security."

Mac scowled. "He *was* a jerk. I'm not impressed with the guy at all."

"Yeah, well, she said his disposition was because of his background."

"Which is?"

"He's—get this, and I quote . . . a *Delta Force Commando*."

Mac cackled out loud. So much so, the two jerked their heads back to see everyone staring at them. Duke started to chuckle as they faced forward.

"Well, I feel safe now," Mac said. "Don't you?"

"Yeah. I think we may need to keep an eye on him."

"Stolen valor?"

"Probably. He may be a vet—could have some experience, but I suspect he's not what he says he is."

9

Tel Aviv, Israel
Market House Hotel

The company had made hotel reservations for the team while they were getting interrogated, then had them take cabs as soon as they were cleared by the Israeli officials. Kadie and Brian stepped from the cab and walked through the hotel lobby. The sun was perched overhead, and they were both hungry. When they checked in to the hotel, the first thing they did was order room service, then took quick showers. By the time Brian finished, the food had arrived. They ate quickly, and both fell fast asleep. Upon waking up that evening, they put their filthy clothes back on and took a cab to the nearest mall. Kadie, still mad about the luggage they left on the runway in Egypt, bought them both some clean clothes. Who knew the airport was controlled by ISIS as well? At least they were alive.

When they returned to the hotel, they passed the bar, and Brian paused. "Hey, there's Duke." He turned and scurried inside.

"Brian, stop! That's a bar. You can't go in there." She hurried after him. Could he go to the bar? It was more like a restaurant than a nightclub. Maybe it was okay. It was, after all, a hotel. It would be okay in the States, so perhaps it was okay in Israel, too.

Duke looked up as Brian approached. "Hey, Brian." He stood and hugged the young man. That impressed her, although the thought crossed her mind that he catered to Brian merely to impress her. It could happen, but she dismissed the notion since it had never happened before. Most men were either dismissive of him or uncomfortable around him. Her college boyfriend went so far as to dump her when Brian came to live with her after her junior year in college.

Maybe this Duke fellow was just a nice guy. She sized him up as she entered the bar. He remained kind of scruffy: unshaven, hair kind of tangled, his clothes—the same he had on last night/this morning. Ugh.

"Hello," Kadie said. Brian sat next to Duke. "We just returned from shopping. We needed new clothes." She held out her two hands that gripped the shopping bags.

Duke smiled. He had a friendly smile. One that seemed genuine. "Well, I was about to order some dinner, then call it a night. Please, join me."

Brian's eyes grew wide. Kadie could tell he was fond of the pilot. "Thank you, but we ate downtown." Her brother appeared sad, and Kadie sighed as she sat down. "But we can visit for a few minutes while you wait for your food." Brian brightened up again. She turned back to Duke. "Did you not have the opportunity to clean up?"

Duke chuckled. "No, I apologize for my appearance. As soon as I went to my room, I received a phone call from the IDF. It appears other agencies in Israel were curious about our experience in Egypt. They were kind enough to meet Mac and me here at the hotel."

"Other agencies?"

"Mossad."

"Oh. Who are they?"

"Israel's version of the CIA. Only better."

"Oh."

"After that, my boss back in the States wanted me to fill out an after-action report on the airplane's damage. They're working on getting an engine for us. They're not sure if they can find one here in Israel or have one shipped in from somewhere else."

"You flew that plane with only—one engine." Brian asked. "You must be—the best pilot in the world."

Duke chuckled again and patted Brian on the back. "Thanks, but we train for situations like that." He leaned in toward Brian. "I may not be the best pilot in the world, but I'm one of the best." And he gave Brian a wink.

Kadie's heart swelled. If he only knew how much he helped Brian. "What's the plan?"

Duke shook his head. "Your *Delta Force Commando* was trying to get commercial tickets for the team to Istanbul, but there is nothing available for at least a week."

Kadie felt her face draw in and her lips tighten at the jab Duke threw her way. Any goodwill he built up, he just destroyed.

"I'm sorry," he said. Her reaction was apparent, her message received. "My opinion isn't a reflection on you. It's on him."

Kadie gritted her teeth, and her eyes narrowed. She wasn't sure why this guy didn't like Curt, but Curt *did* fight the ISIS attackers at the hotel in Port Said *and* the airfield. "How long do you think we'll be here?"

"Minimum, two more days," Duke said. "And that is if they can find an engine locally and a maintenance crew available for them to replace the engine. That would be about a five-hour job. Then we'd need to give it a functional check flight to make sure everything works before we put you folks on board."

"What are we supposed to do until then?"

Duke took a sip of water, then sat back. "I'm going to Jerusalem tomorrow."

Brian's eyes lit up. "Jeru—salem?"

"Yes. I'm going to visit the Garden Tomb."

"Awe you a Christian?" Brian said.

"Yes."

Brian got excited. "I want to go. That is where—Jesus rose from!" He leaped out of his chair and pleaded with Kadie.

She smiled, but she didn't know how to tell Brian they weren't invited. "Brian, Brian, settle down. We're not—"

Duke leaned forward and touched her arm. "You two are welcome to come with me if you'd like."

Brian looked at Duke, his smile stretching across his face. The boy was so happy, he started dancing in place. He hugged Kadie, then rushed over and hugged Duke. Kadie's eyes began to water. She was delighted Brian would get this opportunity. He was going ninety-miles-an-hour when he suddenly stopped and started to sway.

"Brian?" she said. The smile was gone, and her heart skipped. His eyes started to flutter, and his muscles began to spasm as his eyes rolled up in his head. Kadie pushed away from the table as Brian's body went limp and collapsed.

10

Kadie couldn't reach Brian in time. The seizure was bad but hitting the ground would be worse. His knees buckled, and his body twisted as he fell to the ground. At the last second, Duke swooped in behind him and caught his shoulders. He held him there for a moment, then gently laid him on the ground.

"Brian? Brian? Are you okay?" Tears welled in her eyes as she brushed his bangs across his forehead. He was the only family she had; she couldn't lose him. The boy needed his medicine.

"Is everything all right?" Duke sounded concerned.

"He's having a seizure. He'll be fine. If he'd hurt his head, we'd have a bigger problem."

"I'm just glad I was close enough to help."

Kadie held Brian in her arms for a few moments, and his eyes blinked open. He sat up, confused, and scanned his surroundings. She'd seen this reaction many times.

"Brian, are you alright? Do you know where you are?"

Brian nodded and looked at Kadie. "I am okay."

"You need your medicine?" she said.

"Yes."

Kadie rose and gathered her bags. "Let me get him upstairs and give him his Lamictal. I'm sorry."

Duke's forehead scrunched. "It's not a problem. Is there anything I can do to help?"

Kadie shook her head as she steered Brian toward the door. "No, we're fine. Thank you. I'll get back to you about tomorrow."

The two went upstairs to their suite, where Kadie led Brian to his room. She found his medication locked away in the hotel room safe, gave it to him, and put him to bed.

"What time—are we going to—the Garden Tomb?" he said.

Hmm. The trip to Jerusalem had already slipped her mind. She didn't want to go but realized now that she had to.

"I'll go find Duke and ask. Will you be okay while I'm gone?"

Brian nodded. "Teee Veee . . ." He smiled at her in the way that almost always made it impossible for her to say no.

"All right, but only while I'm gone. When I get back, it goes off."

"Okay."

She turned on the television in his room as she walked back into the living area. Stuffing the room key into her pocket, she headed downstairs.

Duke remained where they had left him, halfway through his dinner. He started to stand as she approached, but she stopped him.

"Please don't stop on my account," she said. "I just wondered if the offer for tomorrow still stands?"

"Of course. I think you'll like it. I'm sure Brian will."

Kadie nodded. "He's very spiritual. Most people with Down syndrome are."

"I know. I have had the opportunity of being a buddy at the Night to Shine a few times. What an amazing experience."

Kadie was impressed, though she tried to hide it, that Duke had attended the prom night for people with special needs organized by the Tim Tebow Foundation. What had started off the first year with forty-four churches had grown to almost a thousand.

"Well, thank you for the offer to join you. You're so kind." She thought she saw the gruff pilot blush.

"What faith are you?" he said.

Kadie quivered. She knew the question would come eventually. "Brian is a non-denominational churchgoer." She hesitated, then decided the time had come to put her cards on the table. "I'm not a believer, but I'm willing to go for him."

Duke's eyebrows raised. Yup, he wasn't expecting that one.

"Well, I'm glad to see you support him in his faith."

"It helps him. He likes to pray, and he loves the stories of Jesus."

Duke leaned back in his chair and rubbed his chin as his eyes narrowed. He didn't merely look at her, though—he studied her, sized her up. And she didn't like it.

"What condition does he have?"

"Huh?" Not the question she expected, given her declaration as a non-believer.

"His condition. You said he had to have medication earlier."

"He has a brain tumor. It's terminal. The doctors say he has six to twelve months. The tumor causes seizures. He has them from time to time. If he gets too excited or stressed out, it seems to manifest."

"Oh. I'm so sorry."

Duke struggled with what to say next, and she wasn't in the mood to discuss Brian's condition. "Tell me about yourself," she said.

"Me?"

She giggled. "Yes, silly. You don't expect me to leave town with a perfect stranger, do you?"

Duke smiled. "No, I guess not. Well, hello. My name is Duke Ellsworth. I'm a former Air Force pilot who now flies with Q1 Aviation, a military contractor. That's about it. Now, what about you?"

"Not so fast, fly-boy. What did you do in the Air Force?"

"I flew the AC-130J. It's a special operations bird. We were called Air Commandos."

"Air Commandos? Is that like a Delta Force Commando?" A mischievous grin draped across her face.

"Touché. No, Air Commandos is what we were called. Delta Force would never call themselves Delta Force Commandos."

"You guys sound like a bunch of kids."

Duke chuckled. "You're not far off. Anyway, the gunship flew close air support for special operations troops on the ground—a great plane to fly. I guess I flew it a little too much. At least that was what my wife used to tell me."

"You're married?" Kadie noticed his ring finger. It was empty.

"Was. Now Divorced. She said I spent too much time with my airplanes."

"Kids?"

His eyes started to turn glassy. There was more to this gruff pilot than met the eye. Duke stared at his dinner plate. This was obviously a sore spot; time to help him out. "Princeton."

Duke snapped out of his gaze. "Huh?"

"You asked about me. I graduated from Princeton with a degree in ancient studies. I played volleyball there for three years. After I graduated, I went to Kent State for a Master's in Latin. That's where GDI found me. They offered me this opportunity for the summer. It was the perfect job for my application for a faculty position back at Princeton."

"Impressive. When do you start?"

"I haven't gotten the job yet. If I do, I'll start in the fall." She checked her watch. Satisfied that she'd dodged all the pressing issues and didn't embarrass herself or Duke, it was time to go. "What time do we need to meet in the morning?"

"How about 9:00 a.m.?"

"Nine is perfect." She paused. "You know, I'm only doing this for Brian. I-I don't believe in this. I believe in science."

Duke appeared unfazed. "I understand. I also understand it takes a lot of faith to believe in science."

"Faith?" Her brow furrowed, but the corners of her mouth crept upward. Her eyes grew wide in anticipation of how he would link those two together.

"Hebrews 11:1 . . . Faith is confidence in what we hope for and assurance of what we do not see."

Kadie pursed her lips and squinted; there was more to this man than she originally thought.

11

Kadie and Brian met Duke the next morning in the lobby. Duke cleaned up rather nice, she thought. Clean-shaven, fresh clothes—she caught herself nodding as he walked up. When he flashed a broad smile, she realized she had already been smiling wide.

They greeted each other; then, Duke scanned the lobby. "I hope you don't mind that I arranged for a driver. It's a little more than an hour to Jerusalem and will be easier for someone who knows their way around."

"That's fine," she said.

"Shotgun!" Brian said. "I got—the front seat."

Duke patted him on his back. "You got it, Brian." He turned to Kadie. "Ready to go?"

She nodded, and the trio marched through the lobby to the car outside. The driver's name was Mustafa, a Palestinian living in Israel. Kadie had a few questions for him regarding the state of Israel and was surprised that the man enjoyed living here, as well as the way the Israeli government treated them. His positive response and attitude were something she'd never seen on the news back in America.

After a few minutes, Duke broke the silence. "Kadie, I'm curious. How did you get involved with GDI? No offense, but you are kind of young to be with this outfit."

"I was very fortunate. They needed a linguist with special skills. Let's face it. There aren't that many of us around these days. I guess during their search for someone, the executive vice president for their Science and Technology Division, Doctor Patricia Hastings, reached out to me and made an offer."

Duke nodded. "Impressive."

"She's leading the team in Istanbul. That's who we're going to link up with. Anyway, they wanted someone fluent in Latin and Aramaic. That's me."

Duke's jaw dropped. "More impressive."

Kadie smiled. "I said I wouldn't go without Brian, and I had to be back before the fall. She said she really needed me, and GDI was very accommodating. They covered all Brian's expenses and ensured we had a two-bedroom suite at every location, although the suite in Port Said was dismal compared to the one in Cairo."

"But what is GDI doing here?"

Kadie paused. "I-I can't say. But I can say it's my opportunity to change the world."

"GDI is changing the world?"

Her back straightened, and she clasped her hands in front of her, resting them on her lap. "For decades now, mankind has been using bombs and bullets to impose their will on the rest of humanity. GDI is using science and technology to show people there is another way. We don't have to use violence to get our way."

Duke's brow furrowed. "I didn't see you guys throwing science and technology at ISIS when they were shooting at you the other night. Your GDI guy used a rifle."

"That's not the same thing. We were attacked."

"Precisely. And we responded appropriately. You know, you're dealing with ideologies that have been in conflict for thousands of years. You're not going to change their minds with a hug and a smile."

Kadie sat tight-lipped. She didn't know what to say. This—this pilot tried to shatter her image of what GDI set out to do. They were here to save the world; she just couldn't say how. Here she was, yet again, angry at his ill-informed man. But she wasn't mad at how he treated her. No, she was upset with his opinion. He still believed that violence was necessary to solve problems. She felt there was another way. But GDI used *his* way to get out of their predicament at the airfield, and she was mad because he pointed it out. *Was that, even right?*

After a few more minutes of silence, Duke spoke again. "How . . . how did you realize, at such a young age, that you had this skill for languages?"

She shifted in her seat. "Mom and Dad were archeologists. I traveled with them once I was old enough. Dad said I caught on to the language wherever we went. I began reading at an early age. Reading things most kids that age didn't read. So, they encouraged me, and here we are."

"Are they retired now?"

Kadie shook her head and clenched her teeth. She was still angry at her parents for abandoning them. They left a twenty-year-old girl to raise her thirteen-year-old brother. "When I was junior in college, they were killed in a car wreck. Brian was in the car with them. That's how we discovered his tumor. He kept having headaches after the accident. When they did the MRI, they found a growth around his pituitary gland. He had surgery a year and a half ago, but it's come back worse.

"So, Brian came to live with me while I finished off my undergrad degree. It took me a year longer because I had to lower my course load to help him, which caused me to quit the volleyball team. That would have taken way too much time. Brian earned his high-school certificate of completion the same semester I finished graduate school. It worked out, and I wouldn't change anything."

"You're a good person."

"I love my brother. He's the only family I have left."

Duke reached in his back pocket and pulled out a can of Skoal Wintergreen Long-Cut. He opened the lid and pinched a bit between his thumb and forefinger, then tucked it between his lip and gums.

"That's disgusting," Kadie said, her face drooping.

Duke spit in an empty water bottle. "What can I say? It relaxes me. And dipping is my only vice."

Kadie crossed her arms and stuck her chin out. "I'm sure dipping snuff is hardly your only vice." She turned her body more toward him. "We've talked enough about me. Tell me about you. Why are you doing what you're doing here? Why aren't you in the airlines? There is a world-wide shortage of pilots, you know." She had seen numerous reports on television back in the States.

"When I left the Air Force—" Duke stopped. Kadie sensed something was wrong. He was holding back. He gazed at her, a sadness in his eyes. She felt sorry for him before he ever said anything.

They sat in silence for a moment before Duke continued. "When I left the Air Force, it just didn't make sense to go to the airlines. What purpose did it serve? I figured I've only got so much time left on this planet, and I might as well spend it helping our troops on the ground in combat."

Kadie nodded. "That—that's so noble." They rode in silence for a moment, and she shifted her gaze to the passing countryside. There was nothing but rock.

Rock. That's what this country was—rock. Tan-colored rock against a cerulean sky. It had been carved away over the centuries; the excavation evident. An occasional tree sprouted up out of the crags in the rock, but a forest was nowhere in sight. Occasionally, in the distance, they could see buildings bunched together. As they traveled further into the wilderness, a *Bedouin* would appear wandering in the distance with a camel or a donkey. Fascinating—thirty minutes outside the city, people still lived like they did two-thousand years ago. Except with satellite TV.

Kadie could see why Brian liked this man. She was starting to like him, too. "You certainly impressed Brian with your flying skills. It was exciting how you zoomed in there so fast with all your lights out and no lights on at the runway. We didn't even see you until the last minute before you landed. It was amazing that all that was coordinated in a matter of hours, and you arrived when you did."

"A matter of hours?" Duke looked confused at her comment, then spit in the empty bottle. "That pickup had been planned for three days."

12

Jerusalem, Israel
On the road to the Garden Tomb

Three days? What? How could he have known he was coming for three days?

"Duke, that doesn't add up," Kadie said.

"What doesn't?"

She bit her lower lip as she mulled over the new information. "We were only told that night we were leaving. And it was because ISIS was targeting us." Kadie went on to tell him about Samuel's murder, her chase through the streets of Port Said, and the rapid departure from the hotel that morning.

Duke looked at her matter-of-factly. "I don't know what to tell you. The pickup was coordinated between the CEOs. My boss and your boss are apparently buddies. Mac and I were scheduled to rotate home, so they had us fly the King-Air to pick your team up at the airfield and fly you to Istanbul. We were supposed to fly it back to the States after that.

"We checked with military intelligence before we left Iraq. They suspected that someone occupied the airfield, but they never mentioned ISIS. The only reports of ISIS in Egypt were passive."

"Passive?"

"Yeah. Mild protests, waving a flag in front of a news camera, recruiting—that kind of stuff. But there weren't any reports of any violence on their part."

Kadie stared out the window without speaking for several minutes. *How could they have known?*

"How much longer—Kadie?" Brian broke the awkward silence as he climbed around on his knees, looking backward.

"Brian, buckle back in," she said.

Mustafa, the driver, was saying something in Arabic, pointing at his seatbelt. The volume and tone of his voice indicated he was upset.

"I'm sorry, Mustafa. He gets a little excited sometimes. How much longer before we get there?" She knew they had another thirty minutes, at least according to the GPS on her phone.

"Thirty to forty minutes," the driver replied.

"I can—not wait," Brian said.

Kadie sat back, frustrated. "This is a long ride for a fairytale," she said under her breath.

Duke leaned toward her. "Come again?"

"I go to great lengths to support his fairytale endeavors. We might as well be going to Disney World."

The two spoke in hushed tones so that Brian couldn't hear them in the front.

"So, you're saying God is a fairytale?"

"In my opinion, yes. I deal in facts. There is no scientific evidence that God exists."

"There's no scientific evidence that says He doesn't exist either."

"Sure, there is. Haven't you ever heard of the big bang theory?"

"Yeah, one of my favorite old TV shows," Duke said with a grin.

"Funny. You're afraid of admitting the theory of evolution is what created all this. You people would rather believe in some old man in the sky who does magic tricks to keep you in check. The idea that life on earth began with a small amoeba that turned into a slug and crawled out of the sea and started life as we know it, scares you."

"I thought you said you deal in facts?"

Kadie tensed. "I do."

"But the two main concepts you just named, evolution and the big bang, are theories. You said that yourself."

"So?"

"So, a theory is basically someone's opinion, right? Surrounded by what they consider evidence, but it's not proven. It's just a theory based on information they're choosing to recognize, right?"

Her mind whirled, processing what he was saying.

"Well, yes."

"So, it takes a lot of faith to believe those theories and support them. You don't know that they are factually correct. You use *partial* science as a justification for your position. And you're putting your *faith* in the person who started that theory."

"I don't have faith."

"You do, it's just a little misguided. You think everything that exists on earth, in the universe, is by chance. But that's impossible." Duke was getting louder but caught himself. "The fact that everything that exists is for a reason. *Somebody* had to create this."

Kadie sat back in her seat and fell silent. She wouldn't discuss science for the rest of the trip. She was willing to indulge Brian in his fairytale, but not Duke in his.

13

Jerusalem, Israel
The Garden Tomb

The taxi dropped them off on Sultan Suleiman Street just north of the Damascus Gate of Old Jerusalem. The area appeared like any other part of the city; billboards, bus stops, shops and offices, and cars along the street. If this were the site of the Resurrection, Kadie understood why there were skeptics of the faith. Undoubtedly, the location would be just another tourist trap with rides and shows. Whatever, if it made Brian happy, that's all that mattered.

Kadie, Brian, and Duke purchased their tickets to enter the Garden Tomb. The musty scent of the busy streets gave way to flora and fauna within the walls. A variety of trees, plants, and flowers were scattered throughout, and numerous areas for prayer or reflection were set up with benches for small groups.

It was like they had transported to a different time and place.

The three of them weaved their way through the garden to the back. A tiny arena faced outside the garden toward the side of a small hill. They walked to the rail and gazed across the two-lane road at the rocky slope.

"There it is," Brian said. "The skull!" He raised his hands in triumph.

His enthusiasm made Kadie curious. "What are you talking about?"

"Gol—gotha." Brian stood captivated by the sight. "The place of the skull. It is w-where Jesus was crucified."

"What skull?"

Brian pointed at the hillside, his face glowing with joy. "There—on the side of the mountain. It looks like a skull."

"Brian, that's not a mountain. I'm not sure I would call it a hill." Kadie surveyed the top of the small hill and tried to visualize three crosses. "I suppose this could be the place. It's possible three crosses could fit up there."

Duke chimed in. "Some scholars believe that the crosses may have actually been on the road. Crucifixion was the Roman's way of not only torturing someone before they died but humiliating them as well. This road would have been well-traveled back then, so crucifying Jesus here would have been the ultimate in humiliation."

Brian fidgeted at the knees, up and down. "I want—to see—the tomb."

Duke patted him on the shoulder. "Me too, Brian. Let's go." They turned and walked out of the seating area and meandered along a concrete pathway. Kadie followed behind them. The uneasy feeling she had in the car had long since gone. She had a sense of calm for the first time in days, perhaps even years.

What is it about this place? she thought. *So peaceful, so pleasant. And in the middle of a bustling city. You'd never realize what lay inside these walls.*

They came to a clearing in the garden where a section sat below their level. Kadie shuffled to the rail and looked over the edge. A small line of eight people waited to enter a tiny doorway carved into the side of a hill.

"You coming?" Duke said as he and Brian walked toward the stairs.

Kadie shook her head. "No, you guys go ahead. I'll watch from here." She scanned the area as her brother raced down the stairs. Duke trailed close behind. A smile crept over her face. She was glad Brian came here, particularly since it made him so happy. His faith was strong enough to make her question why she ever lost hers.

"Joseph of Arimathea offered this tomb for Christ," a voice said. She turned to see a man with dark, curly hair, a beard, and a deep complexion standing next to her. "A tomb in a garden where no one had ever been laid."

Kadie studied the man who focused on the entrance to the tomb. Where did he come from? He wasn't here a moment ago. His voice was calm and soothing.

"Joseph wrapped the body in linen, laid it within the tomb, and rolled a large stone across the entrance." The man paused as Kadie stared at the large stone near the entrance. She imagined the scene the man described.

"The Pharisees went to Pilate," the man continued, "and said that while he lived, Jesus had said, '*after three days I will rise again*.' They were concerned that Jesus' disciples would steal his body in an effort to say he had risen from the dead.

"Pilate assigned guards to the tomb and directed the Pharisees to make the tomb secure. A seal was placed across the stone to ensure it was not moved. And yet, Jesus rose."

Kadie shivered at the stranger's words. Thoughts of the most impactful moment in the history of the earth swirled through her head as she stared at one of the two sites that claimed the event. The other site, the Church of the Holy Sepulchre, was the site recognized by the Catholic Church as the true Resurrection site. It also had the stations of *Via Dolorosa*, the route Christ marched through Jerusalem as he carried his cross to Calvary. Maybe they'd go there another day. For Brian's sake, she told herself.

She shifted her focus back to her brother and Duke, who were next to enter the tomb. Duke waved at her, then turned to take Brian's picture at the entrance to the cave. Kadie returned the gesture, but Duke had turned before he saw it. Brian ducked inside, and Duke followed. The stranger next to her was silent.

She waited for several minutes. Long enough for her to start to worry. How far deep into the hill did the tomb go? Could they have gotten lost? Kadie began to walk toward the stairs to find them when Brian exited. She whipped out her phone, but as she snapped a few pictures, she noticed something peculiar. No, not peculiar. Different.

Lowering her phone, she stared at her brother.

He *did* look different.

He looked like a typical, happy teenage boy.

"It's how God sees him," the stranger said.

Kadie blinked and rubbed her temples. Did her eyes play a trick on her? Was the lighting in the garden playing tricks on her? She glanced to her right, but the stranger was gone. Turning to search around her, he was nowhere in sight. Such a man would have stood out in this crowd of brightly dressed tourists, but he had somehow vanished in their midst.

Hmm, must have been in a hurry.

Brian and Duke walked back toward the stairs, where Kadie moved to greet them. She stood at the top of the stairs and waited.

"Are you coming up?" she asked. Kadie couldn't believe the smile on Brian's face. She hadn't seen joy and happiness in him like this in years. If ever.

Brian shook his head. "No, Kadie. Come down."

"I don't want to come down."

"Please—Kadie. For me." His eyes drooped. It wasn't a ploy—he genuinely wanted her down there.

He wants me to go inside.

But I don't want to go inside.

She shook her head, still hesitant.

"Kadie . . ." His voice had that dragging, pleading tone.

She sighed deeply. "Okay, I'm coming." She marched down the stairs, and Brian beamed. The twinge in her knee came back for the first time today, and it slowed her pace down each step. It didn't really hurt, but it became her excuse. Intellectually, she had no reason to enter the tomb; it made no sense. But her brother tugged at her heartstrings. A glance at the gruff pilot showed he sported a subtle smile. Kadie wasn't sure why she checked him—his opinion didn't matter.

At the bottom of the stairs, Brian grabbed her hand. "Kadie, I want you to come into Jesus' tomb with me."

Her mouth opened to rebut his request, but as she locked onto his eyes, an overwhelming sense of joy stopped her. "Okay."

Brian smiled wide and pulled her to the back of the line. She peeked over her shoulder at Duke, who also had a big smile. Outside the tomb, a sense of warmth overcame her. And as the line moved forward and she inched closer, the warmth grew more comforting. She couldn't describe it or quantify it, but emanating from deep within her, it burst outward, bringing joy.

The small opening in the side of the hill appeared to be chiseled out of the rock. To the right of the entrance, a repair job at some point over the years was evident. Blocks of stone, six to eight inches square, were six or seven across and stacked seven high. Outside the tomb, a small trough ran along the front, which would have guided and supported the massive stone once used to cover the entrance.

Two small steps, built from metal and wood, led over the trough into the roughly four-and-a-half-foot tall opening into the tomb. They both ducked as Brian led her through the entrance. Inside the tomb, the area was small and confined, not like anything she had imagined while Brian and Duke were in here. On the right side of the tomb, metal bars protected the area where Jesus had been laid. The area where she and Brian stood held five or six people comfortably, but only two or three could see Jesus' resting place.

The ambient light from outside was the only light source inside the tomb. Kadie's eyes scanned the inside walls, attempting to recall any information from her childhood about the Resurrection. As a child, she had seen Mel Gibson's movie *The Passion of the Christ*. The film focused on the Crucifixion, only touching on the Resurrection, as far as she remembered. But the tomb in the movie *did* kind of look like this.

Brian prayed silently. A smile spread across her face. She was grateful he could be here. The doctors weren't sure how much longer he had on this earth, but if coming here made his last few months better, it was worthwhile.

When he finished, he turned to her. "Okay," he said, "we can go now." He led her outside, and the two stepped into the light, the sunshine partially blocked by the trees in the garden. "I pwayed for you, Kadie. I pwayed you would love Jesus like I do. Because even though you don't, he loves you."

Her eyes watered, and she pulled a Kleenex out of her pocket to clear them. She hugged Brian and turned to walk toward the staircase where Duke stood, the twinge in her knee was gone.

"It's true," Duke said. "Even though you don't, Jesus does love you."

Kadie gritted her teeth. She struggled with her emotions, which welled up inside. "This isn't right."

"What?" Duke seemed surprised.

"I thought Jesus had been crucified elsewhere. Everything is enshrined in the Church of the Holy Sepulcher. The Crucifixion, the Resurrection . . . everything. Christ carried his cross through *Via Delarosa* to Calvary. I was taught that at an early age. None of that leads to here. How can anyone say, with confidence, that this is the location where Jesus was resurrected? How do you know he wasn't resurrected in the Holy Sepulcher? Even *National Geographic* investigated and said that is the true location of the Resurrection."

"I can't say this is the place for sure. But it doesn't matter."

"How can you say it doesn't matter?"

"Because you're arguing *where* the Resurrection took place. You're not arguing if Christ was resurrected. You're acknowledging that Christ rose from the dead, and isn't that what's important?"

14

Jerusalem, Israel
The Mahane Yehuda Market

Kadie, Brian, and Duke strolled through the Mahane Yehuda Market. Duke led the way again, saying he had heard of a good restaurant. She hoped he was right. Brian said he wanted a cheeseburger when they'd left the Garden Tomb, and she didn't know if they'd find one.

"Cheeseburgers aren't kosher," she said, but he didn't quite understand the concept. He thought kosher was a punchline from television.

Duke glanced over his shoulder and smiled. "I think we're going to be all right." He stopped in front of a moderately sized restaurant with a welcome sign over the door: Burger Market.

"Brian, how's this?" he said.

His eyes grew as wide as his smile. "Yes, yes, yes!" He thrust his hands skyward as if he just scored the winning touchdown.

Duke just laughed as he held open the door.

"He's been wanting a burger for three weeks," she said.

"Me too." Duke led the trio inside, where they were taken to a table.

Duke and Brian each ordered a Coke, while Kadie had a bottle of water. As she scanned the menu, she thought about some of the arguments she'd heard over the years about how the *Bible* should be interpreted.

When the waiter brought their drinks, she took a sip. "Duke, if the *Bible* is supposed to be taken literally, why don't we follow it as written?"

"Oh boy, here we go." Duke grinned and sipped his Coke. "Give me an example."

She paused. "Well, the *Old Testament* has many rules. Rules none of us follow." Her mind raced for a moment. "Shellfish. Somewhere in the *Old Testament,* it tells us not to eat shellfish, but we eat shrimp, crab, and lobster. Isn't that sinful? And somewhere it says for women not to wear the same clothes as men, but women wear pants and blue jeans."

Duke's smile grew larger as he set his drink down and relaxed in his chair. The cocky pilot seemed confident.

"When I first began my Christian journey, I had similar questions. I didn't let it hamper me as I explored my faith, and I found the answer quite by accident."

"Okay, I'll bite. What was your accident?"

"Are you familiar with the covenants God made with man throughout the Scriptures?"

Covenants? She had heard the term as a child but ignored the context. "No."

"That's okay. Most people aren't. About two years ago, I found a book entitled, *When a Jew Rules the World* by Joel Richardson. Joel outlines the covenants God made with the Jewish people. There are specifically four he mentions, the first three being the Abrahamic Covenant, the Mosaic Covenant, and the Davidic Covenant."

Kadie's head tilted. The names were familiar, but this concept was new to her.

"The Abrahamic Covenant was made by God to Abraham and his descendants. It was unconditional. A one-way promise. God told Abraham he would give the land of Israel to the people of Israel forever."

"Okay," she said, leaning forward. This was interesting. There's more to this Duke guy than she suspected.

"The Mosaic Covenant was *conditional.* It was made to the corporate nation of Israel."

"Moses."

"Yes, during the time of Moses. God made regulatory conditions for Israel to maintain permanent occupancy of their land."

"But Israel was banished from this land until 1948."

"Yes, they were. The Mosaic Covenant was a two-way agreement, and eventually, the Jews failed to keep their part of the agreement. This is the section of the *Bible* that contains the blue jeans and shrimp argument."

She smiled. "You've heard that before."

"Not in those words, but yes."

"What's the third covenant?"

"The third covenant is the Davidic Covenant. It was an unconditional, one-way promise made to King David. God told David one of his descendants will rise and sit on the throne of Israel."

"Jesus."

"Yes, which leads us to the fourth and final covenant, the New Covenant. It doesn't replace the other covenants—it builds upon them."

She had yet to hear anything that would change her mind, no matter how interesting this history. "So, back to the blue jeans and shrimp argument. The New Covenant built upon the old ones, yet we eat shrimp."

"You forgot—the Mosaic Covenant is a conditional, two-way agreement with the Jewish people. If you do this, I'll do that. I never asked, but I'm relatively sure you're not Jewish."

Kadie hated to admit it, but Duke was right. She'd never thought of it like that. Kadie leaned back in her seat, her mind reeling. "Good discussion."

"I am hungry," Brian said.

"Me too."

"Duke—I would like you to come to my birthday pawty."

The pilot smiled. "Thanks, Brian. I'd like that."

Kadie cringed at the invitation, but knowing it was so far away, she didn't want her brother to be disappointed. She looked over Duke's shoulder and saw the waiter heading toward them. *Good*, she thought, *that should make Brian happy*.

"Hamburger!" he said when his food arrived.

The trio dug in and ate voraciously. Kadie contemplated their conversation during the silence. This stranger, Duke, had sparked questions within herself. Made her look at religion in a different light. Perhaps she *had* been wrong all these years.

"Duke, how is it that a military man like yourself is a Christian?"

The pilot swallowed his food. "Meaning?"

"I mean, after the last conservative president left the White House, the new administration forced the military to remove all forms of religion from the service. Is that why you left?"

Duke shook his head. "No, though I probably should have. The politicization of the armed services accelerated after he left." He paused. "When I was in the military, I was a little too focused on my job. Way too focused. I thought everything was fine. My wife and kids were in the panhandle of Florida while I was deployed. We had a house close to the beach. I thought they would stay occupied while I was away. I thought everything was okay."

"But it wasn't?"

"I-I guess not. It may not have been just that. When I was home in garrison, I wasn't around much either. The commanders always wanted us to work twelve-hour days. I didn't seem to think that was abnormal. It's the way we always did it."

"Twelve hours a day? That's not right."

"No, it wasn't."

"So, as a Christian, how did you rationalize not spending time with your family?"

"I wasn't a Christian at the time. I mean, I was—or at least *I* thought so. I was one of those casual Christians. I went to church on Christmas Eve and Easter. I'd never read the *Bible*. I mean, I'd opened it and read passages, but that was about it. I never let it sink in."

Kadie's head tilted. "So, what happened?"

Duke drained his Coke. "My wife filed for divorce. There was another man, I'm sure. She didn't want anything from me—she just wanted out, and she wanted the kids. Before the divorce was finalized, she had a car wreck. She and the kids were killed."

"I'm so sorry." Kadie started to reach out and touch his hand but retreated at the last moment. Her eyes moistened; if anyone could relate to losing loved ones in an accident, she could. "But yesterday, you said you were divorced."

"I felt that way. It's what she wanted. And it reminds me I need to work at being a better man. I spiraled downward after they died. It got to the point where I couldn't function at work. I drank excessively —very excessively. I sold our house and bought a sailboat and lived on that. I couldn't take care of the house. I couldn't bear going in rooms where the kids had played. I could still hear their voices and see them running through the living room. Part of me honestly hoped that boat would sink in the middle of the Gulf and take me with it."

"That's terrible."

Duke nodded and lowered his head. "The Air Force eventually released me from my commitment. Shortly after that, I discovered I had oral cancer."

"Oh my gosh—I didn't know."

"It's all right. It's my fault. I've come to terms with my disease. Anyway, I had some money in the bank. Drank more, worked less. I became suicidal. It wasn't until an old friend stopped by the docks one day and took me to his house for a couple weeks. He made me sober up. Then he took me to church."

"And the church fixed it?"

"My soul, yes. Not the cancer."

"Must have been a heck of a church."

"It was—and still is. Of course, the church didn't fix me right away, but that first visit made me realize what was missing."

"Which was?"

"I didn't have a relationship with Jesus Christ."

Kadie pondered the comment. Her silence must have told him she was curious to learn more.

"You see, too many people get wrapped up in organized religion. They don't focus on the goals of what that religion is supposed to be —a personal relationship with Jesus. So that's what I focused on. As soon as I understood that Jesus died on the cross for me, to carry the burden of my sins, everything became clear."

Duke gazed into her eyes. She saw a genuine man. A confident man who knew who he was. That was different from anyone she'd ever met in college. And it was different from Curt.

He continued. "Don't get me wrong. This didn't happen immediately. It was a long road. But the immediate impact was I stopped drinking. I did that because I dove into the Scriptures. I couldn't get enough. After a few months of being sober, this job opportunity came open, so I took it."

"Couldn't you work for the airlines? Why come back to the Middle East?" She had asked the question before but didn't know what else to say.

Duke leaned forward, his elbows on the table with his fingers interlocked. "I figured with my cancer—like I said this morning, I only have so much time left. I thought if I were going to fly, I'd do something good with it. We've got guys on the ground in harm's way. My being over here—well, over there—is helping them. And I feel good about that."

Kadie smiled. He *was* a good man. Sadly, the cliché holds. All the good ones are taken. And this one was taken by oral cancer. But she was glad she met him. And Brian certainly became attached. It was nice to have a man he could relate to—and who could relate to him.

They finished eating in silence. Duke picked up the check for everyone and found a driver to take them back to Tel Aviv. Kadie tried to sit up front this time, but Brian insisted on sitting there himself. Then she caught him grinning at Duke. She knew what he was up to. Another long ride in the backseat with the pilot. The boy would never stop trying to be a little matchmaker.

As soon as the car left the confines of the city, Duke turned to her. "What *exactly* were you guys looking for in Egypt?"

15

Jerusalem, Israel
On the road to Tel Aviv

Kadie's heart skipped a beat. *What were they looking for in Egypt?* The one question she hoped he wouldn't ask. "I can't say. Our objective is classified," she whispered.

A smile stretched across Duke's face, and he leaned forward. "Driver, can you put some music on the radio?"

The driver glanced back and nodded, then turned up the music. "This is good, no?"

"It's perfect," Duke said. He leaned back in the seat and faced her. "Okay," he said in a hushed tone. "I've got a Top-Secret clearance. Let 'er rip."

Kadie pursed her lips. He probably did have clearance, but she still couldn't tell him, could she?

In the front seat, Brian had dozed off, his head rolling side to side, oblivious of the music.

Duke retrieved his wallet and produced a civilian Department of

Defense Contractor I.D. badge. The hard-plastic badge had the information and color photo embedded in the plastic itself, not on paper laminated in plastic. The new civilian contractor I.D. card listed his security clearance, and his clearly stated he had a Top-Secret clearance. "Okay, here's mine. Let's see yours."

Kadie bit her lower lip. She never got a security clearance; none of them did as far as she knew. Did she even need one? It had never crossed her mind.

"I-I don't have one."

"That's okay, I've seen this before." The two of them spoke in hushed tones; the music playing in the background kept the conversation from their driver.

"Seen what?"

"Sometimes, NGO's operating abroad will tell their people something is classified. Makes them feel special and keeps them from talking about things. The fear of the unknown, I guess."

"What's an NGO?"

"Non-governmental organization. Outfits like GDI, World Food Bank, and the World Health Organization. You'll also get some black-ops outfits operating under that banner as well."

"Oh." Kadie mulled it over. She shifted in the seat toward him and spoke softly. "Okay, we're searching for a formula."

"Formula?"

"Yes, ISIS has weaponized the hantavirus. We're searching for a cure."

"What's the hantavirus?"

"It's a virus spread by rodents. It starts slow but eventually becomes incapacitating. Fever, chills, abdominal pain, and ultimately kidney failure."

Duke's teeth clenched as he thought about what she said. "Not familiar, but okay. What else?"

Kadie recoiled. "What else? There is no *else*. ISIS has a weaponized version of the hantavirus with plans to artificially create an outbreak. The CIA representative explained that if ISIS could localize the virus and place mass quantities in specific locations at specific times, they could incapacitate almost any place in the world. No city, hospital, or military base was safe."

"Interesting, kind of like a poor man's WMD."

"Yes. There is no modern cure. But there is a legend of a cure from two-thousand years ago in ancient Israel. That's what we're searching for."

"Your company is going to this kind of expense based on a legend?"

"Yes."

"That's nuts."

"Not really. King Solomon's Mines, the Ark of the Covenant. Those are legends."

"Those are movies."

"Movies based on legends."

Duke eyed her skeptically. "So, if the cure is from Israel, why are you searching in Egypt and Turkey?"

"The ancient virus primarily struck Europe and Asia. Because the cure was discovered in Israel and the virus was not documented to be in Africa, those are two of the locations we believe had access to the cure. The legend says the formula was kept in a vase rumored to be in one of several different locations. That's why we have different teams. The vase has Aramaic writing on the side. The formula itself was written in Latin. That's why I'm here. I'm fluent in Aramaic and Latin." She paused. "Greek as well. With a working knowledge of Coptic, which is an ancient Egyptian dialect and Punic, which was used by the Carthaginians in North Africa."

"But Turkey is in Europe."

"Only five percent of it," Kadie said. "The rest is in Asia. GDI is using Turkey as the furthest north they believe the ancient cure might have made it."

Duke appeared surprised. She felt a sense of accomplishment that perhaps she had impressed him.

"That's a pretty extensive background you've got. Didn't you ever go out on a date?" he said.

Her eyes narrowed. "My social life is none of your business."

Duke put his hands up. "Sorry, no offense." He glanced out the window. "So, did this murdered guy find the formula?"

Kadie turned back to the front and shook her head. "That *guy* was my friend, Samuel. That night in Port Said, while Brian and I were downtown waiting for Curt, Samuel called. He said he had discovered something important. What we *actually* were searching for. Something he needed to show me."

"Samuel called you?"

"Yes. He said he was in danger."

"So why call *you*? Do you have a skill he needed?"

"No. Well, maybe. I don't know. Samuel was the team's specialist in carbon dating. He could verify the vase was from the correct period. But we were friends. Closer than anyone else in the group."

"Closer than the Delta Force Commando?"

She started to bite back but stopped herself. "Samuel was like a father to Brian and me. He was skeptical from the beginning. Since he had nothing official to do until we found something, I guess he was investigating in another direction."

"Well, do you want my two cents? At least from the government's perspective?"

"Sure."

"I'm not a government employee anymore, but I have the same security clearance, and I sit through the same intelligence briefings. And I'm sure we've not heard one word about ISIS acquiring any kind of viral weapon. Especially one they planned to unleash on the West."

She pondered this new information. "Are you sure? We had extensive briefings on the disease. We even have team members from the CDC."

Duke shrugged his shoulders. "Don't know what to say. This is the first I've heard of anything like this. Ever. Including my time in the Air Force."

"That's why GDI formed this team. We're here to stop the virus—without bullets and bombs."

"Yeah, except the one guy who discovered this search for a cure might be a hoax is murdered almost immediately."

Kadie backed down. Was he right? Was the search a hoax? What could Samuel have discovered? Who else could have known?

"You know, I watched how your security guy acted when he realized you had Samuel's laptop. He kind of went ballistic, like he found something he thought was long gone."

She thought about the comment. Curt did act strangely. "Perhaps he was just trying to account for company property."

"Maybe. But we left a lot more company property on the runway when we escaped that airfield."

She thought about the stacks of luggage and equipment they'd left. He was right. Inside, her emotions reeled. She didn't know what to think or how to feel. Her head rested against the glass, and she stared in silence at the desert outside for several minutes.

"Tell me about Brian," Duke said.

"What about him?"

"What's with his tumor?"

"After my parent's accident, he had severe headaches. The doctors took an MRI as a precaution to make sure he didn't have a brain injury. That's when they discovered the tumor. They did surgery to remove it, but the tumor came back. It's a high-grade glioma tumor. A Grade 4 Astrocytomas Glioma."

"Astro—"

"Astrocytomas. It can't be cured because it spreads too fast throughout the normal brain tissue. Symptoms are seizures and physical weakness. As it gets worse, he'll suffer memory loss, language problems, cognitive decline, and personality changes."

"I'm sorry."

"We only have another three weeks here. When we get home, he'll start oral chemotherapy with radiation and electric field therapy."

"Will that help?"

"I hope so. There's nothing else we can do."

DUKE SAT ON HIS SIDE OF THE CAR, WONDERING IF HE'D TAKEN THE conversation too far. This girl, no, this woman, was unique. Yes, she was attractive, but what she possessed inside compelled him to get closer to her. Her warmth and thoughtfulness for others seemed to drive her. He wondered why she lost her faith years ago. If there could ever be a chance with her, he would explore it. But like her brother, his time on earth was limited.

Funny. After years of chasing Miss Right Now, never finding Miss Right, he found the first one that might qualify shortly before he would die. He came to grips with his mortality some time back. It wasn't fair, and it wasn't right to get involved with anyone else. Duke's focus was on making things right with God. He had a lifetime of sins to account for. Thankfully, Jesus died to carry that burden for him.

They reached the outskirts of Tel Aviv, and Duke looked at Kadie. Her eyes were closed as she rested her head against the window. She seemed so peaceful. It was a pity she had to go through the things she had in the last few days.

"Kadie." Duke nudged her gently.

"Hmmm?"

"Didn't you say you still had Samuel's USB drive and cell phone?"

Kadie pushed away from the door, centering herself in the seat. She scanned her surroundings, disoriented by waking up in a car. Moments later, as she realized she was on the road to Tel Aviv, she calmly said, "Yes, why?"

"Have you looked at them?"

She shook her head. "I-I haven't had time. Everything's happened so fast, and then we went to Jerusalem."

"But you still have them, right?"

"Yes, they're in my go-bag. That was the only thing I brought on the plane."

"Samuel discovered something that got him killed. Don't you think—"

Kadie sat up straight, her eyes wide. "It makes sense! When I went to his room, an ISIS guy was standing over him, a bloody knife in his hands. He got scared, I guess. He ran out of the room when I showed up."

"I remember."

"That's when I grabbed the laptop, USB drive, and phone. It must have been instinct. My subconscious protecting the company and the mission we're on. I took them to my room, then returned to call the police. That's when the killer came back. He threw a knife at my head. It missed by only a few inches. I turned and saw the size of that thing and decided it was time to go."

"Did the killer come back for the laptop?"

"Maybe. I don't really know."

"And that guy chased you through the city?"

"Yes, along with two of his friends. It took a while to ditch them. The police detained me, then let me go. By the time I returned to the hotel, the police were everywhere. Curt said the decision had been made to go to the airfield."

Duke squinted. "Yeah, for a pick-up coordinated three days prior."

"This is too coincidental," she said. "What should we do?"

"Find out what's on that USB drive no matter what."

16

Tel Aviv, Israel
The Market House Hotel

Kadie, Brian, and Duke arrived back at the hotel shortly after dark, tired from their long day. Kadie and Brian went inside while Duke paid the driver. Curt, his phone stuck to his ear, paced back and forth across the lobby, over the section of glass floor that displayed the Byzantine Church beneath. His animated motions must have chased everyone else from the area. He was not happy about something. When he saw her, his face clenched, and he hung up his phone.

"Where have you been?" Curt yelled at her, the veins in his neck bulging.

She stopped in her tracks. *Where did that come from?* "I-I . . . we went to see some sites in Jerusalem." Kadie nodded toward Duke and Brian.

Curt saw Duke approaching from behind her and grew even

angrier. "You are not supposed to leave this hotel without notifying me first," Curt's voice remained loud and angry.

"Where does it say that?"

"It's understood. That's what you do."

"Says who?"

"The contract you signed. I'm responsible for your safety. You can't go traipsing around wherever you want."

"That didn't seem to be a problem in Egypt."

Before he could respond, Duke stepped between them and stuck his finger in Curt's chest. "Look pal, I suggest you settle down," he said. "You treat this lady with some respect, or I'll relieve some of that tension you're showing on your face."

The two men glared at each other; their faces separated by inches. Curt backed off and stepped to the side to speak. "Kadie, I'm sorry. I have been worried sick about you. With ISIS after us, I was concerned for your safety. I searched for you all day and thought something happened to you. I couldn't bear that."

"Israel is the safest country in the world," Duke said.

"Is that why they have soldiers standing around carrying rifles?"

"That's *why* it's the safest place in the world. I feel safer here than in any U.S. city, that's for sure."

Curt turned back to Kadie. She could tell he didn't like Duke being around. He was jealous—that much was obvious. Spending the day with the pilot hurt his feelings, but she did it for Brian. Surely, he would understand that.

"Curt, we only—"

"Stop," he put his hand up, cutting her off. "We need to return to our rooms. The company says ISIS operatives have found our location. We can't go anywhere without proper authorization."

Kadie became worried. Brian's safety was her primary concern. She ran her fingers through her little brother's hair. He looked angry. No doubt, he didn't like the way Curt spoke to her. Duke, however, had a wide grin. She hoped he wouldn't say anything, and her mind struggled for a way to stop him.

"Who in the world do you get your information from?" Duke said.

"That is ridiculous. Stay in our rooms? Are you nuts? This hotel lobby is more secure than your CEO's boardroom." Duke rested his hands on his hips. "But I don't work for you, so, I think I'll come and go as I please."

Curt stared daggers at Duke. She worried the two men would start to fight.

"You don't work for me," Curt said, "but she works for GDI. And I'm responsible for her. So, when the company tells me it's too dangerous to leave her room, it's too dangerous."

She sensed Duke's confrontation wasn't going to end, and she reached out and touched his arm. "Duke, it's all right. Brian and I are kind of tired. We're going to call it a night."

Duke started to respond when their eyes locked. His emerald-green eyes embraced hers with a longing she had never experienced before. If it were possible for two near strangers to have a conversation by merely looking at each other, they did. The tension melted from his face, and his disposition changed. "Fine," he said.

Curt, smug after getting his way, gestured toward the elevators. "Well, let's go."

The trio walked to the elevators behind Curt. Kadie didn't like the way he spoke to her; it gave her mixed feelings. They stopped on the third floor and went to their rooms. Duke and Kadie's rooms were at the end of the hallway opposite each other. Curt sat in a chair in the middle of the hallway by the elevator.

Kadie opened her door and let Brian inside. Across the hall, Duke stared at Curt sitting near the elevator.

"Thank you, Duke. I-I had a nice time today."

"I'm glad." He looked back at her and smiled. "Me too. Make sure Brian gets some rest. He seems a little tired."

"I will." She started to say more. She wanted to say more. She just didn't know what. "Good night." Closing the door, she locked it behind her. Setting her purse on the credenza, she went to her bedroom and grabbed her go-bag. And as Duke suggested, she reached in and pulled out Samuel's USB.

DUKE PACED INSIDE HIS ROOM, FURIOUS AT THE GDI SECURITY MAN. *This guy is a phony,* he thought. *Definitely not what he says he is.* He went straight to the phone and called Kadie's room.

"Hello."

"Kadie, I apologize for how I acted in the lobby." He paused and thought she might not know who this was. "It's Duke. I'm sorry about our little run-in with Curt. The tension was obvious. I just didn't like the way he talked to you."

"Duke, thank you for that. Curt is looking out for us. I guess as I reflect on the situation, I can see him being worried. We didn't tell anyone we were leaving, and we were gone for hours."

"You don't think the fact you left with me had him upset?" The question came off kind of cocky, which he didn't mean.

"No, no. Well, yes. I'm sure it did. But he shouldn't worry—it wasn't a date."

Duke pulled the receiver from his ear and stared at it. "Right, it wasn't a date," he said. "Hey, did you forget about the USB drive?"

"No, I've got it in my hand."

"Okay, I'm coming over."

There was a pause on the other end. "I don't think Curt will let you do that."

She's right, he thought. "I'll figure something out. See you in a few minutes."

Duke hung up and cracked the door open and peeked down the hallway. Curt lounged in the chair and chatted on his cellphone. Shutting the door, Duke darted out to his balcony. The small area had two tiny metal chairs and a table, the same set-up that was on every balcony in this hotel. Looking over the railing, he estimated it was at least a twenty-foot drop to the ground.

Darkness had settled over Tel Aviv, and there didn't appear to be any activity on the street below them. The moon and stars were hidden by a blanket of thick clouds high in the stratosphere. A low cloud deck would have reflected the city lights like a night-lite reflecting off a bedroom ceiling. Palm trees next to the road blocked the view of his position. Luck was on his side tonight.

Duke studied the hotel's exterior walls and locations of each room, estimating where her room was on the other side. There was nothing from his balcony that continued around the building, but the second-floor rooms did. A tiny ledge ran the circumference of the building. It was small, but it might work. He decided he could do it as long as no one came outside.

He looked across at the wrought iron rails that encased the balconies, then tugged on his. The rail appeared sturdy enough to hold his weight. The brick that covered the second and third floors was textured and uneven, so he would have something to hold on to —he hoped.

I'm a pilot. I'm not afraid of heights. I'm afraid of falling.

The fall wouldn't kill him, but it would likely break a few bones.

Duke climbed the rail and lowered himself to the balcony below. His heart pounded, the danger at the forefront of his consciousness. He put some weight on the rail and tested it. Sweat slid down his face. Balancing himself with the fingertips of his right hand on the wall, he let go of his balcony. His body hugged the brick all the way down, until he stepped onto the second-floor balcony below his room.

After a glance through the glass, the room appeared to be empty. *Better to be lucky than good,* he thought. He slipped over the iron rail and gradually set his weight on the small ledge. The uneven ledge seemed sturdy enough.

Well, here we go.

Duke balanced himself on the ledge and scooted to his right to the curved portion of the building. He was immediately above the front entrance. With no one outside, he slipped past until he reached the corner.

Duke peered over the railing and into the room. It also appeared empty. He hopped the rail and moved to the other side. When he peeked around the corner, he realized the building wasn't symmetrical. Kadie's room was another twelve or so feet further. It seemed far.

And the longer he looked, the farther it seemed. It was then that he recognized another complication.

While this side of the building didn't face a road, it didn't have the palm trees that blocked his movements like the other side did. The odds of someone noticing him increased exponentially.

So much for luck. It was a good idea while it lasted.

He checked back toward his balcony. Any possible retreat to his room was gone. A couple had just walked out on the balcony of the room next to his on the third floor. Neither of them noticed him yet, but if they did, hotel security would be on him in seconds, and he'd be arrested. Curt would love that.

Duke climbed the rail and cautiously stepped onto the ledge. The sidewalk below was empty for now, and he shuffled toward the middle. Below, the lights from the lobby illuminated the ground but cast a subtle shadow on the upper floors. He continued his shuffle, sliding his foot across the ledge. The stress of his actions began to overcome him. Tension overtook his body, and the ledge felt smaller and smaller.

Sweat stung his eyes now, the heat compounding his nervousness. His sweaty palms made it harder to cling to the wall.

Luckily, this side contained two windows, and he used the shutters to keep his balance.

Below him on the street, headlights from a vehicle appeared around a curve and stopped in the street below. Duke froze. He tried to blend in, but the reality was, he was visible if someone focused their eyes upward. Moving slowly was the only way he could make it undetected. He was in the shadows, but he was confident he would be seen if he moved too fast.

His hand slipped on the grip because of the moisture, and he wiped them on his pants. *This was a dumb idea*, he thought. *Next time, I'll just walk across the hall.*

Twelve feet below he heard voices—Arabic voices. He froze. For two long minutes, he stood there, pressed against the wall, praying no one saw him. Afraid to move; afraid to so much as wipe his hands on his pants. He listened, each shallow breath a prayer that he would get through this. And soon, his prayers were answered. The voices stopped, and the vehicle moved on. Guests of the hotel most likely. Duke glanced over his shoulder as best he could, then started to shuffle along the ledge again.

A few minutes later, he reached the balcony on the second floor that sat below Kadie and Brian's room. He hopped over the rail and breathed a sigh of relief. The hard part was over. Or was it? Duke gasped as the balcony lights suddenly turned on.

17

Duke moved fast. He didn't have time to pray, but he had no doubt God was aware of his intentions.

He climbed on top of the iron rail that surrounded the balcony and grabbed the floor above. His feet scampered up the wall until they found the shutters for the doorway. Using that to support his weight, he hauled himself up the iron rail on Kadie's balcony and pulled himself up and over the rail. His left knee smacked the rail hard as he flipped himself on the balcony.

Landing with a thud, he grunted loudly. His feet knocked over the two metal chairs and table. The chairs impacted the cement floor with an irritating echo; the table, fortunately, stayed put. Making noise was the least of his concerns at this point. Survival was his goal. Pain radiated through his knee, but he didn't think there was any damage.

Duke heard the balcony door open from the room next door to Kadie's. By the time he stood and dusted himself off, an older man wearing a sweater-vest and driver's cap stepped out and looked in his direction. Duke's breath came in large gasps, and he nodded at the man.

"Evening," Duke said, wiping the sweat from his forehead.

"*Shalom*," the old man replied.

"*Shalom*. I-uh, I got locked outside."

The older man nodded and sat in his chair. Duke walked up to the glass. Inside the room, Brian watched television. Kadie was nowhere in sight, but he couldn't imagine she left the room—not with Curt sitting in the hall. She must be in one of the other rooms. Before Duke could knock on the glass, Brian saw him and jumped up.

"Duke!" He bolted from the couch and ran to the sliding glass door. Brian unlocked it and let Duke inside. Before he entered, Kadie dashed into the room. The puzzled look on her face when she saw him on the balcony was priceless. She glanced at the door as if to wonder how he came through the room without her noticing.

Duke slipped inside and fist-bumped Brian.

"How did you get here?" Brian asked.

"I walked."

"Wow—that is cool."

Kadie blushed now as she realized the extent he had gone to reach her room undetected. "That was a little dramatic, don't you think?"

Duke shrugged. "Your boyfriend is monitoring the hallway. Seemed like the only option to help you search that USB drive."

"I've been looking at it. So far, nothing." Kadie turned and went to her bedroom. "And he's not my boyfriend," she said over her shoulder as she disappeared through the doorway.

Duke grinned as she left. *That's good news*, he thought. Moments later, she returned with her laptop.

"You can search with me." She smiled at him.

The two sat at the table near the kitchenette, and Kadie moved the day-old copy of *The Jerusalem Post* to the side. Brian brought Duke a bottle of water and joined them for a few minutes until he deemed their project too boring and focused on the television. They searched for the next hour and came up with nothing.

"That seems to be everything on the thumb drive," Kadie said.

"Yeah."

"Should we go back through the documents? Maybe he has something embedded in there somewhere. Maybe a hyperlink within one of the documents, or something like that."

Duke shook his head. "No, I think we need to work smarter, not harder." He paused. "Where's Samuel's cellphone?"

Kadie went back to her bedroom to retrieve Samuel's iPhone. "I tried to open it earlier. Can't crack the password."

"May I?"

She handed him the phone. Duke pulled up the password screen and punched in a series of numbers and pushed the volume buttons at specific points. In a few moments, the phone came to life.

"How'd you do that?" The wonder in her voice was unmistakable.

"Just a little trick one of the IT guys taught me downrange. The spec ops guys use it to open phones in the field when they capture ISIS fighters."

"Isn't that illegal?"

"You want to turn me in?" Duke opened the recent call list on Samuel's phone. The last two calls were on the day of his murder. The final call was to Kadie, just like she said. The other was made an hour earlier.

"I recognize this number," Duke said. "At least where it's from."

"Where?" Kadie closed in.

"Here. Well, not here, but Jerusalem."

Kadie memorized the country code and prefix. It was a quick check against the phone book in the room, and she confirmed it.

"Should we call?" Duke said.

Kadie bit her bottom lip and nodded.

Duke glanced at his watch. It was 8:30 in the evening. He hit the call button and pressed "speaker" as the phone rang. On the third ring, a firm voice answered

"Hello, Samuel. Did you find out anything?"

Duke looked at Kadie and gave her the phone.

"Hello, who is this?" she said.

There was a pause on the other end. "This is Isaac Abelman. Who is this, and why do you have Samuel's phone?"

"I'm sorry to disturb you, Mister Abelman. My name is Kadie Jenkins. I'm a friend of Samuel's."

"Very well. Is he around? He was supposed to call me back."

Kadie closed her eyes for a moment. "I'm sorry, Mister Abelman, but Samuel is dead."

18

Kadie waited patiently for a response. Any response. Finally, Isaac spoke.

"When you say Samuel is dead, do you mean he was murdered?"

Kadie jerked her head toward Duke. His eyes were as wide as hers. *How could he know?* she mouthed silently. Duke shrugged his shoulders.

"Yes, I'm sorry. It was members of ISIS."

"ISIS, how convenient." Isaac's statement was short and possessed a subtle sense of disbelief.

"Sir, I'm sorry. The reason I'm calling is you were the last person Samuel spoke to before he was murdered. I was curious about what you two might have talked about."

Isaac paused on the other end. "I last talked to Samuel while he was in Egypt. Where are you calling from?"

"We're in Tel Aviv."

"Meet me tomorrow at the Israeli Museum in Jerusalem. Noon."

"Israeli Museum at noon. How will I know—"

The line went dead. Kadie focused on Duke, who grimaced.

"He didn't want to talk on the phone," he said.

"Obviously." She set Samuel's phone on the table. "Care to go to a museum tomorrow?"

Duke smiled. He had a friendly smile, she thought. It seemed to knock away his gruffness and made him much more relatable. "Sure. I'll arrange for transportation." He stood from the table. "You know what's at the Israeli Museum, don't you?"

She nodded and smiled also. "Brian, would you like to go to a museum tomorrow?"

He looked over at her, less than thrilled. "Okay."

"It's where they keep the Dead Sea Scrolls," she said.

Brian's head swung toward her. "Really?" he said. "Yes—let's go! Is Duke going?"

"You bet I am," Duke said.

"Awesome. Dead Sea Scrolls." Brian's excitement subsided as quickly as it rose, and he returned to the television.

Duke turned to Kadie. "I need a favor. I need to return to my room, and I'd prefer *not* to go the route I took to get here. Can you peek outside and check if your boyfriend is still sitting out there, guarding your door? I may need to call the front desk and have them run interference."

Kadie snickered. "He's not my boyfriend. But, yes, I'll check." She hurried to the door and cracked it open. When she peeked around the edge, Curt leaned the back two legs of the chair against the wall near the elevators. She closed the door, sauntered back to the phone, and dialed.

"Hello, I'm on the third floor, and there's a man who is loitering in the hallway. He's been there for over an hour, sitting in a chair. I'm afraid to go to the elevator."

"Yes, ma'am. We'll send security there right away."

"Thank you so much," Kadie said. She hung up and turned to Duke.

"You're good," he said.

Kadie beamed. She could be creative and sneaky when she needed to be. "Thank you."

They chatted for a few minutes about their plan for tomorrow until they heard voices down the hallway. Kadie poked her head out the door to find two rather large security men with firearms escorting Curt toward the elevators. She motioned to Duke, who walked unassumingly across the hall, swiped his key, and entered his room. He turned and waved before he shut the door.

Closing the door, she gathered Samuel's USB drive and phone and took them back to her bedroom. She looked at the clothes she had, contemplating what to wear tomorrow when *her* cell phone rang. *I wonder who . . .*

Once back at the kitchenette, she answered her phone.

"Hello, Kadie. How are you doing?"

"Fine, Patricia. What can I do for you?" Kadie was only slightly surprised to hear Patricia Hasting's voice. Their teams were still scheduled to meet up in Istanbul sometime in the next few days.

"Nothing, darling, I was just calling to check on you. I'm sure it's difficult being the only woman on your team. Sometimes it's nice to have a little girl talk."

"I appreciate you checking on me." Patricia made sure Kadie always had accommodations for Brian. She had pushed for her to get the job, after all. "Is there any word on when we'll leave Israel?"

"My people are working on flights to get you here. Currently, there are no seats for the next few days. We're trying to change that. I want to keep you all together, and I don't want to have you all go through another country unless it is unavoidable. Too many issues with Customs and Immigration, you know. Israel alone caused us a lot of problems."

Kadie scrunched her forehead. What problems? She didn't remember any issues other than Curt freaking out over Samuel's laptop. "Has anyone called Samuel's family? Is his body being returned to Israel?"

"We've taken the appropriate steps. We reached out to the embassy, and they're sending a team to retrieve the body from the Egyptian government. Corporate contacted the family and made arrangements for them to receive the body when it gets back to Israel."

"When *he* gets back to Israel."

"Come again?"

"I said when *he* gets back to Israel. Samuel is a person, even though he's no longer with us. You can't refer to his body as *it*."

"Oh, my dear, I apologize. Please don't misunderstand—I've been swamped. I seem to be taking shortcuts everywhere, including my conversation."

Kadie felt a sense of guilt. They'd all been busy. "Don't worry about it. He was a good friend, that's all."

"Kadie, darling, you are the most precious sweetheart. So caring. I can't wait to see you again."

Her eyes shifted side to side, and she glanced at the phone. Awkward. "I suppose we'll be here a few more days, then?"

"That's what Curt tells me. We spoke earlier today." She paused. "He tells me you went adventuring today?"

Kadie thought about the question. It was more of a statement posed as a question. Why did it matter? "We just drove around. Shopping and an early supper." It wasn't a lie technically. She just didn't tell all the details.

"Curt was worried. Please, dear, listen to him. He is our head of security and your safety is his main priority. If something happens to you, I'm going to hold him personally responsible."

"I know." That's a little too much, she thought, but Patricia always came on strong. "Patricia, I'm sorry. Brian needs me in the other room. I've got to go."

"Of course, dear. We'll talk later. Bye, love."

Kadie hung up. Was this phone call too coincidental? A woman she hadn't spoken to in days calls minutes after she makes a call from Samuel's phone. It might have been nothing, but her instincts told her otherwise.

Duke walked to Mac's room moments after entering his own. Curt stood by the elevators, arguing with the two security men. After filling Mac in on what had happened that day, and his experience sneaking into Kadie's room, he contacted the same service he used earlier that day to get into Jerusalem.

When Duke hung up the phone, Mac had a troubled look on his face. "Something wrong?"

Mac's head bounced side to side. "I kept our Delta Force Commando in my crosscheck today."

Duke squinted, anticipating what Mac was about to say.

"He cornered me this morning, asking if I'd seen her. I said no, of course, but I kept my eye on him throughout the day. Sometime after lunch, he snuck into Miss Kadie's room. Snooping around, no doubt. He was only there about two minutes before coming out."

"I don't trust this guy," Duke said.

"Me neither. I'll call some guys downrange tomorrow and ask if anyone knows a Curt Baxter from Delta."

"Good idea. I think the guy's a phony, too." Duke picked a date off the plate on Mac's coffee table and took a bite. "Wish you could have gone to the Garden Tomb. It was amazing." He chewed the tasty fruit and swallowed.

Mac waved a hand at him. "I've been several times. I thought it was more important that you have your *rendezvous*."

Duke felt his face flush, which surprised him. If anyone could do that to him, it was Mac. "It wasn't a rendezvous."

Mac's face sported a subtle grin, hidden in his wrinkled, weathered face. "If it wasn't, it should have been. You're too young to give up on having a relationship, my friend."

Duke's head lowered, along with his voice. "You know why."

"Yes, but that's no reason to give up."

He shook his head. "I'm six years older than her. Besides, even *she* said it wasn't a date. She's just not interested in me. She has the hots for our fake Delta commando."

Mac laughed.

"But we *are* going back to Jerusalem tomorrow. Just to check on a lead on her murdered friend."

Mac grinned. "Sounds like another date."

"It's not a date. Regardless, I need you to run interference. This Curt guy doesn't want Kadie to leave the hotel."

"Not a problem. I'd be happy to." He patted Duke on the back. "God has given us all second chances, my friend. Maybe he's giving you one, too."

19

The morning sunshine spilled between the sheer curtains, the white walls giving the morning sun more brilliance in the small room than needed. Kadie rose from the king-sized bed and went into the bathroom. The black and white checkerboard tile floor was cold, so she threw a towel on the floor to stand on. The oversized, clawfoot tub invited her to take a hot bath, but she was short on time, so she showered instead. She finished dressing, then checked on Brian. Not surprisingly, he was ready to go. When she turned the TV off last night, he went right back to talking about the Dead Sea Scrolls, and his enthusiasm had not waned all morning. He had thanked her over and over. She hoped he would enjoy today, despite their motive of a fact-finding operation.

Kadie breezed through the living room, brushing her hair when she noticed Brian's pill container on the counter, empty.

"Brian, did you take your medicine?"

"I am good," he said, not shifting his focus from his drone. "Kadie, can I take Rupert today?" Rupert was what he named his drone. It was nothing special—he heard the name and thought it was funny.

"I guess so, but you'll have to carry it through the museum."

"O—kay."

She considered contacting Doctor Upton to get more medicine when there was a knock at the door. As she marched to the front of their suite, Brian sat patiently on the couch. It had been one of her major stipulations that he would not answer the door during this trip. She was concerned about his safety; aware he might not always understand others in these foreign lands. A quick check in the peep-hole confirmed it was Duke.

"Good morning," Duke said when she opened the door.

She felt a warm glow as she eyed him up and down. His clothes were pressed, his face clean-shaven, and his hair freshly combed. She glanced up and down the hallway before retreating into the doorway, no sign of Curt.

"You cleaned up kind of nice." She moved back into the living area. "We're ready to go."

Duke entered and closed the door behind himself. "Thanks. I figured you never get a second chance to make a first impression."

She turned and smiled at him. "Well, you did with me."

"I was referring to Isaac."

Her face flushed, then she laughed out loud. Duke started to chuckle as well. Brian took his attention away from the television as the two of them laughed. He began to laugh also, although the expression on his face indicated he wasn't sure why.

Kadie grabbed her purse and walked back to Duke. "Are we ready?"

Duke pulled out his cell phone and casually shook it in his hand. "No. Now, we wait."

MAC WOKE UP EARLY AND WANDERED THE EMPTY LOBBY OF THE hotel. The restaurant had a few people, but most of the hotel guests had yet to circulate. He returned upstairs to his room to wait for Curt to leave his room. Using a chair to prop his door open, he sat just inside the doorway, reading a copy of the *Jerusalem Post*, poking his head out whenever he heard someone leave. At about 8:00 a.m., Curt walked down the hall toward the elevator.

A few minutes later, Mac headed to the elevator himself and rode down to the lobby. He found Curt sitting in a chair, sipping a cup of coffee. When he finished his coffee, Curt went to the restaurant. Mac shadowed the so-called Delta Force Commando for the next hour and fifteen minutes until Duke called.

"You guys ready to go?" Mac said.

"Yeah, we'll be in the stairwell."

"Okay, stand by for my call."

Mac walked by the stairwell door and ensured it couldn't be opened from this side. He found Duke's driver outside and let him know his passengers would be here in a few minutes and would need to leave quickly. Then he turned and headed straight for the restaurant, where Curt sat.

Mac strolled by, pretending not to notice him.

"Where's your buddy?" Curt said.

Mac stopped. "Huh?"

"Your buddy. The other pilot. Where is he?"

"I thought I saw him heading toward the pool on the roof."

Curt smirked and turned his attention back toward his newspaper. His arrogance obvious, but he didn't bite.

"Can't say I blame him, though. With the bikini that girl was wearing, I probably should have followed them. That's something you don't see every day."

Curt's face turned white, and he slowly folded the newspaper. He stood and threw some shekels on the table and rushed to the elevator.

There was no pool on the rooftop. The hotel only had three floors. They'd only have a few minutes. As soon as Curt reached the elevator, Mac pulled out his phone. Curt stepped in, and the doors closed behind him.

Mac hit Duke's number on speed dial. "The coast is clear. Your driver is waiting."

"Thanks, Mac."

"My pleasure."

The trio exited the stairwell and raced for the front door. Duke turned, found Mac, and waved.

Mac waved back as he slid the phone into his pocket and headed to the elevator himself. It was time to make another call.

THE THREE OF THEM SAT IN THE SAME SEATS THEY DID YESTERDAY, THIS time without Brian calling shotgun. On the outskirts of Tel Aviv, Brian peeked into the back seat and smiled. It warmed her heart to see him excited and happy. She wondered how much time he had left before the tumor overtook his daily routine.

"Duke—do you know about—the D-Dead Sea Scrolls?" Brian said.

"I sure do."

Brian went on to explain what he knew of the Dead Sea Scrolls: copies of sections of the *Old Testament* found in jars in a series of caves in southeast Israel.

"The caves awe near the Dead Sea," Brian said.

"I hear the Dead Sea is neat," Duke said. "You float on the surface of the water. You can't sink."

Kadie chimed in. "I would love to soak in that for a few hours. The mud is a great exfoliant."

"The scrolls are kept in The Shrine—of the Book," Brian said, showing them a picture from his cell phone of the uniquely shaped white building continuously cooled with water flowing on top of the roof. "It is like a huge water—fountain."

Duke smiled at the picture on Brian's phone. "That's a neat building."

Brian grinned and turned to face the front. Kadie smiled as the two interacted. Duke was genuinely kind to Brian, and her brother seemed to like Duke. No, he really *did* like him. And her brother had excellent instincts on people's character. She did notice that he never took to Curt this way. Perhaps he saw something she didn't.

"Kadie, did your parents ever come to Israel?"

Her lips tightened. Her parents were a subject she didn't like to talk about. She glanced at Duke and realized he was waiting for an answer.

"Yes."

The gruff pilot was smart enough to realize she didn't want to talk about her parents. The truth was, she still blamed them for leaving her and Brian alone.

Traffic in Jerusalem was a little lighter today, perhaps because they left later than yesterday. Their car drove down a long street, past the U.S. Embassy, until they found themselves at the top of a hill, looking down into a densely populated valley with The Shrine of the Book clearly in sight less than a mile away. In less than three minutes, the driver dropped them at the front of the Israeli Museum.

Duke paid the admission for the three of them, and they walked through the small lobby outside again. Kadie checked the time—they still had an hour to go before their meeting.

"Where are we supposed to meet this guy?" he said.

Kadie shook her head. "I don't know. Back in the lobby, I guess."

Brian ran to the rail they saw outside, Rupert still tucked away in the small Pelican case in his left hand. "Cool," he said. "Kadie come look—at this."

Kadie and Duke joined Brian at the rail. Before them lay a model of Old Jerusalem reconstructed in great detail. The entire model covered an area of about one hundred feet long and eighty feet wide, but the display wasn't linear. Instead, the sidewalk and rails ran around the outline of the city. Several tourist groups stood around the three-dimensional map of the ancient city. The three of them tagged along with one of the groups when an older man who appeared to be an employee approached them.

"*Shalom*. Is this your first time to the museum?" the man asked. Kadie started to ask him if he was Isaac, then saw his nametag: Aaron. Duke looked at her, obviously realizing the same thing.

"*Shalom*. Uh, hi, I'm Duke. This is Kadie and her brother Brian. Yes, it's our first time here. We drove in from Tel Aviv this morning."

"Welcome," the guide said. "I can give you a brief walk-through. This model was commissioned in 1966 by the owner of the Holy Land Hotel in Bayit VeGan. It measured two-thousand square meters and was moved to the Israeli Museum in 2006 at a cost of three-and-a-half million dollars. Based on the writings of Flavius Josephus, it is believed to be an exact replica . . ." Kadie's mind wandered as the man spoke to Brian, who listened with rapt attention.

Duke leaned into her. "We've got an hour. Might as well tag along." Kadie nodded. Brian was fascinated by the model, so as long as he was happy, she was happy. They walked around the model for about thirty minutes, the guide explaining the biblical history of the city.

Brian tugged at the shirt of the elderly guide. "C-can I fly my drone out here and take v-video?"

The guide bent over and stared him in the eye, processing what the boy had asked. He placed a hand on his shoulder. "I don't see why not, as long as you're careful and don't fly it directly over the model. There's not much *balagan*."

"What is *balagan*?" Kadie said.

The old man smiled. "Chaos."

Brian unpacked the drone and the controller, which would hold his iPhone. Tilting and turning the drone in different directions, Brian calibrated the drone and had it flying within minutes. He guided the drone around the model of the city using his iPhone. Kadie detected something was wrong based on the various grunts and moans coming from her brother. The drone landed twenty feet from them on the walkway, and Brian hurried to pick it up.

"Something wrong?" Duke asked.

Brian wouldn't look at him. "I could not make—the video work."

"Oh yeah? Maybe we should have Mac take a look at it. He's a big drone guy."

Brian looked up at him and smiled, then packed up Rupert.

The guide resumed his presentation as they continued around the platform. When they'd made their way back to the starting point, their guide turned to them. "Would you like to see the Scrolls?"

"Oh yes," Brian said.

"Well, let's go."

The four of them walked toward the Shrine of the Book. The magnificent white structure that housed the scrolls resembled an abnormal minaret, a pointed center that swooped down then bulged back upwards around the circumference of the edges. Water was pumped continuously across the glistening top, giving the shrine the appearance of a giant majestic water fountain. Once inside, the guide explained the history of the Dead Sea Scrolls, with Brian filling in the gaps as they walked.

When they reached the round room where the scrolls were kept, Brian ran toward them.

"That is not re—al," he said as he turned back to them. Kadie studied the scrolls with a skeptical eye, although it didn't require one.

"He's right," she said.

"Yes, indeed," the guide said. "The original scrolls used to be displayed here. Years ago, someone attempted to destroy the scrolls by throwing acid on the display. Needless to say, they have been moved to a safer location."

The old man glanced at the clock on the wall. "I hope you enjoyed the tour. It's my lunch break now."

Kadie checked her watch. It was almost noon. "Thank you, we're supposed to meet someone right now, anyway. We appreciate your time, Mister . . .?"

The old man reached out his hand. "Abelman. Isaac Abelman."

20

Jerusalem, Israel
Shrine of the Book, The Israeli Museum

The old man stood in the dark room next to the representation of the Dead Sea Scrolls, a broad smile on his face. Kadie glanced at Duke, who didn't look surprised that their guide had been the man they came to meet.

Kadie wasn't sure if she was furious or fascinated. "Why did you wait so long to tell us who you are?"

The man cradled one elbow in his hand and stroked his goatee with the other. "I was on the clock. I have a job, and everything is *balagan* during work hours. If I were to start talking to you about something other than my job, well, that wouldn't be right." He gave Brian a wink before turning back to Kadie. "But more importantly, nefarious forces are at work. One must determine who is who, before revealing information that has proven dangerous." He turned back to Brian and patted him on the back. "Besides, it's my lunch break, so now we can talk. Follow me."

The old man turned and walked down a dimly lit corridor, leaving Kadie, Duke, and Brian little choice but to follow. He stopped at a lone door and motioned for them to enter. Duke led the way, and Kadie grabbed Brian's hand as they entered the room. Inside stood a large round table with six chairs. Isaac shut the door behind him and invited them to join him at the table.

Kadie began. "Mister Abelman—"

"Isaac, please," he said.

"Very well. Isaac, the reason we called you was because we found your number on our friend's phone."

Isaac shook his head. Kadie could see his expression was grim. "So, he's dead?"

"Yes, he was murdered three days ago. He called you less than an hour before his murder." Her voice wavered. "We were hoping you might have an idea why he was killed."

Isaac's face turned ashen, his hands quivered. He rose from the table and paced across the room. It was a casual pace, his eyes stared as if they penetrated the walls of the room and examined something far in the distance. He walked to the door and checked outside. When he shut it, he locked it this time and strode back to the table with confidence.

"Who are you, people? Why should I talk to you?"

Kadie spoke clear and concise. She explained in detail who she was, the organization she and Samuel worked for, and how Duke joined her on this adventure. Isaac listened intently, asking questions only occasionally. He glanced at Duke from time to time, as if to remind Duke he knew he was still there.

"So," Kadie said, "since we don't have access to Samuel's laptop any longer, we found your number on his cell phone. You were the last person to speak to him alive."

"It seems that *you* were the last person to speak to him alive," Isaac countered.

"Yes," she said, her gaze darting to the side.

Duke pulled out a can of Skoal, pinched some, and stuck it between his bottom lip and gum.

Oh, no, really? Does he have to do that here? Her eyes bulged, and her head tilted. Duke saw her reaction as he was about to spit in a cup. He stopped himself and swallowed instead.

Isaac sat back in his chair and rubbed his forefinger and thumb underneath his bottom lip. He squinted, burning a hole through Kadie's conscience. "What was your organization searching for in Egypt?"

Kadie paused. "I can't say."

Isaac set both hands on the table. "Do you truly believe that a group as unorganized as ISIS is able to get their hands on a virus and then somehow weaponize it?"

So, he knows. He was testing me to see if I'd tell him. "Ye—"

"No," Duke said with a firmness Kadie hadn't heard him use before.

Isaac smiled at Duke. "Neither did Samuel."

Kadie's face flushed, and her eyes grew wide. She set her jaw and breathed deep. They came to the right place.

"Samuel had doubts about what GDI has been searching for from the beginning," Isaac said. "His curiosity—accelerated by the amount of money thrown at the *balagan* project—led him to join the team."

"When Samuel called me, he said he found out what we were *actually* searching for. Do you know what he was referring to?"

Isaac nodded. "I do, and I told *him* as well. Your team is searching for the Aramaic Vase."

Kadie shook her head. How could she have been so foolish to think this museum guide would have more information. "Of course, we were searching for a vase with Aramaic writing on it. The vase contained the formula to cure the disease we're facing. The contents can save the world."

Isaac smiled. "You're right. The contents can save the world. But what you're searching for isn't an Aramaic vase. It's *the* Aramaic Vase. And it won't save the world in the manner you think." Kadie glanced at Duke, who appeared as confused as she felt.

"What's the Aramaic Vase?" she said.

"The vase is a legend by all accounts. A two-thousand-year-old legend. A treasure beyond belief. But the treasure isn't the vase itself. The treasure is what is inside."

"What is—inside?" Brian said, who's interest piqued at the first mention of treasure.

Isaac smiled at her brother and patted him on the back.

"Inside the vase rests the treasure of all treasures. The Pilate Scroll."

21

Tel Aviv, Israel
The Market House Hotel

Mac had successfully avoided Curt for the past few hours—until now. His phone call downrange took up most of his time, and he was eager to discuss the results with Duke. The GDI security man marched straight at him, and he looked mad. As Curt moved closer, Mac confirmed it. Yep, he was mad.

Curt stuck his finger in his face, which Mac didn't like at all.

"You lied to me, you dirtbag," Curt said. "There's no pool at this hotel."

"Hmmm. How about that?"

"Why'd you lie? Where are they?"

"Who are you asking about, specifically?"

"You know who I'm talking about. Kadie and that pilot sidekick of yours."

Mac grinned. "I like to think of myself as the sidekick. Mainly because the hero always gets the girl."

Curt's face turned a deeper shade of red. "They're together, somewhere. Where are they?" He poked his finger in Mac's chest.

Mac snatched the finger and bent it back. Far enough to make him scream without breaking it. "You need to learn to be a little nicer." Mac's smile disappeared from his face. He released the finger, and the GDI man cradled it with his other hand.

Curt turned to walk away. "This isn't over between you and me, old man."

"I look forward to it, junior," Mac said as Curt slinked around the corner.

He was right. This was far from over.

KADIE AND DUKE CAST EACH OTHER CURIOUS LOOKS. BRIAN'S FACE scrunched.

"What's the Pilate Scroll?" she asked. "I've never heard of that."

Isaac crossed his arms. "It's a legend, really. A legend that dates back almost two-thousand years, to when Jesus came to Jerusalem for the final time. Judas betrays Jesus for thirty pieces of silver, and the Pharisees and Sanhedrin arrest him. After Jesus is tortured at the house of Caiaphas, he is brought before Pontius Pilate, the Roman governor of Jerusalem. Pontius Pilate judges Jesus in the Gospels, all four of them, to be exact.

"After Pilate condemned Jesus to crucifixion, there is more to the story than is in the Gospels. Pilate's wife, in addition to the dreams she'd had about Jesus, had been suffering a great illness. Pilate's wife is not named in the Gospels. Origen, in his *Homilies on Matthew*, suggests that her name is Claudia and says she had become a follower of The Way. *The Apocryphal Letter of Pilate to Herod*, written in the third or fourth century, says her name is Procla. This letter proclaims that Pilate and Procla became Christian converts. *The Apocryphal Letter of Nicodemus* also calls her Procla and details her dreams. Regardless of her name, she is the trigger figure in the legend of the Pilate Scroll."

Kadie was fascinated. The old man weaved his tale and placed emphasis where needed. His words rang confident and true. He knew what he was talking about.

"How do you know so much about the *New Testament*?" she said. "Aren't you Jewish?"

Duke leaned in, looking at Isaac. "He's a Messianic Jew."

Isaac smiled at Duke and nodded. "Pilate's wife, we'll call her Claudia. That seems to be the favored name for her in Western culture. Claudia had retrieved Jesus' prayer shawl from the prison guards as they cast lots for his clothing. Before the crucifixion, the Gospel says Claudia warned Pilate—some say she begged him—to let Jesus go. Legend has it that after the Messiah was crucified, Claudia's ailment mysteriously healed. Curious as to how she healed so miraculously, Pilate sought out the Disciples of Jesus. Pilate finds them weeks after the tomb was found empty, gathered on the Mount of Olives in Bethany. He was shocked to learn that Jesus had returned from the dead and was shown the wounds on his hands and side. While there, Jesus tells his Disciples they must wait in Jerusalem until they attain the power of the Holy Spirit. And then he ascends into heaven."

Duke waved his hands. "Wait a minute, wait a minute. There's nothing in the Gospels about Pilate meeting with the Disciples."

Isaac nodded. "That's why it's a legend. Luke chronicled the event at the end of his Gospel, and again at the beginning of the Book of Acts, that time with more detail. No one can explain why the Gospel doesn't mention Pilate being there. Perhaps the Disciples feared retaliation from the Romans if they did; perhaps Pilate asked them not to say he was there, and as men of honor, they respected his wishes."

Brian listened to the story, his mouth slightly open. Kadie wondered if he was able to follow everything Isaac was telling them.

"Regardless, Pilate documents the event on a scroll. The dowels that hold the parchment were said to be made from Christ's bloody cross. This became known as the Pilate Scroll. The scroll is placed in a vase with Aramaic writing on it and sent to Emperor Tiberius in Rome, hence, *The Aramaic Vase*. The legend doesn't reveal what the writing says, only that the scroll within is the treasure. It is believed, however, to be handwritten testimony by the Roman governor of Jerusalem that Jesus had died and three days later rose from the dead. That weeks later, the Roman governor of the province, saw this man he had previously seen crucified, amongst the Disciples. The man truly was the Son of God."

Kadie was flummoxed as the words of the stranger in the garden tomb came back to her. "Why has no one heard of this?"

Isaac ignored the question and continued. "When the vase and scroll reached Rome, the emperor was not having any of it. Legend says he read it and was furious. Emperor Tiberius hides the vase with the scroll inside. He didn't need a revolt in the empire over the one true God.

"This took place around 33A.D., depending on who you talk to. Tiberius remained emperor until March 37A.D. until he died. The cause of his death was never verified. Some say natural causes. Others say it was an assassination by either a Praetorian Prefect or Caligula, who succeeded Tiberius as emperor. Caligula was emperor from March of 37A.D. until January of 41A.D. when *he* was assassinated. *This* conspiracy did involve senators and Praetorian guards."

"Caligula?" Duke said. "What's he got to do with this?"

"Caligula is important because, according to the Eusebius of Caesarea's *Ecclesiastical History*, Pilate killed himself on orders from Emperor Caligula in 39A.D."

"I don't understand the connection," Kadie said.

The old man pushed away from the table and glanced at both her and Duke. "Why would the emperor of Rome order a governor of a small, inconsequential nation to kill himself? Could it be Caligula *also* read the scroll and knew what Pilate had witnessed? The legend—"

"Kadie!" Brian said.

She looked at her brother, who froze for several seconds, then began convulsing.

He was having another seizure.

22

Kadie leaped from her chair for Brian, but Duke beat her there. He lowered him to the floor gently. She knelt next to him and lay his head on her lap. Using the palm of her hand, she rubbed his cheek. It was a mild seizure. He'd had much worse, but even one like this could be harmful if he lost his balance and hit his head. Thank God Duke reached him so fast. She knew better than to sit so far from Brian. He was her responsibility, and she needed to do better.

Self-criticism was warranted; she should have gone back for his medication. The one day they leave without it, and he has a seizure. Fortunately, the seizure gradually subsided. She spoke to Brian softly, running her hand through his hair.

For the first time since Brian's seizure, she looked at Isaac. The corners of his mouth drooped, matching the eyebrows above his watering eyes. She turned to Duke. "We need to go," she said.

Duke nodded. "Can he get up?"

"He should be okay. Brian? Brian? Can you hear me?"

Brian grinned. "Yes—I can heaw you—I'm wight hewe."

Kadie, relieved, exhaled deeply. "He's okay. He's a funny man now."

Duke helped Brian to his feet, and Kadie turned to their host. "Mister Abelman—Isaac—I'm sorry, we've got to return to Tel Aviv so he can take his medicine."

Isaac nodded. "I understand."

"I want to thank you for giving us this information. It's been very enlightening."

"Oh, you're quite welcome. I feel it's important, though, that you know there is more."

Duke wheeled around, balancing Brian as he did so. "More what?"

"More information. More to the legend. More about the Pilate Scroll. More, I'm sure, about Samuel's death."

Kadie and Duke stared at each other, and she could read his mind. She turned back to their new friend and ally. "Are you free for lunch tomorrow?"

THE THREE OF THEM RODE IN THE BACK SEAT OF THE MINI-VAN TAXI TO Tel Aviv. They didn't speak for the first twenty minutes as Kadie cradled Brian, her brother drawing all her attention. He seemed okay for the moment, but Kadie was disturbed that she didn't have his medication. She was cursing herself for letting her brother down.

Duke finally broke the silence. "What is this medication he needs? Can't we find it in Jerusalem?"

"No, it's hard to find. Well, maybe. I don't know. It's called Lamictal. But I don't have a prescription, so even if we did, I doubt they'd give it to me. Doctor Upton has more for him at the hotel. Because we cross so many borders, the company is having Doctor Upton control Brian's medicine."

The brevity and crispness in her response told him this was a subject she didn't want to discuss.

"So," he said, wisely changing the subject, "what do you think about this Pilate Scroll Isaac mentioned?"

Kadie felt unsure. "I don't know. I have a hard time believing it's worth killing someone over. But the legend itself is fascinating."

"So, we *are* coming back tomorrow?"

"Don't you want to? I need to find out what happened to Samuel."

"I'm in. Looking forward to it. I enjoy spending time with you two." Reaching into his back pocket, he pulled out his can of Skoal, opened it, and pinched some between his thumb and forefinger. With the skill of a seasoned pro, he slid the tobacco between his cheek and gum.

Kadie's face morphed into one of shock, disgust, and disappointment. "How can you do that?"

"As I said, Skoal is my one vice."

"You do realize your one vice is killing you?" Her face reflected that she realized how harsh her comment was as soon as the words left her mouth. "I-I'm sorry."

"It's okay. I made a mistake a long time ago, and I'm facing the consequences now. I'm at peace with that."

"You know, if you quit using that stuff, your chances of recovery increase exponentially."

"I'm seeing a doctor when I get back to the States. He's recommending surgery, but he thinks it may have spread to my throat. It's painful sometimes. Mac keeps telling me that I don't need to be over here, but I wanted one last rotation with him."

Her posture relaxed, and warmth emanated from her. "He's a good friend, isn't he?"

"The best."

That brought a smile from Kadie. "Maybe sometimes we need to change something we do for the benefit of those around us."

Duke nodded at the comment and gazed out the window at the vast emptiness. That was his problem. Besides Mac, there was no one in his life to motivate him to change.

23

Tel Aviv, Israel
The Market House Hotel

Duke sat in the corner of the hotel restaurant sipping a cappuccino. His back to the wall gave him a full view of everyone who entered and exited the small hotel. He had spent most of the afternoon getting updates on the status of the airplane; the rest on the antics of the GDI security man, Curt Baxter. The waiter brought him another, and when he looked back up, Kadie had entered the restaurant. She saw him and made her way over. He stood as she approached.

"Good evening, ma'am."

She laughed. "Stop."

"Does your boyfriend know you're here? Don't want you to get in trouble."

Her smile faded quickly.

"Okay," he said. "Bad joke. Join me?"

She sat down, and the waiter handed her a menu. "I came down to get something to take back up to Brian. He's still resting—in front of the TV."

Duke smiled. "He's a good guy."

Kadie nodded. "Yes, he is." She searched the menu for a few minutes, then ordered a to-go plate for both her and Brian. "Are we still on for tomorrow? I'm going to have Brian stay here with Doctor Upton."

That surprised Duke. "Sure, I'm game if you are. I wasn't sure how you were going to handle your restriction."

"I think the best way is to walk straight out the front door right in front of him. That should teach him to talk to me like that."

Duke laughed. "Have you thought any more about what Isaac said earlier?"

"I haven't *stopped* thinking about it. I'm curious. I mean, it's just a legend, right?"

"My experience with legends is they're usually grounded in truth. Are you starting to question your faith? Or rather your lack of it?"

She clasped her hands on the table in front of her, staring at them as she did so. "I used to be a proper Catholic girl. Mass every Sunday, confession, the whole nine yards. When I was seven, my grandparents died. I had a hard time with that. Then when Brian was born with Down syndrome, I couldn't understand that either. I began to question God."

"God has a plan for us all."

Kadie shook her head. "Those are just words. If there was a God, how could he allow all the terrible things that go on in the world? Disease, war, famine, birth abnormalities . . . this is where I lost my faith. When my grandparents died, I was devastated. I couldn't understand how God let them die so young. That event was supposed to have been overcome when my parents announced I was going to have a baby brother. When Brian was born, and I was told he had Down syndrome, I-I didn't know how to handle the drastic life changes I'd experienced as an adolescent." She gazed into Duke's eyes. He felt her pain as she spoke. "I couldn't understand why God let my grandparents die and let my baby brother be born with Down syndrome. I drifted away from the church. My parents were learning to deal with this new issue in our lives and were too busy to go to church themselves. Despite everything that happened, they never lost faith, I guess, but I did. It only became worse when Brian was diagnosed with a brain tumor."

"Yet, *his* faith remains strong."

"Yes, it is," Kadie said. "But that's not abnormal. People with Down syndrome are spiritual. And Brian seems to be at peace with his situation. I don't know how he does it. After our parents died, he started going to a non-denominational church near the campus. They had a Sunday School class that welcomed him with open arms. It seemed to help him."

"He let Christ take the burden off his back. Just like I did."

Her eyes began to water as she struggled with the knowledge of Duke's cancer. "I'm so sorry for everything you're going through."

"Don't be. I'm at peace with myself, too. I'm grateful to spend my last tour helping our troops over here and flying with my best friend. And I'm happy I got to meet you and Brian."

"I'm amazed by how calm you are about all this."

"I don't know why. You see it in your brother every day. Perhaps a relationship with Jesus Christ is something you need, too."

She stared at the table, biting the inside of her cheek. "I must admit, the Garden Tomb was a powerful experience. When I was there . . . I felt something. I can't explain it, but something overcame my body. For one brief moment, it swelled inside of me."

Duke nodded. "Sounds like the Holy Spirit." He could tell she was contemplating what he said.

"What did you do when we returned to the hotel?"

He acknowledged the deflection; perhaps it was time to change the subject. "I checked on our airplane. The new engine is arriving tonight. They'll install it sometime tomorrow. After they do an engine run, Mac and I will take it up for a functional check flight to make sure everything works okay."

"Do you need to stay here tomorrow? I can go see Isaac alone."

"Oh, no, I don't want to miss this. They can install the engine without me. In fact, I'm sure they'd prefer me not looking over their shoulders."

Kadie smiled.

"Look, there's something I wanted to talk to you about." His tone came across as serious, and he could tell she sensed it. "I spoke with Mac after we got back. He did some checking with the Delta guys we know downrange."

"And?"

"Well," he paused. He knew how this was going to go over. "They've never had a guy named Curt Baxter in Delta Force. Ever."

Her face tensed and turned red. And it wasn't embarrassment; it was anger. "I can't believe you. No, no, I can. Of all the juvenile moves you could pull, this one takes the cake. You men are all alike. You try and destroy each other when you can't have something you want."

"What are you talking about? We were just concerned that this guy isn't who he says he is. And we were right! He's a phony."

"Well, maybe he has a different name. Maybe his job was so secret they erased his history from the unit."

"Erased his history?"

"I don't know. You don't have any proof he's not who he says he is other than a phone call."

"A phone call to the source that verified who he is. Or actually, who he's not. The guy is a phony."

The waiter delivered her food to the table, and she signed for it, her hand shaking as she did. Duke couldn't understand why that information made her so angry. Perhaps the two of them were closer than he thought. They didn't seem like it, but who knew.

She picked up the containers of food. "I'm not going tomorrow. I-I don't need to be around any of this macho bravado that you two have going back and forth."

Okay, that explained it. She'd been getting grief from Curt as well. "I understand. I'm going anyway. I'll be down here at nine in the morning if you change your mind."

She said nothing as she turned and stormed out of the restaurant.

24

Duke stood in the lobby at five minutes to nine. Curt sat across the room, staring at him. What a flake. He couldn't understand what Kadie saw in this guy. But who was he to question her choice in men? Her social life was none of his business, and it wasn't like he had a shot with her. No woman would get involved with a man dying from cancer. And he wasn't going to get involved with a woman who wasn't a Christian.

He watched the elevator doors with anxious anticipation. It was almost nine—would she show? Duke didn't know what he was thinking. He hoped she would change her mind and go with him, but either way, he needed to hear more about this Pilate Scroll. The legend was far too fascinating to ignore.

The elevator 'tinged,' and Duke raised his head. Kadie strode out, and Duke gasped. She was beautiful. Her hair was meticulously done, and her fresh face was dusted with just the right amount of makeup. And the sundress she wore over her slender figure took his breath away. He had suspected it, and he was right. She was fit.

"Good morning," he said. "I hoped you would change your mind."

"Yes." She brushed a strand of hair from the front of her face.

"And I'm sorry for my behavior last night. Yesterday . . . there's just been a lot going on, and I'm not handling some of it well."

"I understand. You look very nice, by the way."

She beamed. "Thank you. I'm surprised you noticed."

"Oh, I noticed. You look like you're going on a date."

"We're not going on a date."

"But you *look* like you're going on a date."

"This is not a date."

Duke nodded with a grin. Behind her, Curt leaped from his chair and rushed toward them. Duke looked to the side where Mac stood with one of the guys from hotel security just in case. It was a move he was now glad they prepared for. Hotel security intercepted Curt, while Duke turned and escorted Kadie out of the lobby and into the waiting vehicle.

Once in the car, the driver sped away and then talked incessantly about their destination. Duke appreciated the distraction. He liked talking to Kadie, but he didn't want to come off as too pushy. And he enjoyed watching her share opinions with a third party. She was smart and strong-willed, for sure, and had an opinion on everything. The museum and the Dead Sea Scrolls were no different.

They entered the Israeli Museum at twenty minutes before noon. Isaac was speaking with a group of tourists but acknowledged them with a nod. Duke and Kadie sat on a bench in the shade and waited for the man to take his lunch break.

At noon, Isaac finished with his tour group and greeted Duke and Kadie. The three of them walked back to the same room they spoke in yesterday. Isaac spent the first few minutes re-capping the legend of the Aramaic Vase and the Pilate Scroll.

"Yesterday, you said you had more information on the scroll," Kadie said.

Isaac nodded. "Yes, indeed. It has to do with Constantine the Great."

Duke leaned forward, eager to hear what this scholar had to say.

Kadie turned to Duke. "Do you know who Constantine is?"

Duke's brow furrowed. "Of course. He's the ancient patron of my college fraternity."

"What?"

"Never mind."

Isaac waited until their banter ceased. "The vase and scroll within remained hidden for almost three-hundred years when, in 326 A.D., Helena, mother of Constantine the Great, comes to Jerusalem. While in search of the true cross and other religious artifacts, she hears rumors of the Aramaic Vase and the Pilate Scroll."

"It's here?" Kadie said.

Isaac shook his head. "It was not in Jerusalem yet. She discovered it had been sent to Rome. Upon returning home with a variety of relics and a significant portion of the True Cross, she tells her son about the legend of the Pilate Scroll. Constantine organizes a search for the vase and scroll. The legend says he *finds* it. Different versions say when and where. Some say in Macedonia, some say Egypt, and some say in Rome, but they all say it ended up in the same place—Constantinople. This is the last time the Aramaic Vase was seen."

"That's why the main search party is in Istanbul," Kadie said.

"Yes. Rumors place the legendary vase in Constantinople, which is now Istanbul. Helenopolis, now called Altinova, is in the Yalova Province in Turkey, not far from Istanbul.

"A lawyer in Constantinople, Socrates Scholasticus, born in 380 A.D., chronicles in his *Ecclesiastical History* that Helena finds the three crosses used on Calvary for the crucifixion of Jesus. She touches the pieces of each of the crosses to an ill woman. Miraculously, the woman was healed by the third piece. The healing power of the third piece verifies this is from the cross Jesus had been crucified on. Helena has the nails from this cross sent to Constantinople, where they were incorporated into the emperor's helmet and the bridle of his horse. Pieces of the cross were then sent across the empire and around the globe."

Kadie smiled. "They say if all the pieces of the true cross that are in churches across the globe were gathered together, they could build a boat."

"You're really putting that Ancient Studies degree to work here, aren't you?" Duke said.

Kadie nodded, excited.

"So, the question is, why?" Duke said, happy he didn't have to take his eyes off Kadie. "Why is GDI searching for the Pilate Scroll?"

"I don't know," she said. "But the circumstantial evidence is clear. The personnel, the locations, the cover story . . . they all fit the search criteria for the Aramaic Vase."

"I always questioned this story about searching for some cure to a biological weapon ISIS had their hands on. I have a TS-SCI clearance and have never heard anything about this. ISIS is organized, but not that organized. And there's no way the government would trust a bunch of university academics with such classified information." He turned to Kadie. "No offense."

"None taken," she said. "And I agree. There's something here."

"You're both right," Isaac said. "There is something else. Something that would make anyone leave everything they know and pursue the scroll, despite the fact they could be arrested or put to death."

The two of them looked at Isaac, then at each other before returning their focus to their new friend.

"What's that?" Kadie said.

"The legend states that the Pilate Scroll is surrounded by a treasure. A treasure that's wealth is exceeded only by King Solomon's treasure. Apparently, Emperor Constantine didn't want the Aramaic Vase to stay lost, so he created a reason for others to look for it."

"You're kidding, right?" Duke's disbelief covered his face, but then he relaxed. "It doesn't matter. Treasure or no treasure, the scroll is what's important. A finding like that could change the world."

Isaac stood from the table. "That is what Samuel thought. And he pursued it. One cannot discount where that got him." He looked at them sternly. "You two are in great danger. Tread with caution and trust no one."

Duke started to speak but stopped himself. Isaac left them in the room and returned to work. As thoughts swirled through his head, Duke concluded that Isaac was right. They were in danger.

KADIE AND DUKE STEPPED OUTSIDE. THE EARLY MORNING CLEAR SKY had given way to a gray blanket overhead. In the distance, a sheet of dark gray rain marched toward them. They left the museum with a new sense of urgency. The wind swept through the valley ahead of the front and blew her hair around her face. Her sundress wrapped around her figure, and she lay her hands on her thighs to keep the dress from flowing freely. They found their driver with his vehicle wedged between two large tour buses in the parking lot. They spoke briefly, then headed straight back to Tel Aviv.

No sooner had they climbed into the car, then the rain reached them, pounding on the outside roof as if desperate to get inside.

"Back to Tel Aviv, please," Kadie said.

She didn't want to leave Brian alone any more than she had to. Not because he couldn't be by himself, but she only had so much time left with him and didn't want to waste her opportunities.

Brian coming into their family's life had made them all better people. But her parents' death changed everything. She felt cheated; abandoned. The anger ate away at her for years. It was one of the reasons she worked so hard—to mask the pain and the anger of a twenty-year-old girl who hadn't begun to live life yet.

But something was different here; she had changed. She sensed it. This pitstop in the Holy Land made her rethink her position on God.

She used to say, "Everything happens for a reason." That was a weak way of excluding God or giving Him any credit. *God has a plan. For everyone. We may not understand it or like it, but it will work its way out.*

Duke lay with his head against the glass window, asleep. She did not know how he could sleep through this storm, but apparently exhaustion had gotten the better of him. Still, she wanted company now. There were things she needed to discuss, and so she reached over and punched him in the arm. He bolted upright, unsure of where he was.

"Were you asleep?"

He rubbed his eyes and squinted. "Nope. Wide awake."

She pulled an emery board out of her purse and filed her nails as she spoke. "I was thinking about the Pilate Scroll."

"And?"

"If the Pilate Scroll's last known location was Constantinople, where could it be?"

"That's the million-dollar question, isn't it?"

"Yes." Kadie grimaced and rubbed the nail on her ring finger with her thumb, then began filing again. "How good is your knowledge of the history of Western civilization?"

"My westerns are limited to John Wayne."

Kadie stopped filing and gave Duke her full attention. "Constantinople was Constantine's showplace of the Roman Empire. Yet there is virtually nothing left of this ancient city. Part of the reason is because of the construction. Constantine built the city in record time, but because it happened so fast, the quality of the construction was less than satisfactory. In fact, it started to crumble shortly after the city became inhabited. His brand-new showcase of the Roman Empire was falling apart."

"Okay, so what?"

"Almost a thousand years later, during the Fourth Crusade in 1204, the Venetians raided Constantinople. The crusaders captured the city from the Byzantine Empire and looted the place. Anything that remained of value, particularly any religious artifacts, were brought to Venice."

"As in Venice, Italy?"

"Yes."

"So, where are the artifacts now?"

"The artifacts, and probably the Aramaic Vase, are most likely stored in the basement of Saint Mark's Basilica."

25

Tel Aviv, Israel
The Market House Hotel

Any joy Kadie had as they pulled up to the hotel disappeared. Curt stood outside the lobby. When they stepped out of the car, he pounced on them immediately. He jutted a finger at Duke.

"You," Curt said. "Get to the airport now. Your engine is here, and the mechanics are starting to fix it this evening."

"Where's Mac?" Duke said.

"Your worthless partner is already at the airport, where you should have been hours ago. But you chose to gallivant around the countryside."

Duke turned to Kadie, ignoring Curt's constant jabbering. "I've got to go. Are you going to be okay?"

"Yes, I'll be fine."

Duke pulled out his cell phone. "I need to call Mac, but my battery is dead."

"You can use my phone," she said.

He shook his head. "I'll find him at the airport. There are only so many places he can be. I'll talk to you later, okay? Say hello to Brian for me."

"I will."

Duke spoke to their driver and coordinated a ride to the airport. He climbed in the car and drove off, leaving Kadie alone with Curt. As much as she wanted him to stay with her to keep Curt away, GDI was paying the bills. This time she had to listen.

"Come with me," Curt said. "I have news for you." She gave him a stern look. *Who does he think he's talking to? He's lost any chance for romance with this girl.*

Kadie followed him upstairs to the doctor's room, where Brian stayed for the day. Inside, the rest of the team lingered with smiles on their faces.

"We're heading to Istanbul tomorrow," Curt said to her.

"Will Duke's plane be fixed by then?"

"You're not flying on Duke's plane. GDI has secured commercial travel for you."

Kadie's face went blank. She didn't know how to handle that information. The revelations she had learned in the past forty-eight hours were overwhelming. Knowing they were searching for something other than what they were told? How would she deal with that once they got to Istanbul?

Curt picked up a Federal Express envelope from the table and struggled with the taped over pull-tab. He reached behind his back and pulled out a knife to cut through the top of the envelope.

"You all are booked on the 6:00 a.m. flight to Istanbul . . ." Curt said. His voice drifted off as Kadie focused on the knife. It was a knife she had seen before—inches from her head. The wide blade and narrow handle with the manufacturers' logo inscription seared into her brain.

Curt stopped spewing their itinerary. "What's wrong?"

Kadie couldn't speak. Her mind raced as she put together the pieces of this puzzle.

"W-where did you get that knife?"

Curt paused and studied the knife in his hand as if he had just acquired it. "Oh, you recognize this, don't you?"

Kadie nodded, trembling.

Curt walked to her, tapping the blade flat on his other hand. "This was the knife that was embedded in your wall. I pulled it out to keep as a reminder. I thought you might want a souvenir when all this is over."

He presented the knife to her as if it were some kind of majestic gesture on his part. Kadie stared at the knife, her heart pounding in her chest. She took a deep breath to compose herself. Her eyes locked on to Curt's. For centuries, it has been said the eyes are the window to the soul. Curt's soul was empty.

"No, thank you," she said, shaking her head. She gathered her and Brian's boarding pass and turned to leave the room. There was one thing she was sure of—she was in Samuel's room when the police removed the knives from the wall and door and placed both in an evidence bag. Curt hadn't arrived yet. And she didn't need to be a detective to figure out why he just lied, or why he had a knife exactly like the ones that almost killed her.

Duke was right—the man was not who he said he was.

KADIE HAD BEEN UP MOST OF THE NIGHT, UNABLE TO SLEEP DUE TO THE lie Curt told her and the potential implications it held. She didn't want to believe it, but it was the only possibility. Curt must be Samuel's killer. But why?

Several times throughout the night, she called Duke's room, but he'd yet to return from the airfield. If she had a choice, she would much rather fly to Istanbul with him than with Curt and the GDI team. An uneasiness crept through her body, and she found herself shaking.

Curt had scheduled a 2:00 a.m. bus from the hotel to the airport.

Four hours early was a little much she thought, but it was an early flight, and Israeli Customs could be a challenge.

Brian walked through the room like a zombie. She had woken him up in time to get him ready and help him pack. Once again, he was reluctant to do anything, and her main struggle had been to get him moving. Now they sat in their room, staring at the clock. The last thing she wanted to do was sit in the lobby with the other GDI team members, or worse, alone with Curt until any of them arrived. It pained her to think about her discovery, but at this point, she wasn't sure who she could trust.

At 1:45, she tried Duke's room one last time. No answer. She then had the front desk ring Mac's room. No answer there either. Ten minutes later, she grabbed their bags and ushered Brian to the elevator and descended to the lobby. The team was already in the hotel van. Curt waited inside the lobby for her.

"Good morning, Kadie."

He seemed too chipper for this early in the morning. A little too enthusiastic.

"Good morning. And this is my brother Brian."

She didn't mean to be sarcastic, but the comment flowed out too smoothly. Curt rarely acknowledged Brian while they were on this trip. He really was a jerk. While Brian sensed that from the beginning, she was slow to recognize Curt's true persona.

They climbed on the bus and Kadie searched the faces of the rest of the team, searching for any sign that might reveal something . . .

Most of them dozed gently. When she and Brian took their seats, the van door closed, and the driver pulled away. She glanced out the window at Curt. Odd, she thought. For some reason, Curt remained on the steps of the hotel.

Duke and Mac walked out of the hangar at 4:30 in the morning. They thought getting the engine through customs was going to be the hard part, but it turned out monitoring the mechanics was far more difficult. Thankfully, Mac had an A & P License, making him a certified mechanic on the King-Air. Mac had suggested they hang around while the mechanics hung the new engine, and they were glad they did.

When the maintenance guys tried to sling the chain around the engine, the tension of the chain would have crimped the fuel line, thus ruining the new engine. After a little investigation, Mac discovered the two mechanics had never replaced an engine on a King-Air. Mac and Duke spent the next seven hours monitoring their progress. Closely.

Mac lit up a cigarette, and Duke put in a fresh dip as they meandered out of the hangar. Across the ramp, a group of six people milled around behind a roped-off area.

"Duke, do those folks look familiar?"

He studied the group from a distance: five males and one female. The female had her arm around one of the males. Mac was right. It was the GDI team, and he recognized Kadie and Brian even from this distance. What he couldn't figure out was why the team stood on the ramp waiting for a commercial aircraft.

"What's going on? Do they know something we don't?" Duke said.

"Twenty bucks says our Delta Force Commando pulled a fast one behind our backs. He's not happy you're cutting in on his girl."

"That wouldn't surprise me." Duke spat on the ground. "Any way we can reach them from here?"

Mac shook his head. "Straight across the ramp. But then you'd have the IDF swarming over you."

"Over me?"

"Yeah. This is one I'm gonna let you do on your own."

Duke grinned. "Thanks, partner. You're a lot of help."

"Hey, I've been running interference for you for days now." Mac dropped his cigarette in the bucket of sand next to the hangar door. "Speaking of which, I don't see that clown over there anywhere, do you?"

"No, just the team. GDI must have arranged for them to leave early."

"Most likely that Curt guy, trust me. He's so jealous of you, it's ridiculous."

"Could be," Duke said, reflecting on the incredible revelations they had over the last few days. "But something is up. I'm sure of it."

26

Tel Aviv, Israel
Ben Gurion International Airport

Duke attempted to reach the team on the other side of the ramp but couldn't get through security on the commercial side. He stood at a distance as a Turkish Air 737 pulled up. The pilots shut down the jet's left engine. When the stairs pulled up to the side of the plane, the team boarded. Kadie was the last of them to go up, following Brian. Duke's heart ached, a feeling he hadn't had in some time. The stairs pulled away, the pilots started the left engine, and the 737 taxied out for takeoff. He shuddered and wondered if he would ever see Kadie and Brian again.

Someone went to a lot of expense to get them out of here. Why? What was so important that they couldn't wait another twenty-four hours?

Duke found the airport management office and confirmed his theory. GDI paid for a Turkish Air flight to drop in and pick up the team. None of this made any sense. They would test-flight the new engine this afternoon, and the plane would be ready by tomorrow. They still had artifacts and equipment the team had hand-carried from Egypt on the King-Air. And the weapons Curt Baxter had brought on board as well.

Their company still had them scheduled to fly to Istanbul, then across Europe before heading back to the States. Perhaps they could swing a long stay-over in Turkey. Maybe. But Duke had his doubts.

The two pilots took a cab back to the hotel. It had been a long night, but Duke wanted answers. He went straight to the front desk and had them call Curt's room, only to discover Curt had checked out with the rest of the team.

But he wasn't at the airport with the team. Where was he? Duke's mind reeled as he tried to figure out what was going on. He took the elevator to the third floor and stepped into the hallway. Knowing the team was no longer here gave the floor a sense of emptiness. He glanced at Kadie's door. She and Brian were gone; he wished he could have said goodbye. Duke swiped the card to his room and entered. A blinking red light illuminated the dark room.

His answering service had several messages. There were three messages from Kadie, desperately wanting to speak with him. He played her last one, again.

"Duke . . ." It was Kadie's voice. "GDI has arranged for us to leave this morning. There's so much I wanted to say . . . and I think you were right about a lot of things. I need to talk to you. I don't know who else I can trust. We're heading to the airport. Goodbye, and God bless you."

God bless you? Duke smiled. Perhaps he did have some positive influence on her. The last message was from Isaac, less than an hour ago. Odd. How did he track him down here? Perhaps the old man had contacts beyond Samuel.

"Mister Ellsworth, this is Isaac Abelman. When we last spoke, I told you that you and your friends were in danger. I'm afraid I was more prophetic than I realized. It appears that I, too, am in danger. I have more information for you both. Meet me at work as soon as you can."

Duke hung up the phone. Danger? Isaac? What in the world was going on? He started to call Mac's room, then decided just to write a note and slip it under his door. Rushing to the elevator, he rode down to the lobby and found a driver to take him to the Israeli Museum in Jerusalem. The only thing he added was, "And step on it."

DUKE ARRIVED EARLY. SEVERAL EMPLOYEES SHOWED UP FOR WORK, BUT Isaac was not one of them. At 9:00 a.m., the museum opened, and Isaac was still a no-show. Duke walked up the steps and went to the ticket counter.

"Hello," he said to the familiar woman at the desk. She had sold him tickets each of the past two days, which made her seem as permanent a fixture here as the objects inside. "I'm a friend of Isaac Abelman's. I was supposed to meet him here this morning."

The woman smiled and nodded. "Of course, I recognize you. Unfortunately, we don't know where Isaac is. He didn't report for work this morning. He should have been here at 8:30. We've called his home several times but received no answer."

Duke became worried. "Is your manager here?"

The woman nodded as her pleasantness dissipated. It was clear she detected Duke's concern.

The manager came to the desk moments later. Duke introduced himself and showed the manager his identification and passport. It wasn't necessary, but he was trying to establish some trust.

"I'm a friend of Isaac's. He called me last night and said he needed to talk to me. Said he might be in danger. Do you know where he lives?"

The manager was reluctant to give Duke his address until Duke suggested he also call the police. Convinced Duke was on the level, the manager gave him Isaac's address. Duke ran outside and took a cab to Isaac's home. It was up the hill about two miles away.

Duke paid the cabbie and hurried to the door, which he found cracked open. His heart raced. This was not good, and Duke tensed and clenched his fists, preparing for someone to be in that house. The police were on the way. He knew he should wait for them, but Isaac could be in trouble.

Pushing the door open with his hand wrapped about the front edge of the door, Duke peered inside. The house was quiet. Stepping inside, Duke left the door open to let in some additional light and allow for a quick escape if he needed it. He stood motionless, listening for any signs of someone else in the house.

Nothing.

Duke walked into the middle of the living room. "Isaac?" he called out.

"Uuugghn . . ." The sound came from the kitchen. Duke raced around the corner and saw the old man on the floor in a pool of blood. His body appeared to have several stab wounds in his chest area.

He rushed to his side. The pale and lifeless face stared into the abyss.

"Isaac, can you hear me?" The old man didn't have much time. He had lost too much blood. His eyes blinked, and his mouth quivered. Isaac tried to speak, and Duke moved his ear closer to Isaac's mouth.

"Riddle . . ." Isaac whispered.

"What? What riddle?"

". . . of . . . three . . ."

Riddle of three? What was he talking about?

"To . . . find scroll . . . solve riddle of . . . three . . ."

Riddle of three? What's that? Isaac continued to talk, describing a vase. Not just a vase, *the* vase. Isaac gasped, and the air left his lungs. His head rolled to the side, his eyes open wide and unmoving. He was dead.

Duke stood and surveyed his surroundings. He had two options.

Wait for the police and try to convince them he had nothing to do with this or leave. He had to decide fast, so he chose to leave.

Aware he hadn't touched anything since coming into the house, he remained conscious not to do so on the way out. Passing a coat rack in the living room, he removed the sweater and driver's cap and put them on. Palming the sweater sleeve in his hand, he wiped the edge of the door and slipped outside. No one was in sight, but that didn't mean he wasn't seen going in or coming out. He walked casually until the next block. Just as he made his turn, the police sirens wailed behind him down the street. He made the next right, and as he passed a thicket of trees, he stripped off the sweater and cap and tossed them in some bushes.

Pulling out his sunglasses, he made another left and right turn and found a taxi in front of a restaurant.

"David Citadel Hotel?" he said. It was the hotel Mac had stayed in the first time he came to Israel.

"Yes," the driver replied, putting away his cell phone and activating his meter.

Duke climbed into the back of the cab and rode in silence to the David Citadel Hotel. Once there, he crossed the street to the Mamilla Mall, where he walked the entire length of the mall to the Tower of David on the other end. He picked up another cab and rode across town to the Kidron Valley and the Church of All Nations at the Garden of Gethsemane. There he found another ride to Tel Aviv. He slept most of the way and had the cab drop him off at a restaurant near his hotel in Jaffa. After a short walk to the Market House, he went to his room and collapsed on the bed.

27

Tel Aviv, Israel
The Market House Hotel

Duke awoke to the sound of his hotel room phone ringing.

"Yeah." A tired glance at the clock through the darkness revealed it was 3:00 p.m.

"Duke, the plane's ready for a functional check flight. You ready?"

He recognized Mac's voice and shook the cobwebs from his head.

"Yeah, give me a minute . . . better yet, make it five. I'll meet you downstairs."

Duke rose from the bed. He still wore the clothes he had on yesterday when he fell asleep on top of the covers. Marching straight to the bathroom, he relieved himself, then quickly washed his hands and face and ran a wet comb through his disheveled hair. His thumb and forefinger wiped the sleep from his eyes, and the weary pilot left his room for the elevator.

Downstairs, his friend and partner waited in the lobby.

"You look like crap," Mac said. "Sleep much?"

Duke squinted as the sunlight pushed into the lobby. “A couple hours.” He pulled his sunglasses out of his shirt pocket and slid them on.

“Better,” Mac said, “but you still look like crap.”

Duke grimaced as they exited the lobby and climbed into the waiting car. Mac didn’t question him about anything. Duke suspected his co-pilot wanted him to focus on the flight. When they reached the airport, they walked to the hangar. Duke struggled to keep up with Mac’s pace, which didn’t go unnoticed.

“I’ll take care of everything, Duke. You just crank her up. I’ll do the takeoff, landing, and all the tests.”

“Perfect.” Duke acknowledged the fatigue. Best to let Mac handle everything he could.

When they reached the hangar, they found the mechanics had already towed the plane on the ramp. It had been fueled with the amount Mac had requested and was ready to go. They grabbed their gear and climbed into the airplane. Mac did the walk-around, then climbed back in the plane, and briefed the sortie. Duke followed what he said, nodding and acknowledging when required.

The two pilots took off and flew over the Mediterranean, away from the Class B airspace surrounding Tel Aviv. Mac accomplished the engine shutdown and restart procedures without issue. The engine operated normally. They were hesitant to pressurize the aircraft as they were skeptical of the repair job the guys had done on the bullet holes in the side. Mac suggested they just stay below ten-thousand feet the rest of the trip back to the States. Duke wearily agreed.

Mac landed the plane uneventfully, and Duke taxied back to the hangar. They exited the aircraft and secured the airplane on the ramp.

“You gonna be okay?” Mac said.

“Yeah, just need some rest.” Duke dropped his flight bag on the ground and walked along the front of the wing. “I went back to Jerusalem this morning.”

“What? No wonder you’re walking like a zombie.”

Duke nodded. "I got a call from our friend. He sounded really nervous, which I thought was unusual. Two days ago, he told Kadie and I that we were in danger. Yesterday, he left me a message on my hotel phone and said he was in danger, too."

Mac's eyes narrowed, and his chin stuck out. Duke had his interest.

"I went to the museum before it opened . . ." Duke continued to lay out what had happened earlier that morning, Isaac's murder, and how he had escaped and evaded back to Tel Aviv. His E&E techniques were effective, and he made it back undetected and in good time. But now he was ready for a few more hours of sleep.

In the distance, an Airbus A-330 lifted off from the runway and climbed westward into the vastness of the cloudless orange sky. A myriad of thoughts zipped through his mind. He recapped everything that had happened since they picked up the team in Egypt: the firefight at the airfield, the computer incident at Customs, the 'restriction' to the hotel, and the guy's juvenile behavior toward Kadie.

"You know," Mac said, "Curt didn't get on the airplane with everyone else."

"I know, but he was checked out of the hotel."

Mac nodded. "And now your friend Isaac turns up murdered. Heck of a coincidence."

"Yeah, heck of a coincidence. The guy in Egypt turned up murdered when Kadie waited for Curt to show up for dinner."

"Heck of a coincidence."

Duke watched the A-330 disappear in the distance, then picked up his bag. "Let's get some rest," he said. "We've got an early morning takeoff." Mac patted him on the back with a smile, and the two friends walked through the hangar to find a waiting cab. On the ride to the hotel, Duke had a hard time staying awake. He wrestled through his weariness to come up with a plan on how to handle the situation. *How* was almost a joke. He wasn't even sure what he was up against. But whatever it was, it was deadly.

He needed to get to Istanbul and warn Kadie as soon as possible. GDI was not what they appeared to be.

28

Kadie and Brian checked into their room at the Grand Tarabya Hotel in northeast Istanbul on the edge of the Bosphorus Strait. Numerous ships and boats traveled along the waterway every day, which made Brian happy at first, at least until he discovered the extra-large flat-screen television. The five-star accommodations didn't go unnoticed by Kadie either; she napped for a couple of hours on the most comfortable bed she'd been on in years. As the sun perched high in the sky, she woke up hungry.

"Hey, kiddo. How about we go downstairs for something to eat?"

"O—kay," Brian said. "When is Duke—coming?"

She bit her lower lip and cast Brian a doubtful look. "I don't know. I'm not sure if he's coming here at all."

"Curt does not like—Duke. He is afraid—of him."

Her eyebrows raised as she turned to him. It was an interesting comment from an intuitive young man. She smiled at her brother and ruffled his hair with her fingers. "I know. I've seen it, too."

They marched downstairs to The Brasserie Restaurant for the open buffet and found Curt guarding the door. He wasn't actually standing guard—he sat alone at a table near the entrance of the restaurant, sipping coffee, his eyes tracking everyone who entered. When Kadie walked in, he grew elated.

"Kadie, it's so good to see you," Curt said as he stood.

"And this is Brian," she said, angry that once again, he didn't acknowledge her brother.

"Oh, yeah. Good to see you too, Brian."

Her brother looked away, aware of Curt's insincerity. He had mentioned it before. Now it was all too clear.

"Doctor Hastings called. You need to meet her at the museum. She's eager to talk to you."

"I talk to her every day."

"She wants to talk to you in person. Now."

"We're going to eat breakfast first," Kadie said.

"Breakfast can wait. Doctor Hastings wants to see you now. And you need to be wearing this." Curt handed her a *hijab*.

She wanted to argue, but it was pointless. The culture war would not be won in a hotel restaurant in Istanbul. Taking the garment from Curt, she wrapped the symbol of Islamic oppression around her head.

Kadie sighed, her shoulders sagged. She steered Brian toward the door.

"He can stay here," Curt said, referring to Brian.

Kadie wheeled around, her fists balled at her sides, baring her teeth.

"He has a name. His name is Brian. And Brian is going with me." She turned and stormed out the door, fuming at Curt's insincerity. How could she have been attracted to such a jerk? Duke had warned her about this guy. What did he know that she didn't? What did he see that she ignored?

The museum was almost a mile from their hotel, but they chose to walk. Well, Kadie chose to walk. Brian insisted they take a cab. They were both tired from yet another long night, but Kadie felt the long walk brought her back to life. She glanced at her brother, who was doing fine, but breathing heavily and slowing his pace. His reluctance was starting to show. Perhaps they'd take a cab back to the hotel.

The main building of the Archaeological Museum was a large two-story structure with four massive Corinthian-capped columns at the front entrance. Kadie dragged Brian up the steps into the front door. Once inside, they found Dr. Patricia Hastings in the lobby of the main building discussing something with one of the curators. She, too, wore a *hijab* loosely over her head. When they approached, Patricia's face grew a pleasant smile.

"Kadie, Brian! I'm so glad you're here." Dismissing the curator, Patricia greeted them, arms extended. She embraced Kadie in a long, firm hug, kissing her on both cheeks. And she did the same for Brian, who tried to shy away and giggled at the process. It warmed her heart that Dr. Hastings treated Brian with respect.

"Hello, Doctor Hastings," she said.

"Oh, poppycock, it's Patricia. There aren't many of us girls around, so we've got to stick together." She gently laid her hand on Kadie's forearm.

"Very well, Patricia."

"Let's grab a cappuccino and catch up on things." Patricia led them to the tiny coffee shop attached to the museum. There was no one in line, and she ordered two cappuccinos and a Coca-Cola for Brian. They sat at a small table while the barista fixed their coffee.

The main building was one of three that comprised the museum. Renovated several years prior, it was one of Istanbul's most prominent buildings built in the neoclassical style. Together, the buildings held over a million artifacts, but for some reason, GDI focused on this building to find clues for the hantavirus.

"How was the flight over?" Patricia said. "Any difficulties or complications?"

"It was fine . . . other than the 6:00 a.m. takeoff. We took a van at two in the morning to the airport. It was another night of travel and no sleep."

Patricia appeared genuinely shocked. "My dear, you must be exhausted." She placed her hand on top of Kadie's.

"We're tired and hungry, but Curt—Mister Baxter—said you needed to see us right away."

Patricia waved her hand as if brushing the thought of him aside. "Oh, that's not what I meant. It was more important that you get some rest and nourishment. Sometimes I wonder where I found that man. He just acts on his own."

Kadie wondered if she should tell her what Duke had learned about Curt. Yes, she should. But was now the right time? "While we were in Jerusalem—"

"Yes, tell me about Jerusalem. How was the trip to the Holy Land? I'm so glad you had the opportunity to go. What did you think? Was it everything you expected?"

Kadie abandoned the topic of Curt for now. She needed to think of a way to bring it up. Perhaps tomorrow sometime.

"Kadie?" Patricia searched for an answer concerning Kadie and Brian's visit to Jerusalem. They had been so busy, Kadie didn't have much time to reflect on it.

"It was inspiring."

"Inspiring?" Patricia leaned back in her chair, her eyebrows scrunched together. "I didn't expect to hear that coming from an atheist."

Kadie's head jerked up. "I never said I was an atheist."

"*Au contraire*. The questionnaire you filled out on your application was very specific on religious beliefs. You matched as an atheist. But I'll give you agnostic if that makes you feel better. Thankfully, you're not a believer. You could be arrested for that here if you said that out loud."

Kadie stared at her hands in front of her, tapping her fingertips together one at a time. She did fill out the questionnaire all those months ago. But the events of the last few days made her question her beliefs. She had seen things . . . felt things. Things she couldn't explain. Kadie didn't realize it until now, but perhaps she'd been wrong about God.

"Yes," Kadie said. "A new twist on Don't Ask, Don't Tell."

"Precisely." The glee in Patricia's voice was evident. Odd.

The barista brought their drinks to the small table. Brian eagerly slurped on his Coke, and Kadie added a couple of packets of sugar to her small, caffeinated beverage.

"So, Kadie, my interest is piqued. What did you find so inspiring in Jerusalem?"

Kadie sipped her cappuccino, then set the cup back into the saucer.

"We went to the Garden Tomb. There was—I felt something there. Something I don't think I've ever felt before."

"It's a beautiful attraction. I've heard many people talk about their magical experiences there, but I wouldn't take that too seriously, I've had similar experiences at Disney World."

Kadie's jaw clenched. The comparison seemed offensive at best. "I wouldn't call it magical. It was spiritual. I can't explain it, but the experience is making me rethink my position."

"Really?" Patricia's curiosity bubbled to the surface. "So, you think there is something to Jesus of Nazareth being the son of God? That he was crucified and rose from the dead?"

Kadie pondered the question. Her answer could impact her job. When she signed up, Christians were strictly forbidden. That was mainly because of the countries they operated in. GDI had agreements with the Islamic governments of these countries to operate with impunity. Kadie was confused by the emotions that stirred within her, but the truth found its way out, regardless of the impacts of her beliefs.

"Yes."

29

Istanbul, Turkey
The Archeological Museum

Kadie observed Patricia's reaction to her answer. Her mouth twitched on the left side, and the whites of her eyes grew and crunched her irises, making them appear smaller by the second.

"Yes," Kadie repeated. "I believe Jesus is the Son of God and rose from the dead to cleanse us from our sins." The words didn't flow from her mouth—they flowed from her heart.

Brian stared at his sister, a huge smile spreading across his face.

"Kadie . . . yes!" The boy was excited, and so was she. A life-altering declaration that she had suppressed for years had just been made. Her eyes watered as Brian hugged her. They released their embrace, and she looked back at Patricia, who sat tight-lipped. The twitch was no longer present, and the white of her eyes gone, as her eyes narrowed.

"Well," Patricia said, "I'm not sure what we can do about that. The contract says—"

"The contract doesn't say anything about *becoming* a Christian. The questionnaire says you can't be one to fill out the application because of the countries we are operating in. Nothing says I can't convert while I'm here." Kadie surprised herself at how easily that argument came out of her mouth. She was right, and she knew it. Because when she filled out the application, she wasn't a believer. Only Brian was, and he wasn't coming along to work for GDI. Kadie had made sure she understood everything they'd asked about religion throughout the process.

A faint smile perched on Patricia's face. "You're right." She sipped her cappuccino. "I think we'll be okay. But I'll need to do some digging. I'll call my contact at the embassy this afternoon just to make sure there's no problem."

Kadie studied the executive vice president of Science and Technology. She expected the woman to be a lot angrier than she appeared. They sat in silence for a moment, and Brian slurped his Coke through a straw.

"I want to offer you a job, Kadie."

The coffee cup almost reached her mouth before Kadie returned it to the saucer. "Pardon me?"

"I'm offering you a full-time position with Global Disease Initiative. Or, actually, one of our affiliate companies."

Kadie pushed away from the table. "I—I don't know what to say."

"You have done a remarkable job for us here. I want to keep you around."

"But I haven't done anything regarding my job. I've just—"

"Oh, balderdash. You've done everything we've asked. Not to mention the danger you've faced."

Kadie pondered her comment. How could she have done a remarkable job? She hadn't done anything yet except search for this supposed cure—and that was questionable after meeting Isaac.

"My goal, Doctor Hastings—"

"Patricia, please." Her smile dripped from her face.

Kadie's back straightened, and she clasped her hands in front of her.

"My goal, Patricia, is to return to Princeton and join the faculty there. This trip has been amazing. I've had the opportunity to see some incredible things—"

"And some quite terrifying things, it sounds."

The statement was more on target than perhaps the executive vice president realized. Kadie thought about the last few days. Samuel's murder, being chased by ISIS, the escape at the airport, and her adventures in Jerusalem. The experience had been more than she signed on for. "Yes, some terrifying things as well. But I think given the circumstances," she paused and glanced at her brother, then Patricia, "I think it best that I return to the university."

"But our work here isn't finished."

Kadie nodded. Time to go all in. "I understand. What exactly are we searching for? We've scoured museum after museum. When I was hired, I expected some archeological digs, exploring dark caverns and tombs. But for the last three weeks, I've been a highly paid tourist."

"And being highly paid is a bad thing?"

"No, ma'am. Please understand, I'm very appreciative. But it . . . it just seems like I'm not doing anything that requires my specific skillset."

"Kadie, you're part of a team. Everyone on the team possesses a unique skill set. That's why we brought you together."

"That's just it. *None* of our skills have been utilized, yet."

"And they won't be until we find what we're searching for."

"That's the problem. What are we searching for? Duke said—"

"Who's Duke?"

"Duke is one of the pilots who picked us up in Egypt. He said he'd read all the classified briefings on ISIS, and there's no mention of a biological weapon anywhere."

Patricia let out a long sigh. "Kadie, I recognize young men and their motives. He's trying to win you over. I understand. But keep in mind, he's only a contractor hired by the military to do a crappy job nobody else wants to do. It should be obvious, at this point, the resources GDI has at its disposal. He doesn't have a need to know, so he doesn't. It really is that simple."

Perhaps Patricia was right. She mulled the words over. Maybe Duke didn't have access to the information GDI had received from the government. But how did she know he was a military contractor? Kadie never mentioned it. *Am I thinking too hard about this?*

"What about Samuel?" she asked.

"Samuel?" Patricia's reaction came out tense and loud. Odd.

"Samuel was murdered. Who is looking into that?"

"We have our contacts in the State Department. The embassy is working closely with the local authorities in Egypt to get to the bottom of Samuel's murder and find the killers. The investigation is ongoing."

"But we were told the killer was ISIS."

"Based on *your* eyewitness testimony."

"But why would ISIS target Samuel? A lone man in his hotel room on the second floor of a hotel?"

Patricia stammered. "Well, it, ah . . . it could be anything. Perhaps he made contact with the wrong people in town. Maybe he tried to buy drugs or something else on the black market. He was Jewish, after all. Not a practicing Jew, but Jewish, nonetheless. That, is enough to insult the extremists to spark something."

Kadie couldn't believe what she heard. Patricia essentially gave the extremists a pass for killing a Jew simply *because* he was a Jew. It was the same mentality that led to the persecution of Christians back home.

"No, Samuel was on to something." Oops. That slipped out.

Patricia set her cappuccino in the saucer. Her body tensed, and she leaned forward. "What do you mean?"

Kadie bit her bottom lip. "Samuel thought we were searching for something else."

"Like what?"

"I—he didn't say."

Patricia sighed, her forefinger and thumb resting against the side of her face. "Then how do you know?"

"He called me. He said it was urgent. When I returned to the hotel, he had been attacked. That's when I was chased."

"But you managed to salvage his laptop before the police arrived."

Here we go with the laptop again. GDI has an affinity for that device.

"Yes," Kadie replied. "He said he had something important. I assumed he had sensitive information on the laptop. I mean, we all have sensitive information on these laptops, right? I didn't want it stolen or locked up by the police."

"That was quick thinking. Curt was stunned when he saw you had Samuel's laptop."

"Stunned is an understatement." Kadie recalled the instant Curt transformed in front of her in Tel Aviv. The thin veneer of decency and pleasantness peeled away, exposing himself as what he really was. "He was a jerk."

Patricia rolled her eyes. "Yes, he has his ways. But he's effective."

"What's his background?"

"Curt? He's from Delta Force. Highly recommended, I'm told."

"That's another thing. Duke said he talked to Delta Force members he knows, and no one has ever heard of Curt Baxter." There, she said it.

"My dear, one can't personally account for every single person within an organization."

"No, but..." Kadie hesitated. Duke said Delta Force was an elite group, which inherently made it small. They would know him if he had been a member. "This is different."

Patricia stopped. That got her attention. "Are you saying he's not who he says he is?"

She sure put that together quickly.

"I—I'm not sure what I'm saying. He might be using a false name. Perhaps he padded his resumé to get hired. There's no telling. But Duke assures me no one in Delta Force has ever heard of him."

Patricia's face went blank. Finally, Kadie thought, she said something that registered with the senior executive.

"I'll look into it. If he's given us any false information or misrepresented himself in any manner, we'll take care of it right away.

Mister Thorndike won't tolerate any such action from an employee."

Graham Thorndike was the CEO of Alligynt, the parent company of GDI. Kadie had never met the man, though she had seen him from a distance. He spoke to the entire group before they departed Atlanta and headed for the Middle East, but she never had the chance to say hello up close and in person.

Kadie nodded and took a sip of her cappuccino. The intensely caffeinated beverage had cooled since she first took a sip. The bitterness nipped at her tongue, much like this conversation had flowed—overwhelmingly awkward.

"I look forward to meeting this Duke character someday," Patricia said. "He seems to have made quite an impression on you. Certainly, something I haven't been able to do."

Kadie started to say something, then stopped herself. "I think Brian and I need to return to the hotel. We're both starving and tired." They rose from the table, but Patricia remained seated. "Goodbye, ma'am."

"Be careful, Kadie. Brian, take care of your sister. She's my favorite."

"Okay," he said, looking away.

Kadie cringed at the clingy words Patricia continued to use. But why would she need to be careful? Why here, why now?

As they reached the door of the coffee shop, Patricia said, "You never know who you'll upset when you meddle in other people's affairs."

30

Tel Aviv, Israel
Ben Gurion International Airport

Duke and Mac loaded the King-Air with their gear and conducted a pre-flight. The IDF returned the weapons and other items GDI had left on the plane. The weapons had been disassembled and sealed in a box. Unfortunately, so had the one Mac used. Once everything was secure inside, Duke did a walk-around and inspected the patches the Israeli's made over the bullet holes in the fuselage. Mac accomplished a thorough inspection of the new engine. Duke commented on the excellent job the Israeli mechanics did on the engine and fuel lines.

The plane flew well the day before, but they were extra cautious. Mac had made a few phone calls to get their diplomatic clearance adjusted to fly to Turkey. The original clearance had expired, and they were well outside the standard time required for submission. Sometimes it paid to have friends in high places.

Once ready, the two pilots climbed inside the twin-engine turboprop and started her up. They taxied to the active runway and took off over the Mediterranean, then turned north toward Turkey.

When they leveled off at ten-thousand feet, Duke engaged the autopilot.

"We'll be in VHF contact the entire way," Mac said. "You worried about her?"

Duke looked at his mentor and friend. "Is it that obvious?"

"Yeah."

"I'm just concerned. She's the only witness to this murder in Egypt. The murdered guy had information about why they were *really* in Egypt. She takes his laptop, which freaks out our phony Delta guy when he discovers she has it. We meet Isaac, who tells us what they're actually searching for, then *he* gets killed." Duke returned his gaze out front of the airplane. "Yeah, I think she's in danger."

"That isn't what this Isaac guy said. He said you're *both* in danger."

Duke nodded. "Yeah, but I'm more worried about her. And her brother. I can take care of myself."

"Just make sure you do."

As they approached landfall, the two of them got busier and focused more on flying the airplane. The flight from takeoff to touch-down took two and a half hours, and Duke taxied the King-Air from the active runway to the Tav Genel Havacilik Terminal, where several uniformed customs officials waited. Some of them displayed their weapons openly.

They shut down the engines, and the two crusty pilots looked at each other, unsure of what to do next.

"I'm glad GDI's weapons are sealed in those containers the IDF supplied us," Duke said.

"Yeah, if I didn't know any better, I'd say our pal Curt had this welcoming party staged on our behalf. I bet they were tipped off that weapons were floating around the airplane improperly secured."

As soon as the props stopped spinning, the soldiers surrounded the aircraft and leveled their weapons on them.

"Sometimes, I hate being right," Mac said.

"Yep." Duke breathed deep. "I guess we'll sit here until they can figure out a way to open the door." He set his hands on the dash, palms out. Mac did the same.

"There's our boy." Mac pointed to Curt across the ramp in the background.

Duke shook his head. A minute later, the door to the King-Air opened, and two soldiers entered the plane screaming. Duke and Mac were removed from the airplane at gunpoint and forced onto the tarmac facedown. The soldiers shouted at them in Turkish, which neither of them understood. They stayed there for at least five minutes before anyone who spoke English showed up. By that time, everything had been removed from the airplane.

The Turkish customs office let them eventually stand. He then told them the Turkish government would hold the items until they paid the taxes on them. He checked the manifest and then their cargo. Thankfully, the Israeli ramp crew and customs officials did a great job storing, categorizing, and documenting their cargo.

There was a sense of disappointment among the Turkish soldiers as if the intel they'd been given was bad. Duke and Mac gave each other a silent grin, as the soldiers carried the Pelican cases to the truck where Curt stood.

"That guy is a putz," Mac said. "Wouldn't trust him as far as I could throw him."

"Yep. I guess that was his way of letting us know we need to stay away."

"How'd that work out for him?"

Duke put a hand on his friend's shoulder. "It didn't. Which means we don't have to stay away."

KADIE SAT IN HER HOTEL ROOM AFTER TAKING A SHOWER, THE TOWEL wrapped around her. Her chat with Patricia was not as enlightening as she hoped it would be. Flipping up her laptop, she logged on to the hotel's internet.

Brian walked in from his bedroom.

"Kadie—gross. G-go put on clothes."

She brushed her hand at him. "Hush, don't talk like that."

Brian giggled. "You dress—like that in c-case Duke comes by."

Her face flushed red. She wished Duke would stop by, but she had no idea where he was. Things had evolved quickly, and she needed his perspective.

"I'm afraid that's not going to happen. We're here now. When his airplane gets fixed, I imagine he's heading back to America."

"Oh." Brian turned on the television. "Why don't you call—and talk to him?"

Kadie glanced at her phone on the coffee table. "I would if I had his number." She bit her thumbnail between her teeth; she had only called his hotel room in Tel Aviv.

Brian turned from the television and faced her with a wide grin. "You like Duke."

Pulling the small towel from her head, she rubbed it in her hair as if to help it dry faster.

"Not like that," she said, although she wasn't quite sure. She hadn't thought about it until Brian said something. "We've become . . . friends. He's helping me with something from work."

"You like Duke." Brian returned his focus to the television. "I have his phone number."

Kadie's mouth fell open. *How did he get that?* She rose from her chair and walked between Brian and the television. Brian had a big smile on his face. That rascal—he knew exactly what he was doing.

"Well?" She tapped her foot, her hands on her hips.

Brian laughed, which caused her to laugh also. "It is on my phone." He reached in his pocket and handed it to her. "Duke g-gave it to me. Awe you g-going to call him?"

Kadie stared at the phone in her hand. "No, I think I'll text him." *Or, I'll text him from your phone,* she thought. That would be the best solution. She gritted her teeth and walked into her room.

"Hey—b-bring back my phone," he yelled from the couch.

"Be quiet and watch your movie."

Brian settled back into the couch. "O—kay."

Kadie thought about it for a moment, then typed to Duke:

Hey, where are you?

There was no response for a few minutes, so she walked into the bathroom and started to get dressed. After she put on her underwear and a shirt, she heard a TING on Brian's phone.

I just landed in Istanbul a couple of hours ago. How are you?

Kadie smiled, and her fingers went to work.

Good. We are at the Grand Tarabya Hotel.

After several seconds, Duke responded.

Okay. We'll find it and find you. Tell your sister we need to talk. I've got to go. I'm dealing with Customs. See you soon.

She walked back into the common area where Brian was glued to the television and handed him his phone.

"Okay," she said. "Just so we're clear, *you* texted Duke and told him where we're staying."

Brian appeared confused until he checked his messages. A scowl came over his face, and Kadie instantly regretted her decision.

"Brian, I'm sorry. I shouldn't have pretended I was you."

The scowl intensified, and his head began to shake. It began to shake way too much. Then he started howling.

"What's so funny?"

"Nothing," he said. "You like Duke."

Kadie smiled and shook her head. He pulled one over on her, and she deserved it. And she liked it when he was happy. She bit her lower lip and walked back to the bedroom. Who knew? Maybe she did like Duke.

31

Istanbul, Turkey
Hagia Sophia Museum

Frustrated, Dr. Patricia Hastings descended the steps of the gallery in the Hagia Sophia Museum. The sheer blouse she wore was tucked into her tight slacks; a colorful scarf resembling a rainbow countered the bright white short-brimmed straw hat that perched on the back of her head. Her long, svelte legs were perched in heels that echoed with each step on the marble stairs. Massive chandeliers hung from the ceiling, the circular lights illuminating the marble-covered floor, and the massive, gray-marble columns thrust four stories upward to hold the ceiling in place. Curt stood at the base of the stairs, sipping a bottle of water.

"You're not supposed to have a drink in here," she said, pointing to his bottle of water.

"Sue me." Curt chugged the bottle and placed the cap back on top.

"Where have you been?" she said. Her voice reverberated against the ancient walls.

"Making arrangements. Cleaning things up."

The building was constructed in 537 A.D. by the Emperor Justinian and was the largest cathedral in the world until the Seville Cathedral in Andalusia, Spain surpassed it in 1520. GDI had only received the authority to search the Hagia Sophia Museum two days ago.

Patricia's jaw clenched. Curt had upset her with the way he had handled things so far. "We've made some progress here," she said. "Excellent progress."

"You found the map?"

She shook her head. "No, but we've found instructions. Partial instructions. It's more like a clue we can't figure out."

Curt paused. "Any idea where to start?"

"That's what we need to find out next. We believe the Aramaic Vase is in the hills to the south, in Altinova."

"Helenopolis?"

Patricia beamed. "Yes. The Sator Square provided the key." They had searched the Hagia Sophia to find any documents or manuscripts they could on the Aramaic Vase, and she was more than pleased with their discovery. The Istanbul team of GDI consisted of twenty personnel spread across the city at different locations. With the addition of Team Egypt, their numbers swelled to twenty-six.

Curt set his hands on his hips. "We need to find the map. Then we can be sure."

Her eyes narrowed. "What in the world happened in Port Said? It should have been a routine operation."

Curt gazed at the ground, contemplating an answer. "After the Samuel Jacobson incident, we bugged out. I thought the airport was safe. Who knew ISIS controlled the place?"

"But the pilots handled the evacuation, okay?"

"Yes. Impressive, actually. They flew what the pilot called a tactical approach, whatever that is. Came in low, perpendicular to the runway, and circled around blacked-out. Landed with no lights, no nothing. We started taking fire as soon as they touched down. Guys did a good job getting us out of there."

Patricia walked toward the coffee shop. She never checked to see if Curt followed her. He would be there.

"Why in the world did you go to Tel Aviv?" She stopped and glared at him.

Curt shrugged his shoulders. "Going to Israel wasn't my idea. One of the engines was shot up. I'm not the expert but flying to Istanbul on one engine didn't seem like a good idea. I'm sure they landed at Tel Aviv because we had nowhere else to go. We certainly couldn't land in Syria or Jordan. Those places aren't too friendly to random Americans."

"Why not return to Egypt?"

Curt stuck his hands in his pockets. "I asked the pilot the same thing. His response was, *Don't tell me how to fly my airplane.*"

Patricia pursed her lips and waved at the barista, who nodded. The young girl would bring Patricia her usual cappuccino. "Well, at least the trip through Customs allowed you to discover she had Samuel's laptop."

Curt nodded. "Yes. I can't believe she had it."

Patricia's eyebrows raised, then she exaggerated them even further to prove her point. "Did you ever ask her if she had the laptop?"

After a moment of silence, Curt stared at the ground. "No."

"How much do they know?"

"I'm not sure."

"Them going to Jerusalem—will it hurt us?"

"Unknown at this point. Abelman is no longer a problem." He looked back at her. "She and the pilot . . . they seemed to hang around each other quite a bit. I tried to restrict her to the hotel, but she didn't listen. They've got something up their sleeve."

"Really?" That was something he had never told her before. "You can be a fool sometimes."

He started to speak, then stopped himself.

"Whatever you did, *they* did some investigations on their own."

"Investigations?"

"Yes. On you."

His face tensed, and his mouth formed an 'O.'

"It seems our pilot knows quite a few Delta Force people, and none of them has ever heard of a Curt Baxter."

Curt grimaced and shook his head. "I think we need to move to Plan B," he said. That phase was something she wanted to avoid, but he was right. It was time.

32

Istanbul, Turkey
The Grand Tarabya Hotel

Kadie sat in the coffee shop of the hotel, R.E.A.D., nursing a large vanilla latte. The chair was comfortable yet secluded. At least as secluded as it could be in a hotel lobby. Her *hijab* lay folded on the table next to her latte. She opened Safari on her iPad and searched for Pontius Pilate. There were the usual hits, but she couldn't find any with the depth and breadth she needed.

It was a long-shot that Duke would show. She hoped he would; there were so many questions about everything. The afternoon grew long, and she finished several lattes before her search got any traction. And what she found wasn't what she wanted.

Curt strode into the coffee shop, intense as usual. She couldn't believe how wrong she'd been about the guy. Talk about Jekyll and Hyde. This guy's personality flipped a full one-hundred-eighty degrees.

She tried to make herself small, but Curt had some kind of internal radar that found her wherever she was. Unfortunately, his internal radar didn't work for anything else.

"Kadie, what are you doing here?"

His tone was unusual, considering he had threatened to have her thrown in jail earlier. Apparently, he was Jekyll again, back in his courting persona.

"I'm reading, Curt," she said and sipped her latte.

"What are you reading?" He reached behind her and rubbed her neck behind the collar of her shirt.

"None of your business." She lunged forward at the waist, causing him to release his grip.

Curt started to speak, but she cut him off. "I just want to be left alone to read."

"If that were the case, why are you sitting in the coffee shop?"

Hmmm . . . Curt's a jerk, but he's not stupid. "Brian's watching television upstairs. I didn't want to be bothered by the background noise."

"Well, there are other places you could—"

"CURT! Leave me alone! I'm trying to read."

The few other customers and the barista turned in their direction. She could see him tense up when she blurted his name. That should have sent him a message loud and clear.

"Fine, but you should be wearing your head cover." He wandered off toward the elevator. No sooner was he out of sight than Duke and Mac walked in.

"Duke!" She dropped the iPad on the table and rushed to him. She wrapped her arms around his waist, her head crushed against his chest. Realizing what she'd done, she released him and backed away. "I'm sorry, I—I overreacted."

The tall pilot smiled. Mac did too, more so than his younger partner.

"It's nice to see you, too. Is there somewhere we can talk?"

She nodded. "There's a patio out back on the way to the pool. It's quiet and out of the way. I don't want to go upstairs. Curt just went up."

Duke grimaced. "Yeah, we just came down from there. Brian said you were down here." He paused. "We need to steer clear of that guy for now."

She looked at him, then at Mac, whose face was just as grim. "Duke will fill you in. In the meantime, I'll go check us in."

Duke patted him on the back. "Thanks, Mac." He turned back to Kadie. "After you."

She gathered her iPad, *hijab*, and latte, then led him out to the patio and sat at one of the empty tables.

"So," she said. "What's up?"

"Isaac's dead."

Her eyes bulged. "What?"

A solemn look fell over Duke's face. "I went back to the museum the morning you left, and he never showed up for work. I persuaded the manager to give me his address. When I arrived, he was on the floor, bleeding. Someone stabbed him."

"Oh, my. That's terrible." A dreadful thought crossed her mind. "Was the knife still there?"

"No." Duke breathed deep. "Isaac was still alive, but I couldn't do anything. He did tell me something before he died."

A myriad of thoughts raced through her head. "What?"

"He mentioned something about the riddle of the three. Ring any bells?"

The riddle of the three? Kadie bit her lower lip and contemplated years of information, stories, and legends. She had never even heard of the Aramaic Vase nor the Pilate Scroll, so the riddle-of-the-three fit right in there with them. "I can't say that's anything I'm familiar with, no."

Duke's eyes shifted up and locked on to hers. "I think it was Curt."

Her lips tightened, and she nodded. His expression told her she had surprised him when she agreed with him. No doubt, Duke expected an argument.

Kadie sighed. "When we were at the hotel in Tel Aviv, Curt produced an envelope that contained our boarding passes."

Duke's head tilted to the side.

"Then he pulled out a knife to open the envelope. It was the same kind of knife that the assassin threw at my head in Samuel's room."

Duke squinted. "Anybody can have the same knife."

"No," Kadie said. "When I brought up the knife to him, he said he pulled it from the wall in Samuel's room. I know for a fact he didn't. I saw the police remove *both* knives and take them to the station for evidence."

"He's lying about the knives because he's the one who threw them."

Kadie nodded as she felt the knot in her stomach grow tighter. "I think so. I wanted to believe it's not possible."

"It's possible, probable, and most likely. I'd bet money on it. Kadie, Isaac said you were in danger—"

"He said *we* were in danger.

"Okay, *we're* in danger. But why? Why would he say that having just met us? What would tell him that we were in danger?"

Kadie sat back and lodged her thumbnail between her teeth. Her eyes flitted from the table in front of her back to Duke.

"It has to be the vase," Kadie said. "Samuel learned about the Scroll, and he's dead. Isaac knew about it and told us. Now he's dead. Of course, we're next, right?"

"Yep."

"But why would Curt do this? What does he have to gain?"

"I'm sure Curt is a lowly triggerman. A nobody who's doing the bidding of a somebody. This conspiracy goes way higher than him. Have you googled the Global Disease Initiative?"

"Well, yes, when Patri—Doctor Hastings—first approached me about the job. GDI is a very well-established, well-funded organization. We've received everything we've asked for. They even made accommodations for Brian."

"That's my point," Duke said. "While I think all that is great, who does that? What company in their right mind goes out of their way to give their employees everything they ask for? How many college graduates get a job making six-figures right out of school and a two-bedroom executive suite at every location?"

"I have a master's degree, thank you."

"My question still stands. These guys are dirty. They hid the idea of the Scroll from everyone because it is nobler to find a cure for a virus that will destroy the world than to find an ancient artifact to sell to the highest bidder."

Kadie pushed away from the table. "That is preposterous! There's no way GDI is in this for the money. And who's to say they hid the idea of the Scroll—"

The realization of what she was about to say stopped her in her tracks. Her hands rubbed her upper arms as her skin began to crawl.

Did someone else on the team know about the Pilate Scroll?

33

The lobby was less chaotic than when they first arrived at the hotel. The opulence of the place jumped out at him. The tan marbled floor glistened in the sunlight that pushed through the glass walls of the front of the hotel. Duke approached one of the desk clerks perched behind the curved check-in desk with a deep granite top to pick up his key.

Once in his room, Duke tossed his bag on the white blanketed king-sized bed and admired the view that overlooked the marina next to the hotel. He stripped off his clothes, brushed his teeth, and stepped in the shower. The warm water was refreshing, and the scent of the fresh soap penetrated his nostrils, waking him up.

When he finished in the shower and dried off, he pulled a fresh set of clothes out of his bag and dressed. After he plugged his cell phone in the charger, he grabbed his key and went to Mac's room to ask about going to dinner.

He wanted to bounce everything off Mac one more time because he had no doubt Kadie and her brother were in danger. They needed to leave Istanbul as quickly as possible, whether with them or on a commercial flight. The question was, would she be willing to go?

Duke rapped on the door. When Mac didn't answer, he rapped

again. “Hey, Mac, you in there?” He beat the door loudly, in case his partner had fallen asleep. “Hey, Mac, you awake?”

His first thought was that Mac must have gone downstairs for coffee or food. But he knew Mac would have contacted him first. Duke remembered his cell phone was on the charger and returned to his room to see if Mac called. He moved back to his door and swiped his key. Inside, he checked his iPhone. No messages from Mac or anyone else. He sat on the side of the bed when someone knocked on the door.

Before he could get up, Kadie barged into the room. Still wearing the sleeveless button-up shirt and shorts she had on in the coffee shop, she wasn’t smiling.

“What are—how’d you open the door?”

Kadie held up a small, circular FOB. “Same thing I used to get into Samuel’s room. Works great in this hotel, too.” She stood still in front of the door, her shoulders slumped, her head down. This was not the confident woman he’d come to know. Something was wrong.

“Brian’s missing.”

“What?”

Kadie walked closer, then stopped. Her right hand rubbed the length of her left arm. “After we left the patio, I went to the coffee shop to buy him a latte. When I returned to our room, he was gone. I wasn’t too worried at first, but then I checked with Doctor Upton, and he wasn’t there. I asked everyone on the team, and no one has seen him. That’s when I started to panic. I went downstairs and searched everywhere. I checked with the front desk, the doormen, and even the cabana guy at the pool. Duke, I’m terrified something may have happened to him.”

Duke rose from the bed and wrapped his arms around her. “I’m sure he’s okay. Look, I just tried to find Mac, and he’s not answering his door. Maybe the two of them ran into each other and went to find something to eat.”

Kadie pushed away gently and gazed into his eyes. “Yes.” She hoped that might be the answer as the corners of her mouth slightly curved upwards. “Maybe that’s it.” Extending herself further from his embrace, Kadie moved back to the door. As she reached for the handle, she turned back to face him. "Would you come with me to find them?"

"Of course," Duke said. "Kadie, I was thinking about things . . ."

"Things?"

"Yeah, about this situation. It's not safe to stay here any longer."

"Well, you should leave then."

The corners of his mouth started to curl. He got the sarcasm. "No, I mean, it's not safe for *you* to stay here any longer. You and Brian need to either buy a commercial ticket home or leave with us tomorrow."

She said nothing right away, processing the statement. "You might be right. Things are unfolding at a rapid rate. I—I just want to find Brian first. We'll talk about the rest later."

"Understood."

The two of them left Duke's room and headed to the elevators. They stepped in, and Duke pushed the button for the lobby. Kadie reached over and pressed '4,' the expression on her face serious.

"I want to get Brian's Lamictal from Doctor Upton."

Duke nodded.

The elevator opened on the fourth floor, and they hurried to Upton's room. She rapped anxiously on the door.

"Kadie." Doctor Upton's eyebrows raised. "What a—" He stopped short when he saw Duke standing in the hallway.

"Hello, Doctor Upton. I need to pick up Brian's Lamictal."

"He took one earlier today," the doctor said.

"No, I mean, I need all of it. We're going to leave."

"Leave? What? W-where are you going?"

Duke's eyes narrowed, and his head tilted slightly as the doctor responded to Kadie.

"Is there a problem?" Upton said.

Kadie paused. "We've got an emergency we need to take care of."

"You won't be able to get the medicine through customs without a doctor."

Kadie paused again. Duke wondered if she had thought this one through. "We've made arrangements," she said.

The doctor glanced at Duke, who managed a slight wave from the wrist.

"W-well, okay." Doctor Upton turned and went into the other room and returned with a small bottle. "Can you tell me where you're going?" he said as he handed Kadie the bottle.

"The airport." She took the bottle and hugged his neck. "Thank you for looking out for Brian during this trip. I hope it works out for you."

"What did Doctor Hastings say about you leaving?" Upton said.

"I haven't told her yet." Kadie wondered if she should tell her at all.

Doctor Upton appeared concerned. "Have you found Brian yet?"

"No, but I'm sure he'll turn up. He always does."

"You know, I thought I saw him in a bathing suit with a towel around his neck heading for the pool a little while ago."

Kadie's face drew into a broad smile. It was a pleasant smile that made Duke's heart flutter. "Thank you, Doctor. That saved me a lot of searching."

"My pleasure, my dear. I'm glad I could help."

Duke and Kadie turned to leave.

"You two be careful," Upton said as he closed the door and flipped the deadbolt into place.

They took the elevator to the pool deck and walked outside. Brian was nowhere to be found.

"He's not here," Kadie said.

The worry on her face was evident to Duke. "I don't see him either. Maybe he's inside the hotel still."

"He's not supposed to walk around alone."

"Maybe he got hungry."

"Maybe."

They searched the outdoor grill, and then went back inside the hotel. They peeked in the coffee shop and finally the restaurant. As they meandered through, Kadie let out an exasperated, "Thank God."

Duke scanned the room until he found Mac and Brian sitting in the corner, eating lunch. The small Pelican case holding Brian's drone sat on the table.

"Hey, Kadie," Brian said, waving. "Come sit with us."

"Brian," Kadie said. "I've been looking all over for you."

Brian lowered his head, and his smile faded.

"Sorry, Miss Kadie. I was teaching him how to use the video camera on his drone. We had been out by the pool. When we finished, the boy was hungry, so I brought him down here."

Kadie ran her fingers through Brian's hair. "It's okay. But he knows he shouldn't leave the room without me."

Traces of a smile return to Brian's face as the boy looked up at Mac.

"We need to leave, Brian. Let's go upstairs and grab our things."

"I do not want to go."

"Well, we're leaving," she said. "And I don't have time to argue."

"Leave?" Mac said, looking at Duke.

"Yeah. We'll talk about it on the way to the airport."

Kadie turned to Duke. "We'll meet you downstairs in fifteen minutes."

Duke reached out and tenderly touched her arm. "I think we need to stay together."

Kadie glanced at Brian and Mac, who both seemed confused, then nodded at Duke. Mac threw some cash on the table, and the four left the restaurant and headed upstairs.

34

Kadie and Brian gathered their few remaining belongings and took the elevator up to Mac's room. They had all agreed to meet there, then depart for the airport. Duke would ensure she and Brian boarded an airliner to somewhere; then, they would fly their plane back to the States. Secretly, she wished Duke would fly back with them, but the realities of their situation dictated otherwise.

The elevator door opened, and the two of them shuffled out and walked down the empty hallway to Mac's room. She knocked, and within seconds, Duke opened the door. Once inside, Duke checked the hall behind them, then closed the door.

"Where's Mac?" Kadie said as she turned around.

Duke had a strange look on his face, and put his finger to his lips, telling her she needed to be quiet.

Kadie, curious to what was happening, stood silent. Duke approached her and moved behind her. He reached up to her neck with his hand and pulled at something under her collar. When she turned to face him, his thumb and forefinger held a small circular device about the size of a nickel. Was that what she thought it was? Duke reminded her not to speak.

"How about we watch some TV?" Duke said. He walked to the television, turned it on, and set the device next to it. Then he moved Brian and Kadie close to the door so they could speak without being heard by the small device.

"That's a transmitter," Duke whispered.

"That's what I thought." Kadie spoke softly as well. "I think Curt placed it there earlier before you showed up at the coffee shop."

"Then he's heard everything we've said to this point."

Kadie's eyes drooped. "I'm sorry. We need to get out of here. Where's Mac?"

"He went downstairs already to secure us a ride to the airport. If Curt is consistent, it will be difficult for us to exit the hotel without him seeing us. The biggest thing that can help us is he won't know we are leaving right now."

Kadie thought about what Duke said. He was right, of course. Curt was like a corrections officer, and them leaving would prove to be a challenge.

Duke's phone rang, and he pulled it out of his pocket. The dark black Otterbox case was smudged with dirt, making the cover lighter than it was.

"Yeah, Mac," he said. She could hear Mac's voice despite the television playing across the room, and Duke simply nodded and mumbled responses. He finally said thanks, and he'd meet him outside in the usual place. He slipped the phone back into his pocket and turned to face her.

"Mac stopped on your floor on the way down. On a hunch." Duke continued to talk in hushed tones.

"A hunch for what?"

"When the elevator stopped, he stepped out. Curt and some thugs were kicking in your door."

"Oh, no."

"The good thing is, that device appears to be only a listening device, not a tracker. So, the only advantage we've got is they think we are still in my room. We need to get out of here now. Mine and Mac's rooms will be next."

Kadie nodded. "Brian, let's go."

"O—kay," Brian said. The young man was frustrated; she could tell. He clung the Pelican case holding his drone close to his chest. She was confident he didn't have a grasp on their situation yet. No sense in filling him in until it was necessary. They hurried to the door where Duke checked the hallway in both directions.

"The elevator is not an option. We'll use the staircase." The three of them raced down the hallway to the stairwell. They slipped inside, and Duke paused as soon as the door shut. Kadie also paused and listened. It didn't sound like anyone was in the stairwell, but you never know until you start down. Duke looked at her, nodded, and started down the stairs cautiously. It felt like forever descending from the sixth to the fourth floor. Duke was plastered with sweat, and Kadie felt her heart beating like a bass drum. Brian followed slowly, gripping on the steel rail that followed the stairs to the first floor. They paused on the fifth floor, just in case someone waited for them on the fourth. Hearing nothing, they continued with trepidation. The fourth-floor landing was empty, and they instinctively increased their pace down the stairs.

As they reached the second floor, the silence shattered as Duke's phone rang. He stopped immediately and retrieved it from his pocket, silencing the tone. He gave her an apologetic glance and answered the phone. After a few uh-huh's and okays, he flipped the volume button off and stuck the iPhone back into his pocket.

"That was Mac. GDI thugs are everywhere. He's in a cab at the end of the driveway, but the lobby is filled with GDI."

"What are we going to do?"

"I don't know. This stairwell exits into the lobby. It's probably a hundred feet to the front door from here."

They started down the stairs again and reached the first floor in seconds. To their surprise, there were two doors there—one to the lobby, and one led outside.

"What do you think?" Duke said.

Kadie's head swiveled between the two doors. "I think I'd rather take my chances outside, don't you?"

Duke nodded. Brian did the same.

Duke again led the way as he pressed gently against the door leading to the outside. He squinted as the mid-day sun shoved its way into the dark stairwell. After a few moments, he let the door shut and turned to her.

"It looks like we're on the North side of the hotel. There's a side-walk and bushes next to the building. I'm guessing from where we are to where Mac is waiting in the cab, is about a hundred yards. Could be more, could be less."

"Okay. I like our chances better outside than inside."

"Agreed. You two ready?"

Kadie nodded and checked Brian. He nodded as well. The three of them moved to the door, and Duke again opened the door slowly. After checking both directions, the three of them slipped outside. Kadie went last and ensured the door didn't slam shut. No sooner than the door shut, Duke stopped, then whirled back to face them.

"Get back inside," he whispered as he corralled them back to the door. "There's one of them right there."

Kadie looked at the closed door. There was no handle on the outside to open the door.

35

Kadie grabbed at the flat surface of the door. "We're stuck out here. What's wrong?"

"One of the GDI goons is walking up the sidewalk toward Mac." Duke glanced back and forth. "Quick, get behind these bushes." The three of them darted behind the big bushes between the sidewalk and the building. Kadie was surprised to see there was enough room for them to walk between the two. Duke crouched down and motioned for them to do the same.

"We've got to figure out a way to get around that guy," Duke said.

They sat in silence for a moment before Kadie looked up.

"They obviously are looking for us, right?"

"Seems that way."

"But as far as they know, we don't know that."

"Yeah."

"So, why don't I call Curt and tell him to meet us at the pool. Maybe they will all head that way to meet us. Then we can run to Mac's cab and head to the airport."

Duke mulled over what she said. "It might work." His chin rested in his hand, his thumb tapping the side of his jaw. Then he stopped, and his eyes grew wide. "Brian, didn't Mac teach you how to use the video camera on your drone?"

The boy looked up. "Yeah. Mac is smart. He taught me—a little while ago."

"Do you think you could use it right now?"

The boy paused for a moment, then nodded. Kadie could see he wanted to smile, but he was nervous.

"Brian," she said. "Do you think you can help us?"

He looked at her. "Yeah."

Setting the Pelican case on the ground, he unpacked Rupert and began to align the gyros. He pulled out his iPhone and attached it to the controller. After fiddling with the drone for a minute or two, he turned to Duke.

"Will you go set Rupert out in the grass o-on the other side—of the sidewalk?"

"Okay," Duke said.

The gruff pilot gently picked up the drone and crept to an opening in the bushes. Kadie peered over the top of the bush to the left; no one else was on the sidewalk. To the right, the GDI thug was still walking away from them, about a hundred feet away now. He might turn back at any second and start walking toward them. Kadie hoped Duke was thinking the same thing she was. He needed to hurry.

Suddenly, Duke sprang from between the bushes across the sidewalk, into the open grassy area about twenty feet away. He knelt, set the drone down, and bolted back to the bushes, keeping the GDI man in sight the entire time. Once behind the bushes, he scooted next to Brian.

"Let 'er rip, Brian," he said.

Brian smiled and pressed the controller.

The three of them peered over the top of the bushes as the drone whirred to life. The four propellers made a soft humming sound, and Kadie worried it might alert the GDI man. A second later, it hopped up ten feet above the ground, and Brian focused on his iPhone and sent the drone about a hundred and fifty feet into the sky. It took him a moment to turn the drone in the direction he wanted and lock the camera on the GDI man who was between them and Mac.

"Can you take it around the front of the hotel and see the entrance?" Duke said.

"Okay." Brian maneuvered the drone to the front of the hotel. He had to take a moment to check his surroundings before descending the drone to see the entrance. When he reached the lower altitude where he could see the front door, he turned to Duke. "Watch—this."

He zoomed the camera until he could see the faces of the people standing under the overhang in front of the hotel. As he zoomed in, they identified Curt and one of the other thugs at the front.

"Hold this position here, Brian," Duke said. "Kadie—you ready?"

"You bet." She pulled her iPhone out and dialed Curt's phone. The GDI security man answered on the first ring. Duke and Brian watched on the screen.

"Kadie," Curt said over the phone. "Where have you been?"

"Curt," she said. "I-uh . . . I heard you were looking for me. We're all at the pool right now if you'd like to join us." Duke gave her a funny look, and she shrugged her shoulders with a grimace. "Bye now. See you soon." She hung up and looked over Brian's shoulder.

"It's working," Duke said. Curt and the man with him bolted back into the hotel lobby. "They're heading for the pool. Okay, go back to the guy on the sidewalk."

Brian climbed Rupert higher and turned back toward the sidewalk on their side of the hotel. After a few moments, he was able to lock on the man who still casually strolled along the sidewalk.

"Bummer," Duke said. The GDI man didn't budge.

"Give him a second," Kadie said.

"Your faith is strong, young lady," he said.

"I had a good teacher," she said and smiled at him.

"Look!" Brian said.

He tilted the controller so Duke and Kadie could see better. The GDI man was talking on his phone, then tucked it in his pocket, and started running in their direction.

"Everybody stay low and be quiet," Duke said.

The three hunkered down as the GDI man ran past their position.

"Follow him with the drone, Brian," Duke whispered. He rose slightly to check their surroundings. The GDI man disappeared around the corner.

"He's headed to the pool, too," Kadie said. "Now is our chance."

"Yup, let's go." Duke rose, helped both out of the bushes, and they hurried along the sidewalk.

"They awe all at the pool," Brian said.

Kadie looked over his shoulder. "Now's the time to run." The three of them broke out in a jog until Brian stopped.

"Brian, what's wrong?" Kadie said.

"I have to bring—Rupert home." He pressed the home button on the controller, then started running again.

Good boy, she thought. Ahead she saw Mac's cab pull up, and Mac hopped out of the front seat and waved at them.

"Almost there," Kadie said.

Duke reached the cab first and opened the back door. Brian hopped in and slid to the other side, then Kadie sat in the middle.

"Where's the drone?" Duke said.

Brian stared at the screen for a moment. "It is overhead. It will come down now."

Duke searched the sky. "I see it."

The drone descended quickly and landed with a soft bounce in the grass twenty feet away, and Duke sprinted over, picked it up, and sprinted back to the cab. Mac had climbed back in and shut his door, and Duke reached the cab and climbed in.

"Let's go," he said as he shut the door. He handed the drone back to Brian. "Nice work back there, Brian. You saved us."

Kadie smiled at her brother and ruffled his hair with her fingers. He *did* do good. "Thank you, Brian. You were awesome."

Brian Jenkins blushed and giggled as he sat between them. "I'm a team player."

36

Istanbul, Turkey
Enroute to Istanbul Airport

The four sped away from the hotel in a cab with their few personal belongings in the trunk. Kadie's stress level increased as she sat in the cab. How would running out on GDI impact her career? Would she get fired? Did it matter? She basically quit. Should she call from the airport? Why were they searching for them in the first place? Kadie struggled with her options, which still included turning around and returning to the hotel.

The cab cruised south along the coastline. She had studied the map earlier—the airport was well over an hour away. And the traffic was heavy. Instinctively, she checked her purse for both her and Brian's passports. They remained safely tucked inside. Good thing because it was far too late to go back to the room if she didn't have them.

She turned to Duke. "Maybe we should go to the consulate."

"It's not going to keep them from you. They can enter as easily as you can."

"But there are Marines at the embassy."

"Yes, but your GDI friends seem to have their fingers into everything and everyplace. I'm not sure how safe you'd be there either."

Kadie thought about it and nodded as her face fell.

"What's wrong?" Duke said.

Kadie didn't turn—she just stared at the back of the driver's seat. "I was just thinking about how vulnerable we are, even after we return to the States."

"At least in America, you're on your own turf. You have resources available you don't have here."

She turned to him and nodded, again. Behind him, the highway they paralleled bristled with vehicles. On her side of the car, a mishmash of residential and business buildings. They would leave the back streets and side roads and reach the highway any minute now. That would expedite their travel to the airport, but what was the plan? Were Duke and Mac going with them? Or were they staying here? They would be in danger, too, if they stayed. Regardless of whether Curt wanted them dead because they knew about the Aramaic Vase or because Kadie had an interest in Duke didn't matter. He wanted them dead and would likely carry it out in the most devious manner possible. They'd never see it coming.

"The turn for the highway heading west is about three kilometers away," Mac said. "Then we'll start to make some—" The right front fender collapsed as shattered glass and debris flew into the back of the cab.

Mac was cut short as a truck T-boned the taxi in the front fender and spun the cab halfway around in the middle of the street.

The cab came to a stop; nobody moved for several seconds. Kadie's vision was blurry, and she realized Duke was unbuckling her and pulling her out the left side of the cab.

"Brian," she murmured.

"He's okay," Duke reassured her. "Mac is helping him out the other side. He's not hurt."

Kadie glanced over her shoulder, her vision slowly returning. Within moments, Mac had Brian out the other side. That made her feel better; until the shot rang out.

"Everybody down," Duke yelled. He pushed Kadie to the ground as more bullets impacted the side of the taxi.

"Mac, get him out of here!" Duke grabbed Kadie's hand. "We can't stay here! Let's go!"

They scurried low to the ground until they reached the traffic flow. The gunfire stopped for the moment, but that did not mean the shooters weren't pursuing them. Kadie looked behind her, relieved that Mac and Brian escaped through the crowd on the sidewalk in the opposite direction.

"Who's doing this? GDI?" she said. The fogginess faded fast as everything came back into focus.

"I was hoping you knew." Duke led her across the ten-lane highway, dodging the fast-moving cars until they reached the other side of the road. They paused in the overgrown grass lining the highway, giving them a second's reprieve to find their attackers.

"There." Duke identified two men running on the median. "Well, it's not Curt, but doesn't mean it's not his guys." The two men headed toward them, closing the one-hundred-yard gap in a hurry. One of the men aimed an automatic rifle at them, but the cars passing by robbed him of a clear shot. Numerous vehicles honked, swerved, and slowed when they saw the man brandishing the rifle in the middle of the highway. Kadie squeezed Duke's hand. Her judgment was foggy at best for the moment, making her grateful Duke's wasn't. Whatever he did, his instincts were spot-on.

"We've got to move," Duke said. He turned and ran into the wooded area behind them, dragging her along.

"What about Brian?" she cried.

"He's with Mac. He'll be fine. You won't be any good to Brian if you're dead. We'll call them as soon as we lose these two clowns."

They weaved their way through the trees into an open field. She didn't like leaving Brian, but he *was* with Mac. Could he be trusted? Duke seemed to think so, and for now, that's all that mattered.

"I hope you've still got your volleyball legs. We've got to sprint."

She grinned for the first time. "Try and keep up." Kadie bolted away and stayed a good five yards ahead of Duke across the field. The faster she ran, the more her head cleared. At the halfway point, shots rang out again.

On the other side of the field, they reached a street called Tepecik Yolu. Duke flagged down a kid on a scooter and gave him two one-hundred-dollar bills. The kid happily relinquished the scooter.

"Hop on," Duke said.

"He sure gave that up cheap."

"Probably just stole it." Duke climbed on and cranked the throttle, and they zipped down the street, dust and paper whirling as they sped along the pavement. Kadie pressed against his back, her hands holding tightly around his waist as she peeked over his right shoulder. Her hair danced in the wind as the scooter picked up speed. They raced southeast, weaving through a residential part of the sprawling city. When they reached another major highway, Duke made a left and sped northeast until he approached a T-bone intersection at a soccer field. As he slowed to figure out where to go, bullets whizzed by his head. He jerked the scooter to the right, followed by a small car.

Kadie checked behind them—one of the attackers hung out the window with a pistol. Duke tried to keep the scooter in front of the car to make it harder to hit them. When he reached a roundabout, he let them close. When they were on top of him, he made a sharp right turn on a road that led into a wooded area.

The attackers couldn't follow and had to make at least one circuit on the roundabout. Duke zigzagged on the road, continually turning before reaching a section that was nothing but continuous 'S'-turns. Kadie struggled to maintain her balance on the back and squeezed her arms tighter around his waist.

Finally, the road straightened, and they drove past a large Olympic-sized swimming pool.

"Look," Kadie said. "There's the coast."

The full span of the Bosphorus Strait appeared before them, its surface glistening like diamonds in the sunlight.

"I see it."

Duke gunned the throttle until they reached the street. In front of them, a marina stretched along the coast. He peered over his shoulder. "Care to take a ride?"

"With you? Can I trust you?" She was joking, of course, and she hugged his waist. "Let's go."

Duke slid the scooter into traffic and searched for the entrance to the dock. When he found it, he ditched the scooter around a few others parked on the street. They stretched their muscles and scanned the area for the car that had chased them. It was nowhere in sight.

Together, they hurried down the short stairs to the dock. "I think we need to find a boat and head down the strait to the marina by the airport," he said. "You and Brian should leave with us right now. At this point, that's our best option."

"I agree. We should have done that to begin with."

The two of them approached the slips where the boats moored. "Let me do the talking."

Kadie's eyes bulged. "Why? Because a woman isn't capable of finding a boat?"

"No. Because you're in Turkey, and the culture here is still not favorable to women. The men won't talk to you as readily as they'll talk to me. That's just the way it is."

Kadie backed down and pondered what Duke said. He was right, of course. His comment made her remember her hijab, so she pulled it out of her purse and wrapped it around her head. She lingered at a distance while he approached three different boat owners. On his fourth try, Duke found an older man named Ibrahim who understood a little English. Duke was able to convey they wanted to go down the Bosphorus Strait to the airport. Although the older man urged them to take a longer trip, perhaps following the Strait to the Sea of Marmara, the Black Sea, or the Aegean Sea, Duke stressed that they only wanted to go to the airport. The man relented his push and said there was a small marina south of the airport. Better a small sale than no sale.

The boat was wood; its hull was weathered and worn. The one positive aspect was the motor appeared to be in relatively good condition. The Mercury 25 horsepower outboard motor secured to the transom seemed out of place on the old boat.

Duke paid him cash, and they walked down the steps to the boat. Kadie climbed aboard the old motorboat, and it rocked back and forth. The seats made a crunching sound when she sat. They must have been made by the same guy who made the ones on the bus in Port Said. She settled on the least damaged cushion available in the back of the boat, while Duke and the owner boarded. This man ran some sort of business for tourists, but she couldn't tell what. He didn't have any fishing poles, so he was either a tour guide or a water taxi.

Duke studied the controls as the older man unlashed the ropes from the cleat on the dock. The old man moved behind the wheel, started the motor, and pulled away. Glancing over her shoulder, Kadie saw two men running along the dock toward them.

"Duke!" She pointed behind them.

"I see them." Duke tried to tell the old man to hurry. The boat owner didn't understand, so Duke shoved him away from the steering wheel and took the controls. As he pushed up the throttle and steered the boat away from the dock, the two men opened fire.

All three of them ducked after the first round hit the console. The boat surged as the propeller bit into the dark water, pushing the boat in front of the deep wake it created. A few seconds later, the boat settled with its new condition and accelerated away. The boat owner's eyes widened, and when they were far enough away from the shooters, the old man jumped overboard.

Kadie crouched and moved next to Duke. "Are we technically stealing his boat now?"

Duke shook his head. "Nah, he knows where we're going. He'll find his boat at the marina south of the airport." He paused, then looked at Kadie. "Who are these guys after you? They're persistent as anyone I've ever seen."

Kadie's eyes glistened, and her brows raised. "I don't know. Maybe they're chasing you."

Duke bobbed his head. "Maybe, but not likely." He fished his phone out of his pocket and dialed. "Here, call Mac."

Kadie took the phone, which was ringing by the time she put it to her ear.

"Duke," Mac said, "where are you guys?"

"Mac, it's Kadie. Duke can't talk—he's driving the boat."

"Driving the boat?"

"It's a long story," Kadie said. "Is Brian with you?"

"Yes, he's fine. We're in a cab on the way to the airport. We'll meet you at our airplane."

"Perfect. We'll meet you there as soon as we can."

"Great. I'd love to know how you two can take a romantic boat ride while we're being chased by guys trying to kill us."

Kadie chuckled. "I look forward to telling the story. See you soon. Let me talk to Brian."

"Sure. You two be careful," Mac said.

A moment later, Brian came on the phone. "Hey—Kadie. What are you doing? Why are you—on a boat wide?"

"It's a long story, Brian. I'll tell you all about it at the airport. Are you okay?"

"Yes. M-mac got us away from those bad guys."

"Okay. Stay with Mac until I get there, okay?"

"Yes, Kadie."

She hung up and handed Duke the phone. "They're in a cab on the way to the airport. Mac said to meet them at the plane."

Duke smiled. "Great." He set the throttle at a moderate rate, and the boat moved south along the Strait. The sparkling clear water was mostly still, the midday sun reflecting images from the shore on its surface. The translucent fluid displayed the rocks beneath them and the sharp drop-off into the dark abyss toward the center of the Strait. Duke stayed close to the shore; the draft of the boat not as deep as the larger boats they passed along the way. They relaxed for the first time in an hour, and Kadie leaned against Duke, resting her head on his shoulder. The salty sea spray tickled her nostrils. She sighed and smiled until she detected motion from the side.

Her head jerked as a powerboat lurched forward and turned toward them.

"Duke, look out!"

37

Istanbul, Turkey
The Bosphorus Strait

Duke looked to his left. Instinctively, he cut the throttles and steered his boat to the right. The speeding boat clipped the side of the wooden hull and viciously rocked their boat. The tiny boat swerved as Duke staggered behind the wheel, his hands refusing to let go. Kadie picked herself off the deck and struggled to maintain her footing.

The attackers had stolen a bigger, faster boat, and Duke had to find options. Fast. He scanned every inch of their boat, searching for anything that could be used as a weapon.

"Hang on," he said to Kadie. She grabbed the front console as he shoved the throttle forward and steered the boat to the left. His combat instincts kicked in. Easier than dodging triple-A or MANPADS, that was for sure. He searched for the attackers. Duke wasn't sure if they were skilled boat drivers. He didn't think so based on the initial attack. Why not just pull up next to them and shoot them? That would have been the easy play.

These guys went as fast as they could and tried to ram them—too many movies and not enough time in boats. The odds of damaging their own boat were just as high, but those knuckleheads didn't realize that.

Duke's boat accelerated once he maneuvered out of the choppy wake the larger boat created. Glancing over his shoulder, the assailants set up their boat for an attack on the right side.

"Once I turn, drop to the deck. We're gonna get close to them, and I'm sure they'll be shooting."

"No argument here."

Again, the attackers had their boat at full throttle. Once they turned in to him, Duke cut the wheel sharp, reduced the throttle, then veered back toward their six o'clock position. The thug in the back took several shots but missed wildly. It was difficult to hit a moving target from a moving platform. These guys were thugs, not pros.

Because of their speed, Duke was able to maneuver behind them. He pushed the throttle up, his boat lunging forward as the attackers continued the left turn, circling them. The midnight blue water in the middle of the straight churned into a frothy white, unsteady surface. His throttle at full speed, Duke's boat crashed against the wake behind the attackers' boat and went airborne. The boat landed back in the water with a solid thump, jarring both him and Kadie, who lost her grip and slid to the stern.

Duke pulled the throttle and looked back.

"I'm okay," Kadie said. She crawled to her knees, then stood and moved to the console next to him.

Duke nodded and spotted the attackers to their rear streaking straight for them.

"I guess they learned from the first two attempts. They're coming straight for us."

Kadie glanced behind her. "What are we going to do?"

"I'm working on it." Duke scanned the area as they raced north.

He had hoped to find shallow water in the hopes of getting the attackers stuck, but that didn't appear to exist. This strait was for shipping, and beaches where nowhere to be found.

About a quarter of a mile ahead, Duke saw a barge on the other side of the bridge heading toward them. He maneuvered his boat in the gap next to the barge.

Suddenly, the windshield shattered.

"Get down!" Duke said. He jammed the throttle full forward and ducked himself, weaving the boat left and right, attempting to disrupt their aim. Several shots struck the boat, an occasional lucky shot piercing the console.

Kadie sat on the floor of the boat. She seemed worried, but not scared. "Still working on those ideas?"

A slight grin formed on his face. "Sorta."

He rose and glanced over his shoulder. The attackers hung back to get a better shot at the boat. They trailed twenty yards behind him to the right. The driver had gotten smart and struggled to hold his position. The guy shooting was also getting smarter, taking more time to aim. Either that, or he was running out of ammo.

Ahead of them, the barge started to pass under the bridge. He wasn't sure if the attackers had seen it yet. As they approached the bridge, Duke swung a little to the left, then back to the right, straight for the bridge pylon.

His plan worked. Rather than cut to the left of the boat as they should have, they stayed on the right. Duke swore he heard them scream as he cut back to the left. The attackers cut quickly to the right, going on the other side of the pylon, as Duke's boat zipped under the bridge.

A loud horn echoed from the tugboat pushing the barge, followed by a loud crash. On the other side of the bridge, Duke raced past the barge and tug, then cut behind the slow-moving vessel and reduced his power. Kadie rose from the floor to find the attack boat damaged. The rear of the boat clipped the barge, and a large section was missing. The boat sank in under a minute, the assailants floating among the debris.

"Nice work, Mister Special Operations pilot guy," Kadie said with a nervous smile.

"Yeah, thanks."

"Think that could be the two guys that chased me in Port Said?"

"Don't know—persistent, clumsy, bad shots. I'd say they work for your friend Curt, but I'm not sure yet. It could be the same guys."

"If that was them, they've switched from crossbows to guns." Kadie slid next to him and held onto his arm. "How about we head to the airport?"

She blinked and shuddered slightly. Duke understood her silence and swung the old wooden boat back toward the right bank. They traveled south, under a second bridge that led them into the Sea of Marmara, then turned West. Numerous airliners were flying in low over the water, gear and flaps extended for their landing. In another fifteen minutes, they reached the tiny marina south of the airport. He pulled up to the dock and found an empty spot to moor the boat. Kadie found the rope at the bow, and Duke cut the motor as she wrapped it around the cleat on the dock and collapsed into one of the seats.

Kadie shook uncontrollably, and Duke took her in his arms. When her trembling subsided, he climbed out of the boat and helped her onto the dock. She flung her arms around his neck, sobbing.

"We're gonna be okay," he said.

Kadie didn't respond, but he felt her heart pounding as she squeezed him closer. She finally let go, and for the first time, they checked the exterior of the boat. There were a lot more holes than they realized. Duke exhaled slowly—this attack was too close for comfort. They were lucky. Really lucky.

He gently grasped her hand. "Let's go find Mac and Brian."

Kadie nodded, and they hurried toward the airport.

38

Istanbul, Turkey
The Tav Genel Havacilik Terminal

The cab pulled up to the two-story structure with a glass entrance covered with a smooth glass arch. Duke considered the bright red trim a little gaudy, but he wasn't about to complain. He checked his watch. It had taken them almost an hour and forty-five minutes from the time they spoke to Mac on the phone. Mac should have arrived at least thirty minutes before them, if not more. When they entered the lobby, Duke walked straight to the pilot briefing room, which he found to be locked. He would need to get the magnetic swipe key from the terminal office.

"This is odd," he said. "Maybe they're waiting for us in the restaurant or at the coffee shop." As they walked down the hallway, Duke pulled out his cell phone to call. No answer. Kadie did the same for Brian, but he never answered either.

She gave him a cautious look. "Should I be worried?"

"I'm not sure yet." The expression on his face didn't exude confidence.

When they arrived at the empty coffee shop, Kadie noticed one of Patricia's security men sat alone at a table. He looked Hispanic; a three-day beard covered his face. They walked toward him when the man turned their way. He did not smile; his face was expressionless.

When they reached the security man, Kadie started to speak, when the man offered her a smartphone. "What's this f—oh my goodness!" She shrieked; a noise that would have brought them attention had anyone been there.

Duke looked at the phone in her hand; it was a picture of Brian, held by someone from behind. Duke recognized the background. It was the flight planning room.

"That's the clothes he had on today," she said, her eyes welled up. "What is going on? Was he kidnapped?"

The man made a swipe motion his finger. Kadie swiped to the next photo.

There were more pictures of Brian climbing in a car. The last one showed a pistol pressed against his temple. She gasped, and the tears flowed. With trepidation, she turned back to the security man. "Why?"

Duke didn't need to ask, he knew why. And he knew who. It was GDI.

The phone rang.

"It's for you," the security man said, without ever even looking at it.

Kadie pressed the green icon. "H—Hello?"

"How are you, Kadie?" It was Curt.

"I'm—my—Brian is missing. I think he's been kidnapped." She sobbed as she spoke.

"Put me on speakerphone," Curt said. "Your new boyfriend needs to hear this, too."

Kadie activated the speakerphone, and Duke moved in closer.

"You shouldn't have run away. You've seen what we have to bargain with. I recommend you listen to what I have to say. The only thing you two have left is each other. How romantic. Now, go with my man. You'll be united with your brother, shortly."

Curt hung up on his end.

Kadie shuffled to Duke and leaned against his chest, the tears still flowing. "*He's* got Brian, doesn't he?"

Duke nodded. "They want something. They—" He stopped mid-sentence. A sense of dread overcame him. His skin prickled, and his heart felt like it stopped. "That device, where is it?"

"Device?"

"For the room."

She reached into her pocket and handed him the FOB. "What's wrong?"

"He said, *the only thing you two have left is each other*. That first picture was in the flight planning room."

Duke bolted out of the coffee shop and down the hall. Sprinting across the empty lobby, he reached the flight planning room. When he waved the electronic device in front of the locking mechanism on the door, a green light lit up.

Duke flung the door open and went inside.

39

The room was quiet. The uncomfortable type of quiet that spoke volumes. Duke stepped in cautiously.

"Mac? Mac, you in here?"

He moved further into the room, to the other side of the large planning table, and gasped.

Mac lay on the floor, multiple stab wounds covered his chest.

"Noooo!" he cried.

Duke fell to his knees, pulled out his cell phone, and dialed 911. Nothing happened. Of course, this is Turkey. *What's the emergency number?* He scanned the walls from his position until his eyes fell on a sign that looked like what he searched for. He dialed 112 and one short ring later, someone answered, in Turkish.

"Hello, we need an ambulance at the Genel Havacilik Terminal." Duke paused and lowered his ear toward Mac's mouth.

Kadie screamed behind him. Duke turned and saw the GDI thug with a pistol to her back. He dropped his cell phone next to Mac's body and stood to stop her from getting closer. Tears flowed from her again, the sight of Mac's body no doubt made her fear more for her brother. Duke wrapped his arms around her as she shook, and he fought to stay strong. It made sense now. The chase, Brian missing, his mentor—his best friend, dead. And he knew who did it.

"I'm gonna kill that son-of-a—"

"Duke, no. You'd be just like him," she shrieked. "Brian . . . Curt said to return with this man."

His body convulsed as the anger overwhelmed him. The GDI thug motioned toward the door with his pistol. The three of them left the flight planning room and headed for the exit. They say your mind races through your life experiences right before you die. It does the same thing after a friend dies, but slower, in more vivid detail. And it hurts more. A lot more.

Tears streaked down his face as he relived the experience when he first met Mac in gunships. Mac had been his instructor, and Duke soaked up everything he said like a sponge. The numerous training and combat sorties, exercises, beers at the squadron hooch. Their first deployment together. Duke presenting Mac with the squadron lithograph at his retirement. Mac saving Duke's soul when he was about to kill himself. He was his best friend.

When they stepped outside of the terminal, a car and a second thug was waiting for them.

"Vat haf you been up to?" the man said, a smirk stretched across his face. His accent sounded German. The thug's hand rested on the pistol hidden under his coat.

"Where's your boss?" Duke growled.

The thug sensed Duke's anger and held up the cell phone, the picture of Brian with a gun to his head displayed. Duke felt Kadie tug on his arm. She was right; the game had changed. Mac was gone. It was about getting Brian back now.

TEARS POURED FROM KADIE'S EYES. HOW COULD THIS HAVE HAPPENED? What had she gotten her brother involved in? She squeezed Duke's arm, partly to keep him from overreacting, partly for her security.

"Come with us," the GDI man said. He had a German accent,

Kadie thought, maybe Austrian. The thug turned and moved to the elevator where a second man stood. This one had a darker complexion and a three-day beard. The second man motioned for them to follow him. They did, and the first guy brought up the rear. The small group walked through the lobby and climbed into a waiting vehicle. Once inside the car, black hoods were placed over their heads.

Kadie struggled to see outside the hood, but it was too thick. The car turned too much to be able to maintain a sense of direction. The guys from the boat must have called ahead and had them intercepted. What exactly were these people after? Were they simply a bunch of glorified treasure hunters? Regardless, they were killers.

The drive lasted for about thirty minutes. When they finally stopped, someone helped them out of the car. They kept the hoods on their heads as they walked them into a building. Once inside, they sat in chairs, and their hoods were removed. Across the room, Curt stood with a pistol to Brian's head.

"Brian," she murmured. Her brother's eyes were wide, tears running along the side of his face. Then she clenched her teeth. "If you've hurt him . . ."

Curt's head fell to the side. "Oh, relax, sweetheart. He's fine. He's just crying like the baby he is, that's all."

Behind them, they heard the click-clack of high heels as Patricia entered the room and stood in front of them.

"Patricia . . . I can't believe you're involved in this." Kadie was dumbstruck. "You've got to let us go. Please, we won't say anything."

"I'm afraid it's too late for that, my dear," Patricia said. "You've found out too much, I'm afraid."

"Why'd you kill Mac?" Duke said, struggling against his binding. One of the men behind him clobbered the back of his head with a fist, and Duke let out a loud grunt.

Curt sneered at the pilot. "For fun. I didn't like the guy."

Kadie sniffled, her nose running. "Why did you kill Samuel? And Isaac?"

"I assumed you would figure that out." Curt's response was smug. "It was easy. Sam—"

"You're probably wondering what this is all about," Patricia said, interrupting Curt. It was clear she was in charge. Duke was right—Curt was no more than an errand boy.

"It's certainly not about a cure for the hantavirus," Kadie said.

"No. No, it's not."

"And I suppose the CIA never contacted GDI about any virus?"

"You are correct again. Such a smart girl. All of that was to build the teams we needed. We realized we'd need something big to bring in the brightest minds in the world." Patricia pulled a chair in front of them, five feet away. "Samuel turned out to be too bright. He discovered what we were actually searching for. That was information we couldn't have floating around out there. If the other team members learned we were searching for a Christian artifact, they would have abandoned the project. That's why he was killed. We didn't know who he had been talking to until you led us to Mister Abelman. That's why he was eliminated. He would have talked."

Kadie's eyes stopped watering. "So, you're killing people because of the Pilate Scroll? I don't understand—why is that necessary? You find the Scroll, and you can sell it and get the money you want. You don't have to murder anyone."

Patricia snickered. "My dear, you are so cute. That's why I love you so much—you're so innocent." She rose from the chair and walked around to stand behind it. "We're not after the Scroll to sell it."

Kadie looked at Duke, who had turned to her at the same time. His face appeared as confused as she felt. They both turned back to Patricia.

"If you don't plan on selling the Scroll, then why do you want it?"

"We want the dowels."

"The dowels?"

"The legend says the dowels used in the Scroll were made from the true cross. Jesus' blood is embedded within the wood. The Romans coated the dowels in amber to seal the wood, thus preserving Jesus' blood within the dowels."

"You mean—"

"Yes," Patricia said. She was beaming. Her eyes sparkled, and her smile stretched across her face. "We plan to extract the DNA from the blood sample within the dowels and clone Jesus of Nazareth."

40

Istanbul, Turkey
Global Disease Initiative Mobile Headquarters

"You people are crazy," Kadie said. "You honestly think you can clone the Son of God?"

"We'll see, won't we?" Patricia said. "That's kind of the point. Is he the Christ or the carpenter? We will answer the question that has baffled mankind for centuries. And *I* will be the one who finds the answer. Finally, I will have my seat at the table and solidified my place in history."

Kadie realized this was about ego and pride. Patricia was not who she made out to be either.

Duke tried to stand when one of the thugs pointed his weapon at him. Kadie grabbed Duke's forearm. Someone from behind moved in and tied them to their chairs.

"You do realize," Duke said, "there are at least six movies about dinosaurs that explain why this is a really, really bad idea?"

Curt smirked and started to respond when Patricia put her hand up again. Kadie noticed Patricia had Curt wired like a puppy. He didn't move or speak unless she said so. Duke was right. Curt was no Delta Force soldier. She couldn't imagine one of those guys being a puppet on a string.

"We've taken precautions," Patricia said.

Kadie shook her head. "Precautions won't mean a thing when the general population finds out what you're doing. There will be riots in the streets."

"My dear, there won't be any riots. Christianity is all but illegal in most parts of the world. Creating a clone will only validate why cloning has been banned in most places. We've had systematic evolution in place for decades now. The flooding of Europe with extremists. The spread of atheism and agnosticism throughout the Western world. The destruction of churches, synagogues, museums, and artifacts . . . all by design. By the time word gets out about this, there won't be anyone around to protest. And those that do will be arrested."

Kadie fumed at her words, causing Patricia to pause and smile. "Yes, it's almost complete. When Congress authorized the prosecution of pastors for preaching against subjects the progressives cherished, the criminalization of Christianity was well on its way. In several European countries that have been overrun, it *is* a crime."

"What do you want with us?" Kadie was defiant.

Patricia sauntered back toward her. "We need you to find the Aramaic Vase."

Kadie shifted in her seat. "How can *we* find it? You've had teams searching for over a month, and no one's found it yet."

Patricia set her hands on her hips, and the corners of her mouth perched up. "We've found a code and directions to its resting place. We still need you to decipher the Aramaic and Latin. And you'll do it if you want your brother to live."

Brian's face was flushed, but the tears had stopped. He looked confused, angry, and scared.

"Why am I here?" Duke said. "My employer will want to know what's happened to his aircraft and his crew."

"Why *are* you here, Mister Ellsworth?" Patricia said. "You should have continued on your journey after dropping off our materials. But you chose to reach out to your damsel in distress. An attempt to whisk her off to safety, no doubt. If you'd have minded your own business, your friend might still be alive."

"Still, why do you need me?" Duke said.

"It's simple. We have too many team members here who know nothing about what we are searching for. They'll find their demise eventually in a tomb that collapses around them. Most of their roles, at this point, are inconsequential. But you, Mister Ellsworth, have an airplane I may need. And my lovely linguist is necessary to interpret our treasure. So, it works out well. You two will do the leg work to find the Pilate Scroll. If you don't, the boy dies."

"How can *we* find the scroll?" Kadie pleaded. "We've got nothing to go on."

Patricia's eyes narrowed, and she moved off to her left. One of her goons handed her a large, heavy, leather-covered folder. "We discovered this recently in the Hagia Sophia museum here in Istanbul." She offered the binder to Kadie.

Inside the binder was a single piece of paper ripped at the top but still containing three lines of text. And beneath it—a Sator Square. Kadie gingerly picked up the paper. It had to be, ten, maybe eleven centuries old. Too hard to tell now. Kadie read the writing inscribed in Latin:

It stands among his mother's treasures.

The rivers weave between subtle mountains of granite and stone.

The wedge in the valley leads to the entrance of the city of channels.

The Sator Square was the most intriguing aspect. Why was it there? A Sator Square is an ancient palindrome; the earliest discovery traced back to Pompeii in 79 AD. It consists of rows of five words, each word five letters each. The two words on the bottom are the two words on the top spelled backward. To make the puzzle more interesting, the square accomplishes the same thing vertically:

S	A	T	O	R
A	R	E	P	O
T	E	N	E	T
O	P	E	R	A
R	O	T	A	S

"WHAT DO YOU THINK THIS MEANS?" KADIE STRUGGLED TO WRAP HER head around this. The clues didn't seem complicated, but she was worried about Brian and had difficulty concentrating.

Patricia paced in front of them. "We know Constantine had possession of the Vase and brought it to Constantinople. The question is, where did the Aramaic Vase go after that? And when? *It stands among his mother's treasures* implies Helena. Legend says Constantine built a hidden cathedral in honor of his mother. Most, if not all her treasure, is rumored to be stored in that cathedral."

"And where is that?" Kadie said.

Patricia offered a slight shrug of her shoulders. "We believe the Aramaic Vase and the Pilate Scroll might be in the ancient city of Helenopolis. Constantine built this to honor his mother. It only makes sense that the legendary cathedral is there as well."

"Helenopolis? That's the city of Altinova. It's south of here, not far."

"Correct."

"Why do you think the Scroll is there?" Based off the three lines of text and the Sator Square, Kadie thought the Vase might be in Venice, but they didn't ask her. The last thing she was going to do was stir the pot and put Brian in danger.

"The Sator Square," Patricia said. "When you analyze the words in the square, it is loosely translated to say, *the farmer Arepo uses his plow to work.*"

Kadie was well aware of the interpretation of the Sator Square. She researched it extensively in college and was aware there was much more to the puzzle than the obvious.

"There is a small hill area, south of Altinova. After extensive research, we found that a wealthy farmer named *Arepo* lived in the region over a thousand years ago. We believe the cathedral is on this man's property, in a valley somewhere in that location."

Kadie rubbed her chin. That was a stretch based on what she could tell the paper said. "Are you sure this is the right location?"

"Yes. Without a doubt."

"I don't think it's there. I think—"

"Of course, it is. Why else would we find the clue in Istanbul? This is no coincidence. It's there. Why would Constantine build a cathedral for his mother in someplace other than the city built to honor her?"

Kadie bit her lower lip. Patricia wouldn't listen to her. Best to let this play out. "How does the rest of the description apply?"

"The channels referred to in the passage are the sites on a mountain slope where the water begins to flow between identifiable banks. We believe the geography matches what the writings describe. The Sator Square confirms the farmer's land. Constantine, or his people, wrote this so the Vase would never be lost."

Kadie's head jerked up. "This isn't from Constantine's era."

"Why do you say that?"

"The paper. This is from around 1100 to 1400 A.D. If the paper were from Constantine's era, it would be papyrus or parchment. Paper itself, didn't arrive in Europe until 1150 A.D. when it came to Spain during the Crusades."

Patricia nodded, a blank expression across her face. "Let's get moving."

41

Istanbul, Turkey
On the road to Altinova

Kadie rode in the back of the SUV next to Brian. She had her arm around his shoulders; her hand caressed the hair on the side of his head. Patricia sat up front; the head of the GDI team didn't like her analysis of the paper they had found in the Hagia Sophia, perhaps because it contradicted her conclusion. No matter, they'd find out soon enough.

The small convoy trudged through the dense traffic of downtown Istanbul. In the SUV ahead of them, Curt sat in the back seat, his gun no doubt pointed at Duke in the front next to the German driver. Their hoods weren't used this time, either because they felt it wasn't necessary or because they didn't want to draw attention to themselves. The two SUVs crossed the bridge over the Strait and headed east. They then turned south toward Altinova. After several minutes, the crowds and chaos of the city gave way to the countryside. They turned onto another highway until they passed over another bridge and reached Altinova. The coast stood lined with shipping docks, and they drove through the small neighborhoods and hamlets spread throughout the countryside.

"Where are—we going?" Brian said.

Kadie gazed out the window at the passing terrain. "See those hills to the east? We're going somewhere over there."

"Why?"

"We're going to search for something they call the Aramaic Vase."

"Why g-go look—for that there? W-we saw lots—of vases in the museum."

She turned to look at her brother. "This is a special vase. Inside, it's supposed to hold the Pilate Scroll."

Brian scrunched his forehead, deep in thought. "Oh." Brian seemed content with that answer. "H-how do we know it is there?"

"We don't." Kadie thumbed at Patricia in the front seat. Kadie lowered her voice to a whisper. "She thinks the Vase is here. I'm not so sure."

The caravan of two left the highway and started taking a series of small roads that turned back into a tiny valley nestled between two hills. Something nagged at Kadie, but she couldn't put her finger on it.

"I'm sorry I got us in trouble—Kadie," Brian said. A tear rolled down his cheek.

She wiped the tear away and hugged him hard. "You didn't do anything wrong. These are bad people doing bad things."

"I-I thought you worked with them?"

Kadie paused. How could she explain what was happening?

"I do . . . I did. Let's just say I was tricked into working for GDI. Now that I know what they do, I wanted us to leave with Duke. But they won't let me because they need my skills to get what they want."

Brian nodded. She hoped that made him feel better about the situation. They rode in silence for another twenty minutes before the caravan came to a stop in a dense forest.

Curt stepped out of the Range Rover in front of them and opened the passenger door, dragging Duke out. His hands remained tied behind his back. Her teeth clenched as she imagined how uncomfortable that had to be driving here.

"Let's go," Patricia said over her shoulder.

Kadie opened the door and climbed out; Brian scooted out after her and rushed to Duke. The boy wrapped his arms around the pilot, and Kadie's heart melted

"I found it, Kadie," Brian said. "I-I found what we awe—looking for." His enthusiasm caught her attention.

"What?"

"It is right here." Brian pointed at the round object in Duke's back pocket. "The pilot's Skoal." He laughed out loud, and Duke managed a chuckle, despite his tied hands.

Kadie smiled and started to laugh herself when she saw Curt's head jerk toward Brian.

"What did he say?" Curt exclaimed. His face contorted in anger.

"He didn't say anything," Kadie said. "He made a joke."

Curt drew his hand back and flung it at Brian. Kadie screamed, too far away to help.

Just before Curt's hand slammed Brian's face, Duke leaped between the two, taking the blow on the top of his head before falling to the ground.

Brian's eyes were wide, and he froze. Kadie reached him before Curt could regroup for another strike.

"That's enough," Patricia ordered. Curt backed off his assault on Brian but kicked Duke in the ribs as he lay on the ground. "We still need him. We need them all."

"But he knows."

"They all know, Curt. We passed the point of no return a long time ago. Our only objective is to find the Scroll."

Kadie knelt next to Duke to help him to his feet. "Are you okay?"

Duke nodded. "Yeah. It's only a flesh wound."

"Where?"

"Just kidding. Monty Python joke."

The corners of Kadie's mouth tilted downward. "I'm not so sure we're in the right location," she said softly.

"I'm not surprised." Duke stretched his neck, and they moved over to Brian. "I thought you said this thing was in Venice?" he whispered.

"It seemed like a logical location." Kadie continued to speak in a hushed tone. "But they're interpreting the paper to say the Pilate Scroll is in Altinova."

Patricia's driver stepped forward with some satellite imagery.

"Gather 'round, people," Patricia said, pointing at a map. "Here's where we're going."

42

Altinova, Turkey
The forest hills

Patricia gave a brief synopsis of her plan, and the group headed into the mahogany-brown forest to search for the ancient Arepo farm. Patricia's driver led the way, followed by Duke, Kadie, and Patricia. Curt walked behind Brian, and his driver brought up the rear. The two drivers and Curt all had firearms. Kadie glanced back at Brian. He breathed heavy and constantly looked behind him at Curt. The boy was scared. He clenched the Pelican case with his drone tightly against his chest. Brian was initially reluctant to leave the SUV after Curt's outburst, but Duke had convinced him he and Rupert were needed. The GDI security man had a semi-automatic pistol in a holster, and a pistol-grip shotgun slung over his back. At least Curt didn't hold a gun to his head. For now.

The group meandered along a faint trail that weaved its way toward the base of a small hill surrounded by creaking trees that stretched away from the leafy surface. Birds and small animals scattered as the group trudged through the forest. Small branches and leaves crunched under her boots as she trailed Duke. After about fifteen minutes, the German stopped.

"Listen," he said.

Everyone in the small party paused, heads tilted to focus on any sound. Kadie heard nothing.

The German scanned the back of the line, then beyond them toward the cars.

"Ve are being followed," he said.

Curt looked behind him. "By who? There's nobody back there."

Loping wolves scurried in the distance, too far away to be concerned with their small group.

The German shook his head. "I don't know. I can sense it."

"Okay," Patricia said. "Let's keep moving." She patted Kadie on the shoulder. "Don't worry, dear. He gets a little jumpy sometimes."

They walked for almost an hour before they found a small sapphire-blue stream that sparkled in the sunlight that pushed its way through the foliage. The point man confirmed on the map and satellite imagery that this was what they were looking for. He showed them how the stream trickled west until it widened into a creek, which would broaden further into the channels mentioned in the writing. The farm, he said, would be at the base of the hill where the channel started.

Kadie's eyes narrowed, and she wiped the sweat from her forehead, still skeptical of their plan. She didn't think they would find anything, and she continued to try and wrap her head around this. She would do whatever she could do to help save her brother, and right now, the best thing was to figure out where these guys went wrong because when they reached that location, they were going to be angry.

Curt pushed Brian from behind, calling the boy names and picking on him. The anger welled up inside Kadie until she wanted to take a bat to Curt's head. How could a man be so heartless? How could she have been so blind, so foolish to think he was something else?

Duke checked behind him as well. The anger on his face was evident. Perhaps she'd be better off letting Duke take care of Curt when this is all over. Curt killed Mac, and Duke was not the type of man who would let that go unresolved.

After another hour, they reached their destination—a vast, empty valley between the hills. From here, there was no visible indication of a hidden cathedral.

"Spread out," Patricia ordered. "Everyone start searching."

"What exactly are we looking for?" Duke spoke up, his displeasure evident. He shifted his upper torso; his bound hands no doubt straining his shoulders.

"We're searching for remnants of a building. A cathedral. It could be anywhere around here." Kadie picked up on the intensity in Patricia's voice. The executive vice president was a little too giddy. Kadie knew that would end when they didn't find anything here.

Brian was told to sit down in the clearing while the group searched the small valley. They could attempt to escape, but the group had wandered so far into the forest they would be caught before they found help. While the group began its search, Brian sat at the edge of the clearing and removed Rupert from its container. Kadie stood by as the boy calibrated the small drone, then synched his iPhone to the controller. Within minutes, he had the drone hovering a few feet over their heads.

"Kadie, watch," he said.

She slid closer to him to observe the picture on the tiny screen. He had the camera pointed at them, and Brian giggled. In a flash, the drone climbed upward, above the tops of the trees that surrounded the clearing.

"We can see if there awe any buildings near here."

She smiled at her brother and ruffled his hair with her fingers—what a smart boy. The drone hovered a hundred feet above them, and Brian used his phone to tap out the course he wanted the drone to fly.

When he activated the course, Rupert went to work on the west side of the clearing, showing Brian and Kadie the vast valley from a birds-eye perspective. They would have an answer long before the team found anything.

After about ten minutes, Patricia had noticed they still stood at the mouth of the valley and walked back toward them.

"Ingenious," Patricia said. She stayed there and monitored the drone's flight up the long valley. Unfortunately, it didn't appear any sort of building was anywhere close to here. The drone began its journey back toward their location on the East side.

About halfway to their location, a loud boom, quickly followed by another, echoed through the valley. The video screen went blank.

"What happened?" Brian said. Kadie had a feeling she knew but didn't want to say anything. Patricia gave Kadie a disappointed look and meandered back into the valley. Kadie stared into the distance, but no one other than Patricia was in sight. "Can we go l-look for Rupert?"

"I'm not so sure we would find him, Brian. There's a lot of empty space out there. It might be better that we stay here."

After another forty-five minutes, the group gathered near Brian and Kadie. Duke was the first to arrive, his hands still bound behind him.

"Are you okay?" Kadie said.

"Yeah. Our Delta Force Commando shot at a bird or something out there."

Brian began to wail. Duke turned to Kadie.

"Did I say something wrong?"

Kadie shook her head. "No. Brian had his drone out. We searched the entire valley. On its way back, we lost connectivity—right after the shots were fired."

Duke nodded. He put the pieces together. When the rest of the group showed up, Curt tossed the drone at Brian, missing his leg by mere inches.

"I think this belongs to you," he said. "I thought I was shooting us some dinner, but it turned out to be a robot."

Tears poured from Brian's eyes as he bent down and retrieved Rupert. Kadie wrapped her arm around Brian's shoulders and gave him a reassuring hug. Curt's action was unnecessary—just another opportunity to reveal just who he truly was.

"Okay, people," Patricia said. "Let's make our way back."

43

Altinova, Turkey
In the Arepo Valley

Kadie gazed into the sky as the sun began its journey toward the horizon in the West. Once it became dark, it would be difficult for them to find their way back to the cars. Maybe the darkness would help them escape.

She heard a loud whistle across the valley and saw the Curt waving in the distance. The group wandered toward him.

"Well, it's getting dark," Curt said. "We need to head back to the vehicles." He turned to Patricia. "This was a waste of time. We're definitely in the wrong place."

Patricia fumed at the comment. "This is a process, Mister Baxter. Every potential location we eliminate gets us that much closer to the actual location."

"Doctor," Curt replied, "this was a total miscalculation. We're not even close."

Kadie struggled to fight back a smile as the two compatriots bickered back and forth, clearly angry with each other. Duke didn't hide his smile either.

Curt scowled. "What are you grinning at?"

"Just enjoying the show," Duke said.

Curt thrust a fist into Duke's mid-section, and the pilot doubled over and fell to his knees. He struggled to maintain his balance; his hands still bound behind his back. Curt walked behind him and kicked him between the shoulder blades, sending Duke face-first into the grass.

"Stop!" Kadie rushed to help Duke up. Curt backhanded Brian as she reached Duke. Brian yelped as he fell to his side. Kadie turned to face Curt, her eyes wide and teeth clenched. "What is wrong with you? You're an animal." She helped Duke up and ran to Brian, who was standing up on his own, his eyes burning with anger. The boy had courage despite his differences.

"I never—l-liked you," Brian said, sobbing.

"Oh, shut up, you freak."

Curt was despicable, she thought, and she hated herself for being attracted to him in the past. Kadie steered Brian away from Curt, and they walked toward Patricia. The GDI executive seemed frustrated. The failure of their first and only real clue took its toll.

"What are you trying to do?" Kadie attempted to appeal to Patricia's sensitivity.

"I'm trying to find the Scroll."

"Well, for someone with a Ph.D., you're not being very smart about deciphering these clues."

Patricia's face contorted into a scowl. "What do you mean?"

"You brought me here for a reason. Yet, you had a clue in Latin and never asked me for my interpretation. I told you I didn't think this was the right place, and you ignored me."

"The clues all pointed toward here," Patricia said. "The Sator Square distinctly mentioned Arepo, and it's too coincidental to have an Arepo farm in Helenopolis."

"I agree the Sator Square is an important clue, but I think it's telling us *who* to look for, not where to look."

The anger and frustration on Patricia's face melted away. "Go on." The tone of her voice softened; Kadie could tell she learned from her mistake.

"For the first several hundred years after the death of Jesus, the Sator Square was used by Roman soldiers who considered themselves Christians to identify themselves to each other."

"There were Roman soldiers who were Christians?" Duke said.

"Yes, although they weren't referred to as Christians back then."

"How does the Sator Square identify someone as a Christian?" Patricia said.

Kadie pulled out a pen and paper from her purse and began writing. "The Square, when approached as a giant anagram, presents us with another puzzle." She turned the paper around to show the group what she had done. The letters had been re-arranged into one vertical word and a horizontal word. The remaining letters were placed in each of the four quadrants:

"The Square, when arranged as an anagram, forms a new palindrome, both again using the letter 'N' as the focal point. This time, the letters become two words that form the shape of a cross."

"That doesn't mean anything," Curt said.

Kadie disregarded his comment. "The two words, *Pater Noster*, are Latin. They mean *Our Father*, the first two words of the Lord's Prayer."

Patricia's eyes gleamed. She was starting to understand. "What about the extra letters?"

"The A and the O mean *Alpha* and *Omega*. Jesus said he was the Alpha and Omega, the first and the last." Kadie glanced at Brian and Duke. Brian nodded, and Duke seemed amazed. "The Sator Square wasn't telling us where to look. It was telling us who to look for—Roman soldiers."

"Okay," Patricia said. "I'll buy that. We're looking for Roman soldiers. But the question remains, where?"

"What is the line in the text about the channels?"

Patricia removed the handwritten copy of the message from her pocket. "The wedge in the valley leads to the entrance of the city of channels."

"But it doesn't say channels. It's written in Latin."

Patricia's face was blank. "Canālis."

"Yes. And another word for canālis is canals."

"Surrounded by mountains of granite and stone."

"Buildings," Kadie said. "They're not talking about ancient Helenopolis, they're talking about—"

"Venice."

Kadie nodded. She could see Patricia processing the new information.

"It makes sense," Patricia mumbled. "But then again, it doesn't. Constantinople was pillaged during the Fourth Crusade. The Roman Empire didn't exist anymore."

"True," Kadie said, "but their descendants did. The Venetian Army was contracted to fight on behalf of the Byzantine Empire. When they couldn't pay, the Venetians ransacked Constantinople. Many of the treasures and religious artifacts were looted and brought back to—"

"Saint Mark's Basilica."

44

The journey out of the forest felt as if it took twice as long, but Kadie found comfort in the trek. Curt had backed off his abuse of both Duke and Brian, and Patricia seemed to relax some since Kadie deciphered the clue to reference Venice. The answer had been in front of them the entire time, but it was so obvious they ignored it. Patricia only wished she had deciphered the clues sooner and saved them from this experience in the woods.

They reached the vehicles in a little over two hours, and the sun to the West sat just above the horizon. The seating arrangement was as before, except Patricia told Curt to untie Duke. He protested, but she convinced Curt that Duke wouldn't do anything as long as they had Kadie and Brian.

And she was right. Kadie thought Duke would do anything to protect them. But why? Why did she think that? Did he say he would? No, he had never mentioned anything like that. They never had any kind of discussion about their safety. He'd always been there . . . at least since she'd known him. She trusted his character, and that said a lot.

Kadie settled in the back seat with Brian and gazed out the window. The sun dipped below the horizon as they drove back toward Istanbul. She watched the beautiful transformation of day into night and relished the beauty God had created in the world.

God.

Kadie chuckled to herself. She actually gave God credit for creating the world. Her attention shifted to His Son.

Over the last few days, she had experienced so much so fast. Life and death situations, some of which she still wasn't out of yet. But the most important part was the self-realization that she believed in God and wanted to be saved by His Son Jesus Christ. Was it because she feared the end was near? She didn't want to think so, but maybe. Since they'd met Duke, her curiosity had been piqued, and she began to question her salvation.

She turned to her brother. "Hey," she whispered, "when did you decide you were a Christian?"

His eyes grew wide, and the corners of his mouth surged upward, but he was hesitant to respond.

Kadie looked forward at the two in the front seat. "It's okay," she said softly to Brian. "We can talk."

Brian still appeared fearful, but he did his best to speak in a hushed tone. "I w-was in Sunday school . . . and we sang the song that said J-Jesus loved all the little children in the world. I thought—I'm a little child in the world, and Jesus loves me. It was only fair—that I love him back."

Kadie smiled at her brother as her eyes welled up. It was a simple answer to a complicated question.

"But even when we lost Mom and Dad, you never lost your faith?"

Brian shrugged his shoulders. "God has a p-plan for everyone. After Mom and Dad died, you were there for me—but you c-couldn't be there for me all the time . . . But Jesus was. And he still is. He can be there for you too, Kadie."

The tears that had welled in her eyes now trickled down her cheeks, and she hugged him. "I hope so. I—I want him to. I'm just not sure how."

"I could tell you," he said, "but I might not get it right. You better ask Duke."

Kadie pushed back. “Duke?” Her eyes squinted, and her mouth pursed to the side. “What are you up to, you little matchmaker?”

Brian giggled and hopped in his seat. He turned to look out the window because he tried to hide his big smile and red face.

“Okay, we’ll talk to Duke. He seems to be a good Christian man.”

Brian nodded enthusiastically. “He is coming t-to my—birthday pawty.” She smiled and kissed him on the forehead.

Traffic picked up as they drove closer to the city. She found it ironic that she had decided to accept Jesus Christ as her Lord and savior in a land where she could very well be killed for acknowledging her belief. Yet, that didn’t faze her. As the sun nestled on the water, she wondered . . . would Jesus love her? She had been a nonbeliever for so long, how could she possibly find comfort in a savior she’d mocked and ridiculed? How could God ever forgive her?

THE SMALL CARAVAN STEERED TO THE HOTEL PROPERTY, AND DUKE checked behind him to ensure Kadie and Brian were still there. The SUVs pulled up to the entrance of the hotel so the valets could park them. Everyone stepped out of the vehicles and gathered at the front steps. Kadie and Patricia both had put their hijabs back on, something they usually didn’t do at the hotel.

Curt popped Duke on the head from behind. “Don’t try any funny stuff while we’re here. I’ll kill the girl and her brother without blinking an eye. I might even make you watch.”

Duke turned and stared into the man’s eyes. Curt was telling the truth—he *would* kill them. Right here. But Duke didn’t see a warrior, he saw a coward. A gutless coward who preyed on the innocent to build his ego and sense of power.

“I believe you,” he said.

“Good. You’ve got a lot of work to do. We leave for Venice tonight.”

Duke stopped. “I don’t think so.”

Curt moved in Duke’s face. “I don’t care what you think. We’re getting our bags and leaving tonight.”

"You see, this is why we knew you weren't a Delta guy. You don't have one clue about international travel." Duke's tone dripped with sarcasm.

Patricia moved toward them, her driver behind Kadie and Brian. "What's going on?" she said.

Duke thumbed at Curt. "Dingleberry here wants to fly to Venice tonight."

"Is that a problem?" Patricia said.

"Not if you fly commercial. If you want me to fly, it's going to take some work. And I'm not doing anything until I get some sleep."

"Sleep?" Curt was obstinate.

Duke gave him a look of disbelief. "Yeah, sleep. Unless you want me to doze off and fly us into the side of a mountain."

Curt turned to Patricia. "Let me kill him now, and we'll fly commercial. Please?" His request was more for show, and Duke wasn't impressed.

"No, we need the plane." She turned to Duke. "What do you need to do?"

Duke stood with his hands on his hips, then scratched his head. "Well, I'll need to build the flight plan. Then I'll need to get diplomatic clearance to enter Italy. There's some coordination that needs to take place. But I'm not doing anything until you ensure Mac's body is sent to the U.S. Embassy to be returned home and I get some sleep."

Patricia's eyes narrowed, and she stared at him. "You have thirty-six hours. I'll have the company coordinate your partner being turned over to the embassy tomorrow. Fair?"

Duke nodded. "I'll make it work. In the meantime, I need to go to my room."

Curt shook his head, but before he could speak, Kadie moved forward. "He can stay in Brian's room. It makes sense and will be easier for all of you. There's only so many of you, and it will be easier for you to guard one room instead of two." Duke saw the anger seep out of her, even though what she said made total sense. Not only was he starting to like Kadie Jenkins; he was also beginning to respect her.

45

Istanbul, Turkey
The Grand Tarabya Hotel

Kadie and Brian waited for Duke to retrieve his duffel bag from the concierge's desk. Curt, who lingered close behind them, warned them several times not to speak with anyone in the lobby, or he would kill them. Her eyes glanced around the opulent lobby. Could he get away with something like that? Here?

Yes, easily. All he had to do was say they were Christians, and other than clean up the mess, the government in Turkey would simply look the other way. Sad what the world had evolved into. It was rampant internationally and was slowly being implemented in America.

Duke walked up with his bag. "Shall we?" he said.

"Shut up," Curt said. "Get on the elevator."

The small group shuffled to the elevator and rode to the eleventh floor.

"We're a little higher up," Curt said. "Just in case you want to do your Spider-Man routine again. Makes it a little more impressive."

Duke stared at him blankly. "Noted." Curt must have figured out how Duke got to her room back in Tel Aviv.

The elevator stopped, and they all stepped off on the eleventh floor. Down the hall, one of Curt's men sat in a chair outside their room.

"You work fast," Kadie said to Curt, her contempt unmistakable.

"You should know."

"Don't give yourself too much credit. You're not that impressive for a poser."

Duke busted out howling. Curt turned beet red, and his fists clenched. Kadie ushered Brian into their room, and Duke slammed the door behind them.

"I do not like him," Brian said.

Duke patted him on the back. "Nobody likes him, Brian. So, you've got good judgment."

Brian smiled at Duke and ran into his room.

Kadie set her purse on the coffee table. "He scares me. The things he says . . ."

"You should take him at his word," Duke said. "The man is dangerous, and in more ways than one. He's not scary in the Rambo sense. He's scary because he's the guy that *wants* to be Rambo. He doesn't have the training or the discipline, and he certainly doesn't have the judgment to be a warrior."

Kadie smiled. "He doesn't seem to intimidate you."

Duke shook his head. "No, he doesn't intimidate me. But he does concern me. I don't trust the guy to do the right or noble thing. He's a glorified thug who likes to brutalize and control people. He's pretty tough with a gun in his hand. Without it, he's a nobody."

Brian reappeared in the doorway. "Duke, come check out our room." The boy beamed, and it warmed Kadie's heart to him so happy, particularly under these circumstances.

Duke walked to the doorway, and Kadie followed.

Brian fidgeted, his excitement evident.

"Hey, this looks great," Duke said.

Kadie could tell Brian had come in and moved his things around, so it didn't look like he had his stuff everywhere. It was his way of helping Duke feel welcome.

"You can put your stuff here." Brian opened the top two drawers.

Duke held up his bag. "That's okay, Brian, I can . . ." He paused and sized-up the happy teenager. It was important to Brian that he use the space. "I can put my stuff in one drawer. I appreciate you making room for me."

After Duke emptied the contents of his duffel bag into the drawer, the three of them went back into the living room.

"Duke," Kadie said, "I wanted to talk to you about something."

"Sure."

"Kadie wants to be a Christian," Brian blurted out. He danced around joyfully.

"Brian!" Kadie placed her hands on her hips. She hadn't been sure how she was going to bring it up. Brian just simplified the process.

"Sorry—I got excited."

She turned to Duke. "Can we talk?"

Duke smiled. "Of course."

They sat on the couch, and she discussed the things she had talked to Brian about in the car. Duke listened attentively, asking questions occasionally, but allowed her to do most of the talking. She did notice that when she started to stray off-topic, he steered her back on course.

Then, Duke gave her *his* testimony. He explained his relationship with his wife, the divorce, the death of her and their children. Tears rolled down her cheeks as this man exposed his weakest moments, and his greatest triumphs to overcome them.

"I had to humble myself before God," he told her. "I had been a sinner my entire life and didn't realize it. It wasn't until I reached the breaking point . . . I was suicidal. And a friend introduced me to Jesus Christ. That changed everything."

"I have a hard time seeing the man you describe. You seem so confident, so at peace with yourself."

"I am. But I'm not the man I used to be. I'm better, I think. At least I hope I am. Life's not all about me. It took me losing my family to realize that."

Kadie sat in silence for a few moments. "It was Mac, wasn't it? Mac is the one who brought you to Christ."

Duke nodded. "Yes. Mac not only saved my life—he saved my soul. He was a good friend. My best friend. And that son of a . . ." he stopped himself. "Curt killed him. And one day, he'll pay."

Kadie set her hand on his knee. "What can I do? How can I be saved?"

Duke took her hand in his and gazed deep into her eyes. She felt him exploring her soul, and it made her nervous as she blinked and looked away.

"I'm not a pastor, Kadie, but I know if you repent your sins and accept Jesus to be the Lord of your life . . . If you ask him to come into your heart, to be your Lord and Savior . . . you'll be saved."

"It's that simple?"

"Well, it's the start of the process. Reading the *Bible*, understanding God's Word, living your life as God intended you to live. Being a Christian is not easy. The more you learn, the more you realize how hard it is to be the Christian you want to be."

"Okay," she said, "I'm ready. Help me get there."

Duke nodded and reached out to grab Kadie and Brian's hands. The three of them sat there as Duke prayed, and Kadie repeated after him, accepting Jesus Christ as her Lord and Savior. As she spoke the words, a sense of calm overcame her.

She only hoped she could apply that calm outside this room because the threat to their lives remained.

46

Somewhere over the Mediterranean Sea

The King-Air cruised at ten-thousand feet, bouncing slightly in the turbulence. Duke had considered flying higher, then depressurize the aircraft and put everyone to sleep, but decided against it. He worried something could happen to Kadie and Brian.

The seven of them fit quite comfortably in the twin-engine aircraft. Duke had been able to maneuver getting a diplomatic clearance through European airspace utilizing the call-sign assigned to aircraft back in Iraq. The call-sign was similar to the one used by all aircraft that transited to and from the Middle East Theater. Thankfully, the request went through without much pushback.

One of the GDI goons, the Hispanic man, sat up front with him. Duke had learned his name was Esteban, and the German was Hans. Esteban tried to act tough initially, but once they got airborne, he was like a little kid. Esteban loved to fly, and he seemed to forget he was there to keep an eye on the pilot. Duke did his best to take advantage of the thug's fascination with the flight and build a rapport with the guy. It might come in handy at some point.

They couldn't get approval to land at Tessera, the international airport in Venice, so the next best option was the airport in Treviso, which was about an hour and ten minutes north of Venice. From Treviso, they could take the train to the Venice airport, which would take a few more minutes. Duke had tried to convince them to fly to Vincenza, Italy. Curt somehow knew there was a U.S. Army base in Vincenza and canned the idea.

The flight was long, and by the time Duke had the aircraft inspected by Customs, they all waited for him outside the airport terminal. He was surprised at the pull Patricia and GDI had with foreign governments. With the exception of Israel, GDI operated with immunity at every Customs point of entry they'd encountered. That was an impressive feat.

"What took so long?" Curt said. Every time Duke saw this guy, he wanted to rip his face apart. Images of Mac's lifeless body zipped through his consciousness.

"Customs," Duke replied.

"It doesn't take that long. What are you up to?"

Duke sneered; his fists clenched. Self-control was difficult but necessary. "I'm not up to anything. I have no intention of doing anything that would put Kadie and her brother in any danger."

Curt moved inches from Duke's face. "Let's make sure you keep it that way."

Patricia slid between the two. "Okay, boys, let's not let the testosterone get the best of you. We've got a lot to do today."

The German stooge, Hans, had coordinated transportation to the train station and purchased all their tickets. Duke's head was on a swivel in the train station. *Carabinieri*, the Italian Police, were few and far between, but he was not sure what Curt's reaction would be if the police were notified. Besides, he was curious. What exactly was this scroll they were searching for? Did it possess information that could change the world like Isaac said? Why were *they* looking for it? DNA? No way. That theory played out in *Jurassic Park*, didn't it?

No one spoke on the train to Venice. Duke and Kadie sat next to the window, facing each other. Brian sat next to Kadie. Esteban and Hans covered the aisle seats on each bench. Curt and Patricia sat across the aisle.

The temperature in the train car was cool, but the added silence among them seemed to make it even chillier. He saw Kadie's arms bristled with goosebumps. The GDI team all sat silently, their eyes straight ahead, their hands resting on their weapons hidden under their coats. This was their biggest fear: Traveling with firearms into one of Italy's most prominent tourist attractions, the city of Venice. They could be subject to a metal detector at any point along the way. Would they try and shoot their way out? No telling. But Duke was convinced they would kill Brian first—and that was unacceptable.

When the train stopped in Venice, they were the last ones off. Despite the beautiful city built on numerous tiny islands with canals running throughout, Duke could sense the danger that lurked around him. Kadie followed Duke off the train, her hand gripping his bicep. That wasn't lost on him. She sensed the danger too.

The small group walked to The Hotel Papadopoli. Curt coordinated the accommodations and handed Kadie her key.

"You two lovebirds can room together. I'll take the brat with me."

Kadie's face drooped momentarily as she processed what he said, then the realization of what he planned overcame her, and a fire formed in her eyes and her jaw set.

"Over my dead body," she said as she lunged for Brian.

Curt flung the boy behind him against the wall. "Back off, girly. That can be arranged," he said, grabbing her by her wrists. Esteban moved in behind Curt and took hold of Brian and Hans stuck a pistol in Duke's back.

"You two will be much easier to control this way," he said, releasing her wrists and pushing her back toward Duke. "You wouldn't want anything to happen to the boy."

Kadie backed off, and Duke held her gently, provided some sense of comfort in the face of the obvious threat. He had no doubt that Curt would kill Brian.

The small group headed to their rooms, and then an hour later, everyone gathered in Patricia's suite.

"I've arranged for the three of you to tour Saint Mark's tomorrow afternoon," Patricia said. "I recommend you get some rest."

"Three?" Kadie stood firm. "I don't want Brian involved in this."

Patricia shook her head. "Then it's your lucky day. He's not. Curt will escort you two. There is a hidden stairwell accessible from within the church. Your job will be to find that stairwell. It will take you to the basement." Patricia handed Kadie a sheet of paper with instructions. Duke peered over her shoulder at the handwritten page.

"Where did you find this? Are you sure this is legit?" Duke said.

"It's legitimate," Patricia said. "We have a source inside the Vatican who has assured us of the location of the hidden stairwell. More importantly, he told us how to access the secret catacombs below."

Kadie looked up. No one even knew if there were secret catacombs. "Did they verify the Aramaic Vase is in Saint Mark's?"

"No. They have no idea. Although our source did suggest there are numerous vases in one of the rooms."

Duke piped in. "Numerous, as in more than five?"

Patricia grinned. "Numerous, as in less than two hundred."

Duke and Kadie glanced at each other, and Duke saw the enormity of the task etched on her face.

"Any chance we can walk around the city tonight?" Duke said.

Curt gave him a look that told him, "No."

"I'm sure after the long day of travel, you are quite tired, Mister Ellsworth." Patricia motioned for Hans. "You'll remain in your rooms until tomorrow afternoon. Curt and I will meet our contact from the Vatican and confirm the location of the door before you go." She turned to Hans. "Take them back to their rooms."

"What about dinner?" Kadie said.

"We'll get you something," Curt said. "Unless you'd like to join me on a gondola ride."

"I'd rather starve to death."

"We can arrange that," he said, his jaw clenched, his mouth curled upward.

Duke edged between them and ushered Kadie out the door as he stared down Curt, whose belt bulged where he stuffed a Chinese knock-off carbon-fiber .380 in his pants. Duke knew that pistol tended to jam, but he didn't want to find out if this one would.

PATRICIA TURNED TO HER DRESSER DRAWER AND RETRIEVED A corkscrew, then picked up the bottle of Nebbiolo nestled against the mirror.

"Here, open this," she said, handing them to Curt.

Curt took the bottle and opener and sliced off the metallic sheath that secured the top of the cork. His eyes followed her as she moved across the room to get a wine glass.

"I don't understand why you're protecting them," he said, drilling the screw into the cork.

With the glass in hand, she walked toward him.

"Of course, you don't," she said. "You're too close. You can't see what everyone else sees."

"What's that mean?" He popped the cork and handed her the bottle.

"You're too anxious to kill them. Or least him. I suspect you're mad at her, too, for not picking you in the relationship lottery."

Curt scowled. "I don't think so. The guy is a jerk. Pilots are all alike. They think they walk on water, and they want everyone to know it."

Patricia poured the fine Northern Italian red wine into her glass. She swirled the wine, observing how the liquid clung to the interior. With the glass under her nose, the scent of roses and Bing cherries wafted out from the vessel. Her eyes closed as she sipped the wine, allowing it to dance across her palette. The earthy flavor had a tartness to it yet flowed delicately across her tongue.

"Regardless, ease off the harassment for now," she said. "We need both of them. A threat not followed up on degrades your credibility, and credibility is something we need to keep those two under control."

Curt leaned against the couch in her room. "Fine. So, what's the plan now?"

"Like I said, tomorrow, you take the two of them to Saint Mark's. When they find the vase and the Scroll inside, we're done with her and her brother. We still need the pilot to fly us to Athens."

The DNA lab established by Alligynt Corp had been built in Athens, Greece. Once they had acquired the Scroll, they would go straight to the lab. The DNA experts would fly in from Istanbul and meet them there to extract Jesus' DNA.

"And then?"

Patricia took another sip of Nebbiolo and smiled. "Then, as far as the pilot is concerned, you can do whatever you like."

KADIE AND DUKE HAD WALKED DOWN THE HALL TO THEIR ROOM AFTER Curt shoved Brian into his. He was cruel, plain and simple, and her heart broke for her helpless brother. Her eyes teared up as the door shut behind them.

Hans escorted the pair toward their room. The first thing Duke did when he got inside was lock the door. Then he went to the window. It was permanently sealed, which was unusual for a European hotel, particularly an older one like this.

Kadie stood between the double beds. "I can't stand that man."

"Me neither." Duke turned from the window.

"What do you think?"

Duke shrugged his shoulders. "I think we're kind of stuck here."

"We could just pick up the phone and call the police," she said.

"Yeah. Is that what you want to do?"

"I'd like to, but I worry what Curt would do to Brian."

Duke nodded. "Me too." He grabbed the phone and held it to his ear. "The line is dead, anyway."

They stood in silence for a moment—Kadie surveilled the room.

"Well, this is awkward."

Duke chuckled. "Yeah." He looked back and forth between the beds. "Do you—"

She sat on the one closest to the bathroom. "This one will work."

"Okay. I'll just take this one."

He reached in his bag and pulled out two chem lights and handed one to her. "These are kind of old, but they should still work. I don't think they'll let us take a flashlight into the church. These at least will get past the metal detectors." He paused. "Are you sure we're in the right place?"

Kadie sighed. "As best I can tell from the clues. Someone wanted the vase to be found sometime in the future. It just makes sense, given the history and the clues we have."

"At least your initial hunch was right."

"I hope so," she said. "How are we to know which vase is which?"

"You're the expert. It's supposed to have Aramaic writing on it."

"True, but lots of vases have writing on them."

"Well, we are looking for a *specific* vase." Duke rubbed his thumb and forefinger on his chin.

Her mouth fell open. "Do you have something you'd like to share?"

Duke nodded. "Isaac told me what to look for. It's a medium-sized vase about two-and-a-half-feet tall with four handles. It's formed from an earth-baked clay with a lid made from the same."

Kadie stood from the bed and put her hands on her hips, and she didn't look happy.

"That's kind of important information, don't ya think?" She was louder than usual. "When were you going to tell me about this?"

"Shhh. I didn't say anything yet because it wasn't the time for it. If they thought we had information that specific, they might kill us and go look for it themselves. And it's not like we've had much of a chance to talk."

He was right. The only time they'd been alone, they were either chased by bad guys or looking for Brian. Except for last night, when she became a Christian.

"What about last night?"

Duke appeared flummoxed. "I didn't think it was the right time."

She stepped forward and poked him in the chest. "You don't get to make that call. It's my brother they're holding hostage."

"I know. And I'm as concerned about him as you are. But the more information we control, the safer he's going to be."

"What are you trying to say?"

"I'm trying to say when they get their hands on the Scroll, they won't need us anymore."

47

Venice, Italy
Piazza San Marco

The overcast sky capped the unique city like a beanie on an adolescent—firmly in place, but it could disappear in an instant. The cool afternoon breeze gave her skin goosebumps, and the three of them marched along the backstreets of Venice. Occasionally they passed a waterway and caught a glimpse of happy couples in the gondolas. Kadie wondered when she would make time for a man to ride in a gondola. Her eyes fell on the back of Duke's head. Maybe?

It was a twenty-five-minute walk from the Hotel Papadopoli to the Piazza San Marco, known as *la Piazza*—the Square. Americans usually called it Saint Mark's Square. They headed south out of the hotel, then southeast, through a residential area until they reached the Grand Canal. At the canal, they took a ferry across to *Sant' Angelo*, and from there, zigzagged through more residential areas until they found themselves on the northern side of *la Piazza*, one of the biggest tourist attractions in Venice.

Kadie walked behind Curt, and Duke trailed right behind her. They had been warned that any attempt at escape, or notifying the authorities, would result in Brian getting hurt. Or worse. Kadie and Duke said they understood. They had both discussed it the night before; they knew the danger and made a pact not to make a break for it. But their curiosity was piqued as well. To find a two-thousand-year-old document that validated the resurrection of Christ was enticing.

Kadie took in the spectacle of the crowded Square outside Saint Mark's Basilica. A cruise ship had unloaded its passengers earlier in the day, and *la Piazza* overflowed with tourists, clearly demonstrating its place as the social, political, and religious hub of the city.

They wandered into the center of the Square. To their right, on the southern border, numerous tables lined up in front of Caffe' Florian, the preferred restaurant of the Venetians during the Austrian occupation in the 19th century.

"Follow me," Curt said.

Duke grabbed Kadie's elbow, breaking her concentration on the beautiful spectacle. More pigeons than tourists inhabited the Square, and the noisy birds fluttered out of their way, then back to their spot, as the trio moved across the gray blocks toward Saint Mark's Basilica.

They moved just short of the three tall flagpoles that stood in front of the church. The western façade of the basilica was beautiful. Five arches of molded terracotta, with horizontal moldings, mounted on stone columns. Each arch contained a mosaic relief lined with gold. The central arch over the main entrance was more significant, the gable above displaying a golden-winged lion, the symbol of Saint Mark. Various statues of angels and cherubs lined the roof; the five domes over the primary sections of the church pushed heavenward. Above the central arch, a replica of the four bronze horses the Venetian soldiers brought back from Constantinople stood guard over the plaza.

"It's breathtaking," Kadie said to Duke as they followed Curt to a café on the left side of the square.

Curt sat at a table on the outside of Ristorante Quadri. When Duke and Kadie sat, the waiter was upon them.

"Espresso," Curt said. Duke asked for water; Kadie ordered a cappuccino. Curt checked his watch. They had thirty minutes until they were supposed to meet their tour guide.

Italy, along with the majority of South America, was one of the few remaining bastions of Christianity in the world. Most likely because of the Vatican in Rome. The days of wandering into the church on your own ended years ago. You had to be vetted by a tour group now, and the guide was responsible for his customers while inside.

They sat in silence, observing tourist interactions in the Square. Kadie 's mind drifted back to Brian; she hoped he was okay. She desperately wanted to talk with him about how Curt treated him last night. Was the armed bully as cruel as she suspected? Did he bring her brother to tears again? She and Duke desperately needed to develop an escape plan once they found the vase. Could they bargain with it somehow? Would GDI leave Brian somewhere while they handed it over?

"Don't get too frustrated trying to figure a way out of this," Curt said. "You'll only make yourself miserable. Just focus on the task at hand."

The waiter brought their drinks, and they sat without another word for the next twenty minutes. Curt paid the bill in euros, and the trio rose and walked toward the front of the basilica.

The setting sun behind them cast a colorful display against the glorious cathedral. Curt steered them toward the front entrance, where they would meet the tour guide. The group was limited to twenty people, and their small party of three was the last to arrive.

"*Ciao. Sono contento che tu l'abbia fatto,*" the tour guide said to them.

Kadie nodded and offered a meek smile.

"You speak English?" Curt's voice dripped with disdain.

"I'm glad you finally made it." The tour guide transitioned to English effortlessly. "You're the last ones."

Kadie and Duke glanced at Curt, who looked away as if he didn't hear the guide.

"I'm sorry we're late," Kadie said.

"Do you have your tickets?" the tour guide said.

"Tickets?"

"*Si*, for the tour."

Kadie and Duke turned to Curt, who fished the tickets out of his pocket and handed them over. The guide pulled a hole-punch from his pocket and pierced each of the tickets and returned them to Curt. He gave each of them a portable radio with an earpiece. The guide was older, around sixty, Kadie thought. He wore wrinkled, baggy pants gathered tight around his waist by a belt almost too big. The collared shirt sat underneath the faded yellow vest, which appeared to hold a pocket watch, the gold chain drooping along the front of the vest. On top of all that, a ragged tweed jacket, no doubt identifying him as an academic.

The tour guide identified himself as Armando before launching into a rather extensive background on himself as the sun eased below the horizon.

"All right," Armando said. "Let's get started."

He turned and walked through the front door of the massive church. The interior was a spectacle, while the vast emptiness swallowed them as they plodded through the cathedral. Armando's voice chattered over the radio through the earpiece, competing with the echo of the tourists' nonstop chatter.

The three lingered amongst the other members of the tour. Kadie's eyes darted around the interior of the church. Several different tour groups milled about, making the cathedral noisy. Curt trailed behind them a few feet, watching their every move.

"What are we looking for?" Duke spoke in a hushed tone.

Kadie clenched her teeth. "The south transept."

"Are you sure?"

"Yes. From the corner there, it leads to the treasure of Saint Mark's."

"It can't be in the treasure room," Duke said. "We'll never get access to that."

"Just stick with me," she said. "We have to get to the catacombs."

Kadie's eyes searched the basilica until a slight grin formed on her face.

"There," she said, jutting her head in the direction. "There it is." She left the tour group and slipped across the basilica to the south transept. Duke followed Kadie and scooted next to her, with Curt bringing up the rear.

The three of them approached a relief containing a mosaic within. The area was cordoned off with a red velvet rope. The relief of the disciple with the raised hand beckoned her. Kadie's eyes studied the mosaic from a distance. Duke stood attentively while Curt scanned the area around them.

"Are you sure this is it?" Duke said.

Kadie glanced back at him, her face expressionless, and nodded.

Curt moved in closer. "She's right. You two go. I'll stay up here and run interference."

Kadie's eyes narrowed. "Are you telling me that you're afraid to tour the basement?"

Curt sneered. "I'm not willing to get caught. But if *you two* are caught, your brother's life is in our hands."

Duke stepped between them, taking a protective stance in front of her. "We're not exactly thrilled with the prospect of getting caught either, pal. Of course, that *would* put us in contact with the authorities."

The sneer left Curt's face. "Please don't misunderstand. You two pull anything suspicious—one wrong move—the boy dies."

Kadie moved from behind Duke. "We're not going to do anything. I'll do whatever I need to. Just keep my brother safe."

"Oh, he's safe. You two just need to make sure you keep him that way. Get in, find the Scroll, and get out."

Kadie's eyebrows scrunched, and her mouth tightened. She

turned to the mosaic, her eyes tracing the outline as Curt slid to the side. Duke moved closer.

"And you're sure this is the right place?"

Her eyebrows raised, and her shoulders hunched. "We've got to start somewhere."

She stood with her hands on her hips, her head tilted to the side. She gave Duke a subtle grin, ignored Curt, and focused on the mosaic. There had to be a trigger. A lever, a button, something to open the secret passageway.

She stopped when she noticed the disciple's hand was at eye level.

Looking to the left and the right, she leaned over the rope and pressed her hand against the mosaic. A distinct click immediately followed, and the entire relief shifted slightly, revealing a passageway that descended into darkness.

48

Venice, Italy
The southern transept of Saint Mark's Basilica

Kadie glanced at Duke, and he nodded. In a flash, the two stepped over the thick velvet rope and slipped into the opening behind the hidden door. Duke followed behind her and softly secured the door behind them. The space turned black as soon as the door shut. Duke pulled the chem light out of his pocket and snapped it, releasing the substance within, causing a chemical reaction to create bright green light. Kadie did the same as he moved in front of her. She shook the plastic stick and illuminated the passageway in bright green, luminous light.

Armando's voice rattled over the radio; Kadie and Duke simultaneously turned off their radios. Duke tucked the earpiece in his pocket.

"This could be dangerous," he said.

Kadie nodded. "It's already dangerous."

Not needing to hear anymore, Duke led the way to protect her from whatever lay ahead.

They walked about ten feet and found themselves at the top of a stairwell. Duke checked that Kadie was still there, then started down. She trailed close behind, her hand resting on his shoulder. They slowly descended the stairs, which made a ninety-degree turn about every twelve steps. She felt as if they walked down several stories, but they had no way of knowing, other than the chill in the air and the seemingly endless steps.

When they reached the bottom, the air was damp and moldy with a bitter taste. The steps ended at a hallway with bare light bulbs strung across the ceiling. The soft green glow from the chem lights didn't give them much help, but Kadie managed to find a light switch.

"What do you think?" she said, her finger hovered over the switch.

Duke scanned the area. "These catacombs don't appear to be a secure area. I doubt there's any kind of alarm system down here. If so, we've set it off already."

Kadie flipped the switch, illuminating the series of light bulbs that stretched across the ceiling.

"That makes it easier," Duke said. "Now, all we have to do is find a room with vases."

Kadie cast him an anxious look. "Right."

They crept down the hallway.

"Isaac said the vase was about two-and-a-half-feet-high with no pedestal. Wide at the top and narrowed as it went to the bottom. And it has four handles, one on each side." Duke poked his head into the first "room." They weren't rooms so much as alcoves, vast spaces with arched, open doorways. The first room had numerous statues and paintings.

"The four handles represent the four corners of the earth the Roman Empire was supposed to control," Kadie added. "I don't know why they would put Aramaic writing on the outside, though. It doesn't make sense."

"I thought you didn't know anything about the vase."

"The Romans commonly used four-corner symbology. It represents the empire stretching across the four corners of the world."

Duke shrugged his shoulders. "It's an unusual design. Should make it easier to find."

Kadie nodded.

The second alcove was more like the first. A few vases, none of which matched the description of what they searched for.

"They don't have the fancy climate control here like they do in the Vatican," Kadie said. "I think the items here are more for storage. They've been stuck down here for centuries until someone decides they're worth displaying somewhere."

They picked up the pace. Each alcove had numerous vases, requiring them to enter and investigate. After number six, about halfway down the hall, they discovered an alcove filled with nothing but vases. Tall, short, fat, thin—many with writing on the outside.

Kadie and Duke looked at each other.

"I think we found the right room," Duke said.

"Yes. A perfect place to hide it."

They entered and began their search. There were hundreds of vases. The larger ones in the front blocked much of the light. The two weaved between the multitude of vases, searching for their unique objective.

Kadie's heart pounded. She knew they couldn't stay here much longer. Someone would figure out they were missing and notify the police.

Her eyes danced over the vases, then across the room at Duke. She continued her search and eventually came upon a unique shaped vase with a four-handled top.

"Duke, I think I found the vase."

CURT STOOD NEXT TO THE RELIEF WITH THE DOORWAY BEHIND THE mosaic. He wondered if he looked as impatient as he felt. The fact he'd stayed in one spot for the past fifteen minutes staring at everyone else in the cathedral made him appear suspicious. Armando and their group were on the other side of the cathedral. A security officer approached him.

"Sir, is everything all right?"

"Yes, I'm fine," Curt replied.

"I'm going to have to ask you to move along."

Curt's eyes widened. "I'm fine. I—I'm just enjoying this beautiful artwork." He turned around and faced the relief.

Where are they? They should be out of there by now.

He heard the squawk from the radio, and the police officer muttered something in Italian.

Within a minute, two more officers arrived. One carried a Beretta M12, a 9x19mm Parabellum caliber submachine gun, while both carried the Beretta 92F 9mm pistol.

"Sir," the original officer said, "it's time for you to leave." Curt turned and knew right away these men meant business.

The officer grabbed him by the shoulder and steered him toward the exit. The other two *carabinieri* followed them.

Curt glanced back at the relief as the police removed his radio and earpiece and escorted him outside.

Where are they?

KADIE AND DUKE STOOD ABOVE THE UNIQUE VASE AND GRINNED. SHE knelt and held her chem light up to the side.

"It's Aramaic." She could barely contain the excitement in her voice. Their discovery was two-fold: they found what they came to find, but more importantly, they found what would help her brother.

"The inscription says, *For the message from Pontius Pilate, Prefect of Israel.*" She paused, licking her lips. "That's an unusual inscription to post on the outside of the vase."

"Is this the vase?"

"It has to be. It met the description, and it does contain a message from Pilate. Or least it says it does."

She rotated the vase, and on the other side, a Sator Square was etched into the middle of the vase. Kadie glanced at Duke and smiled.

She reached for the lid. Her fingernails dug under the edge and tried to pry it off.

It didn't budge.

Shifting her grip, she tried again.

"It's stuck. I can't get it to move."

Duke edged closer. "Here, let me try."

Kadie backed off, and Duke pulled on the lid with no success either. He reached in his pocket and pulled out a Gerber utility knife. Duke worked the blade around the circumference of the top, gently prying at the seam of the two.

"I think it's coming loose," he said.

"Keep going."

Duke continued his effort. After another circuit around the top, they noticed some movement.

"It's working," Kadie said.

The lid was a custom-fit within the vase. After prying the lid about two inches, it let out a loud hiss as air entered the ancient vase. Duke removed the lid and handed the vase to Kadie.

Something didn't look right, but she couldn't put her finger on what bothered her.

"The Scroll," she said.

Duke stepped back. "I think you should have the honors."

Kadie moved forward, knelt, and peered inside. She stuck her hand through the mouth of the vase and felt something hard. When she pulled out the object, both were surprised to find a small tablet.

"That doesn't look like a scroll," Duke said.

Kadie frowned as she studied both sides of the tablet.

"I don't understand. This *should* be the Aramaic Vase. The Pilate Scroll should be inside."

"Kadie, it's a legend. Maybe it's been so distorted over the years that a tablet was actually inside the Aramaic Vase and not a scroll."

She held the chem light to the tablet to study the writing.

"Can you read it?" Duke said.

Kadie shook her head. "It looks familiar . . . Like I've seen it before. I just don't . . . Wait a minute." She flipped the tablet over in her hands. "I can't read the writing because it's written backward."

"Backwards?"

"Yes. Very *Da Vinci Code-ish*. This was a common method to hide information back in the day." The Dan Brown novel had been one of her favorites. "We'll need to bring the tablet with us and figure it out at the hotel."

"Are you sure this is the right vase?"

Kadie set the lid back on the vase and turned to Duke. "Well, we have a description of the vase. It's very specific and very distinct. The inscription on the outside and the Sator Square confirms this is what we're searching for."

"But there's a tablet instead of a scroll."

"Yes, and if this isn't what we're looking for, I believe the tablet will tell us the location of the scroll. I thought something was odd when we first saw the vase. See this seam on the side?" She pointed along the length of the vase. "This vase isn't from 30 A.D. It's more like 300 A.D."

"Constantine?"

"Yes. I think before Constantine died, he had the Aramaic Vase moved to a safer location and left clues for people to find it."

49

Venice, Italy
The catacombs of Saint Mark's Basilica

Kadie followed Duke back down the secret hallway and up the squared-off stairwell. They rushed up the stairs, and for the first time, she noticed the stale air made it difficult to breathe. Or perhaps it was just because her heart pounded rapidly. The old chem lights were fading fast, and the darkness began to swallow them. When they reached the top of the stairs, they faced a barren door.

"I can't believe this," Duke said. "We got in relatively easy, but there's no handle or latch to open the door. Duke ran his hands along the edges of the narrow frame. The dissipating chem light only frustrated him as he hovered the illuminated stick near the stone wall next to the door, searching for any type of lever.

Kadie stood anxiously behind him, her eyes desperately seeking an answer.

"Here, see if this helps." She handed him her chem light. Two fading glow sticks had to be better than one.

Duke took the stick and paired it with his. The second stick helped some, but not enough to change their situation.

Kadie watched Duke explore every area around the door, but the more he did, the more she focused on the door. There was nothing that resembled a handle. She pondered the situation for a moment. Could it really be that easy?

It was worth a shot.

"Duke, push on the door."

"I need to find the handle to open it first."

"A handle may not be necessary. Sometimes the answer is right in front of us."

Duke glared back at her as if she told him to do something crazy.

He placed his hands against the door and pushed lightly, then a little harder. There was a slight click, and the door cracked open toward them. Duke turned back to her and grinned.

"You're pretty smart, lady."

Kadie smiled back. "Thanks, but I think it was desperation. Now, let's get out of here." She unbuttoned the bottom button of her shirt that tucked into her pants, slipped the tablet into her shirt, and refastened the button.

Duke pulled the door slowly, trying not to make any rapid motion. He peeked through the crack. No one was nearby. The entrance was hidden from view unless you were in the southern transept. He opened the door enough for the two of them to squeeze through. They stood in front of the same mosaic relief they had used to enter the basement. Duke peered around the corner and quickly brought his head back.

"What's wrong?" Kadie whispered.

"There are police standing to the side. They'll catch us if we step over the rope."

Kadie nodded, aware that the most challenging part of their adventure now lay in getting out of Saint Mark's. Duke peeked back around the corner to watch the police. Seeing the secret doorway still open, she reached behind her to gently close the door.

It shut with a loud, reverberating *click*.

Duke jerked his head back. Kadie's eyes went wide, and she bit her lower lip, the corners of her mouth drooping. No need to say anything—the problem was obvious.

"They heard it," Duke said. "They're coming this way."

"Oh, no."

Duke held her upper arms and gazed into her eyes. "Do you trust me?"

Kadie nodded. "Yes."

"Then follow my lead, okay?"

She nodded again, and before she knew it, he drew her in closer. It wasn't dark, but he became a blur as his arms wrapped around her, His hands roamed across her back, not aggressive but affectionate. Then she gasped.

He was kissing her.

She started to pull away, then realized what he was doing. And she also realized she liked it. A passionate kiss in an ancient, magnificent chapel in one of the most romantic cities in the world was the way every first kiss should be.

She closed her eyes and kissed him back.

"*Che cosa stai facendo*?"

Duke broke off the kiss, and the two of them turned to the Italian police officer who rattled off a variety of angry statements. She understood some of what he said because she knew Latin, but she got lost in the translation due to the speed and emotion of his voice.

"Is something wrong, officer?" Duke said. He played the role perfectly, Kadie thought.

"What are you doing? You must step away from the artwork," the policeman said in broken English. "You are not allowed inside the rope." Duke glanced down at the thick velvet rope draped from post to post as if he'd never seen it before.

"I'm sorry, officer. I didn't notice that."

"How can you not see this is roped off?" The officer waved his hands as Duke took Kadie's hand and stepped over the rope. He turned and helped her over, and they started to leave.

"Where are you going?" the officer said a little too loudly.

Kadie noticed a few people looking in their direction.

"What were you doing over there?" the officer said.

Duke tugged Kadie closer, placed his arm around her waist, and tilted his head at the cop.

"Do you really have to ask? I'm in the city of love with a beautiful girl. Sorry, I couldn't help myself."

Duke smiled at the policeman, and Kadie blushed. Her embarrassment helped sell the deception.

The officer's disposition changed, and he formed a brief smile as he stared at her, his eyes selling him out as they checked her up and down.

Whatever it takes, she thought. *We need to get out of here.*

The policeman nodded and motioned toward the front door. "I must ask you to leave. You have violated the rules of the cathedral."

"Yes, sir," Duke said. "We're sorry." He grabbed her by the hand again and led her toward the center aisle.

Her cheeks flushed again as he squeezed her hand.

"Nice work back there," he said with a smile.

Kadie shook her head. "You're smooth."

Duke feigned surprise. "What? Me? Always better to beg forgiveness than ask permission."

They spotted Armando and the tour group near the entrance to the cathedral. Duke pulled the earpiece from his pocket and handed his radio to Armando as they passed, who looked puzzled, then terrified, that two members of his group were being escorted out by the police. Kadie did the same.

"Great job," Duke said to the tour guide.

Kadie's free hand pressed the tablet against her stomach, her eyes searching the cathedral. "Where's Curt?"

Duke's head swiveled. "I don't see him. Shucks, he would have really gotten mad if he saw you kissing me."

"Kissing you? You kissed me."

He smiled at her again. “I did. But you kissed back.”

“I’m just glad you weren’t dipping Skoal beforehand.”

Duke grinned and raised his eyebrows.

“And I didn’t kiss back,” Kadie said.

“It sure seemed like you kissed back.”

“Well, I didn’t.”

“I’ve kissed a few girls in my day, and I’m pretty sure you kissed back.”

She started to respond, but when they walked out the front door, Curt stood outside, waiting for them. At first, he was expressionless, then his eyes locked on their hands. His teeth clenched, and his eyes tensed. Duke was right. The kiss would have sent him over the edge. He might have shot them right there in the cathedral.

They hopped down the steps to where Curt stood and kept a steady pace.

“Did you get the Scroll?” Curt said, rushing to keep up with them.

“No,” Kadie replied. “But I think we got a clue to where we might find it.”

“Clue? What kind of clue?”

Her eyes darted from side to side. “Can you please be quiet and let’s get out of here? We don’t want to attract any more attention.”

Curt struggled to contain his anger and frustration. He grabbed her upper arm and led them across *la Piazza* toward the hotel. Pigeons scurried into the air as they passed before settling back to the earth

Kadie realized she still held Duke’s hand and let go. Duke appeared disappointed but understood. He didn’t say anything; he only gave a subtle nod.

She swapped hands that held the tablet against her stomach. Her thoughts returned to her brother and the hope that this tablet held the answers they sought.

50

Venice, Italy
The Hotel Papadopoli

Kadie and Duke waited in their hotel room while Curt went to get the others. One of the goons stood outside the door, always on guard. Kadie took the opportunity to find a pencil and a blank piece of paper.

"What are you doing?" Duke said.

"Deciphering a code."

Duke nodded and pulled out his round can of tobacco. He took a pinch and set the can of Skoal on the end table.

Kadie ignored his nasty habit and set the paper over the top of the tablet, rubbing the pencil back and forth, lightly at first, then stronger. The writing on the tablet began to show through. No sooner had she finished, then Curt showed up with Patricia and Brian. Her brother looked scared until he saw her and Duke. Kadie dropped the paper, leaped from the couch, and hugged her brother. The smile on his face said everything.

"Kadie!" Brian said. "I was scared for you. I knew D-Duke would protect you."

She ran her fingers through his hair. "We're fine."

Patricia moved over and placed a hand between the two. "I think we've seen enough of this sappy reunion. How about you solve our puzzle?" The look she gave was less than confident.

Kadie returned to the couch and retrieved the paper.

"We found a hidden passageway that had several rooms on either side. Eventually, we found the vase. Or, at least what we thought was the vase."

"What made you think that?" Patricia said.

"This vase appeared to be made from Constantine's era instead of the time of Jesus," Duke said. Kadie smiled at him, happy he injected himself in this process. It made her feel less alone, and he seemed to sense that.

"Yes," Kadie said. "The construction of the vase is definitely from a later era. Around 300 A.D., from what I can tell."

"Well, that's convenient," Curt sniped.

Kadie ignored his comment and continued. "Inside the vase, we found this tablet with Latin inscription. I couldn't decipher the tablet on the spot because I realized it was written backward. So, we brought it here, and I used this paper to overlay and copy the surface."

"What does it say?" Patricia asked.

Curt snatched the piece of paper. "It still looks like the same gobbledygook crap if you ask me."

He was right, sort of. Kadie took the paper from him and walked to the lamp-stand next to the couch. "I haven't had a chance to look at it yet. As soon as I transferred the writing to this paper, you all arrived." Kadie turned on the lamp and held the paper with the pencil side toward the lamp. The darker impressions showed through the paper, making the text easy to read.

"Clever girl," Duke said.

Kadie appreciated the comment but said nothing. Her eyes shifted left to right, then down the page. The more she tried to interpret the writing, the more she felt her enthusiasm wain. Her feelings must have manifested themselves physically.

"What's wrong?" Patricia said. So much for having a poker face.

"I-I don't know," Kadie said. "It's Latin, but the words don't seem to make sense. There's no complete sentence. Not even a complete phrase. The words don't go together." She began to get worried. They were so close. How could they have a stumbling block like this? She glanced at Brian and wished there was a way for them to run out of the room, complete with a SWAT team that would roll in between them and Curt and his GDI thugs.

Curt picked up the tablet from the table and jostled it back and forth between his hands as if he weighed it somehow. Suddenly, he turned and hurled the tablet against the marble fireplace, the rectangular stone twirling like a frisbee. The tablet impacted the marble with a loud crack and shattered the large stone into several pieces.

"No!" Kadie screamed. She wasn't done with the stone. Maybe she didn't press hard enough. Or maybe she pressed too much. The tablet still needed to be examined. Destroying it was the last thing on her mind. She cast Curt a hateful stare. "I still need that."

"Maybe you brought back the wrong thing," Curt said. "Clearly, you found the wrong vase. And whatever crap you found inside, was designed to send you on a wild goose chase."

"Curt," Patricia said, "You will restrain yourself in the future. I know you're frustrated. We all are frustrated. But your little outbursts aren't getting us any closer to the Pilate Scroll."

The room was quiet. Brian moved to the end table and grabbed Duke's can of tobacco. "I found the pilot's Skoal," he said with a chortle. Kadie smiled and laughed softly, and Duke joined in the laughter as well. Brian was trying to break the tension. His joke was funny before—no reason in his mind it wouldn't be funny again.

Curt was not impressed. "Shut up, retard."

Kadie whirled to face him, and Duke reached forward and pulled her back. She shook herself free and glared at Duke, then stuck her finger in Curt's face. "Leave my brother alone."

Curt's face contorted into a self-righteous smirk.

Brian had wandered toward the fireplace and focused on the pieces of the shattered tablet. He shuffled over and picked up the largest piece. He turned and looked at her.

"There is a message—inside," he said, as he raised the piece and offered it to her.

She moved toward him quickly, before Curt or Patricia could intervene. Partly because she feared for Brian's safety, partly because she wanted to keep this discovery out of their reach. At least at first. Brian handed her the broken tablet, and the first thing she saw was the paper— parchment actually—wedged into the small gap inside the tablet. She tugged at it. The parchment was encased tight within the space. With another significant tug, the parchment broke free, and she slid it from its home for the last eighteen hundred years. She gave the broken tablet back to Brian, who seemed fascinated with his discovery, examining the tight space the parchment had occupied.

Kadie handled the parchment gingerly. Hers were the first human hands to touch it in almost two millennia. The parchment was legitimate; she could tell right away. It was folded into thirds, and she was less than enthusiastic. Nothing they'd found had helped them up to this point. This was going to be another dead end. At least, that's what she thought until she turned the parchment over.

In the middle of the page was a circle of red wax holding the parchment closed. Embedded in the wax was something she recognized right away. She'd seen dozens of photographs of it during her studies, but never a real one. A smile crept across her face.

"Kadie?" Duke said. She didn't respond. She only stared at the parchment in her hands.

She whirled to face the rest of them.

Patricia edged toward her, interested, yet concerned. "What is it?"

She took a deep breath and turned to Duke.

"It's the official seal of the Emperor Constantine."

51

"The seal of Constantine? Are you sure?" Duke said.

Kadie nodded enthusiastically. Duke realized she was convinced that the seal was authentic. His thought shifted from elated discovery to strategic concern. How would this impact their situation? Curt was a loose cannon. No telling what would set him off next. His eyes darted to their captors, but they remained transfixed on the paper Kadie held in her hand.

She shuffled to the coffee table and let the paper balance on one hand as she moved items on the table with the other. With care, she set the discovery on the coffee table, then sat on the floor to examine it closer. The seal still had amazing adhesive qualities, and she tugged carefully at the paper.

"Will that seal damage the paper?" Duke said.

"Parchment."

"Huh?"

"It's not paper. It's parchment. And no, other than a small stain on the other side. I'm trying to remove the seal to keep it intact. There are not many authentic wax seals around from Constantine's time. I've never seen one in person—only pictures from before my parents were born."

Kadie glanced up and around the room before her eyes settled back on Duke. "Do you have your pocketknife?"

He gave her the kind of look that said, *really*? Kadie's eyes drooped, aware of what she had done. Curt approached Duke and held his hand out. Duke reluctantly removed the Gerber from his pocket and handed it to Curt.

Kadie turned to Curt. "I know you have one. Give me your pocketknife, or you can give me his."

Curt looked at Patricia, who nodded.

The phony Delta soldier fished his pocketknife out of his pocket and handed it to her. She opened the blade and probed the edges of the wax seal gently. The blade slipped under the wax a little further each time.

Duke sat patiently as Kadie took her time. She was in her element and knew the importance of being careful. After nearly two minutes, she made a final push, and the wax popped free, fully intact. She slid the seal to the side, careful not to damage it. Folding the pocketknife, she handed it back to Curt. Brian knelt at the other end of the coffee table and anxiously watched his sister work. Kadie smiled at him, then opened the parchment. The writing was still legible, as far as he could tell from this distance. The room was silent, while Kadie's eyes seemed to dance across the page.

KADIE TOOK A DEEP BREATH AS SHE UNFOLDED THE PARCHMENT. HER biggest fear now was the letter falling apart at the folds. She was surprised, however, at the strength of the parchment. The document was in fantastic shape, her fear unfounded. Perhaps it was because there was no oxygen in the tablet. How was that even possible back then? It didn't matter. She needed to translate the contents of the letter and do it fast.

Her eyes scanned the parchment. With every word, a smile crept across her face.

"Well?" Patricia grew more impatient with each moment.

"Give me a minute," Kadie re-read the handwritten letter. The Latin text flowed effortlessly; her eyes started to water as she realized the historical significance of what she had in her hands. It was a unique find, and there was nothing in existence to compare it to.

"It's a short letter from Constantine to his one of his sons, Constantius. He was the middle child from Constantine's wife, Fausta."

"Why write to the second child?"

"I don't know. Maybe he wrote to them all, and this is the only one we've found. Perhaps he thought Constantius would be the one he thought would succeed him as emperor."

"I thought his oldest was expected to be his successor?" Patricia said. *She's done her homework*, Kadie thought.

"Originally, yes. Crispus was the oldest child of Constantine's first wife. That is, until Fausta, his stepmother, seduced him. She wasn't much older than he was—one of the great scandals over the centuries. When Constantine found out, he was more heartbroken than angry, with his son, anyway. He had them both put to death, although not publicly. It was a well-hidden scandal.

"Helena, Constantine's mother, was devastated. The first-born grandchild was her favorite. Crispus' execution was the trigger for her journey to the Holy Land and her quest for the artifacts surrounding the life and death of Christ."

Across the coffee table, Brian's eyes sparkled as she weaved the tale of Constantine's mother scouring Israel for Holy artifacts.

"Enough," Curt said, cutting her story short. "What does the letter say?"

Kadie breathed deep, then read the letter aloud in English.

"Constantius, Naissus is your goal. There you will find the Cathedral of Helena.
In her home and shrine of honor. To locate the vase, you must find its final resting place.
As man emerges from stone, the sun radiates from his head.
The rivers weave between subtle mountains of granite and stone.

The wedge in the valley leads to the entrance of the city of channels.
What was once here is now gone.
It stands among his mother's treasures.
X. P. **α**. ω."

"That's the same information we used at Helenopolis, with some extras thrown in," Curt said.

"Yeah, except without the Sator Square," Duke chimed in. "You know, without the top section, you were over a thousand miles off-target."

Curt cast daggers at the pilot, which again made Kadie fear for their safety. "What does X, P, a, and w mean? They have root-beer back then?"

As Kadie contemplated answering the sarcastic question, Patricia opened her iPad and tapped on the screen desperately. Everyone stopped and watched her, unsure of what she was doing.

Kadie turned to Curt. "It isn't an *X* or *P* . . . they're letters from the Greek alphabet. *Chi* and *Rho*. They are the first two letters from Christ in Greek." She wrote out the translation on a piece of paper.

ΧΡΙΣΤΟΣ = Christos

"These are the actual letters used for the symbol of Constantine. He superimposed the Greek letter *rho* vertically through the Greek letter *chi*. This was the first Christogram, the forerunner of the cross we use today. It's the symbol embedded in the wax seal." She picked the seal up and cradled the delicate treasure in her palm, showing them the emblem.

Duke edged forward. "Wait, are you saying Constantine didn't actually have his soldiers put a *cross* on their tunics?"

"Possibly."

"What are you two talking about?" Curt said.

"The night before the Battle of the Milvian Bridge," Kadie said, "Constantine experienced a divine intervention. It is said he had a dream or a vision of the cross in the heavens. The Greek words *en toútōi níka* appeared with the cross. In Latin, it means—"

"In hoc signo vinces," Duke said. "In this sign, you will conquer."

"Yes." Kadie smiled. "The story says that Constantine had his soldiers put the emblem on their tunics and shields to identify themselves to each other. Constantine's forces went on to win the battle. Whether it was divine intervention or a brilliant strategic move, Constantine gave credit for this sign to God. The victory made Constantine the sole emperor of Rome, and it was the beginning of Constantine's and Rome's conversion to Christianity. Whether it was a cross, or the *Chi-Rho* symbol, or even something else that his troops used, remains unknown.

"The emblem of the cross was used in secret by early Christians before his time. Constantine could have used the symbol *Chi-Rho*. Symbolically, it's the same thing. Historians seem to argue over when the cross was officially adopted as the symbol for Christianity. It's believed it was adopted as early as the third century. Some historians say it didn't evolve until centuries later."

"What about the *a* and the *w*?" Curt said.

"Same thing," Kadie said. "Greek alphabet, but in lower case. *Alpha* and *Omega*. They are the first and last letters of the Greek alphabet. It was also used in Constantine's time with *Chi-Rho*, placed in the spaces formed on the left and right side of the letter *Chi*. Jesus said, *I am the Alpha and the Omega*."

"The beginning and the end," Brian said. "The first and the last."

Kadie nodded at her brother. He was definitely up to speed on his Bible studies.

"The same thing is part of the Sator Square," Duke said.

"Yes, but there's more here," Kadie said. "The line about the man crawling from the stone. It's a reference to Mithraism."

Patricia stopped typing on her iPad, and her eyebrows scrunched. "To what?"

"Mithraism. It was a religion that existed around Constantine's time. Some called it a cult. Regardless, Mithraism had a popular following amongst the Roman soldiers. Officers in most cases."

"What does the clue mean?" Curt said. "Are we looking for a man in a rock?"

Kadie shook her head. "No. But the sentence is included for a reason. There's not much evidence of Mithraism around these days, but what *is* available suggests that the temples the followers worshiped in were all underground."

The GDI team lead tilted her head to the side, a look of confusion on her face.

Kadie inhaled deep. "I think the cathedral might be in a cave."

Patricia gave a subtle nod as her eyes drifted off. She returned her focus to her iPad, typing as feverishly as possible. Eventually, she looked up from her iPad. "Something is wrong. I've searched on my map several times, and there is no such place as Naissus."

Kadie scrunched her eyebrows and fought back a grin. Sometimes she had a hard time accepting the fact this lady had a Ph.D.

"Naissus was the name of the town Helena was from. It was where Constantine's father met her and where the future emperor was born."

"Hence, the first clue which mistakenly led everyone to Helenopolis," Duke said.

"Or on purpose," Kadie replied. Duke nodded.

"But where is it?" Patricia grew more frustrated by the minute. Kadie could tell she was getting more desperate the closer they got to their goal.

Kadie stood from the floor and faced Patricia. "The small town of Naissus is now known as the city of Nis. In Serbia."

Patricia straightened and smiled, then looked at Curt. "See, I knew I made the right decision by keeping her around. She's a wealth of information. Let's get moving. There's a vase waiting for us."

52

The knock on the door was fast and loud. Duke thought it sounded unusual, and he hurried to the door. Kadie stood at the coffee table, while Duke checked through the peephole. It was Esteban delivering their dinner. Hans still stood guard outside. Well, *sat* guard. He had moved the plush chair next to the elevators to right outside their door. Duke opened the door, Esteban entered, set the food on the coffee table, and left without saying a word.

Suddenly, Brian jumped from the couch and ran to the other room. Moments later, he came back out, holding an empty bottle of Lamictal.

"Kadie, I-I can't find my—other bottle."

"What?"

He opened the bottle and poured out the contents. One pill left.

"I will save this—for tomorrow."

"I could swear that Doctor Upton gave us the second bottle."

"I thought so too," Brian said. "But I—can—not find it."

Kadie sensed his worry and wrapped her arms around him. "It'll be okay, Brian. We'll find some at a pharmacy somewhere."

She knew the odds of that were slim, but it was essential to make him feel better about the missing drug. After a few minutes, he went back to his room.

Duke turned back to face Kadie. "I'm sorry to change the subject, but you're sure about this, right? The location of this hidden cathedral?"

Kadie nodded. "I'm sure about what the parchment said. As far as I can tell, the letter is authentic. But when we find the cathedral, there's no telling if the Pilate Scroll is still there—or if it was ever there at all."

Duke put his hands on his hips. "That's what worries me. These characters are getting desperate, and I'm concerned that after this episode, they're gonna have their fill with us."

Kadie glanced at Brian glued to the television and shook her head. Duke understood. No use in scaring the boy any more than he was already. It made Duke furious every time they wanted him or Kadie to do something they stuck a gun to the kid's head.

She walked closer to him, and he held her hand. "Do we even know what we're searching for?" he said. It was a valid question. And while they had some success in their quest, he was starting to feel like Nicolas Cage in *National Treasure.* Every time they moved a step forward, they had to take two steps back.

"At some point after 325 A.D., Constantine built the secret cathedral in Naissus to honor his mother. Who knows why? I'm not sure if anyone other than us is aware this cathedral even exists. Constantine had the Scroll transported from Constantinople to the secret cathedral, most likely for safekeeping."

"But you think this cathedral may be underground, still?"

Kadie nodded. "The idea is not too far-fetched. Mithraism was a religion followed by Roman officers. Perhaps the nods to Mithras were added to motivate Roman officers to have their men build the cathedral."

"Sounds reasonable. Maybe he was going to inter himself in the cathedral."

"No, that can't be it. When he built the cathedral in Constantinople, he planned to have all the Apostles' remains moved there so that he could spend eternity surrounded by the Apostles. So, it couldn't be for safekeeping."

"Unless he was worried about the future."

Kadie's lips tightened, and she squinted.

Duke continued. "I mean, if the Apostles are all buried in one place, wouldn't you want to move *some* things that relate to Jesus somewhere else? Especially an eyewitness account that Jesus rose from the dead handwritten by the man who had him executed?"

"To preserve the faith."

"Yes, just in case they were ever to be conquered."

"Which happened at the end of the Fourth Crusade. The pope organized a Latin Christian crusader army to recapture Jerusalem from the Muslims. Through a series of economic and political events, the crusaders found themselves excommunicated from the Catholic Church, and the ruler they helped take power in Constantinople was overthrown and killed. The crusaders were in a situation where they would now not be paid.

"In April of 1204, they ransacked Constantinople and carried the treasures back here. I'm sure it seemed bad at the time, but two hundred years later, the city fell into Muslim hands and has remained that way ever since. If the Crusaders hadn't brought these things back to Venice, they might have been lost forever."

Kadie clasped her hands together.

"I have an idea," she said. "Perhaps Constantine felt bad because he had his mother's favorite grandchild put to death. Building the secret cathedral was his way of apologizing."

"Apologizing?"

"Or something. I don't know. But it sounds legit." She paused. "I hope it's legit." Her mood grew more somber. "They'll never let us go if it's not. What will they do to Brian?"

Duke leaned in and whispered in her ear. "I think we both know it doesn't matter if we find the Scroll or not. GDI isn't going to let us go home."

Kadie's eyes began to well. As much as she hated to hear those words, she knew he was right. "I've always been bothered by people who ignored God's existence or didn't follow the Scriptures. But whether they were believers or not, when things don't go their way, they start to pray for what they want." She stuffed her hands in her pants pockets and swiped her foot in front of her. "I want to pray for us now." She looked up at Duke. "Does that make me a hypocrite?"

The gruff pilot grabbed her by the shoulders, scrunched down, and gazed into her eyes. "No, it makes you human."

"How are you so calm during all this?" She realized she came off somewhat loud. "I mean, why not just jump these guys, or get some help? Aren't you supposed to be some kind of Air Commando or something like that?"

Duke glared at her. She couldn't tell if he was stunned or angry.

"The time is coming," Duke said. "God has a plan for everyone and everything. Just because I'm a Christian doesn't mean I'm a pushover. You know, Jesus lost it with the moneychangers at the temple in Jerusalem."

"That's a great mindset. How do you gather the willpower?"

"Hebrews 11:1."

Kadie smiled. "Faith."

"We've got to have faith. Confidence in what we hope for—"

"And assurance for what we cannot see."

"Yup."

Kadie straightened her back. "Well, I've got faith we'll find the Aramaic Vase with the Pilate Scroll. We must. It's the only chance we have to save my brother from GDI."

53

Duke spent the rest of the evening planning the flight to Serbia. Again, he needed to grease the skids of the customs folks somehow. They weren't scheduled to fly into the country, and Duke fudged the facts about the flight, their destination, purpose, and itinerary.

Curt had stopped by hours ago to take Brian back to his room and check on Duke's progress. It was well past midnight before Duke finished the coordination to fly the airplane and passengers out of Italy and into Serbia. The route he planned would take a little over two-and-a-half hours. He tried to avoid flying over the Adriatic Sea mainly for safety, but he cut the corner at the northern edge.

He slept on his bed that night and slept soundly. Kadie let him sleep when she awoke in the morning, and he needed it.

Escape was never far from his thoughts, but anything that put Brian at risk was something he was not willing to do. Once they found the Scroll, the possibility of getting away from GDI would be impossible. Curt made it quite clear he would kill the boy anytime and anywhere. Duke believed the man was unstable enough to do it. The GDI goons followed him around the airfield, where he was told not to use the squawk codes for an emergency or high-jacking. Their only hope was the call-sign. Duke continued to use the call-sign assigned to them by the Air Force when he left Iraq. He had deviated significantly from his original flight plan in the past few days. Hopefully, someone in the battle-staff in Baghdad or at Hurlburt Field, would detect it soon.

When they went down to the lobby, Patricia coordinated two separate cabs to the train station, then to the airport in Treviso, where Duke's plane sat. Curt took Brian in the other car to ensure he and Kadie didn't try anything foolish. When they arrived at the airport, Esteban went inside with Duke to file the flight plan. The thug stuck with him like glue and left no opportunity for Duke to slip anyone a message that they were being kidnapped. The rest of the team loaded their gear on the airplane and waited for them on the ramp.

Duke filed the flight plan and walked out to the airplane; his guard close by the whole way. The sky to the West was a deep gray, and the brisk wind of the imminent cold front whisked around them. Curt held Brian in front of him, the pistol in his coat apparent only because Duke knew it was there. The coward—to hold a gun on a person with special needs was unfathomable. He would get his in the end. Duke told everyone to go ahead and climb into the plane while he did his pre-flight. Patricia boarded first, followed by Kadie, Hans, Brian, and Curt. Esteban guarded Duke around the airplane during his pre-flight walk-around and monitored from a distance. Kadie looked at Duke as she entered the doorway of the King-Air, the whites of her eyes capped by drooping eyebrows. He wanted to rush over to find out what was wrong, but he knew. And he didn't want them to know how he truly felt about her. That would complicate things more than they already were. At this point, it was best to appear distant, though no doubt Curt suspected something.

Duke completed his walk around and climbed aboard the dusty King-Air. Esteban came in behind him and sat in the co-pilot seat. After both engines started, Duke taxied to the active runway, then took off to the Northwest, climbing into the darkening sky.

When the King-Air punched through the cloud deck that hovered over Northern Italy at about seven-thousand feet, Duke breathed easier. Once again, the flight plan was filed under a call-sign he used during combat operations in Iraq. He was surprised no one questioned it, despite not having flown to Italy using that call sign.

"What's going to happen when we reach Serbia?" Duke asked Esteban.

"Meaning?"

"Meaning, you guys have a lot of weapons. How do you guys expect to get them through customs?"

Esteban sneered. "Same way we have been doing it. Have the right guy meet us at the airport." The guy shifted in his seat, then adjusted his headset. "Won't be too hard. The airport will be closed when we land."

The flight seemed like it took forever. Duke kept the aircraft at ten-thousand feet for the two-and-a-half-hour flight. The tiny plane bounced and jostled for most of the trip, but he managed to avoid the thunderstorm. They landed at Nis and taxied on the blacked-out tarmac. Duke used his night-vision goggles mounted on his tactical helmet, just like he did back in Egypt. He proceeded with caution, unsure of the layout of the airfield. They shut down, and a well-worn limousine met them on the ramp. No customs, no immigration. Money had its privileges once again.

On the ride to the hotel, Duke sat next to Brian. The boy was sleepy, nodding off occasionally. Glancing at Kadie, Duke flashed her a smile as he tried to read her face. Something bothered her.

The limo pulled up to the innocuous hotel. Hans went into the lobby to fetch their room keys while the rest of the group stayed in the limo. Patricia left the passenger seat of the limo and walked around to the back and climbed inside.

"We'll be going inside soon," Patricia said. "As usual, we don't want you to make a scene. I recommend you go to your room and get some rest. We have a long day tomorrow."

"Where exactly in the hillside do you think we'll go?" Kadie asked.

"We're not going there. We're going to a museum."

"A museum?"

Patricia nodded. "The riddle of the three says there's another vase. That vase should give us the exact location of the cathedral. I'd rather explore that option first before traipsing through the hillside."

"The riddle of the three?" Duke asked. "That's the first you mentioned that." Isaac had told him about the clue with his dying breath, but he had been careful not to mention it. Now, he found out she knew anyway.

"Yes. I wasn't sure it was necessary until now. It's a legend, much like the vase and the Scroll. But we've found one of the vases. And since that vase only contained a clue, it gives credence to the riddle of the three. So, if Miss Jenkins is correct, we should find a second vase tomorrow that points us to where we will find the third."

"I don't understand," Kadie said. "Why three vases?"

"The vase we found was a decoy. Legend says you must use the other two to find the one with the Scroll, but it's hard to say. I think it was simply an afterthought. Someone during, or shortly after, Constantine's reign created the idea, so the location never got lost."

"But it did," Duke said.

Patricia's eyes narrowed. "For almost two-thousand years, but we'll learn soon enough if the legend of the Pilate Scroll is real."

Hans came back to the limousine, and the group piled out. He handed each of them a key. Brian started to walk toward Duke when Curt reached out and snatched him by the collar.

"The kid stays with me," Curt said. "Since it could be our last day tomorrow, I don't want you two getting any funny ideas."

Kadie grit her teeth and lunged at Curt, but Duke grabbed her and pulled her back. "Now's not the time," he whispered in her ear. Kadie relaxed her stance, but her eyes cut daggers through Curt.

"He's out of medication. I need to go to the pharmacy in the morning," Kadie said.

"I don't think there's a pharmacy here," Curt said. "And if there is, the odds of them having what you want is slim to none." The fake soldier steered Brian toward the front steps of the hotel, the rest of the group right behind them, with Esteban bringing up the rear.

The hotel was nothing like they had stayed in before. Opulence was not a priority today. The crew from GDI grew anxious, and their sloppiness began to show. Like a horse to water, they sensed they were close. Every action showed it. The small lobby stood about twenty feet by ten, a tiny front desk, one chair in a corner, and a dead potted plant in another. The single elevator could barely hold three people; two if they had luggage. Their rooms were all on the third floor. Patricia went up first, with Curt and Brian, followed by Hans and Kadie, then Esteban and Duke.

When Esteban and Duke reached the third floor, Hans stood outside, waiting for them, a smirk on his face. Duke walked to the room he shared with Kadie and glanced inside.

Small. Empty. The room was about twelve by twelve, he guessed. It had one bed and one dresser with a fan on top of the chest. No TV, no chair. Very Spartan. He wondered—why the switch in accommodations? Regardless, it was better than some of the facilities he had stayed at down-range.

Kadie must be in the bathroom, Duke thought. *Best to give her some privacy.* "I'll wait here for a moment."

"Go inside," Esteban shoved him in and shut the door.

Duke stumbled in and immediately bumped into the bed as the door closed behind him. As soon as the door shut, Kadie came out of the bathroom.

"I was hiding from that guy," she said. "He gives me the creeps."

Duke nodded. "Not much space," he said, looking over the room. The lone bed, the Serbian version of the king-size, was more like a double-bed in America. Not much room for two people who weren't going to be laying over each other. "I'll sleep on the floor."

"No. No need. We'll make it work."

"Thanks, but if it's all the same to you, I'd feel better about sleeping on the floor."

Kadie sighed and shrugged her shoulders. If he didn't know any better, he would say she seemed disappointed. A lifetime ago, before he had gotten married and was a different person, he would have taken her up on her offer. And he would have made advances on her she might not have been willing or able to resist. But he was a different man now—a Christian man. And he handled situations like this differently than his former self.

Kadie walked back toward the bathroom. "I'm going to take a quick shower." She paused. "I know this is awkward for you. It is for me, too. But I appreciate you being a gentleman. That's rare these days."

She closed the door behind her, and Duke reached in his backpack and pulled out his dopp-kit containing his toothbrush and toothpaste. He found an extra blanket and pillow at the top of the closet. In moments, he made himself a spot on the floor between the bed and the wall. Duke sat on the bed with his back against the headboard as he waited for Kadie to finish her shower.

Tomorrow is the day, he thought. *It's our last chance.*

54

Nis, Serbia
An unnamed hotel

The next morning, Kadie sat on the bed while Duke showered. *He's an honorable man,* she thought. So sad that he had cancer, but he seemed to manage fine. She only wished he didn't still dip that worm dirt. She wondered what he was like before he became a Christian, when he was married, a father, in the Air Force. What happened that drove her away? Was it one event, or an insidious change over time?

A few minutes later, the door opened, and Duke walked out, wearing his cargo pants with no shirt. Her mouth fell open, and she smiled briefly, her eyes drifting down. Hopefully, he didn't see her reaction.

"So, where are we going today?" Duke asked.

"The National Museum Nis." She paused. "I kind of feel like Wyatt Earp on his way to the OK Corral." Kadie raised her head back toward him.

Duke smiled. "Wyatt Earp won that fight."

"I know. I couldn't think of a better analogy." She grabbed her hair with both hands, squeezing her eyes shut. "I just feel helpless, like we're walking into our funeral."

Duke said nothing.

"You said that God had a plan," Kadie murmured. "I hope so because I don't. And I'm guessing you don't either. Please tell me we're not going to die today." Tears rolled down her cheeks.

"Hey, it's going to be okay," Duke slid next to her. He took her face in his hands and wiped the tears from her cheeks. "We are *not* going to die. You've got to have faith. I do. And I've had enough of these guys. The first chance we get, we're out of here."

"I'm worried about Brian. His Lamictal is a preventative medicine. We ran out yesterday."

"That's his seizure medication?"

Kadie nodded. "I hate myself. He has so little time left. I wanted him to experience things, live life, and be happy. I wanted that for him and look at what we've got." The tears continued to flow.

Duke attempted to comfort her with a hug. "Hey, it's not your fault. You did what you thought was the right thing. Under different circumstances, it *would* have been the right thing. No one will fault you for this." He squeezed her closer. "Who knows? When this is all over, you may have quite a story to tell."

She eased away, faked a smile, and stood. "Get dressed. I want to find some coffee before we get started."

Duke put on his shirt, socks, and boots. Once he was ready, Kadie opened the door. In the hallway, Esteban sat in a chair. A small cart sat next to him with coffee cups, a pot of coffee, and a plate of croissants.

"Morning folks," Esteban said, more sarcastic than sincere. "Hope you had a good night's sleep."

Kadie didn't answer as she poured herself a cup of coffee. She noticed no steam rose, and she sipped the bitter black liquid. "Cold," she said, looking at Duke.

"I'll pass," Duke said.

"Yeah," Esteban said. "Maybe you should have gotten up earlier."

Duke picked up a croissant. It was cold and hard. Kadie stared at him as he bit into the crunchy bread. "It's better than nothing."

Kadie grabbed one off the plate. "Where's Brian?" she asked Esteban.

The man motioned down the hall with his thumb. "305. Curt's been up a while. I imagine the kid is up as well."

Kadie marched down the hall and knocked on the door. After a moment, Curt opened it.

"My," he said, "I always imagined how you looked first thing in the morning." He eyed her up and down wantonly. "I must say you do not disappoint."

Kadie ignored him. "Where's Brian?"

"Hey, Kadie," Brian said from inside the room. He rushed to the door and pushed past Curt. Kadie's heart skipped a beat when she saw him. His eyes were red as if he'd been crying. A large bruise covered his left cheek.

"What happened?" Her mouth tightened as she turned back to Curt.

"He bumped his head on the sink last night. It's a shame he's not more careful."

Brian said nothing and clenched his teeth. Kadie had been worried that he would be mistreated. She was right. Her fists were in balls, and her body tensed. They'd sort this out later.

The five of them walked downstairs, where they met Patricia and Hans. Once again, they climbed into a limousine that waited for them out front. The city was dark and bleak. Everything seemed draped in gray hues—buildings, cars, clothes . . . it was depressing.

Twenty minutes later, they reached the National Museum Nis, which sat nestled on a street corner. The one-story façade of the museum was less than inspiring. Tall wooden double-doors with a rounded arch at the top were flanked by square columns, which, in turn, were flanked by rounded Corinthian columns. A depressing color, not quite orange, not quite red, was painted around the columns.

The museum inside was small and uninspiring as well. White marble floors, white columns, white walls, white ceiling—it was a distraction to the eye. There wasn't much inside. Just six collections comprised a little over forty-thousand artifacts. But in the back section of the museum, in the archeology collection, they found what they came for.

Several vases sat on display. Majestically placed in the center of the collection was an Aramaic vase with four handles.

"The vase is exactly like the one in Venice," Kadie said. "But the writing is in Latin."

"Must be more directions," Duke said.

Kadie nodded and turned to Patricia. "This is it."

"You're sure?"

"Yes. It has a Sator Square inscribed on the side."

Hans and Esteban surveyed the area to find out who else was in the museum. Kadie monitored Patricia and Curt cautiously. She trusted no one at this point, except for Duke. How would they get the vase out of here? And if not out of here, how could they at least look inside?

Her questions were answered when Curt walked to the front of the museum, pulled out his pistol, and shot the security guard. The report echoed throughout the museum. When the attendant at the entrance screamed, Curt shot her, too. Hans moved to the front door to guard it.

Patricia went straight for the vase. Kadie watched her closely, then checked Duke, who shook his head.

The GDI VP struggled with the vase but had no success, just like they did in the basement of Saint Mark's. Patricia's frustration built up, and she started to throw the vase on the ground.

"No," Kadie yelled, and Duke lunged for the vase, catching it before it shattered on the floor.

"This may not be the vase you're searching for," Duke said, "but it's still almost two-thousand years old."

Patricia glanced around at their surroundings. "We're in a hurry. What do you suggest?"

Duke carried the vase to a small table and set it down. "Do you have a knife?"

Patricia gave Curt a head nod in Duke's direction. Curt kept a pistol leveled at Duke with one hand while the other extended the knife.

"Look familiar?" Curt said with a devilish grin on his face.

Kadie's eyes locked on the knife. It was the same kind he threw at her head in Egypt. The same kind he opened the envelope with back in Israel. Her stomach turned in knots. Curt killed Samuel and Isaac. He had tried to kill her, too. So desperate to do so, he had chased her through the streets of Port Said—and he wanted her to know it.

Duke took the knife and proceeded to open the vase in the same manner as he did at Saint Mark's. This one appeared to be a little more difficult, but five minutes later, the lid was pulled free.

Inside, Duke retrieved another tablet, similar to the one from the first vase. Kadie's mind raced. Patricia was right—they found the second vase and another clue. How did Isaac know about the rule of three? And how did he know he needed to tell Duke? She kept those thoughts to herself but would talk it over with Duke the first chance she had.

Patricia snatched the tablet from Duke and studied it. Kadie thought it possible she might be able to decipher the message. She was a doctor; she should at least be familiar with some Latin. The GDI VP tossed the stone tablet over in her hands before handing it to Kadie.

She read the inscription, which indeed was written in Latin, then flipped the tablet over to read the other side. Unlike the tablet from Saint Mark's, this one had coherent writing on the outside. When she finished, she glanced at Duke, then turned to Patricia.

"We're in the right place," Kadie said.

55

Nis, Serbia
The National Museum Nis

Kadie continued to mull over their situation as the small group of seven marched out of the museum and piled into the limousine. Patricia was in the lead, followed by Hans, Kadie, Brian, Curt, and Duke, with Esteban bringing up the rear. Patricia pulled out a map right away, and Curt leaned over her shoulder to see what she was doing. The cathedral was just outside town, according to the map.

"We'll go back to the hotel, get a few supplies, and then head out," she said. "It isn't far from here. By this evening, we'll have the most powerful item in the universe in our hands."

Kadie frowned. "What about us?"

"Oh, you're going with us," Curt said. "Don't worry about that."

"And after?"

"There may not be an after." The GDI security man smirked at her, which made her skin crawl.

Kadie paused; Duke was right about Curt. He had been all along. What shocked her was Patricia. The woman turned out to be nothing like the warm, loving academic she made herself out to be. The thin veneer of platitudes and concern was an act. Driven blind by her ambition, Kadie was sure Patricia never saw the consequences of her actions.

The limo weaved its way through the streets and pulled up at the hotel. A Range Rover and Suburban sat out front. "Everyone out, we'll be going in those," Curt said, pointing at the sports utility vehicles. "Hans and I will go get some supplies, and we'll be right back."

"I have to go—to the bathroom," Brian said.

"You can go in the woods," Curt said.

Brian sat and looked frustrated.

"Please," Kadie said. "Let us go inside and use the bathroom. It's been a long morning, and it's going to be a longer day."

Curt snarled and turned back to Patricia, who nodded.

"We'll go back inside," Patricia said. "Same procedures. Nobody try anything stupid."

Everyone went upstairs in pairs, except for Hans, Kadie, and Duke, who went up together. Ironically, they were the first ones back down. Curt came back with Brian, and Patricia and Esteban followed shortly after them.

"Hans," Curt said, "come with me to get our supplies. The rest of you load up."

Duke scanned the streets around the front of the hotel. Empty. Where was everyone in this town? Even worse, how did they find this cesspool of a hotel far from any sign of life? Duke calculated his chances. Curt was walking back and forth from a storage room on the first floor of the hotel. He dropped off backpacks containing flashlights, canteens filled with water, and military MRE's. Hans remained in the back room, no doubt gathering supplies and giving them to Curt. That left only Patricia and Esteban to keep an eye on them. He could handle those odds. Plus, no one watched, Brian.

Curt went back into the room. Kadie and Brian went out to the limo, then Duke with Esteban behind him. Patricia lingered at the limo and spoke to the driver. They walked down the steps of the entrance. Now was his opportunity.

Duke turned and grabbed Esteban and thrust him headfirst into the doorframe. The impact sounded solid, but the move merely dazed him. Kadie turned at the noise, and her body tensed. Esteban swung wildly at Duke, who dodged it and threw a series of rapid blows to his midsection before his iron knuckles slid across Esteban's jaw, sending him sprawling.

Curt, aware of the ruckus, turned and raced down the stairs toward the door, pulling his pistol from behind him. Brian moved out of his way as Curt ran toward the fight, but slipped his foot out slightly, sending Curt face-first down the front steps of the hotel lobby, the pistol flying from his hand and sliding across the street.

Duke landed another blow to Esteban as Kadie and Brian reached the limo.

"Let's go," Duke said.

Kadie and Brian's eyes grew wide, and Duke wheeled around to see two men pointing weapons at them: a Glock 22 .40 caliber semi-automatic pistol and an AK-47 with a wood stock. Duke sighed and raised his hands slowly.

Curt pushed himself off the sidewalk, the side of his face streaked with blood. He staggered over to Duke and threw a hammer-like punch to the pilot's stomach. Duke doubled over in pain, his knees falling hard to the sidewalk.

"I was starting to think you were just a coward," Curt said. "I guess there's a little life in you after all."

Duke looked at Curt, who threw a punch across his jaw, sending him to the pavement. Kadie and Brian rushed to Duke and helped him to his feet. Duke spit blood from his mouth onto the dirty sidewalk.

Patricia walked in front of them, shaking her head. "Mister Ellsworth, you had done so well up to this point. Why do you want me to kill you now?"

"You're going to kill us anyway," Duke said.

Patricia said nothing. The two new men closed in around them, their weapons still aimed at the three of them.

"You must be the guys who followed us in the forest at Altinova," Kadie said to the two new men.

The one with the pistol nodded.

"Were you the two with crossbows who chased me in Port Said?"

He nodded again.

"And attacked us in Istanbul?" she continued.

The one with pistol nodded again, and the other one laughed.

"That was a good move on the boat," the man with the AK-47 said. "Caught us napping."

"You sound American," Kadie said.

"From Chicago."

"You two didn't think I would have more men at my disposal, did you?" Patricia said. "I sent Ray and Cliff here to Egypt once we caught onto Samuel. And they've shadowed us since Istanbul. We're at the endgame now. I brought them in for the finale."

"Thanks," Duke said.

"We'll need their help with the treasure," Curt said.

"Treasure?" Kadie said.

Patricia gave Curt an irritated stare before she turned back to Kadie. "You don't have to play dumb, my dear. The legend of the Scroll is based around the treasure. Constantine apparently tried to set up a small fund for his descendants just in case his empire crumbled around him. The legend of the Pilate Scroll says it is stored in the Cathedral of Helena, surrounded by gold, silver, and precious stones from around the world."

"You won't get any help from me," Duke said.

Curt pressed his pistol to the side of Duke's head. "Give me one reason why I don't splatter your brains on the street, right now."

"Somebody has to fly the plane," Duke said.

"Maybe." Curt leaned closer and whispered. "Maybe we don't need a plane after today."

Duke knew he was done for—assuming they found the Scroll. Curt holstered his pistol, and the two new captors shepherded the three of them into the Range Rover. Once inside, Kadie and Duke sat in the middle row, with Brian between them. Ray sat behind them. Hans and Cliff rode in the front of the Range Rover. Patricia and Curt were in the lead SUV with Esteban. Patricia said she feared Curt and Esteban might kill Duke before they got there.

Kadie could tell Brian needed his medicine. He stared straight ahead and was confused about where they were and what they were doing, both symptoms of an impending seizure. Her uneasiness garnered Duke's attention. She couldn't help it—they were in trouble. Patricia had some far-fetched scheme of cloning Jesus, and Curt Baxter was a psychopath intent on wealth. Their time left alive was limited.

THE TINY CARAVAN SPED THROUGH TOWN, AND WITHIN A FEW MINUTES, was racing through the countryside. Duke couldn't decide if the country was pretty or not. A low ceiling of clouds hung over the town and the countryside outside of Nis. The gloomy overcast painted the landscape in depressingly dark hues, resembling the environment where Hansel and Gretel might have met the witch.

It was a forty-five-minute ride, but once they reached the hills, they slowed considerably. They left the paved road and traveled on dirt roads into a small valley. The SUV bounced and banged along the dirt road; there was no telling how bad the ride in the limo would have been. After twenty minutes, they left the dirt road and rode on grass trails. Duke began to question how much longer they could do that.

Kadie stroked Brian's hair as his head rested on her shoulder. Duke smiled. She really was a good, loving, caring woman. And she was a Christian as well. If he wasn't dying of oral cancer, he might even—

BAM! The Range Rover hit a hole, and the three of them flew forward and impacted the front seat.

"Ugh!" Kadie blurted, lacing her arms over her face. Brian landed between the two with a yelp.

Hans and Cliff exited the vehicle. Hans radioed the SUV ahead while Cliff opened the back door.

"We'll walk from here," he said, pointing his pistol at them as they piled out of the back of the SUV.

They trudged along the tattered path to the Suburban, which was now two-hundred yards ahead of them. Sunlight peppered through the trees, barely lighting their trail. Esteban stood next to Curt and Patricia, who were engaged in an intense conversation regarding the hidden cathedral and what they might expect to find.

56

Nis, Serbia
The hill country

The scent of the fresh pines tickled Kadie's nostrils. Despite the cool air, sweat beaded across her forehead and the nape of her neck. She let go of Brian's hand and pulled her small elastic scrunchy off her wrist. Gathering her hair behind her head, she tied it into a ponytail.

Kadie trudged through the forest with the group, holding hands with Brian. Towering pines surrounded them as they followed the trail, which became more difficult to follow about forty-five minutes ago. The overcast cloud deck dissipated, and sunlight trickled through the dense forest, like flakes of snow for the first snowfall. The group stretched over a hundred feet as they shuffled single file and meandered through the woods. Their feet constantly slipped on the damp rocks and grass, the soles of their shoes losing the battle with Mother Nature.

Brian didn't look well and had been out of his Lamictal for two days now. His complexion started to turn pale last night and remained so today. Lack of Lamictal wouldn't do that. Maybe it was the stress. They had not talked about what was going on nor when it might be over. Brian could sense what was happening but didn't know how to communicate his thoughts. Shoot, neither did she.

She wondered whether this would be another dead end. Would they find another clue that led them somewhere else? So much information had been found, they were fortunate to piece it together the way they did. But that begged the question—did they piece it together correctly? How would Patricia and her men handle the disappointment of another setback? Clearly, they had no qualms with killing.

At the base of a small hill, Ray, the point man, stopped and hollered at Doctor Hastings. The rest of the group, Kadie included, hurried to where the man stood.

"It's the cave," Patricia said. "We've found the entrance."

"Maybe," Curt said. "Let's give it a look, shall we?"

Everyone zeroed in on Ray's position as they removed the vines and limbs that covered the entrance.

Patricia beamed from ear to ear. "Finally. This quest has taken so long." Ray worked frantically at the cave entrance to clear the debris. On his hands and knees, he shined his flashlight into the dark entrance.

"There's nothing there," Ray said. "The cave is only about five feet deep."

"Maybe the entrance collapsed," Curt said.

"You can see for yourself," he said, standing and offering Curt the flashlight. "It's a tiny natural cave. Nothing manmade about it."

Curt snatched the flashlight and knelt at the entrance. He mumbled a few unintelligible words while he peered into the cave, then pulled out and tossed the flashlight back to the man.

"Let's keep searching," Patricia said.

"Sure would have been nice to have a drone to help us find what we're searching for," Duke said as he glared at Curt. The Delta Force impersonator answered with a non-verbal gesture.

The group spread out once again. The more they wandered around, the more Kadie convinced herself this was a waste of time. The thoughts plagued her consciousness. What if they were in the wrong place?

Thirty minutes later, a voice echoed across the open field.

"I found it!" Esteban yelled on the North section of the hillside.

Once again, the group gathered at the location. This time, it looked more probable.

Kadie and Brian arrived at Esteban's location. Sure enough, it was a cave. A cave with a manmade door at the entrance about ten feet away. She inhaled deeply, mulling over the fact that she could be wrong—this might turn out to be the correct location after all.

Duke and Cliff reached the cave, followed by Curt, Patricia, then Ray. Curt pushed his way to the front.

"Has anyone tried the door?" he said.

"No," Esteban said. "I was waiting for everyone else."

"Move," Curt said, approaching the door. He eyed it curiously as if it were a puzzle to be solved. Kadie studied the exterior of the door. There didn't appear to be any cipher or cryptic writing. Curt reached for the handle, but the door was locked. He glanced back at Patricia, frustrated. Curt turned back to the door and ran his hands over it, pressing against the surface. Then, he leaned his shoulder into it. Eventually, he stepped back and kicked the door next to the lock.

His foot went through the door, ripping the lock and handle away from the doorframe. Curt pressed against the door and pushed it open, making a loud creaking noise. Kadie's nose wrinkled as a stench wafted through the entrance to the cave; worse than any garbage dump that she had been around. Whatever they uncovered didn't smell pleasant.

Duke leaned into her. "Decaying flesh, maybe? Must have been airtight in there."

Cliff slid his backpack off his shoulder and removed several flashlights, which he handed to everyone but Kadie, Brian, and Duke. Kadie wondered how they were going to resolve the unspoken issue. If there was a treasure in the cathedral, would they simply use them as pack mules to lug more riches out of the cathedral back to the SUV? With the Range Rover totaled, there definitely wouldn't be any room for extra passengers *and* treasure. They'd all be shot and left there no doubt.

The point-man turned on his flashlight. The bright LED beam made the cave appear as if it were bathed in daylight. The carved-out walls had several pictograms and symbols on the walls, but Kadie couldn't tell what era they were from. She detected a more pressing problem.

"Okay," he said with a smile. "Let's go check it out."

Kadie didn't budge. "I can see spiderwebs from here." She shook her head at Patricia. "I don't do spiders."

Ray pointed his pistol at her. "I'm afraid you do now."

She shivered and searched Duke's face for a sign that everything was going to be okay. He seemed—peaceful. Was that the sign? He seemed ready for whatever they faced. Duke took her hand in his and patted it gently before Patricia pulled her away. The two new guys led the group into the cave, then Patricia, who pulled Kadie by the arm, followed. Brian was reluctant to go, and Curt shoved him into the dark passage. Brian yelped and started to wail. Duke lunged forward and put his arm around Brian to calm him down. Curt was right on their heels; Hans and Esteban brought up the rear. After about twenty feet of descending trail, the ground they walked on gradually turned into a crude set of stairs carved into the stone.

Kadie paused on the stairs, allowing Brian and Duke to catch up. The interior of the cave was just that—a cave. Kadie thought this might be a dead-end until he heard Patricia scream. They hurried forward to see what happened. When they arrived at the crude landing on the staircase, Ray and Patricia stood over a pair of skeletons. The flesh had long ago withered away.

"How did they get here?" Kadie said.

Ray shook his head. "No telling."

Duke moved forward to examine the corpses. "How did they die?"

Curt arrived and panned his flashlight around the ground and along the walls. "Maybe some kind of boobytrap. You know, like in Indiana Jones."

"It's *Raiders of the Lost Ark*," Brian said.

"Shut up, Elmer Fudd," Curt said. "Whatever. It doesn't matter."

Kadie clenched her teeth and steered Brian away from Curt, toward the back of the group that now stretched far apart, single file down the crude staircase.

"The steps are slippery," she said to Brian.

They walked with caution until they reached the bottom of the stairs and the path leveled out. Kadie took a sip of water out of her canteen and then gave Brian some.

A loud crack came from the front of the line, but from her position, she couldn't see anything. There was just a sickening crunch echoing throughout the chamber.

"Everyone freeze!" one of the point-men yelled.

Kadie thrust her back against the cavern wall, pushing Brian back. A rolling cloud of dirt and dust swirled in the air, blinding everyone in the tunnel.

"Brian, shut your eyes and breathe through your shirt." Kadie grabbed the top of her shirt and pulled it over her mouth, filtering out the dusty air. Brian copied her actions.

It would be a few minutes before the dust settled. Nobody moved. Kadie kept her eyes closed and breathed through her shirt to keep the dust from getting in her lungs. Patricia was right in front of her, and after about a minute, she turned the corner and screamed. The others rushed forward.

Bright LED flashlights cut through the dust-filled air like laser-beams through outer-space. When Kadie edged forward around the corner, one of the point-men lay crushed underneath a large, hand-cut stone that had served as a boobytrap for the cathedral. It was Ray. Dead.

The grizzly sight was too much, and she turned into Duke, flinging her arms around his neck. He responded by wrapping his arms around her waist.

"It's going to be okay," he whispered.

Brian stared at the scene, the only visible portion of the man being his feet, like the wicked witch in *The Wizard of Oz*.

"I recommend we proceed with caution," Patricia said as she rounded the corner. She knelt and retrieved the dead man's flashlight and pistol. It was the first time Kadie ever saw Patricia carry a gun.

"Flyboy, you lead the way," Curt said, motioning with the pistol in his hand. "Just in case." Hans gave Duke a flashlight, then he gave one to Kadie, and Brian, as well. Perhaps they felt it would be safer with more eyes searching for boobytraps.

Duke looked at Kadie and moved to the front of the small group, stepping around the stone that crushed one of their captors.

"You two are next, sweetheart," Curt said, shoving her and Brian forward.

Kadie grabbed Brian's hand, and they trailed Duke down the dark passage. They aimed their flashlights ahead of Duke to help him see. The cave meandered in different directions and widened and narrowed at various spots. Occasionally, a marker carved in the stone indicated the followers of Mithras built the passage. Pictograms illustrated a rising sun, a man climbing out of a rock, a man with sunbeams radiating from his head—all pointing to Mithraism.

They stumbled across three more skeletons. Kadie suspected they were from the same group but couldn't verify it. Again, there was no way to identify how the people died.

After five minutes of walking through the small tunnel, they reached a door. Not just any door—a six-foot-tall double-door, hand-carved out of stone.

"It's not the ornate door I'd expect a cathedral to have," Duke said to her.

"Remember," Kadie said, "the cathedral was most likely built by soldiers who followed Mithras. They were known for carving their temples out of stone. The elaborate and symbolic structures you've seen built by the Catholic Church weren't built until almost a thousand years after this. So, for the time, this was quite elaborate."

Duke pointed at the standard on the door. Rows of it covered each door. "Look familiar?" he said.

"Chi-Rho," Kadie replied. Both doors were adorned with the Greek symbol referencing Jesus. Each door had twelve rows of six symbols each. She ran her fingers over one of the raised standards of Constantine and shoved the door. It didn't budge. Duke joined her and pushed, then Curt, as well as the two thugs.

"It must be locked," Patricia said, stepping back, setting her hands on her hips. "But there doesn't seem to be a keyhole anywhere." Curt gave her a look that spoke volumes. Of course, it's locked. That's why it won't open.

The phony Delta Force operative ran his hands along the seam between the two doors and along the edges of the entire doorway. He beat on the doors and hollered.

"We'll come back with dynamite," Curt said to Patricia, his frustration clouding his judgment.

"No, you won't," Duke said. "Not if you want to live."

Curt shot him a deathly look.

Duke continued. "If you try to blow anything up down here, the entire structure will most likely collapse. And the Scroll, the treasure, this entire cathedral, will be destroyed."

"Well, how do we get inside?" Curt was yelling now, his hands twirling around, making gestures that had nothing to do with their predicament. Hans examined the door while Esteban and Cliff stood near the stairs, guarding everyone.

Kadie moved away from the door, looking around at the surrounding wall. Moving toward the entrance, her foot bumped something. She whipped her flashlight beam at the ground and shrieked.

A skeleton sat leaning against the wall.

Duke and Brian rushed over.

"That's not good," Duke said.

Brian didn't seem as concerned. "Cool. Another skeleton."

Kadie slid the beam up and down the dried-up bones, the garment long rotted away. "Let's hope he just sat here too long, trying to figure out how to open it."

"Maybe he was k-killed by poison darts," Brian said with a grin.

"Not funny, Brian," Kadie said. She knew *Raiders of the Lost Ark* was one of his favorite movies, but an ancient trap had just killed a man. They were in real danger.

Duke traced his flashlight along the rock walls. "Doesn't look like there's any boobytraps built into the rock. It looks like the guy died of something else, but there's no way to tell."

They moved back to the doors and watched Curt struggle to find a way in. No one said a word for a few moments until Brian spoke up.

"I know how to open it."

Everyone stopped and looked at him. He stared at the door, his hands on his hips. The poor boy was sweating profusely, but his eyes were wide, his focus astute.

"Shut up, retard," Curt said. "I think I liked you better when you cried and didn't want to go anywhere."

Kadie ignored Curt's disgusting comment and moved toward her brother. "Brian?"

Brian looked up at her, as serious and confident as she'd ever seen him. "It is like the clue said—Alpha and Omega."

"Alpha and Omega?"

Brian nodded enthusiastically. "Yes—Alpha and Omega. The beginning and the end—the first and last."

Kadie shook her head and looked at Duke, who shrugged his shoulders. She turned back to Brian. "I don't understand."

Brian walked between the people blocking his access to the doors. "Alpha and Omega. The beginning and the end—first and last."

He reached up to the top left of the door to the first standard. After working his hand along the surface and around the circumference, they heard a loud click. He then moved to the next door on the bottom right, bent down, and worked that standard the same way. Again, a loud click and the two doors opened inward slightly.

Everyone, including Curt, stared at Brian, this time with admiration.

"Way to go," Duke said, giving Brian a fist-bump.

Brian responded with his fist and blushed. "Thanks, Duke."

Kadie ran her fingers through his hair, and he giggled and batted her hand away.

"Enough of the feel-good, lamentations," said Curt, shoving Duke in the back. "It's time to put your money where your mouth is."

Kadie and Duke looked at each other. *I don't know whether to laugh or cry,* she thought. She started to smile but contained it. Kadie pushed the door open and stepped confidently through, her flashlight cutting into the darkness. The door creaked on the ancient hinges that hadn't moved in centuries.

"Keep an eye out for more boobytraps," Duke said with a chuckle. But it wasn't a joke.

She was worried about the same thing.

57

Nis, Serbia
The cave entrance to Helena's hidden cathedral

This portion of the cave had a stuffy, musty scent. Kadie stepped through the doorway, panned her flashlight around the small enclosure, and sighed heavily. This situation has turned out to be one new puzzle after another, and she was well past her tolerance level. The only thing that kept her going was the safety of her brother. Instinctively, she crawled against the wall. Brian and Duke trailed her.

She traced the beam of her flashlight around the next room. The space was taller than the one outside. In front of her, an intricately carved wooden door curved at the top in the form of an arch. The walls on either side of the door were only five feet wide, and again, only the rock wall of the mountain made up the sides and top of the room. This must be the entrance to the cathedral.

Kadie found an ancient torch mounted against the wall. Shining her flashlight beam on the tip, it was clear the torch had been used in the past.

"Anybody have a lighter?" she said.

The goon behind Brian stuck his hand into his pocket and handed the lighter to Kadie. She sparked the lighter, and a flame danced out of the top. Kadie stood on her tiptoes and stretched to light the torch. The flame caught right away, and the blaze illuminated the space far better than their flashlights.

"We might need this," she said to Duke.

"I'll get it," he said.

Duke pulled the torch free from its mount. A loud grinding sound shattered the silence, followed by a scream that became more distant by the second.

When they whipped around to face the threat behind them, all the group was accounted for except one. Hans was gone; his weapons lay next to a massive hole in the center of the floor. Duke shuffled to the edge and stuck the torch over the middle, but that didn't do much of anything. Kadie pulled up next to him and shone her flashlight down the hole. It was deep. Too deep to see anything the LED flashlight beam could reach. There were no sounds coming from the pit, either. With their numbers decreasing rapidly, Kadie wondered if any of them would ever get out.

The tiny group gathered around the hole. Peering into the abyss, they realized that saving Hans was impossible. Curt was the first to step away, and he grabbed Kadie by the upper arm.

"Come on, sweet cheeks," he said and shoved her forward. "You can lead the way."

Kadie grimaced at him and tried the door handle. Hmm, unlocked.

She opened the door and peered inside behind the high-powered flashlight.

"Is it safe?" Patricia asked through the door opening.

Kadie glanced over her shoulder and nodded. "It looks like more of the same. There's another door. But this one is wooden."

Patricia and Curt poked their heads in and used their flashlights to search the new space.

"See if it's unlocked," Patricia said to Kadie as she edged toward the wooden door.

Kadie turned without acknowledging and walked to the door. Her hand shook as she grasped the handle, which was a large circular piece of iron that hung waist high on the door. With the iron ring firmly in her hand, she gave the handle a good tug and the door opened outward. The rusty hinges gave way with a loud groan, just like the stone doors they had found earlier. The seal the stone doors created must have preserved the integrity of this wooden door over time.

Shifting the flashlight beam into the new room, she stepped inside. The bright LED flashlight cut through the darkness like a hot knife through a stick of butter. What she saw took her breath away.

They found it—the Cathedral of Helena.

Her heart raced, and her skin tingled as she stood inside what resembled an ancient cathedral. Not the glorified cathedrals lined with ornate statues and gold trim, but a cathedral from the fourth century. One designed and built during Constantine's reign, but vastly more stunning.

The doorway led to the center aisle of the cathedral. The pews were simple stone benches, but they were hidden. No, not hidden—covered. Covered with riches so vast, she thought she was on the set of a movie. Her flashlight raced over various treasures: statues, staffs, trunks overflowed with gold coins, precious stones, fine linens draped from one row to another. And vases. Hundreds of vases spread around the cathedral.

Her initial assessment was the church was unfinished, and she was right. As she walked her beam around, she could see the ceiling had yet to be completed further toward the front.

"Holy smokes," Duke said behind her. She saw another flashlight beam dance around the room. Then another and another, until seven total beams explored the interior of the cathedral.

Kadie found a bowl near the entrance; liquid pooled almost to the rim. Holy Water? Dipping her finger in the liquid, she rubbed the viscous substance with her thumb and forefinger, then sniffed it. Oily. Definitely not Holy Water. She glanced at Duke. "Well, here goes nothing."

She took the torch from Duke and dipped the flaming end into the liquid, igniting the bowl. Instantly, the bowl erupted in flame, illuminating the back of the church. On the other side of the aisle, she found another bowl and lit that one. Esteban took the torch from her and scurried to the front of the church, lighting every bowl filled with oil he could find. In minutes, the interior of the cathedral bristled with illumination, the firelight dancing off the golden treasures within. Esteban returned, giddy as a schoolboy.

Curt, Esteban, and Cliff talked excitedly back and forth, unfazed by the fact their team had been reduced by forty percent.

Kadie watched them grow more and more animated as they talked. She sensed their situation was about to take a turn for the worse.

She was right.

58

Nis, Serbia
Inside the Cathedral of Helena

Patricia stood in the center aisle of the ancient cathedral, her heart pounding. She couldn't believe she found it. The treasure was more than she imagined when Graham Thorndike first proposed the project to her. She had seen movies where the hero and heroine find the cavern filled with riches; sure, the fictional representation has been impressive. But nothing compared to the real thing. She caught herself being distracted from why they were here in the first place. They were here for the Scroll.

She pulled her eyes away from the glorious treasure before them and focused on Kadie. The girl looked gorgeous in the flickering firelight, but her attention was on something other than the treasure. Kadie stared at Curt and his men. Patricia realized she might have a problem on her hands.

The two men seemed to be arguing with Curt. No, they weren't arguing, they were—negotiating? No, they were coming up with a plan, and a moment later, Curt looked at Patricia and nodded. The two men followed his gaze to her.

Curt left the men and approached Patricia.

"We're going to be rich," Curt said behind her. He had lost focus of his role. Hidden treasure tended to do that.

"Let's not forget what we came here for," Patricia said, but her eyes sparkled at the treasures before her. "We are here for the Pilate Scroll. We've got to search for it. That's what Mister Thorndike is paying us for."

"Well, that's part of the problem. Mister Thorndike isn't here, and your girl and her pilot friend can look for the Scroll. Me and the boys have made a decision."

"Have you now?"

"We figured, considering what we've found—fifty-grand isn't quite enough to cover our time and trouble for this little trip. It's time to renegotiate our contract."

A crisp smile streaked across her face. "Did you tell your men that you're making ten times that for this little trip?"

Curt shook his head. "No need to rub it in. We're here to finish the job. We're well aware of what Mister Thorndike said. But the boys think we should be able to keep anything we can carry out of here."

Patricia crossed her arms. This was completely against Mister Thorndike's orders. Any treasure was to be explicitly claimed on behalf of Alligynt. Something to do with the legalities of individuals transporting the treasures out of one country back to the United States. She figured it was to cover the costs of the massive expedition. The amount of the treasure here made her believe there was more than enough for Alligynt.

"Do they now?"

"Yes." Curt paused. "And I agree with them." He turned and motioned with his arm across the expanse of the church. "Look at all this. We all can carry as much as we can out of here, and Mister Thorndike won't miss a thing. Besides, if we don't find the Aramaic Vase with the Scroll in here, we all, including you, go home with nothing."

"What about our guests?" She glanced at Kadie, her brother, and the pilot.

"We can use them to carry our treasure to the Suburban. After that, they're dead weight and will occupy space in the car. I'll kill the pilot and the retard, no problem. I figured I might have to fight you over the girl." He sneered at his comment.

"No need to be sarcastic," Patricia said.

She mulled the words in her head as she gazed across the ancient cathedral. Yes, finding hidden treasure did change things. And it wasn't like she had a choice. They weren't asking her permission—they were letting her know the rules had changed. It was the only way, at this point, that she could maintain some semblance of control.

Plus, she finally began to admit to herself, she wasn't going to leave here empty-handed. Her goal when this journey began was career enhancement, triggered by the fame and fortune that would come from the discovery of the DNA of Jesus of Nazareth. If they didn't leave here with that, there would be no career enhancement or fame. She would have to settle on the fortune that she could carry out of here.

"Okay," she said. "You've got a deal."

59

Kadie had remained frozen in her position. She could only imagine what was being said. But whatever it was, she knew it wasn't good for the three of them. Patricia and Curt finished their discussion, and Curt gave his men a thumbs up, and the two captors ran past her, gleefully exploring the contents of their discovery.

"Start looking for the vase," Curt said as he strutted past her.

Kadie watched him wander off to the left side of the cathedral. Duke and Brian walked up behind her.

"I guess they renegotiated their contract," Duke said.

"Looks that way." Kadie placed her arm around Brian.

"So, we found it?" Duke said.

Kadie nodded. "This is the Cathedral of Helena. The interior appears to be incomplete. Perhaps when she died, Constantine stopped working on it."

"Why would you say that?"

"I don't know—just a hunch. You know, when Helena went on her quest to the Holy Land, she did it to get away from the empire. She was heartbroken by a series of events."

"I guess everyone has their problems," Duke said.

"Constantine must have built this cathedral to prove to his mother that she was still the most important person in his life. To build this in the town where she was from, where he was born, speaks volumes. Most likely, neither of them ever set foot in here. But the treasures he stored here . . . I don't know if it was to pay for the place to be built, or to store things for a rainy day."

"I'm thinking a little of both," Duke said. "The vase. Is it here?"

"I hope so," she paused. "For all our sakes." Her eyes scanned the vast interior. The underground cathedral was massive, almost three-quarters the size of Saint Mark's. It would take some time to search this place.

"Why don't we split up?" Duke said. "We'll cover more ground that way. If you find the vase, don't call out. Come get me, and we'll check it out together."

Kadie nodded.

"Brian, you go with your sister. Keep her safe."

"Okay—Duke."

Duke split off to the right, and Kadie and Brian began to search on the left. Kadie took a moment to explain to Brian the size and shape of the vase they searched for. He reminded her he had seen the vase in the museum earlier. Vases were tucked away in every nook and cranny in the cathedral. Occasionally, she checked on Duke across the church. He searched as desperately as they did.

Their captors, however, seemed oblivious to their actions. Even Patricia and Curt were swept up in the emotional upheaval that comes with the discovery of a fortune in hidden treasure. Was it possible they might forego their original plan? Creating clones from human DNA had been experimented on for decades. To create a clone of Christ seemed so . . . unholy. She said a silent prayer and begged God to forgive her, Brian, and Duke for their role in this diabolical scheme.

A few rows ahead of her, Curt's eyes bulged, and a devilish smile stretched across his face. He emptied his backpack and began to fill it with gold coins. The fake soldier lifted his backpack and cursed aloud when he realized it was too heavy for him to carry a long distance. He removed some of the contents, then took the backpack to the entrance and set it on the ground. Curt gave Kadie an unassuming glance as he walked by. He was preoccupied with his newfound riches.

At the front of the cathedral, Patricia wandered to the left transept, acquiring several small gold statues, plates, and cups. Esteban and Cliff hastily collected their booty without being so selective. Kadie thought the two henchmen seemed uninterested in the three of them right now. Greed tended to change people, but unfortunately, in the end, the ones with the guns tended to win.

The search went on for ten minutes when she felt a tap on her shoulder. Duke stood behind her, his forefinger to his lips. She got the message. Duke found the vase. Kadie turned and walked to Brian and whispered in his ear to follow her and Duke.

The trio moved two-thirds of the way toward the front on the right side. There, hidden in plain sight, was an ancient, two-and-a-half-foot tall vase with four handles and Aramaic writing on the outside. Just like the previous two vases, this one also had a Sator Square underneath the inscription, but this Sator Square was different. Hand-carved with a different tool than was used for the Aramaic inscription. This Sator Square was added after the fact to help identify its importance.

Kadie smiled. "You found it," she said.

Duke nodded. "What does the writing say? The same as the other two?"

"No, the text is different." Kadie read over the inscription, then reread it, just to be sure. "It says, *For Emperor Tiberius. The manuscript within is written by my hand. May you read and comprehend. Pontius Pilate, Governor of Judah.*"

Kadie looked over her shoulder to check on their captors. They were all still absorbed in collecting their treasure, even Patricia. She was surprised the executive was so easily distracted, but then again, the treasure was tempting. With the vase in their possession, now was the time to escape. She watched Curt continue to move bags of gold coins near the entrance of the cathedral but looked in their direction every time he dropped off a bag at the door. There was no way they could escape without getting shot before reaching the entrance. But even if they reached the door, they'd have to race through the tunnel, and if they made it through the tunnel, they'd be stuck in the forest. Her eyes watered as she thought of the fate they faced. She turned back to Duke, who struggled with the lid. "Can you open it?"

"The lid is secured like the other two. The problem this time is I don't have my Gerber."

"I have a knife," Brian said and pulled a beautiful double-edged blade with gold grip from his pocket. Kadie shook her head and smiled. He must have picked it up as they searched. Smart boy.

Duke chuckled and took the knife. He worked the blade in the seam, around the edge, until the lid began to creep up. The lid slid up quickly. His experience with the two previous vases had paid off.

Kadie moved closer as he finished. Gradually, the lid popped free with a deep hiss as oxygen entered the vase for the first time in at least eighteen hundred years. Duke rested the lid against a wall and peeked inside.

60

Kadie moved closer, her head hovering over Duke's right shoulder. Duke turned his head to her and smiled. "I think we found the Pilate Scroll," he whispered.

He reached inside and pulled out a cloth-covered object.

"Is that a blanket?" she said.

Duke held the white cloth with blue trim in his hands. "No, it's a Jewish prayer shawl. I'm willing to bet this prayer shawl belonged to Jesus. Claudia must have taken it from the guards before they tortured him."

"It looks brand new."

"Must be a heck of a vase." Duke shrugged his shoulders, unwrapped the shawl, and gave it to Kadie, who turned and handed it to Brian.

"Hold this," she said. "We don't want to lose it."

Kadie looked back at Duke, who held a scroll in his hands. The Scroll consisted of two dowels with the papyrus rolled on each stick, meeting toward the middle. The Scroll also appeared to be new. At least, as new as a scroll could look in biblical times.

Duke had a smile on his face as he passed the Scroll to Kadie. "Here you go. It's what we've been searching for."

Kadie flashed a smile. "I know. It's what happens next that concerns me."

Duke nodded. His grim expression said everything. "Hebrews 11:1."

Confidence in what we hope for and assurance about what we cannot see. Kadie hoped God had a plan because Duke didn't, and neither did she.

A ribbon wrapped around the center of the two dowels of the rolled-up Scroll kept them together. The clasp of the ribbon contained a small metal emblem with *Chi-Rho* engraved on the surface.

"Constantine's standard," Kadie said. Duke and Brian nodded. "He must have placed this seal on the Scroll when he read it."

Carefully, she removed the metal clip and ribbon and slipped it into her pocket. When she unrolled the Scroll, her eyes grew wide. The text was handwritten in Latin, the ink still bold and vibrant. The papyrus looked so new; she could see how it had been intricately woven together.

"Well?"

Kadie unrolled the lengthy scroll to the point where she could read the entire message. Her eyes danced across the page.

Noble Excellency,

Greetings! I pray this letter finds you in good health. There has been much upheaval in the state of Israel as of late. One of their own, a prophet named Jesus, a Nazarene, claimed to be the son of the Jewish God. Such a claim created an uproar amongst the elders of the Jews. He was brought before me, and they insisted he be crucified. After much debate and internal struggle, I granted the wishes of the elders and washed my hands clean of their efforts.

My wife had recently converted to a follower of The Way, the religious doctrine this Nazarene professed. She had a fatal illness, and despite that, received dreams about this prophet and the persecution he faced from his people. While the prophet was under arrest, my wife spoke to him, and he blessed her. We don't know why or how, but her illness went away.

She begged me to spare the prophet, but the decision had been made. The prophet Jesus was crucified and died on the cross. The earth physically shook when he died, cracking the ground beneath him. I saw it myself. He was buried in a tomb, and because there were rumors that he would rise from the dead, I posted guards outside his tomb. These men were some of my finest, as we could not have someone steal away his body.

Yet within three days, the prophet's body disappeared. His followers claimed he rose from the dead. This was impossible, I thought. But my soldiers never saw anyone enter the tomb, or the prophet's body removed. Over the next few days, my wife explained the premise of this "Way." I believe this is what saved her. To learn more about this prophet Jesus, I sought out his followers. Several weeks after the disappearance of the body, I found his Disciples meeting on a hill outside Jerusalem. I approached them and inquired about this man Jesus. They claimed they had seen him on several occasions prior, risen from the dead. While I was with them, something happened that can only be described as miraculous.

Jesus, the prophet I had condemned to death weeks before, appeared on the hill with us. I personally verified the holes in his hands and his side from his crucifixion. We ate, and the Nazarene told his followers they would receive the Holy Spirit. When we finished, Jesus rose into the sky and disappeared into a cloud.

I was stunned. Everything the followers said about him was true. This man had been crucified by my hand, yet three days later rose from the dead. I saw the man die on the cross, yet I saw him standing among his followers several weeks later. The prophet had no animosity or anger toward me. He forgave me for doing, in his words, what was necessary.

Jesus of Nazareth truly is the Son of God. That experience persuaded me also to become a follower of The Way and the son of the one true God. I urge you to share this message with the people of the Roman Empire.

Pontius Pilate, Prefect of Israel

. . .

Tears streamed down Kadie's face; Duke and Brian moved in front of her. Brian wiped the tears from her face with the corner of the shawl.

"What's wrong?" Duke said.

"I've been such a fool my entire life. I let my pride rule my actions." She sobbed heavily. "I've wasted so much time. Will God ever forgive me for being such a sinner?"

Duke put his arm around her. "That's kind of what this is all about, isn't it?" He put both hands on her shoulders and gazed into her eyes. "It's not how you start, Kadie. It's how you finish."

Brian held her hand. "What does it say?" he said.

Kadie told them what the Scroll said, and that she believed it to be authentic.

"I wish Mac was here to see this," Duke said.

Kadie nodded.

"How come it looks so new?" Duke said.

Kadie shook her head. "I don't know." She glanced at the shawl that Brian had draped around his shoulders. "Perhaps something inside the vase preserved the papyrus and the shawl."

"But you're sure the Scroll is authentic?"

"Yes. If it's a fake, it's the best fake in the history of deception. Every detail is perfect for the period." She paused. "Duke, we've got to figure out what to do. This finding must be shared with the world. This is proof that a real and significant historical figure was an eyewitness to both the crucifixion and resurrection of Jesus Christ. Pontius Pilate saw the wounds in Jesus' hands, feet, and side just as Thomas did. This—this will change everything."

Duke nodded. "I agree, but we've got to get out of here first. Alive. And we've got to take this with us."

"I don't think you need to worry about that," they heard from behind them. Kadie recognized the voice immediately.

She turned to see Patricia, a wry smile on her face, pointing a pistol at them.

61

Kadie stared down the barrel of the Kimber 1911 pointed at her. The chrome-plated pistol glistened in the flickering sheen of firelight. It resembled a cannon at a firing squad —out of place in her tiny hands.

"Well," Patricia said, "it seems you found what we're searching for." Her tongue wet her lips, and her eyes never moved from the Scroll. Several heavy gold necklaces she found in the church hung around her neck, and her pockets bulged with treasures.

Kadie gave a hesitant nod.

"Give it to me."

Cautious, Kadie handed the Scroll to Patricia. The executive vice president of GDI unrolled it in both hands; the pistol still clasped within her right. The woman's eyes danced around the ancient papyrus and examined the dowels. She rolled it back up and tucked it under her arm.

"It' a fake," she said.

Kadie shook her head. "I don't think so. The construction is too perfect for that era."

"It looks brand new. The Pilate Scroll is almost two-thousand years old." She pulled the Scroll out with her free hand. "This is not that old."

"Patricia, this is the document—"

"Stop playing games with me." Her voice raised several octaves. "The dowels are supposed to be coated with amber. There's nothing like that here."

"But that's a legend. It doesn't mean that's what it actually is."

"The dowels are made from the cross Jesus was crucified on," she screamed. "The DNA of the most popular man in world history is embedded within the dowels of the Pilate Scroll. These appear like they were purchased at an arts and crafts store."

Kadie studied the ends of the dowels extending from the Scroll. They were hand-carved and skillfully sanded. Custom fitted and sturdy, far from anything that could be bought in a store. Patricia's expectations were clearly something else. The older woman aimed her pistol at Kadie.

"I'm tired of you screwing around. You're going to tell me the location of the Pilate Scroll, or I'll shoot you all right here."

The woman was serious but delusional. How was *she* supposed to know the location of the Scroll? Did Patricia think they brought a substitute with them and swapped it out? Kadie glanced at Duke, who focused on the pistol. She turned to look at Brian, who's eyes were glassy and unfocused.

"Brian?" Kadie's heart skipped a beat. He was unresponsive.

"Uuuuungh." It was only a sound, but a sound she'd heard many times before. His body became rigid for a few seconds, then convulsed. He fell, his head impacting the stone wall with a loud smack. Kadie raced toward him as he collapsed. She grabbed him before he hit the ground.

"Oh, please," Patricia said. "Save the theatrics for someone else."

"He's having a seizure," Kadie said. *How long has it been since he'd had any Lamictal?* She laid Brian on the hard floor of the cathedral. A small gash oozed blood on the right side of his head, dripping down his face. She put him gently on the ground, whispering words of comfort while his body shook for a few more seconds.

Dear Lord, don't let the poor boy die here. Not like this. Not now.

As Kadie turned back to Patricia, Duke rushed toward the GDI executive VP. She whirled the pistol in his direction and squeezed the trigger.

BOOM!

The roar of the .45 caliber round echoed across the underground church. Duke lunged at Patricia as she fired. His face flinched as the bullet ripped into his arm, spewing blood from the wound. His momentum thrust him forward, and he was on top of her in a flash. Duke knocked the gun out of her hand and reached for the Scroll, but the pain in his arm seemed to keep him from putting up much of a fight.

Patricia wrestled away from the wounded pilot and ran to the pulpit. Duke spied her pistol on the floor and dove for it just as her accomplices stopped what they were doing across the cathedral. Esteban was on top of him immediately, wielding a jewel-encrusted sword. Duke swung the .45 caliber in his direction and fired. The sound reverberated again throughout the church as the man crumpled to the ground, dead.

Kadie could feel the vibration of the shot in her feet, her ears ringing from the noise.

Curt and Cliff opened fire in their direction. Every pull of the trigger multiplied the sounds from the excellent acoustics inside the church. Duke took cover behind one of the royal chairs and a chest filled with treasures. Kadie shielded Brian as best she could. She jerked her head to the right when a small piece of the ceiling fell a few feet from her.

There was another loud crack, and both Kadie and Duke looked upward. The ceiling began to split from one side to the other.

"Duke, the ceiling is collapsing," she said.

"Yeah, I see that."

DUKE SHIFTED HIS GAZE FROM THE CEILING AND PEERED AROUND THE edge of the stone pew. Cliff stepped away from the ceiling debris. He wandered aimlessly in the open, exposed; his side bled profusely, his weapon still clenched in his hands. He must have been struck by something that fell from the ceiling, the gaping wound causing him to lose focus.

Unseen by the thug, Duke took aim. Despite the "fire lamps" in the cathedral, it was a challenge to line up the sights on the 1911. *This would be an excellent time for night-vision sights*, he thought. *Who buys a Kimber 1911 and doesn't put night-vision sights on the thing?* With the forward and aft sights centered on the thug, Duke squeezed off three more shots. Cliff's chest exploded as the .45 caliber slugs ripped into him. His rifle clattered on the ground as he curled over and collapsed.

Curt swung his rifle in Duke's direction and started spitting hot lead. Duke dove to the floor, rolled under a stone bench, and crawled forward as deadly 7.62 rounds peppered the stonework around him. He flinched and yelped when he rolled on top of the bullet wound in his arm. *Won't make that mistake again*, he thought. Duke then ejected the magazine to check his ammo—a double-stack, thank God. Eight more rounds.

The ceiling continued to crack and crumble, its stability worried Duke. They needed to get out of there fast. Every time someone pulled the trigger in this underground cathedral, they created a cascading series of sounds, all of which deteriorated the structural integrity of the ceiling.

Duke checked Kadie and Brian. They still hugged the floor, though it appeared they were uninjured from this firefight. He couldn't tell Brian's condition, but it didn't look like he was moving. The space shook with every shot fired in the underground church, which meant only one thing.

"Kadie, we've got to go!"

"We need the Scroll!" she hollered back.

Duke could see Patricia hiding behind the ancient pulpit; the Scroll still clutched in her hands.

Having failed to hit Duke, Curt changed his position to get a better shot. This left him briefly exposed, and Duke squeezed off a few rounds in his direction. The powerful 1911 spewing lead sent Curt back behind his cover. A glance at Patricia confirmed she had yet to move. Duke started to holler at Kadie when the floor vibrated. The floor to the cathedral rumbled, and treasures stacked in the pews tumbled to the floor as more chunks fell from the ceiling. His mind reeled at what was happening when a loud, roaring rumble ripped through the cathedral. That could only be one thing.

Earthquake.

62

Debris rained around them and Kadie shoved Brian under the bench as the floor shook. She knew exactly what was happening, having been in an earthquake in Mexico City at age ten. The feeling of helplessness was something she had never forgotten; the terrifying experience seared into her consciousness.

Patricia screamed as the earth made a giant ripping sound. Vast sections of the ceiling crashed to the floor around them. The entire section of the cathedral where Curt had been, was destroyed and the shooting stopped. A deep crevice lay in its place, filled with rubble.

When Duke's head popped up above the stone pews between them, Kadie must have smiled because he grinned back at her before returning his attention to Patricia.

"She's gone," he said.

Duke stood and bolted to where the pulpit once stood while Kadie struggled to lift Brian off the floor. The poor boy was semi-conscious and couldn't keep his eyes open. They clamored to their feet and limped to the center aisle, where Kadie sat Brian at the end of the pew. Kadie rushed to where Duke lay on his stomach, looking down into the crevice.

She reached the front of the church and glanced in the direction where Curt had shot at them from. He was nowhere to be seen. The massive crevice ran from his side of the cathedral to the front where Patricia had been. Peering into the giant crack in the earth, she found Patricia clinging to the side of the crevice. One hand tightly gripped the Scroll, the other, hung on to the jutting rock.

"Patricia, give me your hand." Duke reached over the edge, straining to get closer to her.

"I-I can't," she cried.

Kadie knew Patricia couldn't remain there much longer, particularly if there were another tremor. "Patricia, hand me the Scroll," she said. "You need to use both hands to get out."

The executive vice-president of GDI shook her head. The fool.

"Give me the Scroll so Duke can pull you out," Kadie said, reaching deep into the crevice. Duke stretched for her, finally grabbing the arm that held the Scroll.

Huge pieces of the ceiling and the earth above crashed to the floor of the church. Duke pulled upward, and Patricia managed to get footing higher in the crevice.

"We don't have time," Duke said. Patricia was closer now, allowing him to grab her other arm and pull her up to the ledge. With Kadie's help, they pulled her and the Scroll to safety. Another ripping sound above and more debris fell on the spot where Curt had shot at them. Duke rolled in that direction to check the damage, and suddenly there was Curt standing over him. The GDI security man aimed his pistol at Duke's head, and Kadie screamed. Suddenly, a bright, white light burst through the darkness in the ceiling, blinding her.

KADIE SCREAMED, AND DUKE SHIFTED HIS FOCUS FROM THE PISTOL pointed at his head to her. She was looking toward the ceiling of the cathedral, but he couldn't see what she saw in the darkness. There were more screams, and Duke turned back as Curt's pistol fell to the floor. Curt shook violently as light emanated from his eyes and mouth as if his body cooked from the inside. The blood-curdling scream that Curt let loose was cut off, and the light became beams shooting out of his body, extending four to six feet in every direction. Static electricity raced around his body for a few seconds, then the beams stopped. Curt stared at Duke, his eyes pleading, the internal pain he experienced unbearable.

Duke wanted to jump to his feet and punch the guy, but whatever —or whoever—was killing him wanted him to suffer. Veins in Curt's neck, face, and forehead abnormally pulsated. He moved a hand toward his head, his mouth open; attempting to scream yet unable, his eyes wide with shock. His hand started to disintegrate, the ash of what was once his body falling to the ground. He was being killed slowly and forced to watch it. Even worse, he was being forced to comprehend it. A fitting death for such an evil man.

Duke turned back toward Patricia, who experienced the same fate. The Scroll lay still at her feet and appeared to glow. Duke reached his hand out to grab it but jerked it back as the glow intensified. In a matter of seconds, the Scroll disappeared or disintegrated. He wasn't sure of anything other than it was gone.

The walls of the cathedral seemed to peel away as the collapse of the structure increased. With no more time to waste, Duke pulled Kadie to her feet, the wound in his arm aching as he did. She froze when the second tremor ripped through the church.

"Kadie, come on," he said. He rushed to the center aisle to grab Brian when he realized she wasn't behind him. She stood frozen right where he had left her. He hurried back, grabbing her upper arms in his hands, and studied her face. It was if she were looking through him. "Kadie, are you okay?"

Kadie wrestled free, her fingers splayed and her hands in front of her. She shook her head, her eyes staring in the distance. "I-I can't see."

"I've got you." Duke grabbed her hand and towed her to where Brian sat. She struggled to keep up with him, stumbling with every other step.

"The light—the light blinded me."

Duke didn't have time to argue—or judge. He didn't know what light she was talking about. Maybe she was struck on the head or got something in her eyes, but it didn't matter—they needed to escape now, or they would all end up dead.

"The Scroll?" Kadie said. "Where is it?"

"It's gone," Duke said. "We've got to get out of here. Wait here. I'll get Brian."

Duke knelt by Brian. The young man was unresponsive. Not wasting any time, Duke picked up Brian in a fireman's carry over his shoulders, the pain in his arm making him groan out loud. Something sharp poked him in the shoulder, and he set Brian back down. The boy had the gold-handled knife in his pocket. Duke removed the knife and stuck it into his cargo pants, then lifted Brian back up in the fireman carry. Once Brian was on his shoulders, Duke realized the prayer shawl from the vase was missing. No time to search for it now.

"Kadie, we're right in front of you. Reach out and grab the back of my belt." He felt her grasp behind him. "Don't let go. We've got to get out now."

"Where is everyone else?"

"Gone."

"They left?"

"No, they're dead."

Kadie paused as her grip tightened on his belt. "Can you see?" she said.

"Yes, let's go."

Duke led her along the center aisle, now littered with debris and fallen treasure. He talked her over and around obstacles as they went. They reached the tall, double-wooden doors, and a loud rumble again occurred behind them. In front of them was the pit that claimed one of GDI's men. The ledge on the sides was big enough to walk by, but with him carrying Brian and leading Kadie, it was risky.

"Kadie, we're approaching the pit outside the cathedral, remember?"

"Yes."

"Okay. I'm gonna walk slow. We're gonna stay as close to the side as possible. Take small steps and be careful."

"All right."

Duke shuffled cautiously along the side of the pit. It was about ten by ten feet. He tried to use his right hand to grab anything on the side of the cave. It didn't help much.

He felt a tug on his back and a quick yelp from Kadie, then a greater tug.

"Ouch!"

He swayed as he started to lose his balance but managed to hug the wall. Kadie must have stepped off the ledge. "You okay?"

"Yeah. I slipped and smacked my knee."

Duke took a deep breath. They were in a precarious situation. If she stumbled into the pit, she'd take him and Brian with her. There was nothing Duke could do to prevent them from falling in. "Take your time and try to stand back up. The ledge we're on is about two feet wide. Let me know when you're ready to move again."

"Okay."

Duke held his breath as she tugged on the back of his belt. He sensed she was positioning herself closer to the wall, and he breathed easier when he heard her sigh.

"I'm ready," she said.

"We're halfway there. Try to hug the wall. I'm gonna go slow, okay?"

"Okay."

"Let me know when you're ready to start moving." Duke hoped it was soon. The entire underground structure was shaking, and they didn't have much longer.

"I'm ready," she said.

They shuffled along the edge again. Slower than he wanted, but more cautious. After a few more seconds, they cleared the pit.

"Okay, we're past it," he said, and they picked up their pace.

Duke felt like Lot and his family racing out of Sodom, and he wasn't about to become a pillar of salt. As they hurried through to the stone door that brandished the *Chi-Rho* symbols, it sounded like the entire ceiling of the cathedral collapsed. The force of the destruction blew dirt, dust, and debris out the doors, through the small holding area and stone door, past them and up the first ten steps.

Duke covered his face as the dust cloud engulfed them but continued forward. He kept his pace until he reached the first step of the stairs. Kadie still clung on to his belt, and he shifted Brian on his shoulders.

"We're at the staircase," Duke said. "I'm going to try not to go too fast."

"I'm right here."

His foot found the first slippery step, and he began his climb. After the first few steps, he grunted, the weight of Brian starting to take its toll. He tried to open his eyes every few steps. The dust cloud gradually decreased, and eventually, the light from the entrance outside beckoned him forward.

There hadn't been any rumbling since the ceiling collapsed, but he feared another earthquake tremor. Were those even common in this part of the world? He struggled up the steps, past the landing, and finally reached the slight ramp that led to the entrance.

They reached the outside, and when the fresh air tickled his face, he smiled briefly.

"Thank God," Kadie said. "We made it."

Duke didn't slow his pace. "We've got to get Brian to a hospital. You, too. You must have gotten some debris in your eyes."

Kadie didn't say anything as they picked up the pace along the trail in the forest. They stumbled continuously in the high grass, falling victim to dense roots and large branches alike. Five minutes later, they reached the Suburban.

"We're here," Duke said. "You can let go while I stick Brian in the backseat." He felt Kadie release his belt, and Duke bent over to stand her brother up against the side of the SUV. The weight off his shoulders made him feel much better, but his arm was growing numb from the wound. Opening the door, he helped the semi-conscious Brian into the seat and buckled him in. He took Kadie by the hand and walked her around to the other side. She had a pleasant calm about her as if she'd accepted her condition. Duke opened the door for her, and she climbed in.

"I've got this," she said as she moved into the seat next to her brother and buckled in. Duke grinned. She was a tough one, unwilling to let someone do something she could do herself, even when she couldn't see.

He shut the door and hurried into the front seat. His eyes searched everywhere. Uh-oh.

"Do you have any keys?" Kadie said.

"No."

"What are you going to do?"

"Improvise."

Using the knife he found on Brian, he pried off the bottom cover to the steering wheel column. He worked quickly and with purpose. Once free, he found the bundle of wires and pulled them out. Separating the two he wanted, the knife severed both wires, and he stripped them. He used the two ends against each other to start the ignition, and the engine roared to life.

"You've done this before," Kadie said from the back.

"Maybe once or twice."

"You *are* a real commando."

Duke grinned but said nothing as he put the car in reverse. He backed up, straightened out, put the Suburban in drive, and raced down the trail. Swerving around the damaged Range Rover, he accelerated and headed toward the main road. The Suburban bounced them around on the forest trail. Ten minutes later, they reached the paved road.

Duke checked the rearview mirror as they sped toward the hospital in Nis. Kadie held Brian in her arms and ran her fingers through his hair. Duke smiled and returned his focus to the road. His faith—their faith—paid off.

EPILOGUE

Birmingham, Alabama
The Kirklin Clinic of UAB Hospital

Kadie sat in the waiting area outside the Neurology Center on Floor 2 at the Kirklin Clinic. The facility at the University of Alabama at Birmingham was one of the best in the country. Brian's appointment wasn't scheduled for another month, but after the incident in Serbia two months ago, the doctor encouraged her to bring him in sooner.

The better part of the last hour, Kadie had paced back and forth toward the glass front, constantly checking outside by the large fountain in front of the building.

Brian had insisted on going in alone. For most of the tests, he would be alone anyway, but the doctor understood what he wanted. Brian wanted to be in control of something; it gave him a feeling of independence. So, he always went in by himself first, and the doctor would follow up with Kadie at the end.

Today, he was getting the full treatment: MRI, CT scan, X-rays.

Based on the seizure and head injury he experienced in the cathedral, the doctor wanted to know exactly what was going on in there. Brian had X-rays done in Nis for his head injury, but they didn't show anything abnormal. Kadie's vision had slowly started to come back later that same day. She couldn't explain why or what happened, and the doctors said she was perfectly fine.

They had quite the experience there and were grateful to be alive. Brian had the adventure of a lifetime and Kadie . . . well, Kadie found what she had missed most of her life: God.

And then there was Duke. Brian had become quite attached to the swashbuckling pilot. He was the male figure her brother needed since their parents died. And Duke sincerely liked Brian; the two genuinely got along. Duke had saved both of their lives that day, and that wasn't the first time either. His bullet wound, courtesy of Patricia, was superficial at best and didn't seem to bother him afterward.

They had stayed in contact for the first few weeks after they returned to the States, but that turned to a trickle until Brian's appointment was changed. The last time they had seen each other was at Mac's funeral over a month ago.

Brian had begged her to call Duke to come to the doctor's appointment today. She was hesitant at first. Duke had his own life, and both had plenty of issues to sort out after the adventure involving Global Disease Initiative and the Pilate Scroll.

The Global Disease Initiative headquarters, of course, had plenty of questions for her before they lawyered up when she posed questions of her own. The government had plenty of questions for Duke as well, like, why did he use government call-signs to fly to Turkey, Italy, and Serbia? They accused him of illegally transporting firearms, but they couldn't prove anything. And his company, of course, wanted their King-Air back. Duke had flown back to America commercial with Kadie and Brian. The King-Air remained on the ramp in Serbia.

The gruff pilot promised he would be here, but an hour after Brian's scheduled appointment time, Duke was still a no-show. Her heart ached for Brian, who was clearly disappointed. But Kadie was lying to herself—she was disappointed too. She had grown quite fond of the pilot. If he didn't have *his* health issues, maybe . . .

Her thoughts were interrupted when the elevator door opened across the expansive waiting area, and Duke walked through. He glanced around until he finally looked in her direction. She gave a subtle wave, and his eyes locked on her. *Oh my, he looks good.* Duke wore a suit and tie, which she could never have imagined. Clean-shaven, hair combed, and a radiant smile.

"Hello, Kadie." Duke wrapped his arms around her. "I've missed you guys."

They embraced in a hug, and she couldn't stop the tears. She couldn't explain them either.

Kadie sobbed. "We've missed you, too." She pulled away and gazed at him. "Thank you for coming."

Duke put his hands to her face and wiped away the tears with his thumbs. "I'm sorry, I'm late. There was a traffic accident on the interstate north of Montgomery. I was worried I wouldn't make it at all."

They caught up on what each had been doing for the last two months. Duke asked her about the incident in the cathedral that blinded her. The ceiling had collapsed, but it didn't expose the cathedral to the outside. It had been dark, and no light had been present from the outside. She told Duke she thought she had died that day. The bright light . . . and a voice that said, "Welcome home, Kadie." Duke explained what happened to Patricia, Curt, and more importantly, the Pilate Scroll. She struggled with the idea that they indeed experienced something supernatural. Even the earthquake seemed limited to the cathedral alone as no quake was felt anywhere else in Turkey that day. How did they explain something like that without being called crazy? They had mutually agreed that they would not mention the events of the collapse . . . for now. Mainly because they had no proof of their story except for the metal *Chi-Rho* clasp she had tucked into her pocket.

She tried to change the subject. "I appreciate you coming. I realize you have your own issues to worry about." Duke had to see his doctor about his oral cancer once they returned to the States. He had discussed the seriousness of the disease on their way back to America. She had no idea he was that bad, nor had she known he planned to quit flying upon his return because of the impending treatments. The man did mask his ailment well. Even now, he had a grin on his face. You'd never know he was dying of cancer.

"That's what I wanted to talk to you about. I—"

A loud creak came from behind, and they both turned to see the door to the doctor's office swing open. The neurosurgeon walked out with a clipboard in his hand and a grim look on his face. *Oh no*, she thought. *I can't handle this.*

The doctor stopped in front of her.

"Kadie," he said. The doctor glanced at Duke and nodded. Duke reached out and shook his hand.

"I'm Duke Ellsworth, friend of the family."

The doctor shook his hand and turned back to her. "Kadie, I don't know how to say this . . ."

Kadie felt her legs grow weak, and her knees buckled. Duke placed his arm around her shoulders to stabilize her.

Saving me once again.

She glanced at him. The pilot still grinned from ear to ear. She's about to get terrible news, and the jerk keeps smiling. His ability to comprehend what's going on around him is lacking.

"Kadie," the doctor said. "Brian is completely healed. He's okay."

"Yes, I understand. But it's been two months and—"

"No, I guess I'm not making myself clear. There is no indication of the tumor. I'm not sure how to explain it. It's not showing up anywhere. We've done every test twice, and every test came up negative. We compared his films today with past films. I wish I had an explanation other than a miracle, but I don't. It has to be an act of God. The tumor is gone."

Tears streamed down her face. But Duke? The man's grin seemed even more full now. Could he have known? How?

At that moment, the doors swung open again, and Brian came strutting through, his arms pumping up and down like he had just won the Olympics.

"I don't have no tumor," he was singing. "I don't have no tumor."

When he eventually focused on them, and his eyes grew wide. "Duke!" He ran to the pilot and hugged him.

"Hey, Brian," Duke said.

The doctor spoke briefly to Kadie. He wanted Brian to have a follow-up in three months and encouraged her to get a second opinion just to be sure, but he was confident their machines were accurate. The boy's tumor was gone.

When the doctor left, the three of them stood hugging, laughing, and crying, and praising God for the miracle they had just experienced.

Kadie stopped and turned to Duke. "You've been sporting a mischievous grin since you got here. Did you know something?"

"That's what I wanted to tell you. I didn't want to say anything until Brian was done, but Kadie, my cancer is gone. I'm one-hundred percent cancer-free. No more smokeless tobacco for me. I've kicked the habit forever."

Her mouth fell open. "How?"

"I'm not one-hundred percent sure," he said, "but I have my suspicions." Duke went on to explain the story from the Book of Matthew when a woman touched Jesus' cloak and was healed by her faith.

"The prayer shawl wrapped around the Scroll must have belonged to Jesus," Duke said. "We certainly *believed* it belonged to Jesus. We touched it and were healed. It was our *faith* in Christ that healed us. It's the only answer."

"Two miracles," Brian said.

"Yeah, bud. Two miracles."

Kadie sobbed.

"What is wrong—Kadie?" Brian said.

"I—I wish . . . oh, it's dreadful for me even to think about it. But you hear about how Jesus healed the lepers. I—I just wish you didn't have Down syndrome."

Brian eased over to her, took her hand in his, and looked in her eyes. "Don't cry, Kadie. Jesus m-made—me this way. I do not need to be cured. I-I'm special." He reached up, and his fingers lightly stroked her face. "God sent me here—to save you."

Kadie burst into tears once again and squeezed her brother. God *had* sent him here to save her—to save her soul. He had been showing her the way for years. Unfortunately, it took this event for her to see the light.

After a brief amount of time, she backed away and ran her hand along her blouse and slacks, then wiped the tears away with the back of her hands.

She turned to Duke, her hands on her hips. "I don't understand. We all touched the shawl. It cured your cancer. It cured Brian's tumor. Why didn't I get cured of anything?"

Duke approached her and put his arm around her shoulder.

"Maybe Christ healed your heart," he said.

Once again, the floodgates opened, and Kadie poured out her emotions. They all sat for a few minutes until she could compose herself. Christ *did* heal her heart, and he showed her the way. Brian had been the catalyst for most of her life, but Duke was brought into their lives for a reason. That was clear to her now. She only hoped *he* knew that as well.

"I think a celebration is in order," Kadie said. "How about we get lunch?"

"Sounds great!" Duke said. "I owe you a celebration lunch for your Princeton job."

Kadie's head lowered. "Yeah, about that . . . I didn't get the job."

Duke looked stunned. "What happened?"

"GDI . . . or rather the parent company, Alligynt. They made a phone call, and suddenly the job was no longer available." Her shoulders sagged, and she felt her eyes well with tears. Crying for her brother was one thing, but she didn't want to cry for herself. Not here.

Duke stood in front of her and put his hands on her shoulders. It calmed her some, mainly because every time he did it, something positive came out of it. He hunched down in front of her to get her to look at him. It worked. His smile warmed her heart.

"Kadie, you need to channel your energy into your faith. Make *that* your work."

Her head tilted. "What do you mean?"

"I think you should write a book about our experience."

"Really?"

"Of course. Do you remember why you joined the team at GDI to begin with?"

"I do. It was a noble effort. We were going to change the world with science and technology, not bombs and bullets. But we were a team working together for the good of everyone."

"Kadie, now *you* have a platform to share your experience and your message. Have a little faith," Duke said with a smile. "Sometimes, it only takes *one* person to change the world."

THE END

ACKNOWLEDGMENTS

First of all, I want to thank the good Lord for letting me play on this big blue marble called Earth, for as long as I have. I was once one of those 'casual Christians' Duke talks about in the book. My Christian journey has been a long and joyful one, but the more I learn, the more I realize I don't know. Thank you, Lord, for not giving up on me.

I want to thank my wife, **Kim**, for making me want to be a better man and a better Christian. The main character in this book, Kadie, was named after a good friend of ours, **Kadie Whitard.** Miss Kadie passed away a few years ago, but the life she lived as a Christian inspired me to name my heroine after her.

I can't remember exactly when the idea for this story came to me. But I do know when the idea for *a* story did. The Pilate Scroll, is of course, a fictional artifact. Its origin is what makes the story so much fun. In May of 2018, Kim and I were on a tour of Israel, led by **Governor Mike Huckabee** with his Blue Diamond Travel group. It was a first class operation that opened our eyes to the Bible like nothing else could. This was a very historic time in Israel, as we were there for the 70th Anniversary of the nation of Israel, and the American Embassy moving to Jerusalem. We were probably on the second day of the tour and I told Kim, "There's a story in here somewhere. I've just got find it." Well, I never found the story—it found me. And once it did, it flowed faster, and more effortless than any story I've ever written.

I don't remember when or where the idea of a Down syndrome character came from. I'd worked with **Tim Tebow's** "Night to Shine" that our church hosts which had given me some insight to the character as I began to develop him. Once I decided what I was going to do, I reached out to a friend of mine from high school, **Bill Johannessen**, whose son Will, is Down syndrome. I explained to Bill what I was trying to do, and sent him an outline of the story. I didn't want to exploit the character, but rather show he was a person who was relevant to the story. Bill's assistance was invaluable, as he helped throughout the process, from outline to final product. It has been said that the mark of a good character, is that if you remove that character, the story totally changes. And that's what happens with our character, Brian. If he's gone, *The Pilate Scroll* is a different story. I also want to thank the folks at the **National Down Syndrome Society**. Their assistance in fleshing out my character, Brian, was very helpful.

Writing a Christian Thriller was a little out of my wheel-house. I'd read a few over the years and I wanted to make sure this book was three things: relevant, Biblically sound, and not overly preachy. I wanted a fast-paced adventure story that contained a message of the Lord's salvation. And I think I got it. I want to thank the people who assisted me in this aspect: **Pastor Karl Stegall; Gene Mills, President-Louisiana Family Forum**; and my fellow Christian authors **David Jeffers, Jason E. Fort**, and **James R. Hannibal.** David is the author of *Man Up! What the Bible Says About Being a Man!* Jason is the creator of Fortress Books, and James is also a fellow pilot and the author of the multi-award winning Christian Thriller, *The Gryphon Heist.*

The Pilate Scroll is not real. Claudia's life-threatening illness is fiction and Pilate searching for and finding the Disciples is fiction as well. And of course, Pilate writing about Jesus' resurrection on the Scroll, and sending it to Emperor Tiberius is fiction. The back-story involving the Emperor Constantine is all true, with the exception of him finding and hiding the Pilate Scroll, which of course is fiction. Extensive research was done, and a great deal of information was derived from **D.G. Kousoulas's** book, *The Life and Times of Constantine the Great.* The journey to the Holy Land by Constantine's mother is true, but her learning about the Pilate Scroll is fiction, and Constantine's building the secret Cathedral of Helena is fiction.

Thank you to another high school friend, **Doctor Vince Tullos** for your medical expertise, and special thanks to my niece, **Tyler Jeter,** whose pharmaceutical expertise was vital to the story.

Thanks go to my good friend and fellow Ghostrider, **Dick Clark**, for his input on King-Air operations.

A story isn't a novel until it's written, and I've got a team of trusted agents I need to thank for ensuring my garbled thoughts have morphed into an entertaining novel. My go-to guy, as always, is my good friend and fellow pilot, **Scott Tyler.** Scott has a way of finding those nuanced issues that smooths out all the rough edges; and he's not afraid to tell me when I'm wrong. **Rob Rolfsen,** a good friend from college, is a living, breathing encyclopedia, who points out so many different facts about so many different things. Thank you to my special, dear friends **Rickey and Debbie Heroman, Mike Burton, Richard and Becca Overton,** my son **Derek**, and my daughter **Lydia** —thank you. Thank you for my Beta Reader team from my newsletter group, **Terrie James, Netta Pickering,** and **Richard Mott.** Your insight and inputs helped immensely. My friend and fellow author **Gary Westfal** also assisted in identifying those easy to miss author mistakes. And once again, special thanks to my editor **John Briggs.**

Finally, I want thank you, the reader. I hope you enjoyed reading this book as much I enjoyed writing it. May God Bless you and yours!

ABOUT THE AUTHOR

M.B. Lewis is an Amazon #1 International Bestselling Author, and his books have also been on the Bestseller lists on Barnes and Noble Nook and Kobo platforms. The author of the award-winning Jason Conrad Thriller series has been on numerous author panels at writer's conferences such as Thrillerfest, The Louisiana Book Festival, The Pensacola Book and Writers Festival, and Killer Nashville.

A 25-year Air Force pilot, he has flown special operations combat missions in Bosnia, Iraq, and Afghanistan in the AC-130U Spooky Gunship. Michael is currently a pilot for a major U.S. airline.

A proud Christian active in his community, Michael has mentored college students on leadership development and team-building and is a facilitator for an international leadership training program. He has participated as a buddy for the Tim Tebow Foundation's "Night to Shine" and in his church's Military Ministry program. Michael has also teamed with the Air Commando Foundation, which supports Air Commando's and their families' unmet needs during critical times.

While his adventures have led to travels all around the world, Michael lives in Florida with his wife Kim.

Follow Michael Byars Lewis:

www.michaelbyarslewis.com

www.facebook.com/mblauthor

michael@michaelbyarslewis.com

www.ingramcontent.com/pod-product-compliance
Lightning Source LLC
Chambersburg PA
CBHW020606310726
48979CB00008B/1365/J

* 9 7 8 1 7 3 3 0 9 8 9 3 9 *